T0265772

EAT, DRINK AND DROP DEAD

EAT, DRINK AND DROP DEAD

T.C. LoTempio

**SEVERN
HOUSE**

First world edition published in Great Britain and the USA in 2023
by Severn House, an imprint of Canongate Books Ltd,
14 High Street, Edinburgh EH1 1TE.

Trade paperback edition first published in Great Britain and the USA in 2023
by Severn House, an imprint of Canongate Books Ltd.

severnhouse.com

British Library Cataloguing-in-Publication Data
A CIP catalogue record for this title is available from the British Library.

ISBN-13: 978-1-4483-1002-9 (cased)
ISBN-13: 978-1-4483-1053-1 (trade paper)
ISBN-13: 978-1-4483-1001-2 (e-book)

All Severn House titles are printed on acid-free paper.

Typeset by Palimpsest Book Production Ltd.,
Falkirk, Stirlingshire, Scotland.
Printed and bound in Great Britain by
TJ Books, Padstow, Cornwall.

Dedicated with love to my good friend Hilary Anderson in Newton New Jersey – the woman behind Hilary Hanson!

ACKNOWLEDGMENTS

As always I would like to thank my agent, Josh Getzler, and his assistant Jon Cobb, for all their efforts on my behalf. A special thanks to my buddy Cathy Collette for always believing in me. And a shout-out to my cousin, Paul Ferrante, for everything he's done to help me publicize my books!

I would also like to thank my editor, Rachel Slatter, for catching my mistakes and helping to make this book the best it can be, and the whole team at Severn House for taking a chance on Tiffany Austin. I hope everyone comes to love her as much as I do!

ACKNOWLEDGMENTS

ONE

'You've got the best job in the world, Tiffany. You get to eat for a living.'

I raised my glass of sangria and smiled at the girl seated across from me. 'I certainly do, and I owe it all to you.'

Hilary Hanson blushed right to the roots of her blonde pixie haircut. We'd been friends ever since fifth grade, when she'd rescued me from Dean Whittaker trying to stick a frog down the back of my sweatshirt. We were inseparable all through high school and when we both went our separate ways to college, swore to keep in touch. Over the years we'd managed to maintain our friendship, in spite of the distance between us: Hilary in our hometown of Branson, Georgia, and me in The Big Apple. When she'd told me six months ago that the magazine she worked for, *Southern Style*, was thinking of hiring a food critic for their digital magazine, I hadn't thought I'd a prayer in the world of landing the job. I had no journalism experience whatsoever, and my creative writing skills were rudimentary at best. What I did have, though, was a degree from the CIA – that's Culinary Institute of America, folks, not the government agency. I was a qualified chef, and a darn good one, if I had to say so myself. Up until six months ago I'd been the assistant head chef at one of New York City's premier hotels. Why'd I leave? Well, let's just say I'd been on the losing end of a very complicated love triangle, and let it go at that.

Hilary had arranged an interview with her editor for me, and imagine my surprise when I found out that Dale Swenson, the editor of *Southern Style*, was the very same Dale Swenson who used to pull my ponytail and tease me unmercifully in the fourth grade. Thankfully he didn't grill me too much on why I was seeking a food critic position rather than another assistant head chef one. Rather, most of the interview was spent with Dale explaining all about the sister digital companion to the long-standing print one, and just what they were looking for. While their print circulation was steady, they weren't immune to the growing popularity of digital versions. The job, he said, would consist of maintaining a weekly blog for the digital version, and writing a monthly column for the print one. After an hour or so of reminiscing, he'd agreed to my taking on the column on a six-month trial period – and that period was up at the end of this week.

I set my drink down and fiddled idly with the edge of my napkin. 'I'm trying to think good thoughts, and not freak about over what might happen Friday.'

'Oh, you've got nothing to worry about.' Hilary made a lazy circle in the air with her hand. 'Your monthly column in the print magazine is fantastic, and your food blog's been a bona fide hit right from the get-go. Everyone I've talked to says your restaurant reviews have been spot on, and they love your Friday recipes. You're a shoo-in.'

'I'm not so sure,' I said. I tucked a stray auburn curl behind one ear. 'Marcia Allen told me the other day she heard the board wanted to cut back some of the columns. If that happens . . .'

'Oh, no one listens to Marcia,' Hilary declared with a care-less wave of her hand. 'She thinks because she's an executive admin to Enzo Manchetti, she's got some sort of an "in". All she does is parrot stuff she gets from Marketing, and it's never right. Anyway, they always threaten to cut columns at the end of the fiscal year.' Hilary tapped at her chin with one long, red nail. 'Although . . .'

I looked at her sharply. 'What? You know something. Spill it.'

'It's only a rumor. I heard it from Twyla Fay, though, and her info is usually pretty accurate.'

I frowned. Twyla Fay Thorpe wrote the Household Tips N Tricks column for *Southern Style*, and was known to be somewhat of a gossip maven. 'What's the rumor?'

Hilary fidgeted in her seat, then leaned in close to me and whispered, 'They are thinking of cutting one column in particular.' She paused. 'Jenny Lee Plumm's.'

'Jenny Lee Plumm's?' I gave my head a brisk shake. 'That

can't be true. I thought Society N Style is one of the most popular features?'

'The column's popular. It's the columnist who's not,' Hilary said with a chuckle. 'I heard Ms Plumm's been acting quite the diva lately, and the higher-ups aren't too pleased.'

'I find that hard to believe,' I said. 'I thought I heard she had some big board member on her side?'

'Yeah, Jeremy Slater. He retired two weeks ago.'

'Oh? I hadn't heard that. Kind of sudden, isn't it?'

'Not really. Slater's wife was never thrilled with either Jenny Lee or her husband's support of her. She's been after him for quite a while now to pack it in. Anyway, some uncle of hers who lived in Boca Raton died a few months ago, and apparently he was quite fond of Mrs Slater. He left her his mansion in Boca and a million dollars in stocks and bonds.'

I let out a low whistle. 'Whew. That's a life-changing amount.'

'Yep, and Mrs Slater apparently decided it was time for a change. She put her foot down and told Jeremy he had to choose: either her or the magazine . . . and Jenny Lee. Needless to say, Slater chose cushy retirement in Boca.'

'Can't blame him. I imagine Jenny Lee was upset.'

'Oh yeah. Nothing she could do about it, though. Her sex appeal can't hold a candle to Eunice Slater's newly revitalized bankbook.' Hilary tapped on the table for emphasis. 'With her staunchest supporter gone, trust me, it's only a matter of time. The rest of the board listened to Jeremy because he was the senior member but, believe you me, first opportunity they get, I bet Jenny Lee's out on her well-shaped derriere.'

'Her leaving might certainly open the way for hiring me, but I hate to think I'd get the job at her expense.'

'Oh, sweetie.' Hilary laid her hand over mine. 'Sometimes you can be so naïve. Do you think for one minute if the roles were reversed, Jenny Lee would feel an iota of guilt at her good fortune? Of course not.' She picked up her glass and waved it in the air. 'Regardless of what happens to that witch, I've no doubt that Friday night we'll be celebrating Bon-Appetempting's permanent success.'

I couldn't help it, I laughed. 'From your lips to God's ear.'

'Hey, Twyla Fay said you're a shoo-in, and that's the next best thing.'

Our waiter, a tall, olive-skinned man with bushy eyebrows and lips turned down in what appeared to be a perpetually stern expression, appeared just then to describe the specials, all of which sounded tempting. 'I'll have the cornbread tartlets with tomato and lima-bean relish to start,' I said when he'd finished. 'For the main course, I would like the garlic chicken.'

'I'd really like one of everything, but I guess I'll start with the Southern-style fish tacos,' Hilary said with a smile. 'For the main course I think I'll try the Southern fish stew.'

'Excellent choices,' the waiter said as he held out his hand for the menus. As I handed him mine, I added, 'Could we get a dish of polenta for the table? And a small platter of the sriracha beef lettuce wraps?'

The waiter wrote my request down without comment, but I saw his eyebrows rise ever so slightly. The second he was gone, Hilary leaned into me and whispered with a giggle, 'I think we shocked him. He must think we haven't eaten in days.'

'I don't care what he thinks. This place's name is Bueno, Bonito y Barato. Translation: Beautiful, Delicious and Cheap. I want to see if the food lives up to the name.'

Another waiter appeared, refilled our glasses of sangria. We clinked them in the air, and then drank. I was just setting my glass back down on the table when I heard Hilary's sharp intake of breath. 'Whatever you do, don't look to your left,' she hissed.

What's your first reaction when someone tells you that? Of course, you look, and that's exactly what I did. And I sucked in my own breath sharply at the tall, statuesque figure I saw framed in the restaurant's doorway.

None other than Ms Jenny Lee Plumm herself, dressed to kill in a tight little red number cut low to emphasize her generous – ahem – twin assets.

'Didn't I tell you not to look?' Hilary chided. Her own head was bent down and her hands were busy folding and refolding her napkin. 'But since you are, what's she doing?'

I turned my head slightly away, but I still had a pretty good view out of the corner of my left eye. 'She's leaning on the counter and talking to someone standing behind her. She'd better be careful or her girls are gonna spill out all over the . . . oh, goodness!'

'What, what!' Hilary almost jumped out of her chair. 'What's the matter?'

My hand shot out, grasped Hilary's arm. 'Sit down,' I rasped. 'She's not alone. There's a man with her.'

Hilary cut me an eye roll. 'Oh, geez. That's no news flash.'

'Ordinarily that would be true, but in this case the guy she's with is Frederick Longo.'

Hilary's brows drew together. 'Who's Frederick Longo?'

'You wouldn't know him unless you were a confirmed foodie. He's one of New York's premier chefs.' I scrunched my lips into a pensive expression. 'Whatever is he doing here in Branson, and with her?' As far as I knew, Frederick Longo was happily married, and from what I knew of his wife, I didn't think she was the type to condone infidelity.

'I have no idea, but . . .' Hilary had glanced over in their direction, and now swiftly turned her head. 'Heads up – they're coming this way.'

I immediately became immersed in searching through our overflowing breadbasket for a roll. It proved to be all in vain, though, for a few seconds later a shadow fell across the table.

'Well, well. Fancy meeting you here.'

I looked up into wide blue eyes and a perfect Grecian nose framed by a mass of perfectly coiffed platinum-blonde hair that might or might not have come out of a bottle, it was hard to tell. Ruby-red lips parted, revealing impossibly white and straight teeth that I still wasn't certain were caps or real. 'Why Jenny Lee Plumm,' I heard myself say. 'I could say the same thing about you.'

She looked at me in much the same manner that a cat would regard a plump, juicy mouse caught between its claws. 'Why, I'm here for the same reason you are, darling. I've been dying to try their food ever since they opened. And I brought an expert with me.' She indicated Chef Frederick with a sweep of her arm. 'Chef Longo, meet Tiffany Austin and Hilary Hanson.'

Longo nodded politely to Hilary, and then fixed me with a penetrating stare. 'Tiffany Austin? Not the same Tiffany Austin who worked at the Madison Hotel? You were Leonardo Puccini's assistant, if I recall correctly.'

Heat seared my cheeks, but I forced a pleasant smile to my lips and nodded. 'You have a good memory.'

He tapped at his temple. 'Hasn't failed me yet. You were, or should I say are, an excellent chef. I remember Ronald insisted I sample your specialty, that veal chop in that remarkable sauce.'

'Yes, I remember Ronald loved that dish,' I murmured. Ronald was Ronald Marki, the hotel owner. 'Veal alla Madison.'

'Yes. That sauce was superb. I was so disappointed when they pulled that entrée from the menu after you left. They do serve a similar dish now, and the sauce is good, but nothing like yours. Perhaps one day you'll consent to share your secret with me.' Longo's eyes gleamed at the memory and I shifted a bit in my chair. I hadn't thought about that dish since I'd left New York, and with good reason. There was indeed a secret connected with it, but it was one I could never share with Longo, or anyone else for that matter. After a few moments of uncomfortable silence, Longo cleared his throat. 'I must tell you, Ronald was devastated when you left so suddenly. The whole cooking staff too.'

Out of the corner of my eye I saw Jenny Lee lean forward, a viper's smile on her lips. I tried to make my tone casual as I responded, 'Oh, you know. It was just time to move on.'

Jenny Lee arched a brow. 'Hm. One would think you'd have moved on to another restaurant, rather than write a food blog.'

I thrust my jaw forward. Jenny Lee knew how to push my buttons, all right. 'Believe it or not, being a chef is an extremely stressful job, as I'm sure Chef Longo can attest to. I was getting burned out, and wanted to try something a bit different.'

Jenny Lee switched her gaze to Longo, who nodded. 'That is true. A female chef has to work harder than a man to achieve success. The work is brutal and it can be a most stressful situation, especially if you work for a perfectionist, which Leonardo Puccini most certainly is.' He shot me a kind smile.

'I'm sure it won't surprise you to hear he's gone through three other assistants since you left.'

Only three, I wanted to say, but I kept my mouth shut. Jenny Lee, however, was another matter. 'Three? My, he must be difficult to work for.'

Longo chuckled. 'That's putting it mildly. I understand, though, that Ronald's son Jeffrey has stepped up his game quite a bit. Leonardo always had a soft spot for him, and apparently he's been taking Jeff under his wing, teaching him a few things. The lad's turned into quite the chef, which pleases his father no end.' He turned to me. 'You worked with him when you were at the Madison, didn't you Tiffany?'

'Yes, we worked together.' I'd tried to keep the tremor out of my voice, but I wasn't very successful. I noted Jenny Lee watching me like a hawk. 'I always thought he was very talented.'

'But?' Jenny Lee drawled.

'There's no but. Why would you think that?'

Her lips curved into an almost feline smile. 'Behind every story like that, there's usually one heck of a but.'

I shook my head. 'Not this time. When I was there, I could see that while Jeff was truly talented, he lacked confidence. I'm glad he's finally realizing his potential.'

Jenny Lee frowned and cocked her head. 'Maybe I am off. Maybe the real story is you, Tiffany.'

'Me?'

'Yes. I still can't get over the idea that you'd rather write a blog than cook. I can't help but think there's a bit more behind your leaving New York to come back here than meets the eye.'

'Sorry to disappoint you,' I said lightly. 'It's just as I said. The competition was keen and I was getting burned out. I needed a change of pace.'

Longo smiled thinly. 'See, Jenny Lee. Not everyone has deep, dark secrets.'

Jenny Lee's gaze slid over to Chef Longo and their eyes met. Something – I wasn't quite sure what – seemed to pass between them, because Jenny Lee's cat-ate-the-canary smile got a bit wider and Chef Longo's face darkened. But it only lasted a moment, and then it was gone, so quickly that I wondered for a moment if I'd truly noticed anything. An uneasy silence hung over the table for a moment afterward and then Jenny Lee said brightly, 'Chef Longo might soon be a permanent fixture around Branson. He's been asked to fill Jeremy's slot on the board of directors.'

'Really?' I noticed Hilary giving me a look out of the corner of my eye and studiously ignored her, turning my attention to Longo instead. 'You'd be a wonderful asset to the magazine, but wouldn't you miss New York?'

'Not as much as you might think,' Longo said with a rueful smile. 'I confess, I was a bit surprised when I was approached, but the more I thought about it, well, I guess I came to the same conclusion you did. It's time for a change. Of course, it's not a done deal yet. My appointment must be voted on and approved.'

'A mere technicality,' Jenny Lee said, with a snap of her fingers. 'I'm sure the board knows a good thing when they see it.' She fixed her gaze on me. 'I hope you're around to witness it,' she said sweetly.

Longo frowned and looked at me. 'Are you leaving the magazine, Tiffany?'

I shot Jenny Lee a look and then turned to Longo. 'I hope not,' I said. 'I was hired on a six-month trial basis, which is up the end of this week.'

'Yes, and there have been rumors of budget cuts, so you know how that goes.' Jenny Lee spread her hands. 'LIFO. Last in, first out, right.'

'I'm sure Tiffany's work will speak for itself,' piped up Hilary. 'I've worked for *Southern Style* since I graduated college, and while I've seen them cut columns, I've never seen them cut a popular one.' She looked at me with a wide smile. 'Why, I heard Callie tell Dale only yesterday that they can hardly keep up with all your fan mail.'

'She did?' I stared at my friend. This was the first I'd heard about a surplus of fan mail. I wondered if Hilary weren't exaggerating just a bit to irritate Jenny Lee.

'Oh yes.' Hilary bobbed her head so hard her gelled spikes shook. 'Apparently the column you wrote last week resonated with quite a few people.' She tossed a smile in Jenny Lee's direction that resembled more of a sneer. 'Actually, more like *tons* of people.'

'The one about McCaffrey's Tavern closing?' McCaffrey's, a popular tavern on Branson's east side, had always been regarded as a version of Cheers, the place where everybody knew your name. The owner, Silas McCaffrey, had recently inherited some money from an aunt and decided to close up shop and move out West. I'd gone to the farewell party and I knew the article I'd written had been pretty well received. 'Funny, Dale didn't mention—'

'He's probably saving it for your review,' Hilary cut me off with a handwave. 'Maybe he doesn't want you to get a swelled head, you know, like other people.' She slid another sly glance in Jenny Lee's direction.

Jenny Lee's attention, however, was focused on me. 'How nice your little article got so much attention,' she drawled. She smiled, but I noted that it didn't reach her eyes. She laid her hand on Longo's arm and said, 'I receive quite a bit of fan mail as well. Women are always writing me, asking for fashion and makeup tips and wanting news on the latest styles.' She glanced briefly at me and then turned to Longo. Butter practically melted in her mouth as she declared, 'You know, even if they cut Tiffany's blog, the restaurant reviews don't have to disappear. It wouldn't be much of a stretch for me to include some in *my* column.'

Hilary raised an eyebrow. 'But you're not a professional food critic.'

'Well, neither is Tiffany,' Jenny Lee said coolly.

Hilary and I exchanged a glance. I couldn't fault Jenny Lee there.

There was an awkward pause, and then Hilary cleared her throat. 'That's true, Jenny Lee,' she said, 'Tiffany isn't a professional food critic. What she is, is a pro chef. A review from her would carry far more weight than one from you, because she's more qualified to pass judgement.'

Jenny Lee's face darkened and she leaned forward. I was afraid for a moment that she might strike Hilary, but after a second she seemed to compose herself and her slim shoulders lifted in a shrug. 'I guess we'll just have to wait and see what happens Friday, won't we?' she remarked in a taut voice.

Hilary leaned back and crossed her arms over her chest. She glared at Jenny Lee. 'I guess we will.'

Thankfully, our waiter chose that moment to return with our appetizers. As the waiter set our plates in front of us, Chef Longo made another low bow. 'Sorry, we did not mean to interrupt your dinner,' he said to me. 'I'll be in town for a while. Perhaps we can have lunch. Catch up on things.'

'That sounds divine,' Jenny Lee cut in. She craned her neck around the room. 'We can make plans later. Right now, though, we should get to our table. Where is that hostess – oh, there she is.'

She turned on her heel and hurried off. Longo watched her go, and then looked at me. 'I suppose I should follow her,' he said. 'It was lovely seeing you, Tiffany. I hope everything works out for you with your job at *Southern Style*.'

'Thanks. I do too.'

He inclined his head toward Hilary, and then turned. He started to walk away, then spun around and came back to our table. He leaned over me and whispered, 'Don't worry. I'll make sure it's only the two of us at lunch.'

I didn't know just how to respond to that, so I just smiled and nodded and didn't say a word. Longo made another swift bow, and then he took off after Jenny Lee. Hilary leaned across the table. 'Wow! What do you make out of all that drama? Hanging out with award-winning chefs isn't exactly Jenny Lee's style, is it?'

I picked up my knife and tapped it against the table. 'No, but maybe she's heard the rumors about being dumped and thinks she can make an ally out of Longo. An endorsement from him would practically guarantee her secure employment, I'm sure.'

Hilary grinned wickedly. 'Her machinations might not do her any good, though. I thought he seemed a bit uncomfortable around her.'

I chuckled. 'So you noticed that too, eh?'

Hilary shook her head. 'It was hard not to.' I popped a tartlet into my mouth, chewed for several seconds, and then washed it down with a sip of water before answering. 'Chef Longo came into the hotel kitchen once or twice. He was friends with Ronald Marki, the owner, and Leonardo, my boss.' I paused. 'In Leonardo's case, maybe friends isn't quite the right word. They were more like colleagues, or genial acquaintances. They respected each other's abilities. Anyway, Longo was always very pleasant and respectful to me.'

'Well, all I can say is it's a good thing Longo doesn't know the real reason you left that hotel and New York. That way he can't spill it to Jenny Lee.'

I threw up both hands. 'She can't ever find out. She'd manage to twist it all around and it would end up being a disaster of epic proportions, not only for me, but for Jeff.' I sighed. 'I couldn't do that to him.' I eyed my friend. 'You do know that you're the only other person, besides myself, who knows what happened.'

'Yes, and I appreciate the fact you trusted me enough to confide in me. Don't worry, I'll never tell.' Hilary mimed locking her lips and throwing away the key. Her gaze was pensive as she asked, 'Have you ever wondered what might have happened if you'd stuck around. Told Jeff the truth about why you broke up with him? Heard his side of the story?'

I rested my chin in my palm. 'Have I ever wondered if I did the right thing? You bet I have . . .'

I could remember what happened like it was yesterday. Dinner service was over for the evening, and it was nearly midnight. I was alone in the kitchen, making notes for the following evening specials. I'd looked up to find Leonardo standing in the doorway, his face dark as a thundercloud, arms folded across his broad chest. 'That new dish of yours was quite a hit,' he said, his tone rough.

I glanced up from my notes. 'You mean the Veal alla Madison? Yes, it was, wasn't it?'

Leonardo's eyebrows drew together. 'I understand the patrons liked the sauce in particular,' he said.

I smiled. 'I'd like to take the credit for it,' I said, 'but the thanks for that go to Jeff Marki, not me. The sauce was his genius twist on a popular recipe.'

Leonardo's gaze was cold. 'Is that what he told you?'

Something in the tone of his voice sent a chill up my spine. 'Yes. Is something the matter, Leonardo?'

'You bet something's the matter.' Leonardo pounded his fist against his palm and then took a step toward me, his expression dark. 'So, tell me . . . is this a conspiracy against me? Are the two of you in cahoots?'

I looked up from my notes and frowned. 'What on earth are you talking about?'

He folded his arms across his chest. 'I think you know.'

I pushed my notes off to one side. 'No, I really don't. Enlighten me, please.'

His gaze bored into mine. 'You really don't know?' As I shook my head, he shot me a chilly smile. 'That so-called genius twist on the sauce was never Marki's idea. It's mine!'

I gasped. 'Yours?'

'Yes. I developed it a few years ago. Obviously your little protégé slash boyfriend found a way to steal my recipe and use it on your new dish to impress you.'

I strove to keep the quiver out of my voice as I said, 'You must be mistaken, Leonardo. Jeff would never deliberately steal your recipe, or anything else.'

'I beg to differ,' growled Leonardo. 'Jeff can be lazy, true, but he is also young and ambitious, and eager to make an impression, particularly on his father . . . and you. He would steal, and he did.'

'That's an absurd accusation,' I said. 'Think about it, Leonardo. How would Jeff have gotten his hands on your recipe?'

Leonardo folded his hands across his chest and scowled deeply. 'An enterprising fellow, looking to curry favor with his boss and his girlfriend, would have found a way.'

I thrust my chin out. 'You're wrong.'

'Am I?' Leonardo unfolded his arms and took a step toward me. 'Perhaps you are not entirely innocent in this yourself. You could have been aware of what he'd done and looked the other way.'

I gasped. 'I would never do that.'

'No? Love makes us often do things we ordinarily wouldn't. You might have thought using that sauce would bolster Jeff's confidence.'

I squared my shoulders and my chin went up. 'I don't see how using a stolen sauce would bolster Jeff's confidence. You're grasping at straws. Besides, you have to know that I would never condone stealing in any form,' I said. 'This all has to be a mistake.'

'That it is,' Leonardo sneered. 'And Jeff made it. Once word of this gets out, it could do serious damage to his career, his credibility . . . and yours.' His gaze bored into mine. 'However, there might be a way to avoid all this. Sweep the whole unpleasant incident under the rug, so to speak.'

I shifted in my chair. 'What is the way?'

He raised a finger in the air. 'First, you must quit immediately.'

I had to fight to keep my jaw from dropping. 'Me? Why should I quit? I told you, I had no idea . . .'

'It doesn't matter. Who would believe you weren't aware of what he'd done especially when the dish is such a hit!'

I swallowed. There was no doubt in my mind Leonardo wouldn't hesitate to besmirch my reputation as well as Jeff's. 'Fine. I'll hand in my resignation first thing in the morning.'

'Good.' He paused. 'That's not all. You must break off your relationship with Jeff. Tell him you never want to see him again.'

'Why on earth do you want me to do that?'

'I have my reasons. Quit your job and end your relationship with young Marki, or I will waste no time in making an announcement. What is it to be?'

I felt tears sting the corners of my eyes. 'No announcement,' I mumbled. 'I'll break things off with Jeff.'

'Good. Do it tonight.' He turned to leave, then paused. 'Oh, and one more thing. This little conversation must stay strictly between the two of us. You must never mention it to anyone, especially Jeff or his father. If you do . . . all bets are off.'

'Don't worry,' I spat. 'I want to forget this conversation ever happened as soon as possible. I'm leaving here with my dignity intact.'

He gave me a self-satisfied smile. 'A wise decision. I always knew you were a smart girl.' He paused and then added, 'For what it's worth, Tiffany, you are an excellent chef.'

He turned on his heel and left, slamming the kitchen door behind him. I stood and stared at the closed door for a few moments, then laid my head down on the counter and wept . . .

'Tiff? You OK?'

I started at the sound of Hilary's voice and shook my head to clear it. 'Sorry. I guess I went back in time for a bit.'

She shot me a sympathetic smile. 'You were thinking about what happened with Jeff?'

I hesitated, then nodded. 'Yes. In hindsight, I suppose I should have confronted Jeff about Leonardo's claim but, to be honest, back then I found Leonardo too intimidating. I had no doubt that he would have done his best to ruin not only Jeff's reputation but mine as well. And I have to admit the thought did cross my mind that Jeff might have somehow gotten his hands on that recipe. He was a bit on the lazy side, but he was eager to make a good impression on his father. Ronald Marki had never quite approved of his son being a chef.' I sighed. 'I did what Leonardo wanted. I broke up with Jeff that night, and the next day I quit my position. There was no way I could work for Leonardo anyway, after all that. I walked out and never looked back.'

'So to this day you still don't know if Leonardo's claim was true or not. If Jeff really did steal his recipe.'

I took a deep breath to compose myself. 'I'm sure Leonardo's claim was all a sham, but it doesn't matter anymore. That ship has sailed.'

'What makes you say that?'

I exhaled a deep breath. 'Because I saw Jeff and Fiona's engagement notice in the *Sunday Times* last week.'

Hilary's hand shot out to cover mine. 'Oh Tiff! I'm so sorry. Why didn't you call me?'

I shrugged. 'No point. Like I said, that ship has sailed. Seeing that announcement made it all crystal clear. Even if Fiona begged and held her breath till she turned blue, there's no way Leonardo would let his precious daughter marry a man he considered a thief. That's when I knew he lied about Jeff stealing that recipe. He knew I'd do just about anything to keep him from getting hurt. He lied to get me out of the way so Fiona would have a clear field with Jeff.'

Hilary's lips puckered. 'Boy, what a cad.'

'Yes, he is,' I agreed. 'But it all worked out for the best. I've got a brand-new life here in Branson, and a new career. To be honest, I'm glad I'm no longer a pro chef. It can be a very toxic industry.' I fluffed out my napkin and laid it across my lap. 'Enough of this. Let's eat, shall we?'

We ate in silence for the next few minutes. The tartlets were divine: buttery and fresh all in one bite. The Caesar salad was delicious too, the lettuce crisp, the dressing tangy. As I ate, I could feel myself calming down. Food always had that effect on me.

The server returned to collect our empty plates and then the main course rolled in. The garlic chicken was superb, seasoned just right, succulent and tender. I stole a bit of Hilary's fish stew and found that to be divine as well. I jotted notes on my phone in my lap as I went along. Three bites into the polenta, I reached down and undid the top button on my pants.

A different waiter sidled up to our table and placed shiny dessert menus in front of us. He was younger and seemed far more affable than the other man. 'I don't know,' I murmured. 'I'm pretty stuffed.'

'Are you sure?' He pointed to a picture on the menu. 'We have strawberry whipped cream pie in a graham cracker crust, and a delicious key lime cheesecake. We also have fried ice cream, chocolate, vanilla or pistachio, and the traditional favorite, flan. The flan's on the light side,' he added with a wink.

Both Hilary and I groaned, and Hilary made a show of rubbing at her stomach. I smiled up at him. 'Do they taste as good as they look?' I asked.

He leaned forward and said in a stage whisper, 'Better.'

'Sold. I'll take a slice of the strawberry cream pie and the cheesecake to go,' I said. I looked at Hilary. 'What about you?'

Hilary passed her menu over to the waiter. 'You've talked me into it. Make that two orders to go.'

The waiter gave us a knowing smile and withdrew. I took that opportunity to glance over at the table where Jenny Lee and Chef Longo had been seated. To my surprise, it was empty.

I got Hilary's attention and inclined my head toward the empty table. 'When did Chef Longo and the Dragon Lady leave?'

Hilary suppressed a chuckle. 'When we were about halfway through the polenta. From the little I saw, they appeared to be engaged in an argument.'

I raised an eyebrow. 'Really? That seems odd. I didn't think Jenny Lee would deliberately alienate someone who could prove a possible ally.'

Hilary shrugged. 'I mean, I could be wrong, but I don't think so. Jenny Lee's face looked like a thundercloud and Chef Longo's not much better. They paused over there, by the bar. He laid his hand on her arm and she shook it off and marched away.'

I shook my head. 'And you didn't alert me? I would have liked to have witnessed that.'

'It all happened very fast. Jenny Lee marched off in one direction and Chef Longo in the other.'

'Curious. I didn't think they'd known each other long enough to fight.'

'With Jenny Lee it only takes a nanosecond, you know that.' Hilary shot me a mischievous grin. 'Maybe he made a pass at her and it wasn't well received.'

I chuckled. 'If anything, it was probably the other way around.'

The waiter returned with two large plastic bags. He set one in front of each of us, and then deposited the check square in the middle of the table. I picked it up, looked at it and let out a low whistle. 'Good thing these review meals are comped to the magazine's account,' I said. I whipped out my wallet and slid the company credit card into the case. 'So much for the cheap part of the name. The meal was definitely pricey, but worth it.'

Hilary ran her hands along her curvy hips and let out a soft moan. 'Man, I am so fat! I have got to lose ten pounds. It's all your fault, you know. Have I mentioned that getting free food is one of the best parts of your job, and by extension, mine?'

I looked pointedly at the bag in Hilary's hand. 'You could have said no to the dessert goodie bag, you know.'

She sighed. 'I know. I'm weak. No willpower. So shoot me.'

'No thanks.' My gaze swept over her. 'You're not fat, you know, no matter what you think. You're curvy. There's a difference.'

'Yeah? Tell that to Arleen.' Arleen was Hilary's sister. The girls were total opposites. Hilary was five two, big chested and curvy, and Arleen was five ten, long wavy blonde hair and thin as a rail.

'Arleen is too fixated on appearance.'

Hilary pulled a face. 'I guess she has to be.' Arleen wanted to be an actress and was a drama student at Mercer University. She'd recently gotten rave reviews for her portrayal of Blanche in the university production of *A Streetcar Named Desire*.

'Exactly. She can look like a stick if she wants. But you, my friend, have substance.'

'Yeah, well, I'd still like it if I were about fifteen pounds less substantial.'

The waiter took the packet containing my card and returned in a few minutes to drop it back in front of me. I signed the slip, adding a generous tip, and then slid the card back in my wallet. I reached for my plastic bag. 'OK, time to go.'

We scraped back our chairs and headed for the lobby. 'So what's the verdict? Four stars? Five?' Hilary asked. 'Personally, I'd give it six.'

'So would I.' I grinned at her. 'But I'll let you know definitely after I sample that cheesecake.'

We walked outside and I paused for a moment, taking in the beautiful Georgia evening. 'It's a perfect night, isn't it,' I remarked. 'No humidity, not a cloud in the sky . . .'

I stopped as the sound of angry voices reached our ears. I glanced over to my left and sucked in my breath. Jenny Lee Plumm stood there, her face like a thundercloud, her hands on her hips. She was engaged in a rather heated argument with a tall, swarthy-looking man.

Hilary poked me in the ribs. 'Oh, ho, maybe that's the reason she dumped Longo. She was double-booking dates.'

I frowned at the couple. 'He doesn't look like her type, does he?'

'Heck no. This guy looks like a bouncer. See that bump on his nose? I bet it's been broken a few times. Definitely not her type.' Hilary gave her head an emphatic shake. 'She's usually on the arm of a guy who could pass for a *GQ* model. He does seem familiar though,' she added, tapping at her chin. 'But I can't place him.'

A dark convertible suddenly screeched to a stop next to them. I was too far away to tell the make, but it looked expensive. A woman was driving it, but the scarf she wore wrapped around her head and the dark glasses made discerning her identity impossible. I expected the man to get in the passenger seat, so I was surprised when Jenny Lee opened the door. Before she hopped in, though, she raised her fist at the man. Her voice was loud enough so Hilary and I heard every word.

'You'll be sorry, Roberto. Mark my words, you'll pay!'

Jenny Lee slid into the passenger seat. She leaned over, whispered something to the driver, and then the convertible sped off like a rocket.

'Hah. It's not me who'll pay!' Roberto shouted into the wind. I started to turn away, but something made me look back. I bit back a gasp as I saw Roberto make a cutting motion across his throat, then turn on his heel and vanish into the night.

TWO

I dropped Hilary off and then drove the twelve blocks to the little cottage I called home. My Great-Aunt Melanie, my father's only sister, had left it to me when she'd passed two years ago. She'd had no children and had always looked on me as the daughter she'd never had. I'd originally intended to sell it, but after last year's events I was glad that I'd never gotten around to it. When I'd left Georgia for the Culinary Institute, I had no plans to return. I'd thought my life, personal as well as professional, would be in New York. I had to admit that old saying of my aunts was right: sometimes the Universe did work in mysterious ways.

I pulled into my driveway and sat for a moment, admiring the house. It was like many others in this section of town, a Tudor-style cottage with arched doors, a thatched roof, cross gables and even a small turret. Lush tendrils of ivy crawled up the walls on either side. I exited the car and made my way inside. My aunt had also left me all the furnishings, and so far I hadn't changed one thing. The damask sofa and loveseat in the living room seemed a perfect complement to the dark paneling and beamed ceiling. The wine and gold Aubusson carpet, antique highboy and tasteful oil paintings gave it a homey touch, I thought as I glanced around.

And so did my roommate, the Siamese, who right now lay curled in a ball on the wingback chair.

As if on cue, Lily raised her dainty head and let out a loud, throaty meow. She rose, stretched, then hopped down, walked over to me and started to circle around my legs.

I bent down and gave her a pat on the top of her light brown head. I'd always wanted a Siamese and had adopted her from a co-worker at the Madison whose purebred had a litter. I'd named her Lily after Lilian Jane Veley, who co-founded the official Siamese Cat Club in 1901. She had all the traits typical of the breed: warm, affectionate; a real 'people cat'. She also had the distinctive Siamese loud pitch and, true to the breed, could be extremely vocal and demanding, depending on the situation. Lily's means of conveying her wants ranged from gentle mews to loud, raspy calls. More than once I'd considered renaming her 'Chatterbox'.

I looked into her wide, unblinking blue eyes. 'Hello, Lily. Are you happy to see me, or just itching for dinner?'

Lily sat back on her haunches and meowed throatily, as only a Siamese can.

I laughed. 'OK, your vote's in. What about your brother? Where's he at?'

'Woof!'

I turned just as a tan and black bundle of energy hurled himself at me. Cooper was my King Charles Cavalier rescue puppy, just under a year old. When I'd moved back to Branson with Lily, I'd promised myself that I'd get one of those dogs. I'd always been a sucker for their sweet face and even temperament. Fortunately Lily also proved to be a fan. Cooper's first night home, she'd actually cuddled up next to him in his doggie basket. I caught Cooper and hugged him to my chest. He swiped his pink tongue across my chin. 'Woof,' he said again.

I set him down on the floor. 'OK, then. Dinner it is.'

I dropped my light jacket on to the loveseat and headed down the short hallway to the kitchen, my furry children close at my heels. I don't mind admitting that, next to my bedroom, the kitchen is my most favorite room in the house, and the only one that I'd redone. I'd replaced the old, worn cabinets with beautiful oak ones; taken out the old stove and refrigerator and replaced them with stainless steel, top-of-the-line models; put in a dishwasher and a new garbage disposal; and had a marble island complete with drawers for my cooking utensils and pots and pans erected right in its center. Directly above the island was a wooden hanging stemware rack which boasted my collection of crystal wineglasses. This new kitchen was one any professional chef would envy, and I should know. I'd designed it after the one in the Madison Hotel.

I set the bag with the dessert from the restaurant on the counter, opened the refrigerator and removed a small container. Of course, being a chef, the first thing I'd done after I'd adopted

Lily was to look up healthy recipes that I could make for her. No way was I giving her processed cat food! This was one of her favorites – tuna patties. A chef's dream, healthy and easy to make. I took out two, put them on a dish, and set them in front of her. Lily butted my hand with her head, a signal that she was grateful, and then hunkered down in front of the bowl. The sound of her contented slurping told me all I needed to know.

Next came Cooper's dinner. I took out another container and removed cut-up lean chicken breast accompanied by cooked green beans, squash and cauliflower and put a generous helping in his bowl. He looked at me with his limpid brown eyes and then hunkered down next to his sister. I smiled at the sound of his tail thumping against the parquet floor.

Children fed, I poured myself a tall glass of merlot and retreated to the living room. My laptop was still on the King Louis desk in the corner where I'd left it earlier. I picked it up and carried it over to the sofa. I took a long drink of wine, then set the glass on a teak coaster on the low mission-style cocktail table and leaned back on the sofa, tucking my legs under me. I balanced the laptop carefully on my lap and opened my Word program. I'd gotten into the habit of typing my reviews out on Word before transferring them to the blog. It made editing easier, for me anyway. I stared at the blank screen and blinking cursor for a few moments, then began to type:

> After you turn down Pine Street and stumble four blocks West, you'll come across one of Branson's hidden jewels: Bueno, Bonito y Barato. Don't be put off by this restaurant's hole-in-the-wall appearance. In this reviewer's opinion, it more than lives up to its name.

I paused, nibbling at my lower lip. I had loads of words of praise I wanted to say about the food, but one important aspect was still untried. I set the laptop off to the side and returned to the kitchen. Lily and Cooper had scarfed down their dinner and now Cooper was curled up in his doggie bed, snoring away. Lily was on the counter, washing her paws. She fixed me with a wide blue stare as I reached for the bag I'd dropped on the far end of the counter, watching me as I pulled out the plastic container containing the two cakes. She minced over, sniffed at it as I opened the utility drawer and removed a fork.

'Sorry, kiddo.' I waved the fork in the air. 'This isn't good for animals. Maybe not humans either. I haven't sampled it yet.'

Lily blinked, then hopped down from the counter, trotted over to her bed next to Cooper's, turned around twice and then lay down, her back to me.

I laughed. 'Yeah. I didn't believe that either. I mean, how could something that looks this good possibly be bad, right?'

I'd learned, though, never to judge a meal or a dessert on looks alone. Plenty of items that looked absolutely divine had ended up tasting either bland or just plain horrible. I had a feeling, though, that these cakes wouldn't fall into that category. I pulled a plate out of the cupboard, cut off a small piece of each, then stuck the rest of the desserts in the fridge. I carried the plate back into the living room, resumed my place on the couch and dug in.

'Oh my God,' I moaned after tasting the strawberry pie. 'This should be illegal.' Ditto the cheesecake. Needless to say, I scraped every morsel from my plate, then set it on the table and picked up my laptop. Once again, though, my fingers hesitated over the keys. I found my thoughts returning to Jenny Lee Plumm and the scene I'd witnessed outside the restaurant. So, instead of continuing on with my review, I called up Google instead and typed 'Jenny Lee Plumm' into the search engine. A link to her website came up, and I clicked on it.

The home page consisted of lots of photos of Jenny Lee, taken at different stages of her modelling career. Her bio page didn't tell me anything I didn't already know. I suspected that it had been written by her publicity man a while ago. There was no mention on it of her new position on *Southern Style*, but on the 'Favorite Links' page the link to Society N Style was right on top. I clicked on it and noted that the blog hadn't been updated for a few days, which was odd – Jenny Lee was usually a fanatic about that. The longest she'd ever gone without an update had been twenty-four hours, and that was only because she'd had a bad cold. I shrugged, thinking it might be due to her preoccupation with other things – Chef Longo, perhaps, and how to snag that permanent spot.

I closed out of the website and typed in Jenny Lee Plumm – Images. A whole page came up, and I scrolled idly down it. The top few rows were more of the same model shots that appeared on her website, but further down were some photos of Jenny Lee taken with other people. I noted one of her with Susan Lucci at an awards dinner, and another one with Hillary Clinton. I sucked in my breath, though, at an image on the very last row. It was Jenny Lee, dressed in a short teal and white chiffon dress. She was hanging on the arm of a dark, swarthy man in a tuxedo. He was in profile, but he strongly resembled the man she'd called Roberto. I clicked on the image to enlarge it and glanced at the caption beneath the photo, which wasn't much help: *Jenny Lee Plumm and friend at opening of Le Cirque in Branson*. Their arms were intertwined, and the rapturous look on Jenny Lee's face was certainly not indicative of a volatile relationship.

Something had happened to change things. What?

I hesitated, and then hit the print button. I had absolutely no idea what I was going to do with this photo, but something – call it my female intuition – was telling me it just might come in handy someday.

THREE

'So, today's the big day, huh? Don't be nervous, now, darlin'. Everything's gonna be fine.'

Twyla Fay Thorpe grinned at me from the doorway of the little cubbyhole I'd called my office for the past six months. A short, stout woman who had the fiery red hair of Lucille Ball and the personality of Mary Tyler Moore, she was always friendly and upbeat, with a 'glass is half full' outlook on life. In addition to being *Southern Style*'s resident gossip maven, Twyla was also known around the office for her flashy, over-the-top outfits, and today was no exception. The bright orange and fuchsia kimono-style dress she wore could probably be seen on Mars. Her handbag and shoes were a muted tangerine shade. The shoes I liked, in spite of their color. Strappy sandals with a four-inch heel, I figured them to be either Louboutin or Jimmy Choo. Both definitely out of my price range. Twyla's late husband had been a successful financial advisor and had left her pretty well off, so she could well afford designer shoes.

I shot her a smile. 'Thanks Twyla Fay. I have to admit, I didn't get much sleep last night.'

Twyla Fay tossed her head, causing the dangling orange and lime crystal earrings in her ears to bobble back and forth. 'Well, I don't know why! That blog of yours is a sure-fire hit, sugar, there's no doubt about it.' She put both hands on her ample hips. 'If anyone around here should be worried about steady employment, it's the Queen of Siam.'

I couldn't hold back a chuckle at Twyla's bluntness. 'You mean Jenny Lee.'

Twyla Fay let out a loud snort. 'No other. Her blog is popular, but so is yours. In fact, I'd dare to say out of the two, yours wins hands down. Most people I know would rather read about trendy eateries or delicious simple recipes than who around town is dating who.' She closed one eye in a broad wink. 'All one has to do is stop in at Lavish Locks to find out that info, anyway.'

I stifled a laugh. Twyla Fay certainly didn't pull any punches, and she was right. The little hair salon, owned by Minnie Mae Draper, had earned the nickname of 'gossip central'. 'That's true, but there's more to her column than just that.'

'Not all that much more, if you ask me.' She ran her hands down the sides of her outfit. 'If I need fashion tips, I'll consult the ladies down at the Magnolia Boutique.' Twyla Fay leaned in a bit closer to me. 'But what really does the little witch in is her sparkly personality. She's crude and rude to most of the staff around here, treats them like they're her indentured slaves. Someone needs to tell her the Civil War ended long ago, and she's not Scarlett O'Hara. Mark my words; if anyone's getting cut around here, it's her.'

'They wouldn't cut her and hire me,' I said. 'That wouldn't be fair.'

'Life isn't fair, sweetness.' She reached out and squeezed my hand. 'What say we meet up at Trends at five for a celebratory drink? My treat. Who knows? I might even spring for dinner.' She gave me a wink, then turned and hurried down the hall before I could answer.

'Either way, I'll definitely need a drink,' I muttered. I called up my calendar and looked at my appointments for the day. I was free until the Friday staff meeting at eleven. Now might be an excellent opportunity to have a friendly chat with Jenny Lee. If she were in, that is. She hadn't made an appearance at the office all week, and when she did was notorious for never arriving before ten.

Jenny Lee's office was situated at the other end of the long hallway. I started down the hall, deep in thought as to just what I could find to chat about with Jenny Lee. The weather? The latest fashion trends? Her taste in men? I was jolted out of my reverie by the sound of an angry female voice.

'You can't do this to me! You haven't heard the last of this.'

I glanced up and saw that I was in front of Dale's office. The door was closed and the shades drawn, but that angry female voice had definitely come from there. Curious, I stepped closer. I could hear the distinct rumble of a male voice, pitched far lower than the female's, but I couldn't make out what was being said. I was just about to step away and continue down the hall when the door was suddenly jerked open, and an angry-looking Jenny Lee stood framed in the doorway. She looked startled at first, and then her perfectly shaped lips compressed into a thin line and her eyes took on a chill worthy of an Arctic iceberg.

'What are you doing, snooping?' she practically yelled. 'Or are you here to gloat?'

I shook my head. 'Jenny Lee, I have no idea what you're talking about.'

She made a tsking sound deep in her throat and glanced back over her shoulder. 'Yeah, yeah. We'll see who has the final word around here. Even if I have to rattle some skeletons to get it.' Her head swiveled back in my direction, and she shot me another dagger look before pushing past and nearly toppling me over. I was just about to hurl an angry retort at her retreating back when I felt a hand on my shoulder. I spun around and looked at Dale, who appeared totally unfazed by Jenny Lee's parting threat.

'Tiffany, I'm glad you're here. It saves me the trouble of having Callie look for you. Come in, please.'

I went into the office and paused, uncertain. He shut the door and waved his arm. 'Have a seat.' I went and sat in one of the two leather chairs in front of his massive redwood desk. Dale seated himself in his leather chair, leaned back. 'I'm sure you know what today is.'

'Sure. It's Friday.'

He laughed. 'It's also the day when your trial period is up. Tiffany, I'm very pleased to tell you that the board has decided to make your position permanent – if you want it, that is.'

For a second I couldn't say anything, and then I stammered, 'What? Oh . . . that's great.'

Dale looked at me, and then let out a soft chuckle. 'Is that all you've got to say? I find that hard to believe.'

'I guess I'm in shock,' I replied. I cocked my head at him and scooted to the edge of my seat. 'So, who do I have to thank for this?'

He laughed. 'Yourself, although I will admit I did put in a

rather glowing recommendation, if I do say so myself. Don't sell yourself short, missy. You write an excellent column.' His phone rang and he frowned. 'Excuse me.' He pushed down on the intercom. 'Callie, I told you to hold my calls . . . oh, all right.' He glanced at me with an apologetic look. 'Sorry. It's Henderson from Security. I'll only be a minute.' He picked up his other line, and true to his word, the conversation was very brief. After a few minutes he hung up and turned back to me. 'Sorry about that. Now, getting back to the business at hand, we can't get over how your blog has grown in popularity over the last six months.' He held up both hands. 'No pressure.'

I shot him a playful grin. 'Dale, if it wouldn't be unprofessional, why, I could kiss you right now.'

His eyes twinkled. 'I won't tell if you won't,' he said. I looked at him sharply, but his expression was impassive. He held out his hand. 'I guess, though, we'd best settle for a simple handshake.'

I clasped his hand firmly. 'You and the board won't regret this decision, Dale. I've got lots of ideas for the blog going forward.'

'I'm sure you do,' he said with a smile. 'Feel free to share some of them at our staff meeting. I'm sure the rest of the staff will be interested.'

'I will.' I looked down at my hand, still firmly clasped in his. He looked down too, and then released it with a sheepish grin. I flexed my fingers and waited a few seconds before I said, 'I didn't mean to eavesdrop on your conversation with Jenny Lee, I hope you know that. But she was so loud, it was impossible to ignore her.'

'No apologies necessary. I get it.' He picked up the paperweight on his desk, moved it from one hand to the other. 'I guess I might have reacted the same way, if I'd got fired.'

'Oh, no!' I'd risen from my chair, and now I dropped back into it with a thud. 'So the rumors were true?'

'Yes. She didn't take it well, as you heard.' He set the paperweight down, rose and eased one hip against the corner of the desk. 'Her numbers have declined rather sharply the past few months, and the board didn't feel that they could justify keeping her on any longer.'

I looked at him searchingly. 'There's more to all this than just declining numbers, isn't there?'

He hesitated, and then nodded. 'Yes. Her attitude's also gotten worse. She was always obnoxious, but since Jeremy left even more so. There have been a few . . . incidents. I can't share the details, but suffice it to say that between the declining numbers and her protector gone, it was the right time to take action.'

I let out a breath. 'Poor Jenny Lee.'

'That's so typical of you, Tiffany.' Dale bent down and tilted my chin up with his forefinger so he could look into my eyes. 'You feel sorry for her, don't you?' Without waiting for an answer he went on, 'Of course you do. That's the type of person you are.' He released my chin and went back behind his desk. He sat in his chair and laced his fingers in front of him. 'Here's a piece of advice, Tiff. Save your sympathy for someone who deserves it.'

I couldn't argue that point. 'I suppose you're right,' I conceded.

'Of course I am.'

I started to rise from my chair but Dale held out his hand, motioned me to sit. 'Before you leave, I'd like to run some-thing by you.'

I nodded. 'Sure. What?'

He let out a breath. 'It's an idea the board was tossing around. How would you feel about doing a piece on the blog, maybe once a month, sort of a who's-who around town is frequenting what restaurant, what they think of the food . . .'

I stared at him. 'Turn it into a sort of gossip column you mean? To take the place of the one Jenny Lee did? What's next? One on what all the top chefs are wearing this year?'

'Oh, I'm sure you wouldn't have to go that far,' Dale said quickly. I noted his cheeks had flushed a bright pink. 'Although you might make mention of any designer duds you happened to notice.'

I bit down hard on my lower lip. 'Look, Dale, I'm not a gossip maven, and I'm certainly not the style or fashion guru that Jenny Lee was. If that type of thing is what the board wanted, then they shouldn't have fired her!'

Dale's hand shot out, covered mine. 'Hey, hey, calm down. It's only talk right now. I'm not saying anything's going to change, but if it were . . .?'

I sighed. 'Would it matter? I'd do it, of course, but I wouldn't have to like it.'

'Please don't worry about this. It may never happen. I just wanted you to be aware the possibility exists.' He gave my hand a brief squeeze, and then released it. 'You know, Tiff, you've got a quality Jenny Lee never had: likeability. People like you, and they trust your opinion. If you tell women to wear their bedroom slippers to church service, I'm betting they'd do it.' He couldn't suppress a grin as he added, 'Besides, you're a much better writer than Jenny Lee could ever hope to be.'

Something in the tone of his voice set off a little warning bell in my head. 'Dale, did you mention any of this to Jenny Lee? About rolling certain elements of her column into mine?'

He hesitated, and then nodded. 'Yes. She was getting rather loud, protesting that without her there would be no society slash gossip column, so I told her what the board was considering. Don't worry, I also made sure she knew we hadn't discussed it with you.'

Jenny Lee's venomous reaction to me made a little more sense, now. 'I'm sure that doesn't matter,' I said with a large sigh. 'If I was on her blacklist before, I probably head it now.'

'I think I might hold that dubious honor,' Dale said. He coughed lightly and then said, 'I won't take up any more of your time. I imagine you've got some notes to go over before the staff meeting?'

'Yes, sir, boss.' I got up and smoothed down my skirt. As I turned to leave, though, I was struck by another thought. 'What did Jenny Lee mean when she said she'd rattle some skeletons if she had to? It almost sounded like a threat.'

He glanced up from his computer with an enigmatic expression. 'I guess it did, didn't it? Well, I'm not worried about her, and you shouldn't either.' He made a shooing motion with his hand. 'Go on, get out of here. Go call your family. I'll bet they're anxious to hear the news.'

He turned back to his computer and I took that as my cue

to leave. As I exited, I saw Twyla Fay and Callie Johnson, Dale's admin, talking in low tones at her desk. They looked up as I passed, and both gave me a thumbs up. Twyla Fay held out her hand, palm up, all five fingers extended, which I took as a reminder of her offer for a drink. I smiled and nodded at them and continued on down the hall to my office. Once inside, I shut my door, kicked off my heels and did my version of a 'happy dance' – somewhere between a polka and a frug. Then I flopped into my chair, fished my cell phone out of my tote and called my family. The call went straight to voicemail, which wasn't unusual. My parents were both retired English professors and spent a good deal of their time travelling. I left a euphoric message and then hit the speed-dial number for Hilary. When her voicemail clicked on, I said, 'Hey! When you get in, come right to my office! We've got celebrating to do!' I tapped my phone against my chin, debating whom to call next, when I heard a soft tap-tap at my door. I knew it couldn't be Hilary – she would just open the door and walk right in. 'Come in,' I called.

The door swung open, and I started as I recognized the figure framed in my doorway. 'Chef Longo?'

Longo smiled at me. 'Hello, Tiffany. I heard the news, and just stopped by to offer my congratulations.'

'Thank you.' I motioned to a vacant chair. 'Won't you come in, sit a few minutes?'

'Don't mind if I do.' Chef Longo stepped inside and settled himself in the chair. He smiled, revealing his even white teeth. 'I had no doubt you would snag the spot,' he said. 'Might I say it's well deserved?'

'You might. I'm sure there are some who would disagree.'

'Oh, I don't think so.' He fiddled with the edge of his navy and white checked tie. 'From what I've seen, you're pretty well liked around here. Unfortunately I can't say the same about Jenny Lee.'

'You've heard, then?'

He nodded. 'I have to tell you, I was not surprised. From what I was told, this has been a long time coming. The only reason it didn't happen sooner was because Jeremy Slater always took her side.'

'And now he's gone,' I said. 'I can't say I'll miss her, but I thought she wrote a pretty good column. I always looked forward to reading her fashion tip of the week.'

'That's very generous of you, more than she deserves, I'm sure. Anyway . . .' He waved his hand in a dismissive circle. 'Enough about her. I came by to offer my congratulations, and also to tell you that my appointment to the board has been approved.'

I offered him a wide smile. 'That's great. Congratulations to you as well.'

'Thank you,' he murmured. His eyes twinkled as he added, 'One of my first suggestions will be to expand the food section. One thing I've learned, everyone loves a good recipe, and most people do fancy themselves amateur chefs.'

'I couldn't agree more. That's why those cooking contest shows are so popular,' I said with a vigorous nod. 'I do have some great ideas I can't wait to put into motion.'

'I am sure you do. Trust me, the better woman won.' He glanced at his watch. 'I must be getting on. I did mean what I said the other night, though, about us having lunch. Are you free today?'

'No, I'm sorry. Our staff meeting is today and they usually provide lunch for us.'

'Oh. Well, some other time, then.'

'Absolutely.'

Longo left and I leaned back in my chair. Something in his tone when he spoke about Jenny Lee made me think their dinner the other night hadn't gone as well as Jenny Lee had hoped. Longo had apparently seen it for what it most likely was – an attempt to cultivate his support. I had to admit, though, I was looking forward to Longo being on board. Having a pro like him in a position of power would definitely bode well for my blog.

I spent the next half-hour writing down notes for ideas for several new articles, one sparked by my talk with Longo. It was for a new monthly feature on my blog called 'Recipe of the Month'. I planned to have readers send in their recipes in a variety of categories, and I'd sample and choose the best one to be featured. Corny? Maybe, but I was certain it would bring a lot of foodies out of the woodwork – and over to *Southern Style*.

I saw it was quarter to eleven. I rose and picked up my trusty notebook. I didn't want to be late for my first official staff meeting. I stepped out into the hallway, but instead of turning right and heading for the conference room, something made me glance in the opposite direction, over toward the bank of elevators. I sucked in a breath at what I saw.

Longo and Jenny Lee, standing in front of the elevators, and they seemed to be engaged in a very heated conversation. Without giving it a second thought, I turned and started walking toward them. They were both so engrossed in what they were saying, neither one of them looked over. I stopped about ten feet away. There was no one else around, and their voices had grown louder, so I could make out pretty much what they were saying.

'You are just upset because your little trick did not work on me,' said Longo. 'In the future, I'd thank you not to poke your nose where it doesn't belong, as you did with Slater. If you ask me, the man's lucky to be out from under your thumb.'

'Careful Fred,' Jenny Lee said with a sneer. 'Poking my nose into people's business is what I do best. And I always get what I'm after. Always.'

'If I were you, I'd be very careful. Very,' growled Longo. 'Because if you interfere, I will have no choice but to retaliate.' Then he turned on his heel and stalked toward the door marked STAIRS.

Jenny Lee watched him go, her face twisted into what I could only describe as an evil expression. In that moment, she reminded me of every Disney villain I'd ever seen in my life. Quizzing her about that photo could wait, I decided. Maybe forever. Jenny Lee jabbed at the elevator button. The doors opened, and she stepped inside. I turned to go, and once again something made me look over my shoulder.

As the elevator doors closed, I saw Jenny Lee staring straight at me. If looks could kill, I'd be pushing up daisies right now.

FOUR

'Why, oh why do you worry about that witch when everything's going your way right now?'

I looked over at Hilary, sprawled across the spare club chair in my office, and managed a weak grin. 'You didn't see the look she gave me, like she held me personally responsible. I know she's not going to take this lying down.'

'There's nothing she can do about it,' Hilary declared matter of factly. 'The decision's been made, the die's been cast. She's been canned, and she's gonna have to learn to live with it.'

Memory of Jenny Lee's run-in with Longo flitted through my mind. 'I doubt it's going to be that easy.'

'Stop borrowing trouble.' Hilary sat up straighter in her chair. 'I'm tired of talking about that no-talent hack. Let's talk about something pleasant, like your new brilliant idea.'

I perked up instantly as I recalled the reaction I'd gotten at the staff meeting. 'They all did seem to like my "Recipe of the Month" idea, didn't they?'

'And why not? I for one think it's a fab idea. If there's anything a home cook likes, it's a contest, and this one is destined to be a sure-fire hit. Why, you might single-handedly be responsible for improving *Southern Style*'s circulation!'

'Wouldn't that be something,' I said with a laugh. 'For now, though, I'll just take my small victories where I can get them.'

'Do that,' Hilary urged. 'And please, please, stop feeling sorry for Jenny Lee. Let it go! Next thing I know you'll be making chicken soup and going over to her apartment, spoon-feeding her, rubbing her back and combing the want ads, trying to find her another job.'

'Oh, I wouldn't go quite that far. I'm sure she can find her own job without any assistance from me. She must have plenty of connections.'

'Yeah, and they're probably all overcome with glee at her situation. Get it through your head, Tiff. This woman is not a nice person. Why, if the devil were a woman, he'd be Jenny Lee.'

I bit back a chuckle. 'She's not that bad.'

'No, she's worse. Trust Auntie Hil, will ya? Don't make the mistake of underestimating that witch.' Hilary glanced at her watch and rose from the chair. 'Well, kiddo, I've got to split. Dale wants me and Mac to cover that photography exhibit at the museum this afternoon.'

My eyes twinkled. 'That sounds like a real hardship. How'd you wangle that assignment?'

Hilary could barely suppress a grin. Mac was Mackenzie Huddleston, a six feet four hunk of man who looked like the real-life version of Clark Kent minus the glasses. In addition to being heart-stoppingly handsome, Mac was an excellent photographer who'd won quite a few awards, the most recent one for a photoshoot he'd done in Africa. He'd gotten the job on *Southern Style* courtesy of his aunt, Margaret Huddleston, a wealthy Branson dowager who was on the magazine board. 'I was just in the right place at the right time, for a change,' she said. 'I'm the envy of everyone right now, even if it is only business.'

'I know Jenny Lee would be green. I heard that she tried to corral Mac into going to several society parties with her, but no sale.' I'd silently applauded him, thinking that knowing Jenny Lee, she'd had more on her mind than just business.

'I guess you didn't hear,' Hilary said with a sigh. 'They did date, for at least a few weeks, anyway. But Nancy Marchand saw them two weeks ago at Bistro Niko and she said it looked like the bloom was off the rose, so to speak. They spent most of their time glaring at one another across the table.'

I thought about the scene I'd witnessed between Jenny Lee and Longo, and about Roberto. 'She doesn't seem to have much luck with men.'

'Her inner barracuda comes to the surface, no doubt. Well, I'm off. Maybe I can pry some details out of Mac.' She rolled her shoulder. 'He might need one of these to cry on, ya know? Cheerio! Oh, and don't forget – Trends at five. Twyla Fay's got quite the little party planned.' Hilary gave me a jaunty wave and then was gone.

My cell started to chirp, so I reached across my desk and scooped it up. I saw my parents' number on the display, and pressed on the answer button. 'Hello, Mom? Dad?'

'Hello, Punkin!' My dad's voice, loud and cheerful as always, boomed out. 'We got your message, so I presume congratulations are in order?'

'Yes, thanks. I went to my very first staff meeting as a permanent member just a few hours ago.'

'That's wonderful, dear.' My mother's calm, controlled voice came over the line. 'We're happy for you . . . as long as that's what you truly want.'

I could hear the slight note of doubt in my mother's voice. She'd always inspired me to cook, and she'd been thrilled when I graduated from the CIA in the top third of my class. I knew she'd loved telling people her daughter was a chef at the prestigious Madison Hotel in New York, and I also knew how disappointed she'd been when I'd returned to Branson and sought a non-cooking position. My parents have always been of the mindset that their children should learn from their mistakes – case in point my brother's three failed marriages – and seldom doled out advice. I knew, though, that it was killing them, particularly my mother, to follow that credo with me. I'd thought about confiding the truth, but I knew that would mostly entail a lecture, and I hadn't felt like hearing it. I put a bright note in my own voice as I responded, 'It sure is! And guess what! They loved my idea for my first feature as a permanent columnist.'

I went on to describe my Recipe of the Month idea. Both Mom and Dad greeted it with the enthusiasm I'd come to expect of parents who wished their only daughter had stuck with the career course she'd originally chosen. We exchanged a few more pleasantries, talked about the status of some family members, including my brother's latest flame, and then my father said, 'Your mother and I would like to give you a little party to celebrate your good fortune. Any chance you can come home soon? Like maybe this weekend?'

My nose wrinkled at the thought of one of my parents' famous parties. I usually ended up in the kitchen doing most of the cooking. As if she were reading my mind, my mother said, 'Don't worry, Tiffany. You can leave your apron at home. I plan on having Hodges Catering come in. We just need a date from you.'

'Um, well, can I get back to you on that? I think this weekend's going to be out. I've got a lot to do for the magazine. Maybe I can get away next weekend. Can I let you know Monday?'

'Sooner's better than later,' said my mother. 'After all, we have to make arrangements. How about Sunday by noon?'

I sighed. When my mother took that tone, it did no good to argue. 'Sure.'

'Don't forget now,' my father added. Hah, like they'd let me. We exchanged some more pleasantries and then I hung up. I'd just slipped my phone back into my tote bag when my office door flew open and who should be standing in my doorway but Jenny Lee Plumm! Her cheeks were red and her eyes were blazing. Without waiting for an invitation, she marched inside, slammed the door, and stood towering over me, her hands on her hips. Judging from the expression on her face, she wasn't here to offer her congratulations.

'So,' she snarled, 'I hear that you're going to be taking over my blog as well! Talk about pouring salt in the wound!'

For a second all I could do was stare at her, and then I found my voice. 'Th-that's not true,' I stammered.

Her eyes widened. She thrust her hands into the pockets of her black silk jacket. 'That's not how I heard it.'

'Well, how you heard it is wrong.' I pushed my chair back and stood up. My normal height of five foot six was no match for Jenny Lee's Amazonian proportions. In the four-inch stilettos she wore, she had a good eight inches on me, maybe more. 'I have no intention of taking over your column. I admit, Dale asked me to consider it—'

'Of course he did,' Jenny Lee interrupted. 'Dale is a weakling, Tiffany – haven't you figured that out yet? He's a stooge of corporate. He'll do anything they ask of him, and if they decide they want gossip mingled with restaurant reviews, then that's what you'll do.' She sniffed and crossed both arms over her chest. 'Me, I was never a slave to them. I marched to my own drum. Pissed 'em all off.'

'And look where that got you,' I couldn't resist saying.

'Because my leverage was gone. But I'll get more,' she hissed.

I looked at her, puzzled, and then I remembered the remark Longo'd made about Slater being out from under her thumb. 'Like the leverage you had with Jeremy Slater?'

She frowned. 'What do you know about my relationship with Jeremy?'

'Not too much,' I admitted. 'But it's no secret the two of you were close.'

'Close, yeah, we were . . . once. That's all over with now. A closed chapter. You know what they say – all good things must come to an end.'

An uncomfortable few moments of silence passed, and then I cleared my throat. 'Look,' I said, 'I'm sorry you got fired. I truly am.'

She thrust her hands back into her jacket pockets . . . 'You know, I think I believe you mean that.'

'I do. I hate to see anyone lose a job. Even you.'

'Is that because of what happened to you in New York?'

I looked at her sharply. 'That was an entirely different situation. I did not get fired.'

'No, you quit, and rather abruptly. Why? What scared you away?' She paused. 'Or should I ask who?'

I started. 'Nothing and no one scared me away. You just said it yourself. I quit of my own free will.'

Her eyes narrowed into thin blue slits. 'It's true you quit. Freely? I have to wonder. Tell me, Tiffany. Just why does a girl who graduates at the top of her class from one of the finest culinary schools in America, and lands a dream job assisting one of the most prestigious chefs in New York, suddenly throw it all away to come back to her hometown and write a food blog?'

'Didn't we have this conversation already?'

'Yes, you've said you were burned out. Stressed out. And Fred backed you up. But guess what? I don't believe you.' Her arm suddenly shot out and she pointed a long fingernail right under my nose. 'You have something to hide.'

I took a step backward. 'You're nuts. What could I possibly have to hide?'

She tapped her nail against her chin. 'I don't know . . . yet. But rest assured, I'll dig it out.'

'You're wrong,' I said, but my voice sounded weak and hollow, even to my own ears. 'There's nothing to dig out.'

Jenny Lee threw back her head and laughed. 'Of course there is, Tiffany. And I'll find it eventually. Right now, though, I've got bigger fish to fry. I tried to impress this upon Dale, get him to intercede with the board on my behalf, but my pleas fell on deaf ears.' She leaned in closer to me. 'I've got my finger on the pulse of a story that will let me write my own ticket. Anywhere I want. *Vogue*, *Glamour* . . . or bigger maybe. *Newsweek*, *Times*.'

One thing about Jenny Lee. She always thought big. 'Those are premier magazines. What sort of story are you after?'

She waggled her finger in my face. 'Oh, no. This has to be kept super quiet until I have all my ducks in a row, which is going to be very, very soon. So you can rest easy, for now. Right now I have no time to expose your dirty little secret but – rest assured – once I have what I want, you're next on my list, followed by your high school crush.'

With that, she crossed back to my office door and jerked it open. I lunged for her, grabbed her arm just as she stepped into the hallway.

'Jenny Lee, please,' I said. 'Drop your silly vendetta against me.'

She gave me a black look. 'Why should I?'

I hesitated and then said, 'Because it could result in hurting innocent people.'

'Do you think I *care*?' she snarled. 'Did anyone care about me getting hurt? Sorry, Tiffany. It's every woman for herself.'

I stood staring at her for a moment. I'd always thought Jenny Lee unbelievably selfish, but this went way beyond that. If she started digging into my past, she'd be playing with people's lives, and I just could not let that happen. 'Please, just listen to me.'

She held up one hand, traffic-cop style. The other she slid into her jacket pocket. 'Sorry, Tiffany. I have no interest in what you're going to say, and I imagine it will be something intended to throw me off your scent. Well, guess what! I can't be thrown off. I intend to make your life as miserable as you've made mine.'

'I haven't made your life miserable,' I protested.

Her brow arched. 'But of course you have. Your goody-goody presence makes my life miserable. Knowing that you have my job at *Southern Style* makes me miserable.'

'I didn't steal your job,' I cried, but Jenny Lee wasn't listening.

'Of course, there is a way you could set things right,' she purred. 'You could quit, and recommend to the board that I take your place. If you did that, why, I might reconsider.'

My jaw dropped and I stared at her. Obviously losing her position at *Southern Style* had affected her mind. 'I can't do that,' I said.

She shrugged. 'Well, then, I can't halt any investigation I might pursue into your background. Learn to live with it.'

I reached out to grab her arm, but she pivoted away. I followed her into the hallway. 'Jenny Lee, please. Don't do this,' I said.

Jenny Lee's answer was to turn her back and start walking swiftly away.

'Jenny Lee, please.' The words were out of my mouth before I could stop them. 'You are impossible! What if the roles were reversed? What if I started digging into your past? Starting with Roberto?'

Jenny Lee stopped stock-still in the middle of the hallway. She turned and gave me a piercing glance over one shoulder. 'And just what do you know about me and Roberto?' she growled.

'I know the two of you had a heck of an argument Monday night,' I shot back.

Jenny Lee turned, and for a moment it seemed to me she'd lost her composure. It lasted only a brief second, though. The next instant her shoulders squared and she held her head high, chin thrust forward. 'Don't be a goose. I have arguments with men all the time. It makes the making up so much more fun.'

I should have let it go, but instead I hurled back, 'It didn't seem like a run-of-the-mill argument to me. Roberto seemed very angry.'

'Oh, what do you know?' she snapped. 'When was the last time you had a date? The Stone Age?' She started to turn, and then suddenly spun around. 'That's it, isn't it? You left New York and that restaurant because of a man! Now I just need to find out what man!'

I sucked in a sharp breath. 'You . . . you're wrong.'

'The hell I am.'

She turned with a gleeful expression on her face and started back down the hall. Impulsively I shouted after her: "Jenny Lee, don't. You . . . you'll be sorry.'

She paused and looked over her shoulder. 'I think it will more likely be the other way around. Unless you plan to hold Roberto over my head. That will get you nowhere, I assure you.'

She turned and resumed walking. I shouted at her back, 'Jenny Lee, please listen to reason.' She kept on walking. I cried out, 'Oh, I could just *kill* you for being so stubborn.'

No reaction whatsoever. I imagined she must hear that phrase many times in the course of a day. I shook my head and, as I turned back to my office, saw several staff members duck their heads and walk swiftly away.

'Swell,' I muttered. My gut instinct told me to run after her and make a big public apology, but in the end pride won out, and I stomped back into my office and slammed the door.

In retrospect, I probably should have gone with my gut.

FIVE

Five o'clock found me sitting at a table in Trends. The pub was a favorite of the magazine staff, probably because it was only two blocks away from the office. It was located in a single-story redbrick building which at one point in time had been a firehouse. The current owners had redesigned the entire interior, but left the fireman's pole in the center as a conversation piece. It boasted dark pine walls on which were 'trendy' posters of movie stars, both vintage and current, singing groups and the like, and pine-plank floors that were covered most nights in peanut shells from the complimentary bowls of shelled peanuts that graced the bar and all of the tables. The tables themselves were also carved out of dark pine. I'd reviewed their bar items the very first week I'd started on the magazine. I'd given their mini cheesesteaks with peppers and onions a five-star review, as well as their jalapeño poppers and kick-butt chili. They also made a mean Cajun burger – fourteen ounces of pure Angus beef topped with Cheddar cheese and infused with special Cajun spices. My mouth watered just thinking about it.

I looked around at the lively group gathered around the large, round table. Marilyn Monroe in her *Seven-Year Itch* white dress smiled down at us from the wall. Twyla Fay was there, of course, and she'd brought Minnie Mae Draper along. I was at the head of the table and Hilary sat beside me. Across from us was Dale's admin, Callie Johnson, two other admins whose names I couldn't remember, and Serena Post and Gerilyn Dodge from the Art department. I nudged my friend. 'Where's Mac?'

Hilary's lips settled into a pout. 'He said he had another appointment he couldn't break, but if he got done in time he'd be here.' She sighed. 'He didn't say so, but I got the vibe it had something to do with Jenny Lee. Some guys never learn.' Her glum expression morphed into a sly one. 'Dale's coming.'

'Dale? Really?' I didn't know why that should surprise me, but it did.

'He had some sort of meeting with Security at four fifteen, and then he said he had something he had to take care of, but he'll be here.'

'It's probably about the new alarm system. I heard him talking to Henderson when I was in his office.'

'That's probably it, then.' Hilary shot me a mischievous grin. 'He said he wouldn't miss a chance to celebrate your good fortune.'

'Whoa, whoa, slow down, Dolly Levi,' I said. 'Dale and I are just friends, nothing more. He's my boss, for goodness' sakes.'

Hilary snorted. 'Like you'd be the first girl who ever dated her boss.'

Or the boss's son. 'Yeah, well, those situations seldom work out.'

Hilary's face fell as she realized what she'd said. She slapped at her forehead with the palm of her hand. 'Oh, what a goose I am. It totally slipped my mind. I'm so sorry, Tiff.'

I could see she felt bad, so I just waved my hand. 'Forget about it. I have. Let's just have a good time.'

Donna Fallafel, a cheery young girl who'd waited on me several times before, came over with a tray laden with drinks. She set a frothy concoction in front of Hilary. I looked at it curiously. 'What's that? Not your usual Sloe Gin Fizz.'

'No, I thought I'd be daring tonight.' Hilary ran her finger along the rim of the glass. 'It's called a Pain in the A***. A combo piña colada and rum runner. I took the liberty of ordering you one,' she added, as Donna set a similar glass in front of me. 'Tonight's your night to be daring, Tiff!'

'Thanks, but I think I've been daring enough for one day,' I said dryly. 'Or haven't you heard?'

'About the little spat you and Jenny Lee had earlier? Of course I heard. Everyone's heard.'

I slumped in my chair. 'Terrific. And I'd hardly call it a little spat. Even though she manages to push all my wrong buttons, I can't believe I actually threatened her.'

'Oh, that.' Hilary gave a dismissive wave. 'Like no one else has ever uttered those words to her! Now come on.' She gave me a poke in the ribs and raised her glass. 'Put Ms Personality Not out of your mind. This is a celebration, remember?'

'With you here to remind me, how could I forget?' I picked up my glass, clinked it with hers, and took a sip. 'Wowza!' I cried, setting down my glass. 'That's strong!'

Hilary grinned. 'Good for what ails you.'

We were all midway through the second round of appetizers, which included the popular mini cheesesteaks and jalapeño poppers, when I noticed a familiar figure walk into the bar area. As my gaze locked with Frederick Longo's, he inclined his head imperceptibly, then took a seat at the far end of the bar. I popped my andouille mini-dog into my mouth and pushed my chair back. Hilary turned and gave me a questioning glance.

I pointed to my empty glass. 'Little girls' room,' I said.

Hilary nodded. 'Don't be long. I'll have a refill for you when you get back.' She glanced at her watch and frowned. 'I wonder what's keeping Mac and Dale. Dale at least should have been here by now.'

'His meeting probably ran overtime. You know what a workaholic Dale is,' I said. I gave her shoulder a squeeze and made my way over to the far end of the bar. There was an empty stool next to Longo, and I slid on to it. Longo turned to me and smiled. He pointed to the glass of red wine in front of him. 'May I order you something?'

I shook my head. Truth to tell, I was still a bit woozy from the Pain in the A***. 'I'm good, thanks.'

He stole a swift glance toward the table where my friends were all chattering away. 'I went to your office to talk to you, and was told you were here. I assume you are celebrating your good fortune in being made permanent?'

I nodded. 'Yes. Would you like to join us?'

He picked up his glass, took a sip of wine, and then set the glass down. His long fingers curled around the stem. 'No, there's somewhere I must be.' He turned toward me, and his gaze bored into mine. 'I had a very unexpected call earlier, from Jenny Lee.'

'Oh. No doubt she wanted your shoulder to cry on. She told you she'd been fired?'

'No, but she did not have to. As a board member, I had been apprised of it.' He cleared his throat and went on, 'Jenny Lee wanted to know what I knew about you, and your position at the Madison; specifically if I had any idea why you'd left their employ so suddenly.'

'I see.' I felt a lump rise in my throat. 'What did you tell her?'

He shrugged. 'Seeing as I do not know anything, I wasn't very helpful. Not that I would have been anyway,' he added, his features shifting into a dark scowl. 'Then she asked me if I could give her some names of people she might persuade to reveal what they knew about you.'

Beneath the bar counter, I clenched and unclenched my fist. 'Did you? Give her names?'

He laughed. 'Of course not. I told her to Google you and no doubt names of people you'd been acquainted with would pop up. She said she'd done that already, but she was looking for someone who might not perhaps be a matter of record.' Longo shrugged. 'I told her that whatever silly vendetta she had against you should be forgotten, and her efforts would be better concentrated on trying to find another job. And then I hung up on her,' he said with a slight smile.

'She paid me a visit earlier today. She blames me for her misfortune. She told me she's going to keep digging until she finds something she can use against me.'

The corners of Longo's lips drooped down. 'Tiffany, I am so sorry. But that's how that woman operates.' I looked at him, and he coughed lightly. 'It didn't take long to see through her. She thinks she's clever, but she's actually pretty transparent.'

There was a bowl of peanuts on the bar. I reached out and took a fistful. 'Chef Longo, do you know the reason she was fired?'

'I believe it was her numbers, her Q-rating they call it. The board did not believe she was bringing in enough readers to justify her exorbitant salary. And there was also the feedback from other employees, and some readers.' His lips twitched slightly. 'She offered to take a pay cut, but the board would not hear of it. I fear that – without Jeremy in her corner – Jenny Lee is not very well liked.' He tapped his forefinger on the bar. 'As I said, her motives are transparent.'

'She said that if I quit and recommended she have my position, she'd leave me alone. I said no, quite forcefully, I'm afraid. From what you've just said, though, I doubt my endorsement would have carried any weight anyway.'

Longo's tone was sympathetic. 'You quitting would not have made a difference, and Jenny Lee knew that. She was trying to goad you.'

'Well, she succeeded.' I leaned in a bit closer. 'I overheard you say to her that Jeremy was lucky to be out from under her thumb. Did she have something on him? Is that why he supported her?'

Longo looked down at his glass. 'Jenny Lee had something on quite a few people, and Slater was no exception, I'm sure. I do not know what, if anything, she might have held over his head, but apparently it wasn't anything serious.' He paused and then added, 'I heard about your little . . . argument. I can't say as I blame you for what you said. I would probably have reacted the same way.' He looked straight at me. 'I just wanted to alert you she's out for blood.'

'I figured as much. She said once she finalizes this other story she's working on, I'm next.' I sighed. 'Quite frankly, I have no idea what else I can do to discourage her.'

Longo regarded me over the rim of his glass. 'Is there a particular reason she should be discouraged? Is there something in your past she could dig up that would hurt you?'

He sounded genuinely concerned. I paused, unsure if I should confide the truth about Jeff to Longo or not, but the decision was taken out of my hands as Dale suddenly appeared behind us. 'Hey, sorry I'm late,' he said. He glanced around the bar area. 'Where is everyone? I thought this was a party?'

'It is,' I said. I slid off the stool and smiled at him. 'We've got the big table in the open area. Callie saved you a seat.'

He looked at me, then at Longo. 'Hello, Fred. Will you be joining the party?'

Longo pulled his wallet out of his breast pocket, dropped

a twenty on the counter, and then slid off his stool. 'Regrettably, no. I have an urgent appointment that I cannot break.' He looked at me. 'We'll finish our conversation another time. Congratulations again.' He inclined his head, then turned and made his way out of the tavern.

Dale watched him go and then turned to me. 'He's a bit of a strange duck, isn't he?'

'He's a top chef. They're a breed unto themselves.'

Dale raised an eyebrow. 'You were a top chef, and you're not half as mysterious as Fred.'

I laughed. 'I was an assistant chef, and I certainly don't consider myself a top one. That title is reserved for the likes of Gordon Ramsay, Wolfgang Puck and Frederick Longo.'

Dale made a low bow. 'I stand corrected. So, what were the two of you talking about? It seemed like an earnest conversation.'

'My encounter with Jenny Lee earlier today.'

He eased his elbow against the bar. 'What encounter is this? The one where you threatened her with bodily harm?'

I balled my hand into a fist and gave him a light punch on the shoulder. 'Yes, smarty. Apparently Jenny Lee was quizzing him about my time in New York. She's determined to dig up dirt on me.'

'Yes, that does sound like Jenny Lee's MO,' Dale remarked. 'This time, though, she's up against a losing proposition. Someone should tell her not to waste her time. If anyone ever had a squeaky-clean background, it's you.'

I flushed. 'Thanks.'

Dale studied me for a moment. 'That's the truth, right? There's nothing Jenny Lee could uncover that would hurt you, is there?'

I had the feeling what he was really asking was, *Is there something in your past that could end up being an embarrassment to the magazine?* Once again, I was unsure how to answer. And once again, the decision was taken away from me as another familiar figure emerged from the restroom area.

I gripped Dale's arm. 'Oh my gosh! It's him.' I breathed.

'Ow!' Dale extricated his arm from my grasp. 'Watch those nails, missy. And who's him?'

I tried to make my tone sound casual, but it was hard with all the excitement that suddenly bubbled up in my gut. 'Just a guy I need to talk to.' *For my own preservation*, I added to myself, *just in case I need to fight fire with fire.*

Dale raised an eyebrow. 'Oh?'

I thought I detected a note of jealousy in Dale's tone. Ordinarily that would have pleased me, but I couldn't fixate on that now. Roberto was on his cell phone, speaking quite animatedly. I could tell from his expression and the set of his jaw that the call wasn't a pleasant one. Was he talking to Jenny Lee, I wondered? Abruptly Roberto shoved his phone into his jacket pocket and headed for the exit. I gave Dale a little push. 'You go on over to the table. I'll just be a minute.' Before Dale could utter a word of protest, I'd moved across the room toward the exit door. I stepped out on to the street and looked first right, then left.

No Roberto. Once again, he'd vanished. I sighed and retraced my steps back inside. I noted that, in my absence, Mac had also arrived. He looked a bit harried but none the worse for wear, and Hilary and Callie appeared to be mesmerized by the story he was relating. I slid back into my seat and noted that, true to her word, Hilary had gotten me a refill. I picked up the glass and took a hearty swig, which earned me a curious glance from Dale, who was seated across from me. I shrugged and took another hearty sip.

Sometimes a gal's just gotta do what a gal's gotta do. In this case, it was get buzzed.

The party started to break up around eight thirty, after I'd been presented with a huge slice of the special dessert of the house, Mauna Loa cheesecake. It was a delicious concoction of cream cheese flavored with flaked coconut and topped with chocolate-dipped macadamia nuts and cherry sauce. Even with Hilary, Callie and Dale helping me, I felt ten pounds heavier and had to keep snapping the waistband on my pants. Dale helped me on with my jacket and offered to take me home, but I declined. It was only a fifteen-minute walk to my house from here, and truthfully I felt the walk in the fresh night air would do me a world of good and help to clear my mind. Hilary teasingly made sure I could walk a straight line before she – and Mac – took off for the Blue Goose, a nightclub over in Castle, the next town. Well, why not, I thought. It was Friday night, after all. I was glad someone had a life.

As I walked, I pondered what Longo had told me about Jenny Lee. She certainly seemed determined to 'get me'. The problem with that, though, was there was nothing to get, not really, and innocent people could get hurt in the fallout if she started asking questions of the wrong people. It seemed, though, that there was nothing I could do to change her mind.

And then I felt my phone vibrate in my pocket. I whipped it out and sucked in my breath as I saw the name of the text sender: Jenny Lee. The message was short and to the point:

> *We have to talk about things. Meet me at Barry's Café at 9:30. Sharp!!!!!*

I frowned. Barry's Café seemed an odd choice for a meeting. It was located off the main drag on a side street, about a five-minute walk from Trends. Barry's was a popular gourmet coffee spot, always crowded. It was small with very few tables, although their counter boasted a pretty large seating area. It would be packed at this hour, but maybe Jenny Lee wanted an audience for whatever it was she wanted to discuss. All the exclamation points at the end of the text irritated me. I definitely wasn't up to another confrontation similar to our earlier one. Of course, there was always the possibility that maybe she'd had a change of heart. Or maybe she needed a shoulder to cry on about Roberto. As fast as that thought entered my brain, I dismissed it. Jenny Lee wasn't the type to have a girl-to-girl chatfest. I looked at the text again. *We have to talk about things.* What things could she mean, unless . . . she'd managed to discover the reason I'd left New York. But how?

'A snake like her must have ways of getting information out of people,' I muttered. I looked at my watch. It would be tight, but if I power-walked, I might even get there in time.

It was almost ten thirty when I let myself in the front door of my house. Cooper was there to greet me, his tail wagging briskly, and I remembered he was overdue for a walk. Lily was curled up on the back of the sofa. She opened one eye at my approach, purring softly when I ran my hand gently down her back, then closed it again. I'd phoned Mrs Wiggins next door to feed them, and I could see that she'd done her job, but I'd neglected to mention taking Cooper for a walk. The spaniel danced merrily around my legs as I pulled his leash from the hook by the door and fastened it to his collar.

Because it was so late, and also because I was beat, the walk was going to be a short one, just up and down the block. As Cooper pranced along, sniffing at everything in sight, I mulled over the events of the evening. The one uppermost in my mind was getting stood up by Jenny Lee, who'd been the one to text *me* to meet *her* in the first place.

'What was up with that, dissing me after practically ordering me to meet her at nine thirty sharp with many exclamation points, no less?' I asked Cooper, as the spaniel sniffed at a spot under a large elm tree. 'No doubt she's playing mind games. Making me wonder whether or not she managed to turn up something. She probably never had any intention of meeting me.'

I remembered the hurried conversation Roberto had before he'd left Trends. Had he been speaking with Jenny Lee? He'd looked upset, almost furious. For that matter, who was Longo's mysterious appointment with? Could he have been meeting Jenny Lee? If so, why? At least there was nothing Longo could tell her about why I'd left New York. No, the only one who could say anything to smear me would be my old boss, Leonardo. And since I'd kept up my end of the bargain, he'd have no reason to say a word . . . or would he? With Leonardo, one never knew.

Done with his sniffing, Cooper tugged at his leash, an indication that he wanted to go home. I was all for that idea. The kitchen clock read eleven p.m. when we came in the back door. I took Cooper's leash off and he immediately trotted over to his doggie bed, turned around twice, lay down and promptly shut both eyes. A few seconds later I heard the sound of snoring.

'Ah, for the life of a dog, or a cat for that matter,' I said with a chuckle. My head started to pound again and I was pretty sure it was due in a large part to the generous alcohol in the Pain in the A***. I put the kettle on the stove for tea and vanished into the bedroom, changing into my favorite flannel pajamas, a soft pink and grey print of dogs and cats. I slid my feet into fuzzy gray mules and pulled on a pink bathrobe. I glanced at myself in the mirror. God, all I needed was curlers in my hair and I'd really be a fright! If Dale saw me now, he'd probably head for the hills.

I poured myself a cup of Earl Gray and sat down with my laptop at the kitchen table. I didn't feel sleepy anymore – I attributed that to my walk with Cooper – so I decided I might as well get some work done on next week's blog. I planned to kick off my new 'Recipe of the Month' feature with something simple that everyone could join in. I didn't want it to look like the feature was aimed at experienced home cooks, so I planned to invite my readers to submit their recipes for pizza. It sounded more complicated than it was – with all the premade pizza dough and crusts available, making a tasty pizza was actually something the least skilled cook could accomplish. I was just about to type the intro when Lily came caroming into the kitchen and jumped right into my lap. 'Ow-Orrrr,' she cried in her shrill Siamese voice.

'Lily, what's wrong?' I asked. The cat jumped on to the counter and stood there, her back arched, her tail bristling. The next instant I heard a knock at the back door. Cooper raised his head as I got up to answer it. 'Down boy,' I cautioned as he started to rise. 'It might not be anything.' Even as I said the words, though, I realized how silly they sounded. It was after eleven at night. It had to be something!

Cooper didn't heed my command and followed me to the door. I peeped out through the curtain and I could make out the distinct forms of two men. Cooper let out a low growl as I twisted the lock. I held up my hand in a 'stop' gesture to him. He backed away, definitely not happy. I opened the door and peered out. 'Can I help you?'

A tall man in a tweed blazer turned and looked straight at me. He had thick dark hair, an unruly lock of which fell across his forehead, and a strong, firm jaw. Eyes blue as the sea bored into mine. 'Are you Ms Tiffany Austin?'

I frowned. 'Who wants to know?'

The man reached into his blazer pocket and pulled out a shield. At the same time the other man moved forward into the light, and I could see that he was a uniformed police officer. 'I'm Detective Eric Dalton and this is Officer Farraday. We'd like you to come down with us to the police station.'

Just like that? I thought. I looked down at my attire. Dalton smiled, revealing perfect white teeth. 'We'll wait for you to change.'

My head shot up. 'May I ask why I'm being summoned to the police station at this hour?' I asked. I knew I sounded belligerent, but quite frankly at that moment I didn't much care. Police always had an adverse effect on me, even though I'd never committed a crime.

The smile vanished from Dalton's face, and he tipped his chin. 'We have some questions,' he said.

I still wasn't inclined to be cooperative. 'Regarding . . .' I prompted.

Dalton's next words nearly made me topple over. 'Regarding the death of Jenny Lee Plumm.'

SIX

For a few seconds all I could do was stare open-mouthed at the two men. Finally I found my voice. It came out a high-pitched squeak. 'D-death of Jenny Lee Plumm? She's dead?'

Dalton's head inclined in a nod. 'Yes.'

My hand went to my throat. 'Oh my God. What happened? Was it an accident? Or something health-related?' I didn't think Jenny Lee had a heart condition, or anything like that, but then again we'd never discussed the status of her health, or anything else of a personal nature.

His dark eyes gleamed as his sharp gaze swept me up and down. 'If you wouldn't mind, we just need to ask you a few questions. As I said, we'll wait while you change.'

I glanced down at my pj's and fuzzy slippers and coughed lightly. 'I-I . . . sure, I guess so.' I started to shuffle off, and then turned abruptly. 'Is going to the station really necessary?' I asked. 'I mean, you could come in, I could make some coffee and you could ask me what you need to here.'

The corners of Dalton's lips twitched ever so slightly. 'A tempting offer, to be sure, but our superior specifically requested we bring you in.'

That didn't sound good. 'Do . . . should I call a lawyer?'

Dalton shrugged. 'That's entirely up to you. As long as you have nothing to hide . . .'

He let the sentence with its unspoken implication dangle in midair. 'I'll just be a few minutes,' I said tightly. I turned without another word and left them standing on the back porch. I hurried upstairs to change, followed closely by Cooper and Lily. They hopped up on my bed and watched as I shrugged out of my pj's and into a pair of black jeans and a comfortable scoop-necked wine-colored sweater.

'Why on earth do they need to question me about Jenny Lee?' I muttered as I ran a brush through my mane of thick auburn hair. They wouldn't need my opinion on a heart attack or a car accident, would they? This only left one possibility, which I resolutely refused to think about right now.

I gave Cooper a kiss on the nose and dropped another one on Lily's forehead. 'I'll be back soon, I hope,' I said. I hurried downstairs and joined the two men on the porch. We walked in silence down my short driveway to the cop car parked at the curb. I saw some lights go on in the neighboring houses and figured people, no doubt, were peering out from behind their curtains, curious as to what was going on. I was rather curious about that myself.

It was a twenty-minute ride to the police station from my house, but we made it there in half the time. Detective Dalton parked the car and strode ahead of us into the station. Officer Farraday came around to my side of the cruiser to open the door. I hopped out and followed him in silence into the building, a large gray edifice that had always reminded me of a prison. Somehow it didn't surprise me that the interior wasn't much better than the exterior. The walls were painted a hideous greenish-blue hue. It reminded me of the hospital, where I'd visited my father when he'd had his heart attack some years earlier. Not exactly cheery, but then again I supposed police stations weren't exactly meant to be that way.

Dalton was waiting for us at an elevator bank at the end of the hall. We shuffled inside and Dalton pressed the button for the second floor. We exited and walked down another long hallway to a door at the very end. A bronze placard on it read 'Conference Room 1'. Dalton pushed open the door and motioned for me to enter. As I stepped over the threshold, I noticed another man seated at the long conference table that took up most of the room. I recognized him immediately. Chief of Detectives Philip Bartell had recently received a Good Citizen award from the mayor and, believe it or not, had been featured in *Southern Style* a few months ago in none other than Jenny Lee's column as one of the Ten Most Eligible bachelors in Broward County. He'd previously been head of the Birmingham, Alabama homicide division. Rumor was they'd made him an offer he couldn't refuse to relocate to

Branson. Bartell was attractive, in a rough-and-tumble sort of way. His chiseled features and unruly shock of hair had always reminded me of my favorite movie actor, Clint Eastwood. He lifted his head as I approached and his eyes, a stormy gray, bored into mine.

'Ms Austin. Thank you for coming.'

Damn, but with that slow, sexy Southern drawl he even sounded like Clint. I slid into the chair opposite his. 'You're welcome, but I really didn't have much choice.'

Bartell ignored that remark and leaned back in his chair. He flicked his gaze over to a water pitcher on the table. 'Would you like a glass of water?'

I shook my head. 'No thanks. I'm fine.'

'Very well.' He laced his hands underneath his chin. 'I understand the hour is late, so I'll get right to the point, Ms Austin. How well did you know Jenny Lee Plumm?'

I snuck a quick look over at Dalton and Farraday, who'd taken seats at the opposite end of the table. Their expressions were impassive, like they'd been carved out of granite. I cleared my throat and looked Bartell straight in the eye. 'Not all that well,' I said. I was surprised at how steady my voice sounded, because my stomach was doing flip-flops. 'We both worked at *Southern Style* up until today, but we really had very little contact with each other. I saw her at the staff meetings once a month.'

'I see.' Bartell leaned forward a bit. 'You say you both worked there until today?'

'Yes. I was hired on a temporary basis and was made permanent today. Jenny Lee was . . . let go.'

Bartell pulled a notebook and a pen out of his pocket and started to scribble in it. 'You mean she was fired.'

I squirmed a bit in the chair. 'I was trying to be kind, but yes, she was terminated. Apparently her column wasn't as popular as the board hoped it would be.'

'I see. And she was bitter about this? Blamed you for her troubles?'

'She blamed me, yes, among others.'

'Others?'

'She was also angry with our editor, Dale Swenson.'

Bartell tapped his pen against the desk. 'Would you describe your relationship with Jenny Lee Plumm as volatile?'

'I wouldn't say that we had a relationship. As I said, I only saw her once a month in the staff meetings, and elsewhere only fleetingly. As a matter of fact, I've seen more of her today than in the entire six months I've been at *Southern Style*.'

Bartell set his pen down, tented his fingers beneath his chin. 'Where did you see Ms Plumm today?'

'Once in Dale . . . in Mr Swenson's office, after he delivered the news. I was outside, in the hall. She came out, saw me, said something like, "I guess you're pleased," or words to that effect, and then walked off. I saw her later on in the hall again, talking to Frederick Longo, our newest board member.' I paused. 'And then the last time was in my office.'

Bartell picked up his pen. 'She came to your office?'

'Yes. She lashed out at me. She said that I had her job now, and she was going to delve into my past until she found something that would ruin me.'

Bartell scribbled in his book. 'That made you angry.' It was a statement, not a question.

'Not angry as much as frustrated. Jenny Lee was impossible to reason with.'

Bartell glanced up, and his icy gaze bored into mine. He set down his pen and leaned back in his chair, arms folded across his chest. 'OK, how *frustrated* were you?'

I wondered how much I should reveal. Something in Bartell's manner made me think he already knew everything there was to know about my altercation with Jenny Lee. I swallowed and said, 'Jenny Lee was being more stubborn than usual, and mean. She was fixated on finding something that would ruin me. We had a brief altercation in the hallway and I'm afraid I lost it.'

Bartell didn't look up from his furious scribbling. '"Lost it?" Could you be more specific?'

I swallowed. 'I told her I could kill her, or words to that effect.'

Both of Bartell's eyebrows rose. He leaned forward and picked up his pen again. 'So you threatened her.'

'Yes . . . I mean no, of course not. I didn't mean it,' I added quickly. 'It was just something that came out in the heat of the moment.'

'I see. And this . . . altercation. What was it about?'

'I told you, she was fixated on finding something that would ruin me. I was trying to convince her not to.'

For a moment, you could have heard a pin drop in the room, and then Bartell cleared his throat. 'Ms Austin, were you aware of anyone else who might have felt animosity toward Jenny Lee Plumm?'

I twisted my hands in my lap. Should I mention the arguments I'd overheard between Jenny Lee and Fred Longo? They were probably nothing, and I hated to drag Longo into anything. Finally I said, 'Your little notebook wouldn't be big enough. Jenny Lee wasn't very well liked by anyone at *Southern Style*, that I can tell you. From what I've heard, half the female population of Branson didn't feel very kindly toward her. Jenny Lee could be a flirt and a tease. As for anyone else, I have no idea.'

'You mentioned her being angry with Dale Swenson?'

'She was angry over being let go. She didn't have a history with Da . . . with Mr Swenson, if that's what you're asking.'

He continued scribbling. 'How about any drug or alcohol problems? Money issues? Any problems with boyfriends?'

Roberto came briefly to my mind, but I shook my head. 'Sorry. I have no idea.'

'You're certain?'

'Yes.'

Bartell set down his pen, and a thick silence settled over the room. Finally he leaned across the table toward me. 'Was that the last time you saw Ms Plumm?'

'Yes.'

'And you didn't hear from her any more today?'

'No . . . wait.' I scrubbed one hand along my jawline. 'That's not true. She texted me, at Trends.' When Bartell didn't comment I went on, 'She texted me that she wanted to meet at Barry's Café to discuss *things*.'

'Things? What sort of things might that be?'

'I have no idea. She wasn't specific. I waited there till ten, but she never showed up. You can check with the waitress on duty. She served me a latte and I told her I was waiting for someone.'

'Um-hm.' Bartell scribbled something in his notebook, then his head jerked up and he pointed a finger at me. 'You were there until ten?'

'That's right.'

'And Ms Plumm sent you a text?'

'Yes. Around nine fifteen, I think.'

He frowned, and then nodded. 'OK. You said that you were at Trends when you got this text?'

'I'd just left. As I mentioned, I was put on staff permanently today, so a few of us got together to celebrate.'

'And I take it Ms Plumm wasn't invited?'

'No, she wasn't.' I leaned forward. 'Can't you tell me what this is all about? Just how did Jenny Lee die? Was it some sort of accident, or a heart attack?' I demanded.

'Sorry, I'm not permitted to share that information.' Bartell looked me square in the eye. 'What I can tell you is that, at the moment, her death is classified as suspicious.'

I twisted my hands under the desk and blurted out the thought uppermost in my mind, the one that had refused to leave me ever since the police had appeared at my door. 'You mean it's possible she might have been . . . murdered?'

Bartell leaned back in his chair and tented his fingers underneath his jaw. His gaze bored into mine as he answered, 'There's always that possibility, yes.'

Considering the questions he'd been asking, that announcement shouldn't have come as a surprise. Still, actually hearing the words made a sickening pit start to form in my stomach. My throat was dry and tight but I managed to get out, 'Look, I might have threatened Jenny Lee but it was just something said in the heat of anger. I was upset that she wouldn't listen to reason. You have to believe me. I disliked her, sure, but I would never have actually killed her.' More silence. 'Do I need a lawyer?' I squeaked out.

Bartell pushed back his chair and stood. He was easily over six feet – if I had to guess, I'd have said at least six foot three. His tone was surprisingly gentle as he said, 'Ms Austin, you are not accused of anything. Our investigation is just beginning. But we will be in touch with you again. I assume you know what that means.'

I smiled weakly. 'Don't leave town, right? Don't worry, I have no trips planned.'

'Good to know. We'll need you readily available until our investigation is complete.'

'So that means what? I'm considered a person of interest?'

Bartell blew out a breath. 'You've gotta love all these cop shows on TV. Don't read more into this than there is at the present time, Ms Austin.' He inclined his head toward the door. 'You're free to leave. Good night.'

I rose shakily from the chair. 'Good night.' I started for the door, but Bartell's voice stopped me.

'If you should think of anything else . . .'

I looked at him over my shoulder. 'I'll be sure to call you,' I ground out, and then I bolted from the room and walked swiftly back down the hall. I heard footsteps behind me and I turned my head to see Dalton and Farraday right behind me. No one said a word as we all got into the elevator and rode back to the first floor. We exited the elevator, and walked in unison to the front door.

'Farraday will be glad to drive you back home,' said Dalton.

'No thanks,' I said. One ride in a squad car was enough for me to last my entire lifetime. 'I'd much rather walk, thanks.'

Dalton's gaze bored into mine. 'Are you sure? Rumor has it there might be a murderer out there, you know.'

I smiled thinly. Apparently Dalton, unlike Bartell, had a sense of humor. 'I'll take my chances, thanks.'

They both followed me outside. I turned and started walking in the opposite direction without another word to either of them. When I reached the corner, I turned and looked back. Apparently they'd given up on me quickly, because neither of them was anywhere to be seen.

I rolled my eyes skyward. 'Free at last,' I murmured, and threw my arms wide. Dramatic? Sure it was, but I felt I deserved a little comic relief after my ordeal at the station. I'd actually felt as if I couldn't breathe. And then it hit me.

Good Lord. It was possible Jenny Lee had been *murdered*. And they were questioning *me*.

I glanced at my watch. 12:35. I reached into my jacket pocket and pulled out my cell phone. I dialed Hilary's number, and she answered on the second ring. 'Hey, what's up,' she asked.

'Are you still at the Blue Goose?'

'Actually, I just pulled into my driveway.' She paused. 'Tiff, is something wrong? You sound terrible.'

I glanced down the street. 'Feel like meeting me at the Stumble Inn?'

'The Stumble Inn? What are you doing there? That's all the way over by the police station.' Her tone held a note of suspicion. 'What's going on, Tiff? You said you were going straight home.'

'I did. I was summoned out.'

'Summoned out? By who?'

'It's too much to go into over the phone. Will you meet me or not? I'm buying,' I added.

'Well, then how can I refuse?' Hilary said. 'I'm calling an Uber. I'll see you in ten.'

SEVEN

I walked across the street to the Stumble Inn and pushed through the door. The bar, with its white frame, gray trim, and dark wooden shutters might have received an accolade or two as one of the top twenty bars in the United States, but it still didn't look like much, which was probably part of its charm. The bar owners had gone for the kind of simple décor that could only improve with spilled beer and peanut shells on the floor.

I found a table for two at the rear of the bar. I laid my jean jacket across one of the chairs to hold the table, not that it was necessary. While the bar was packed, the seating area was only half-full. I made my way to the bar and ordered two margaritas and a bowl of peanuts. As I waited at the bar, I listened to the band, which consisted of a mandolin and a banjo player. Even their rendition of 'Piano Man' wasn't plucky enough to keep my conversation with Bartell from burning through my brain. *You know what that means, right? Yeah. Don't leave town.*

I glanced around, checking out the room for any familiar faces, although I doubted I'd find any. A couple of women, attired in tight dresses, were shimmying in front of the band. To my right, four guys in well-worn T-shirts and jackets were arguing over who'd end up winning the National League pennant this year. Judging on voice volume, I suspected they'd spent quite a bit of time here today arguing on that subject. I was relieved when the bartender arrived with my order, and slid an extra ten across the counter for him. He pocketed it and flashed me a grateful smile.

I'd just brought everything to the table when the door opened and Hilary hurried inside. I noted that she'd changed from her earlier attire to jeans and a comfortable, dove gray sweatshirt. She saw me and made a beeline for our table, slid into a chair, grabbed the margarita and took a long swallow.

'Whew,' she said, waving her glass in the air. 'I haven't been here in a long time. I'd forgotten just how fantastic their margaritas are.'

I picked up my own glass, took a sip, and I had to agree, the drink was excellent. 'Thanks for coming. I'm so glad you did.'

Hilary clinked her glass with mine, and we set them down on the table. She leaned forward and propped her chin in one hand. 'OK, I'm here. You said it was too much to go into over the phone, so spill. What happened tonight?'

I ran my finger around the rim of my glass. 'Jenny Lee's dead.'

'WHAT!' She raised her arm, balled her hand into a fist and pounded at her temple. 'I'm sorry. I could have sworn you said Jenny Lee is dead.'

'I did,' I said calmly. 'Murdered, apparently.'

Hilary flopped back in her seat. 'YOU'RE KIDDING!'

'Ssh,' I cautioned as I saw several heads swivel in our direction. Hilary picked up her glass and downed the entire contents in one swift gulp. She set the glass down and craned her neck in the direction of the bar. 'Something tells me I'm gonna need a refill.' She picked up her glass and waved it in the direction of a frowzy-haired waitress. As the woman approached, Hilary picked up my half-empty glass and handed both of them to her. 'Two more, fast. And make them doubles.' As the waitress shuffled off, Hilary held up her hand. 'Not one more word till we get those drinks.'

We didn't have long to wait. Less than five minutes passed before the waitress returned with not only fresh drinks, but a new bowl of peanuts. Once she'd departed, Hilary took a long swig of her drink and grabbed a fistful of peanuts. 'OK, I'm listening. What the heck happened?'

I explained how I'd come home and started to work on my 'Recipe of the Month' idea when Dalton and Farraday had shown up. 'They said they needed to question me in relation to the death of Jenny Lee Plumm. They took me down to the station and then Bartell took over.'

'Wait . . . Bartell?' Hilary's voice came out a loud squeak. 'As in Philip Bartell, one of Branson's ten most eligible bachelors?'

I shot my friend a stern look. 'Yes, but that's beside the point.'

Hilary pretended to swoon. 'I can see why you'd get flustered. Philip Bartell – whew!' She made an exaggeration motion of fanning herself.

'Anyway,' I said firmly, 'during my grilling by Bartell, he mentioned Jenny Lee's death was labelled suspicious – a possible homicide.'

'Holy merde.' Hilary's hands went to her throat and she twined her fingers around her red crystal necklace. 'Did he say anything about how she actually died?'

'Not one word.' My lips twisted into a rueful grin. 'Actually, he said he wasn't at liberty to discuss the details.'

'Oh, all cops say that.' Hilary waved her hand in a circle. 'Maybe she died of natural causes and Bartell only said that to get a reaction out of you.'

'I wish that were the case, but unfortunately I don't think it is,' I said. I felt the knot in my stomach grow tighter as I related the details of the interview to my friend.

'They can't seriously consider you a suspect, can they?' she said when I finished.

'I hope not,' I said. 'I did threaten to kill her, though.'

'But you didn't mean it!' Hilary's lips pursed. 'He really told you not to leave town?'

'No, he said that I knew what being available for more interviews meant. I added the part about not leaving town, but Bartell didn't deny it.' I brushed my hand through my mass of hair. 'I asked if I needed to consult a lawyer, and he said that I wasn't accused of anything. He didn't say accused yet but I could just sense it.' I released the hunk of hair I'd grabbed and scrubbed my hand across my face. I turned to Hilary and said in a hushed tone, 'He knew.'

She stared at me. 'He knew? Who knew? And what?'

'Bartell. I had the distinct impression he knew about my altercation with Jenny Lee all along. That must be why he had his men pick me up.'

Her face took on a puzzled expression. 'Don't be ridiculous, Tiff. How could he possibly have known that?'

I shrugged. 'I have no idea, but I'd bet next week's paycheck that he did. He didn't react when I mentioned the text I got from Jenny Lee.'

'Aw, that doesn't mean anything,' Hilary said with a brisk wave of her hand. 'He's a cop. They're trained to not react.'

'Maybe so.' I closed my eyes and tried to think. 'Jenny Lee texted me at nine fifteen, so let's just say she died sometime between then and ten. His men came for me around eleven thirty. He might have had time to interview someone before me, someone who told him about the incident in the hall.'

'O-K,' Hilary said slowly. 'But who could it have been? No one would do that. Everyone at the magazine loves you.'

'Yeah, well, quite a few people heard me yell at Jenny Lee that I could kill her earlier today. Maybe someone actually thinks I made good on it.'

'Do you remember who heard you?'

I shook my head. 'I know there were quite a few people milling around the hall. Honestly, I was just so embarrassed by the whole thing that I ducked back into my office as quickly as I could. I didn't pay much attention to who was standing around.'

Hilary took another sip of her drink. 'Ordinarily, in a situation like this, I'd say that Jenny Lee was the one who ratted you out. But seeing as she's dead . . .' Her shoulders shook in a shudder. 'I wouldn't worry too much about the police focusing on you, though. I'm sure once they start digging into Jenny Lee's life, they'll have more suspects than they can handle. Practically every woman in Branson, for starters.'

I snapped my fingers. 'I can think of a good possibility right off the bat,' I said. 'The mystery man, Roberto.'

'Oh, yeah!' Hilary's eyes shone. 'We heard him threaten her, remember? Actually, we heard them threaten each other.'

'But I saw him make a cutting motion across his throat at her,' I added. 'And I saw him in Trends, earlier tonight, having a heated conversation on his cell phone.'

'Do you think he was talking to Jenny Lee?'

'I don't know.' I closed my eyes, trying to visualize the scene. Abruptly my eyes flew open. 'What time did Mac arrive?'

'About quarter to six, I think. Why?'

'Mac was at the table when Roberto left. Man, I'd love to know more details, starting with just where they found the body. Maybe that would give us a clue as to who might have done her in – and who might have blown the whistle on me.'

'Well, it's a sure bet you won't find that out from the police,' said Hilary. She was silent for several seconds, her fingers tap-tapping on the table. At last she turned to me. 'There might be another way to get the info you need.'

I leaned forward. 'I'm listening.'

'Two words. Howard Sample.'

I wrinkled my nose. 'Howard Sample? Isn't that the guy you dated last month? The one you said was a real snooze-fest?'

'None other.'

My eyes narrowed. 'I believe you said that you wouldn't be caught dead with him anywhere again, pardon the poor choice of words.'

'I did say that, yes, but you are my very best friend and this is an emergency. No sacrifice is too great.'

Hilary pulled out her cell phone and punched in a number. I started to say something but she held up her finger and pressed it against her lips, a sign to remain silent. A few seconds later her voice dropped to a low, sexy drawl. 'Howie? It's Hilary Hanson. How are you?' She nodded, rolled her eyes and then said, 'I've been just fine, thanks. Missing you. Why haven't you called?' More eye rolling. 'Oh, you silly goose. I was just busy with work, that's all. As a matter of fact, my phone's been on the fritz for a couple of weeks now. That's probably why I never returned your call.' She listened a few moments and then purred, 'I'd love to see you again too. How about breakfast tomorrow? You're free? Great. See you at Ida's Diner at eight.'

She hung up and threw me a Cheshire cat smile. Totally bewildered, I spread my hands. 'What was that all about?'

Hilary waggled her finger at me. 'You are just about the only person in the world I would put myself through the torture of having breakfast with that guy for. But I promise you, I'll get some information about Jenny Lee Plumm out of him.'

I was still bewildered. 'What on earth could Howard Sample possibly tell you about Jenny Lee?'

'Lots, I'm hoping, since he said he couldn't talk too long. He has a lot of work to do tonight on something that just came in. Or, I should say, someone.'

I shook my head. 'I'm sorry, I'm still lost. How exactly is Howard going to help with regards to Jenny Lee's death?'

'I'm sorry, Tiff. I don't think I ever mentioned what Howard does for a living. It's part of the reason I never returned his calls. I just thought his job was too creepy.'

'Creepy? For God's sake, what does he do?'

Hilary's Cheshire smile got wider. 'He's the assistant county coroner.'

We finished our drinks and left; after all, Hilary had to be up early for her big date with Howard. He was supposed to have the entire weekend off, she said, but he'd gotten an emergency call to come in. Hilary was supremely hopeful that Jenny Lee was the emergency.

'He probably won't tell you very much,' I'd cautioned her as our Ubers pulled up and we said our goodbyes.

'Hey, at this point, every little bit of intel helps, right?'

Since I was ninety-nine percent sure I was the prime suspect, I'd had to agree with that assessment. Home again, I twisted my key in the lock and pushed open the side door. Cooper and Lily were right there. Cooper's tail was wagging so hard his entire body shook. Lily sat next to him, watching me with her big blue eyes, then came over and wound herself slowly around my legs. I bent down, gave Cooper a pat on the head and scooped the Siamese into my arms.

'You two are just what I need right now,' I murmured into Lily's soft fur.

I carried Lily into the living room, Cooper close at my heels. I sat down on the sofa, Lily on my lap. Cooper jumped up and wiggled next to me, settling himself against my hip. I leaned my head back and closed my eyes. I didn't want to think of the evening's events, but it was impossible. I found myself replaying my conversation with Bartell. The more I thought about it, the more certain I was he'd known all about the 'threat' I'd uttered to Jenny Lee.

'Someone had to tell him, but who?' I muttered. Where had Jenny Lee been when she'd sent me that text? She'd wanted to meet me at Barry's Café. Had she been there? Or somewhere else? Had she been alone? And just how had she died?

I moaned. 'My head hurts,' I said. Cooper immediately sat up and started to lick my face. I grinned and took his head between my hands. 'Thanks, boy. I can always count on you and Lily.' I sighed. 'Since sleep's practically impossible, I might as well try to get some work done.'

I transferred a sleeping Lily from my lap to the couch next to Cooper and walked over to the desk to get my laptop. I brought it back to the couch, set it on my mission-style coffee table, and booted it up. I opened Word and pulled up the file entitled 'Amateur Recipes'. I typed for a few minutes, then sat back and read the results:

> *Home Cooks! Now's the time to shine!*
> *Enter Bon-Appetempting's First Pizza Challenge!*
> *We're looking for your original recipes for homemade pizza! The three best will be featured on our blog, and participate in a cook-off to win a grand prize! (details to be ironed out)*
> *Fill out the form and submit to us by 30 September.*
> *Get your chef's caps on and let the cooking commence!*

I sat back and surveyed my handiwork. Rough around the edges, to be sure, but it had promise. I'd tweak it more after I spoke to Dale. I'd mentioned having a grand prize and a cook-off when I'd pitched the idea, so it shouldn't be too much of a shock. I hit the save button and felt something cold and wet brush against my wrist. I looked over at Cooper.

'Not bad, considering my mind's pretty much elsewhere, huh?' I asked the dog.

Cooper looked at me with his big brown eyes. 'Woof.'

'That's what I thought.' I straightened and Cooper jumped back up on the couch next to me. He laid his head in my lap and I stroked his soft fur. Lily – spread out as only a cat can on the couch's arm – opened one blue eye.

'I can't help thinking about Jenny Lee,' I murmured. 'Especially since I get the sense I could be pretty high on Bartell's suspect list. Who might have wanted her dead?' I leaned forward and called up a blank Word document. I titled it 'Suspects in Jenny Lee's Murder', and then looked at my two companions. 'Let's make a list, shall we?'

Cooper barked in agreement, and Lily let out a soft merow.

The first name that came to my mind, of course, was the mysterious Roberto. His motion of slicing his throat had pretty much said it all. He was angry at her, but angry enough to kill? Judging from what I'd seen, the answer was a resounding yes. I considered adding Mackenzie Huddleston's name to the list but in the end rejected it. He and Jenny Lee had dated, but he didn't seem all that broken up about it. In fact, from the way he'd flirted with all the women at the table tonight, I'd have to say he was well over Jenny Lee. Besides, he'd been at our table in plain sight from six fifteen till almost nine and left with Hilary. If anyone had an iron-clad alibi, it was Mac.

The next name I jotted down was Frederick Longo. There was something there, although I wasn't quite sure just what. They'd argued at the restaurant Monday night, and again on Friday. What was it Longo had said to her? Something about her little tricks not working. Had she attempted to blackmail him into going to the board and trying to get them to change their minds? Or was there something else? And if so, was it enough for Longo to kill her over?

'Two viable suspects that I know of,' I murmured. 'And God knows who else. Longo intimated she had dirt on lots of people. Jenny Lee had way more enemies than friends, that's for sure.'

And thinking about Jenny Lee's lack of friends brought sharply to mind the woman in the convertible who'd magically appeared to pick her up Monday night. Who was she and what was her relationship to Jenny Lee?

And did she have a reason to want her dead too?

I typed 'Mystery Woman' underneath Longo's name and

frowned. After a moment I added my name and Dale's too. I knew I was innocent, and I believed Dale was as well, but in the eyes of the police, whether I liked it or not, I was relatively certain we were both on their list. Even though Bartell had tried to downplay it, how could we not be? After all, we'd both had arguments with Jenny Lee the day of her death. She'd threatened Dale, and I'd threatened to kill her.

One thing I knew: if I wanted to get our names off that list, I had to home in on the real killer – and fast.

EIGHT

S ometime during the night I'd stretched out on the couch and fallen asleep. I was jarred from my slumber by a furious pounding on my front door. Cooper, who'd been snuggled at my feet, immediately hopped down, ran over to the door and started to bark. Lily, snuggled on the top of the couch, lifted her head, yawned, and promptly went back to snoozing.

Fully awake now, I swung my feet off the couch and made my way to the front door. I peered out through the side curtain. I looked down at my spaniel and said 'Relax, Coop. It's Dale.'

Cooper stopped barking but continued to stand watchfully by my side as I unlocked the front door and swung it wide. Dale nodded and pushed past me into the foyer, where he turned to regard me with dark eyes. 'You look like hell,' he said.

'Gee thanks.'

Cooper, apparently satisfied I wasn't in any mortal danger, gave another loud yip and scurried off in the direction of the kitchen. Lily rose from her supine position, stretched, jumped lightly to the floor and followed suit.

I chuckled and looked at Dale. 'Mind if I feed the children first?'

'Not at all. As a matter of fact, I wouldn't turn down a cup of coffee.'

'Fine. The Keurig's on a timer, so it should be on. There's a selection of pods right next to it.' I ran my hand through my tousled hair, conscious of my grubby appearance for the first time. It didn't seem to bother Dale, though. He followed me into the kitchen, laid his keyring on my counter and busied himself at my Keurig while I spooned food out for the 'kids'. Canned tuna for Lily, and a fresh chicken and spinach mixture for Cooper. I refilled their water bowls and noted that Dale had also made a mug of coffee for me as well as himself. I sat down next to him at the kitchen table and, while he debated between Splenda and regular sugar, I took a long sip of the hot brew – Newman's Special Blend, my favorite.

'Aah, that's better.' I glanced at the clock on the wall, saw it was just seven thirty. 'So, what brings you by so early on a Saturday morning?'

Dale took a sip and then set his mug down, wrapped his hands around it. 'I wanted to make certain you were OK after last night.'

I looked at him sharply. 'Last night?'

His expression grew wistful. 'You don't have to play dumb with me, Tiff. I know all about Jenny Lee's death. The police questioned me at length too.'

I felt an immediate sense of relief that I hadn't been the only one in Bartell's sights. 'Was it Bartell? What did he tell you?'

'Not much. At first he only told me she was dead, but when I balked a little bit he said there were certain things about her death that made them classify it as suspicious. He didn't cough up any details, he just wanted to know what I knew about her background, if I was aware of anyone who might have wanted her dead, or threatened her recently.' His cheeks flushed a delicate shade of pink. 'He asked a lot of questions about you.'

My stomach lurched. Could it have been Dale who blew the whistle on me? 'He did?'

'Yep. Wanted to know about your background, how you were doing at the magazine. I told him we'd gone to grammar and high school together, and I could vouch for your character.'

'Thanks.'

He tapped his spoon against the rim of the mug. 'Don't thank me yet. He asked me about your relationship with Jenny Lee; specifically, that little catfight the two of you had yesterday.'

'He asked you about that?' I felt a bit relieved. If Bartell had quizzed Dale, then that meant Dale hadn't been the one to tell him about it. 'I wouldn't call it a catfight,' I protested. 'It was more of . . . a disagreement.'

'A loud disagreement. Anyway, I told him that what I knew

was third-hand or second-hand at best, I didn't actually witness it, but he wanted to hear it anyway. He asked me if I thought Jenny Lee could have provoked you into threatening her and I told him absolutely. Threats aren't your style. Why, you'd never hurt a fly.'

'Gee thanks. Didn't they say the same thing about Norman Bates?'

'Yep, but you're way prettier.'

I made a face at him. 'It does bother me that he seems to be fixated on our argument and more specifically, my remark. I can't imagine why, unless—'

'Unless you're suspect number one?' Dale finished. 'I can't believe that. There must be loads of other people who had better reasons to want her dead than you. As a matter of fact, you don't even have a reason.'

I tucked my leg under me and cradled my mug. 'So you wouldn't consider her threat to delve into my past and ruin me a motive sufficient enough for murder?'

He snorted. 'Maybe if you had a checkered past, which you don't . . . do you?'

'What do you think?' I countered. Before he could answer I went on, 'I think Bartell knew all about that incident before either of us were dragged down there. I'd love to know how he found out so quickly.'

Dale ran a hand through his hair 'Well, if he had Jenny Lee's phone in his possession, that could explain it.'

I paused, mug halfway to my lips. 'Her phone?'

Dale nodded. 'Jenny Lee had a habit of always leaving the record button on whenever she had conversations with people. To avoid her being misquoted, she always said. Do you remember if she had her phone with her when she came to your office?'

My eyes slitted as I thought. 'I didn't see her phone,' I said at last. 'But I remember she kept fiddling with her jacket pockets.'

'Well, there you go. She probably had it in her pocket.'

I set my mug down. 'If that's true, Bartell would have gotten an earful. He also would know that she goaded me into making that threat, so why keep harping on it?'

'Because that's what cops do. C'mon, Tiff, you know that. After all, you used to be a big fan of *Law and Order*.'

'Yeah, and Bartell does remind me a little bit of Jerry Orbach – personality, not looks.'

'I figure they must have found Jenny Lee's phone, because Bartell knew all about my meeting with her.' His lips twisted into a rueful smile. 'I knew she was recording everything, and yet I let myself fall into her trap.'

'Don't tell me you threatened to kill her too?'

'Actually, I told her that if she tried to make any trouble over her termination, I'd cheerfully strangle her with both hands and not look back.'

'Ouch. Well, don't beat yourself up. That woman managed to push everyone's buttons and rub them the wrong way. I bet if we took a survey, more than half the magazine employees would have reacted the same way.'

'That's probably true.' Dale pushed his mug off to one side and twisted his hands in front of him. 'Bartell knew all about her parting threat to me. Wanted to know if there was anything in my past that I'd been afraid she'd dig up. I told him no, and he should feel free to check me out. I'm sure he wasted no time doing so,' he added with a wry grin.

'Well, I guess I like the idea of him finding out via the phone rather than someone ratting on us,' I said. 'What I'm most curious about, though, is just how she died.' I snapped my fingers and started to rise. 'The morning paper. Maybe there's an account in there.'

'Nope.' Dale shook his head. 'There's a mention of her death below the fold on page one, but it doesn't say the manner of death, just that her body was found late last evening and the police are investigating. The story's very brief, no details. It doesn't even say where the body was found.'

I sat back down and touched my finger to my lips. 'It's like they're trying to keep everything about her death a deep, dark secret. Why, I wonder?'

Dale shrugged. 'Who knows? I'm sure Bartell has his reasons. Anyway, I do believe it's customary for police not to reveal all the details in a murder investigation. Hallmark evidence, I think they call it. It refers to certain aspects of evidence they feel are unique and case-sensitive, and which will help them trap the killer.'

'Maybe so. I'll tell you this, though – I don't like being under suspicion, not one bit.'

'Me either.'

'Did he tell you not to leave town?'

'I believe his exact words were, "Stick close to town, in case we need to question you further."'

I picked up my spoon and absently started to stir what little coffee was left in my mug. 'Someone should really steer this guy in the right direction,' I said with feeling.

'Away from us, you mean? Well, I'm all for that. Anyone in particular you want to direct him towards?'

I tapped my spoon against the rim of my mug and set it down. 'Actually yes. Frederick Longo.'

Dale's brows knit together. 'Longo? I thought he was a friend of yours?'

'He was a friend of my former employer. He's more like an acquaintance to me.'

'Hm. It certainly seemed as if there were more to your relationship than that. When he met with the board and was told his appointment was approved, I understand he was quite effusive in his praise of you and your blog.'

I found it hard to keep the surprise out of my voice. 'He was?'

'Yes. He said that your blog was a credit to the magazine and he'd be glad to support any endeavor you undertook. He believes that expanding the food section is key to increasing readership.'

'Of course he'd feel that way, he's a chef,' I said. 'He might be right. I mean, look at the popularity of cooking shows. That's one of the reasons I wanted to kick off that contest.'

'I remember. I have it on my agenda to discuss Monday.' He let out a soft chuckle. 'Assuming, of course, Bartell doesn't have one or the other of us in jail by then.'

'Bite your tongue,' I said. 'I'm innocent and so are you. I'm not so sure about Longo, though. I overheard him arguing with Jenny Lee twice.'

Dale turned sideways in his chair and stretched his long

legs out in front of him. 'If that's what you're basing your suspicions on, I'd rethink them. Jenny Lee has probably argued with practically everyone on the *Southern Style* staff a million times, and God knows who else. They can't all be suspect.'

'True, but I got the sense from what I did overhear that there might be more to Jenny Lee and Longo's relationship than her just trying to butter him up so he'd intervene for her.' I tapped at my chin. 'It sounded to me like she'd tried to dig up something on him but failed, and he was warning her not to try again.'

'Why? Because there was something for her to find? Or because he just didn't want to be bothered by her?'

'Maybe one or the other, maybe both. Who knows? I do think, though, that their relationship bears further investigation.'

'I'm not so sure about that,' said Dale. 'Longo's the type Jenny Lee liked. Rich, successful, a good-looking older man . . .'

'Longo's married,' I pointed out.

'So was Jeremy. That little detail never stopped Jenny Lee,' Dale responded. 'I think she found out he was being considered for the director position and she just got him in her sights, decided to work her femme fatale charms on him. And when that didn't work out, she lashed out by threatening to do what she did best – dig up dirt.'

'Like she did with me, and Lord knows how many others.'

'Bingo.'

'Were you aware Jenny Lee was also dating Mac Mackenzie?'

Dale leaned back and stretched his long legs out in front of him. 'Yeah, for like a nanosecond. I think the real attraction for Jenny Lee was the fact Mac's aunt was on the magazine's board. As for why Mac would have dated her . . . well, you know. Do I have to draw you a diagram?'

I pulled a face. 'Not really.'

We were both silent for a few minutes, and then I pointed at Dale's empty mug. 'Need a refill?'

He held it out and flashed me a grateful smile. 'If you wouldn't mind. I find I'm in need of a larger jolt of caffeine than usual this morning. I've got to meet Detective Dalton at the magazine office in an hour. They want to search through Jenny Lee's office. For all the good it'll do them,' he added. 'She kept that office barer than Mother Hubbard's cupboard. I told him they'd probably have better luck searching her home office.'

'I'm sure that's on their agenda. Bartell struck me as a very thorough individual.'

I picked up both mugs and walked over to the Keurig. While the coffee was brewing I asked, 'Did Jenny Lee have any women friends that you know of?'

Dale looked at me. 'What an odd question. I doubt that very much.'

'Why?'

'Well, judging from the way she interacted with the women at the magazine, Jenny Lee wasn't the type to have girlfriends. Every time I saw her, it was always in the company of a man.'

'That doesn't mean she didn't have a close woman friend,' I said. I brought Dale's mug and his keys over to him, set them down, and then went back for my own mug. 'I can think of one, at least.'

He looked at me, surprise evident on his face. 'Really? Who?'

'I don't know her name,' I confessed. 'But, Monday night, when Hilary and I ran into Jenny Lee and Longo at that restaurant I reviewed, we saw her having an argument with another man when we were leaving. A woman in a dark convertible picked her up.'

Dale spooned some sugar into his mug, picked up his spoon and stirred. 'Now that is interesting. I didn't think Jenny Lee had any girlfriends.'

I shrugged. 'Maybe she's a relative? Did Jenny Lee have any sisters?'

Dale frowned. 'She was an only child, but I think I remember her mentioning a stepsister who lives in California. I'm not sure how close they were, though.'

'Well, whoever this woman was, Jenny Lee seemed glad to see her and jumped right in the convertible. They took off like a pack of wild dogs were after them.'

'That does sound very mysterious. What did this woman look like?'

'I have no idea. She had on a scarf and sunglasses that hid her face.'

'A real mystery woman, eh? So, what? You think this woman might have killed Jenny Lee?'

'At this point I don't think anyone should be ruled out, no matter how far-fetched the possibility might seem.'

'Agreed.' He lifted his hand and ran it through his hair. 'What about the man you said Jenny Lee was arguing with? Maybe he's a suspect.'

'Funny you should say that. He's my other possibility. I only know his first name, Roberto, but I found a photo of them together on the Internet.' I crossed the room to where I'd thrown my tote the night before and started rummaging in it. 'I had the photo in my bag. I wanted to show it to Jenny Lee but I never got the chance . . . Ah, here it is.'

I pulled the photo out. It had gotten a little crumpled, so I smoothed it out and passed it over to Dale. 'He does look rather sinister, don't you think?'

Dale stared at the photo with an odd expression on his face. At last he looked over at me. 'You said his name's Roberto?'

'Yes, I heard her call him that. Hilary heard it too.' I stared at Dale, who'd grown pale. 'Do you know him?'

Dale set the picture on the table. In a low voice he said, 'I don't know him personally, but I've definitely seen him around the magazine. If you were there more than one day a month, you probably would have too.'

'He works for the magazine? That must be how they met,' I cried. As Dale remained silent I added, 'Well, don't keep me in suspense, Dale. Who is he?'

Dale cleared his throat and then said in a hushed tone, 'His name is Roberto Manchetti.'

'Manchetti. Hm, yes, he does have an Italian look about him. Manchetti,' I repeated it again. 'Why does that name sound familiar?'

'Because you've probably heard it.' Dale was pale, and his tone was hushed as he added, 'It's a well-known name around the magazine. Enzo Manchetti is the chairman of the board of *Southern Style*. Roberto is his son.'

NINE

Dale left shortly after dropping that bombshell, and I sat for a while at my kitchen table, trying to make sense of what I'd learned. One thing I had to say about Jenny Lee: she sure didn't waste time with small potatoes. She went straight for the top: Slater, and Roberto Manchetti – and who knows, maybe even Roberto's father? Could that have been what they were arguing about? I dismissed the last possibility as soon as it entered my mind. From what I knew of Enzo Manchetti, Jenny Lee Plumm would be the last person on earth he'd be attracted to.

I replayed my interview with Bartell in my mind. He hadn't confirmed that I was a suspect, but he hadn't done much to discourage that notion, either. I wondered if they did indeed have Jenny Lee's phone and, if so, what other information they might have gleaned from it – the identity of Roberto, perhaps? If Bartell did have her phone, and if she had recorded our meeting, he'd have heard about Roberto. Of course, he'd have also heard Jenny Lee's theories on my past as well, which might give me a motive for murder in his eyes.

Arriving at a decision, I jumped up, grabbed my purse, and rummaged through it until I found the card Bartell had given me. Then I fished my cell out of the bag. Cooper and Lily were both spread across the kitchen floor, watching me. 'Hey, he said to call if I thought of something right?' I said to them. 'I thought of something. Bartell should know about Roberto's connection to the magazine, right?'

Both animals cocked their heads at me and didn't utter a peep. I took that as silent agreement and punched in Bartell's number. My call went straight to voicemail.

'Detective Bartell, this is Tiffany Austin. You might remember me from last night, or rather earlier this morning. You had me brought in for questioning regarding the murder of Jenny Lee Plumm. You, ah, you told me to call you if I thought of anything and well . . . I have.' *Oh, gee, Tiffany, smooth!* I hesitated. I couldn't make any references to Jenny Lee's phone. What if the police didn't have it? I swallowed and continued, 'I don't recall if I mentioned this or not, but Monday night my friend Hilary and I saw Jenny Lee having a rather heated argument with a man named Roberto. I've since learned something about him you might find interesting. I'll be waiting for your call.'

I hung up, flung the cell off to the side and scrubbed my hands across my face. I peered out from between my fingers. Lily and Cooper were both sitting there, staring at me, and I swear I saw both of them shake their heads.

'I'm sorry,' I yelped, pulling my hands from my face and rubbing them along the sides of my pj's. 'I got nervous, OK. Anyway, it's something I'd rather speak to Bartell about, not his machine.'

Both Cooper and Lily yawned and lay down.

I sighed and glanced at the clock. Nine a.m. Hilary was probably still at breakfast with Howard Sample. Hopefully it would be successful and she'd find out some details but, until I heard from her, I had to keep busy, and I knew just how.

I'd been promising the owner of Po'Boys Anonymous for several weeks now that I'd stop by to sample their new brunch menu. I'd already tried their famous po'boys for lunch – several times, in fact – and had given them a well-deserved five-star review.

For those not familiar with this traditional Louisiana dish, a po'boy is a sandwich that almost always consists of meat, usually sloppy roast beef or fried seafood that can include shrimp, crawfish, oysters and crab. Bob and Nita Gillette, the owners, served 'em up on baguette-like French bread and they usually sold out of one variety or another well before lunch hour was over. I had to admit that, in spite of everything, I was salivating at the thought of what delicacies might be in store for me on their new brunch menu.

Po'Boys Anonymous was about a five-minute walk from the magazine office. I showered and dressed in black jeans (elastic waist) and a comfortable rose-colored Hacci cold-shoulder top that flared out at the waist, perfect for hiding bulges from an overindulgent meal. I grabbed my purse, said goodbye to the children (who were still snoozing), and drove the short distance to the gray slate building that housed the offices of *Southern Style*. I parked my car in the employee lot, which was pretty full for a Saturday, and walked the two-and-a-half blocks to the restaurant. As I approached the low-slung gray slate building, I could see through the large plate-glass window that it was busy. Nearly every table was full. There was a counter in the side window that had stools facing the street, and that was almost full as well. As I walked toward the entrance, some birds swooped down to settle on the wide flower box underneath the picture window. They chattered gaily as I pushed open the door.

I paused on the threshold and sniffed the air appreciatively as delicious aromas wafted toward me. There was a printed menu displayed on a large blackboard to the right of the main counter. The breakfast items were traditional Southern break-fast staples: biscuits with sausage gravy, golden grits casserole, Southern breakfast scramble and chicken and waffles, country fried steak and strawberry bread. The lunch offerings made my mouth water too: in addition to their full range of po'boys, there was Southern macaroni and cheese, Southern red rice with shrimp, salmon patties, Southern fried catfish and crab and shrimp gumbo. I whipped out my cell and snapped some photos of the overflowing platters that I was certain would soon disappear, judging from the line that was starting to form.

Nita Gillette was just refilling the platter of catfish. She looked up, saw me, and immediately set the platter down and walked around to greet me, arms outstretched. 'Tiffany! My dear, you finally made it to our brunch!'

I hugged her back and then inclined my head toward the counter. 'Yes, but Nita, I don't think you even need a review from me. Look at this place! You're packed!'

Nita blushed. 'Oh, thank you, darlin' but you're wrong. We all need a good review, and one from the best food critic, not to mention a premier chef, can't hurt us one little tweeny bit.'

I smiled. 'That's so good of you to say.'

'Well, it's true . . . Honey, look who's come to sample brunch. Tiffany Austin.'

Bob Gillette, a big hulk of a man with shoulders like an Atlanta Falcon linebacker and huge, beefy hands, stepped forward and enveloped me in a bear hug as well. When we pulled apart he took my hand and pumped it up and down. 'Miss Tiffany, it's a pleasure. I'm sure we owe our booming business to that glowing five-star review you gave us a few months ago.'

'That's true,' Nita agreed. 'Why, we've been so busy since we introduced that new menu, we hardly have a moment to ourselves. Yesterday we were so busy we were both here till almost eleven at night with no breaks.'

'I'd like to take credit for that, but I think your food is the real key.' I paused and made a motion of sniffing the air. 'It smells so good in here!'

'That's Nita's gumbo,' Bob said proudly. 'Her mama's recipe. There's a secret ingredient in there that she won't even tell me.'

'Women have to have some secrets,' Nita said demurely. She leaned toward me and said in a half-whisper, 'He just wants to find out if I pilfered some of his home-grown herbs. But I'll never tell.'

Talking about secrets made me think of Jenny Lee, and I did not want to think of her right now. I just wanted to enjoy my brunch. I glanced around the room. 'Looks like every table is taken,' I observed.

'Not every table,' said Bob with a wink. 'There's one in the kitchen that Nita and I eat at. Of course, if you don't want to eat back there, I'm sure something will open up soon.'

'Are you kidding?' I grinned at him. 'I was a chef, remember? I always ate in the kitchen. Lead the way.'

I followed them through the swinging door into a kitchen area that was so spotless, I could have eaten off the floor. Two chefs in white hats busied themselves at the large double burner stove, while two others busied themselves chopping lettuce and tomato, no doubt for the huge bowl of garden salad I'd noticed on the counter. Nita ushered me over to a small table set for two in the corner. It reminded me of the table in *Lady and the Tramp*, with its red and white checked tablecloth, gleaming silver and white plates, and hurricane lamp in the center. Bob swept up both plates and bustled toward the stove.

'A little of everything for her, honey,' Nita called after him. She sat down in the chair opposite me and smiled. 'I certainly hope you enjoy it.'

'I'm already writing a rave review in my head, just from the aromas alone,' I assured her. 'I'm only sorry I didn't get here sooner.'

'So are we,' Nita laughed.

Bob appeared and set two heaping plates in front of me. Then they went about their business and left me to mine – eating! I dug blissfully into the perfectly cooked chicken and waffles and popped some catfish into my mouth at the same time. All the food was superb and, by the time I'd cleaned both plates, I was very thankful I'd worn the elastic waist jeans.

'I guess you didn't like it, huh?' teased Bob as he removed my plates. Both of them looked as if they'd just come out of the dishwasher. He peered closely at one of them. 'By gum, it looks like you even ate the silver etching.'

'Don't tempt me,' I laughed. 'I'm wondering if I can give you the first six-star review ever.'

'We'll take it,' laughed Nita. 'We've always liked firsts.' She set a plate in front of me that boasted a humongous hunk of pie.

I groaned. 'Oh, Nita, I don't know if I can.'

'Hey, this is my grandma's special pie. Peanut butter crème. Just take a taste, and if you like it, I'll box it for you to have later.'

I picked up my fork. 'I'm gonna have to start buying the next size in jeans.'

I popped a piece of the pie into my mouth, rolled my eyes. 'Oh. Soooo good.'

'Great. I'll box some slices up for you.' Nita picked up the plate. 'How about a nice cup of coffee to finish?'

'That sounds good.'

Nita brought back a good-sized box that I figured contained more than two slices of pie, along with two mugs of coffee. She put the box and one mug in front of me and then sat down opposite me, cradling the mug in her hands. 'Time for my break anyway,' she said. We both sipped the coffee, which was strong and delicious, and then Nita said, 'So, what's new with you, Tiffany? How's it going at the magazine?'

'Very well. I was appointed to the permanent staff yesterday.'

Nita clapped her hands. 'You were! That's wonderful. Isn't that wonderful, honey?' she asked her husband as he hurried past with a tray.

'Sure, sweetie.' He paused. 'What's wonderful?'

Nita tittered. 'Tiffany's food blog is now a permanent feature in *Southern Style*.'

'Oh, congratulations.' Bob set down the tray and held out his hand. 'Sorry, Tiffany, I didn't realize that you were employed on a temporary basis.'

'It was a six-month trial. Apparently my numbers were good enough to make it official.'

'Numbers,' he sighed. 'Sales and numbers. Everyone seems to live and die by them, don't they?'

Nita gave a small shudder. 'Don't talk about dying, Bob, especially after what happened last night.' She turned to me. 'We heard that some poor woman got murdered last night.'

I nodded. Good news certainly traveled fast here in Branson. 'Yes. Jenny Lee Plumm.'

Bob and Nita exchanged a quick look. 'So it was Jenny Lee Plumm that was killed,' said Bob. When I nodded, his face darkened. His eyebrows drew together, giving him a thunder-cloud effect. 'Well, good riddance, I say.'

Nita patted her husband's arm. 'Now, now. We shouldn't speak ill of the dead.'

Her husband's lips twisted into a grimace. 'Don't get me wrong. I'd like to feel bad, but I just can't. That Jenny Lee Plumm wasn't a nice person.'

I took another sip of my coffee. 'I didn't realize you knew her.'

'Oh, we didn't actually *know* her,' Nita said quickly. 'She just came in here a few times.'

'Yes, and always with some disparaging remark to make. If it wasn't the food, it was the décor. She even wrote us up in that society column of hers a few months ago.' Bob let out a snort. "Places in Branson to Avoid", I think the article was called. And do you know, she had the nerve to come in here the day after it came out. Can you imagine?' His cheeks reddened as he added, 'I gave her a tongue lashing she wouldn't forget, and then I showed her the door.'

My eyes widened. 'You threw her out?'

'Oh, not bodily,' Nita hastened to assure me. 'But he definitely got his point across.'

'She didn't even care that she could have ruined our business,' Bob declared. 'She yammered all the way out, threatening retaliation.' He looked at his wife. 'I guess we don't have to worry about that now – not that we ever were,' he added quickly.

'Thank goodness people put more stock in your review than her article,' Nita said with a nod. 'But I have to agree – it's tough to feel bad about a person like that. She was evil.'

'Jenny Lee wasn't very well liked,' I agreed. 'I hate to say it, but I'm sure there were few tears shed.'

'That's probably true,' Nita said. 'I have to admit, I'm a bit curious as to how she died. It might have been an accident, but that Detective Bartell didn't seem to think so.'

I paused, my mug halfway to my lips. 'Detective Bartell?'

Nita nodded. 'Yes, I thought I mentioned he was in here this morning for coffee with that nice Detective Dalton.'

'Ah,' I said. 'Is that how you found out about the murder?'

Nita's cheeks brightened a bit. 'Well, yes. I wasn't eavesdropping on purpose, mind you, but when I brought over their orders, I caught snatches here and there. I didn't know they were talking about Jenny Lee, though.'

I hitched my chair closer to Nita's. 'Just what exactly did you hear?'

'Not that much,' Nita admitted. 'I did hear something curious, though. Detective Dalton said, "Between nine and nine thirty", and Bartell said, "Can't he be more specific?" Then Dalton said he'd ask again, and then he said something else to Bartell, and both Bartell's eyebrows rose and he said, "You're serious?" Dalton laughed and then he said, "Well, at least she died eating something she loved."'

I frowned. 'She died eating something? You mean she choked to death?'

Bob let out a snort. 'Couldn't have been Jenny Lee if that's the case. The woman ate like a bird. Pecked at her food.'

'Maybe she was really hungry and gobbled it down,' suggested Nita. 'I've seen a few people have close calls that way. Oh, well. It'll all come out eventually. Whether we liked her or not, Jenny Lee was a public figure. People will be interested in the details.' She paused. 'There was another man in here who seemed interested in what the two detectives were saying as well. He tried to act like he wasn't listening, but I could tell he was.'

I leaned forward. 'Could you describe him?'

Nita's lips scrunched up as she thought. 'He was good looking, but not in a conventional way. He had a muscular build. To be honest, he kind of reminded me of a bouncer.' She smiled at me. 'Can I get you anything else, honey?'

'No thanks. I'm good.'

I downed the rest of my coffee, set down my mug and pushed back my chair. 'Thank you for everything,' I said. I started to reach for my purse but Nita's hand shot out and she pushed it away.

'Don't be silly. This was a business lunch, after all. You were reviewing our new brunch menu.' She closed one eye in a wink. 'I'll just send the bill to the magazine.'

'Thank you, but I'd have given you an excellent review even if I paid. I haven't had a brunch this good in a long time.'

'We'll take as many good reviews as you want to give us,' chuckled Bob. 'Y'all come back soon.'

'Definitely,' added Nita. I was halfway to the door when she called after me, 'Oh, and if you should hear any more details on what happened to Jenny Lee, let me know. I have to admit, I'm curious.'

'However she died, I hope it was painful,' Bob growled.

I picked up my purse and headed for the door. I was a little taken aback by the venom in Bob's tone when he spoke of Jenny Lee, and I couldn't help but wonder: could he be a suspect?

TEN

B ack out on the street I paused, letting what I'd just learned sink in. I found it a bit hard to believe that she'd choked to death, because Bob was right. Jenny Lee ate like a bird. She chewed her food ad nauseum. I'd seen it firsthand at staff meetings. So, if she hadn't choked to death, that left only one other possibility.

Whatever she'd eaten had been poisoned, which also indicated her death hadn't been accidental. It had been premeditated. But by whom?

Roberto Manchetti came to mind. Nita's description of the man so interested in the detective's conversation could fit him. Of course, if he shared a history with Jenny Lee, it would only be natural he'd be curious about the details of her death. Unless, of course, he'd been the one to end her life, in which case, he might be interested in just how much the police knew. I'd sure be interested in where he might have been on Friday night.

Nita said a timeframe of between nine and nine thirty had been mentioned. But Jenny Lee had texted me at around nine fifteen, so that meant she had to have died between nine fifteen and nine thirty. Her death must have been swift. I glanced around. This section of town was chock-full of eateries. Chances were good that Jenny Lee had been at one nearby, but which one? I needed to find out more details about her death.

I leaned against a lamppost and whipped out my cell. I punched in Hilary's number, glancing at my watch as I did so. I distinctly remembered hearing her make plans to meet Howard Sample at eight, and it was nearly noon. She must either be having a really good time, or she was hard pressed to wrangle some info out of him. When my call went to voicemail, I groaned out loud. I left a message: 'Hil, it's me. I found out some info that might relate to Jenny Lee's death. Waiting for your call.'

I tossed my phone back in my bag and looked around. It probably wouldn't hurt to just check out some other eateries in the immediate vicinity. I walked slowly up and down the street, pausing every now and then to look at a different establishment. There was a wide range of restaurants along the strip, anything from luncheonettes to elegant eateries. What one might Jenny Lee have chosen? And was she alone, or had she met someone? Hilary would have said Jenny Lee didn't have friends, but I could think of one at least: the mysterious woman who'd picked Jenny Lee up the other evening.

I passed Emmaline's Market and had a sudden desire to make shrimp gumbo for dinner. Lily and Cooper would approve, especially Lily. I went inside and spent a half-hour looking at all the delicacies Emmaline Carey had crammed into her tiny store. I finally loaded my market basket with all the ingredients I'd need to make a New Orleans-style shrimp gumbo: celery, green peppers, cayenne pepper, shrimp, and andouille sausage. After deliberating a bit, I decided to add fresh crabmeat as well. I added a loaf of crusty French bread, a sack of Buffalo Blue for Cooper and a Friskies for Lily and made my way to the checkout counter. As I approached, I paused and blinked twice. Nope, I wasn't seeing things.

Philip Bartell was standing in line, tapping his foot impatiently. Even though the line at the adjacent counter was shorter, I sidled over to stand behind him. He glanced casually over his shoulder, and then did a double take as recognition kicked in.

He inclined his head slightly. 'Ms Austin.'

I shifted the market basket in my hands. 'Detective Bartell. Fancy meeting you here.' I glanced at the items he'd laid on the counter. 'Doing a bit of shopping, I see.'

He turned and eyed my overflowing basket. 'Not as much as you.' He pushed his few items further up on the counter. They didn't take up much space, actually. A Cadbury chocolate bar, a can of shaving cream, a container of milk. He motioned to me. 'That looks heavy. Please, lay them down.'

He didn't need to ask me twice. I noted he eyed every item I set down. 'I had a hungering for gumbo,' I said. 'I thought I'd make a nice hearty New Orleans one.'

His eyebrow lifted. 'I imagine, considering your background, that it will taste delicious.'

'Oh, it will. Count on it.' I gave him a wide smile. 'I could save you some, if you'd like.'

Much to my surprise, he smiled back. 'That's very generous of you, but I'm afraid I have to decline.'

'No problem.' I tried to make my tone light as I added, 'I guess there's some sort of regulation against taking food from possible murder suspects?'

The smile faded, and he didn't answer for a few seconds. Then he said, 'I enjoy cooking myself, but I'm afraid I don't have much time to indulge these days.'

I couldn't keep the surprise out of my voice as I remarked, 'You cook?'

'Yes, and I'm not half bad. Not as good as you, I'm sure, but . . .' He patted his stomach. 'Well enough for a bachelor, I suppose.'

'Oh, I believe you. It's a well-known fact that male chefs dominate the restaurant world. Of course, that doesn't necessarily mean they're the better.'

The cashier started ringing up Bartell's items. He put the milk and shaving cream in a plastic sack. The candy bar he unwrapped and bit into it as the cashier announced, 'That will be seven eighty-four, please.' He fished his wallet out of his jacket pocket and handed over a ten. He took another large bite of the chocolate, chewed and swallowed before taking the proffered change.

I eyed the half-eaten candy bar as the cashier started to ring up my items. 'Don't tell me that's your lunch?'

'No, I grabbed a burger at some joint a few blocks from here.' He popped the last of the caramel Cadbury into his mouth and balled up the wrapper. 'My first dessert.'

'Dessert!' I'd totally forgotten. I'd intended to pick up the ingredients for Bananas Foster, something I hadn't made in a while. As I noticed my bill growing, though, I was relieved I hadn't. As it was, I'd have just enough to pay for what I did purchase.

Bartell was still standing off to the side, eyeing me. 'I'll bet you could whip up a mean crème brûlée,' he said.

'I've been known to.' I handed the cashier the entire contents of my wallet – three twenties. After receiving a five and some change back, I picked up my two plastic sacks. 'Tonight, though, I'll have to settle for vanilla ice cream and strawberry sauce. I've got some strawberries in the freezer. I can defrost them and whip up a good sauce in my Vitamix.'

'I've got chocolate ice cream in my freezer. And I think I've got some marshmallow sauce left. That'll be my second dessert later on tonight – if I get home at all. It looks like I have another late night of work in front of me.'

We exited on to the street and Bartell reached for one of my sacks. Hefting it into his hand he gave a perfunctory nod. 'Where are you parked? I know you couldn't have walked here, you live too far away – or did you want the exercise?' His gaze raked over my body, and I felt my cheeks sear with heat.

'I'm parked in the lot behind *Southern Style*,' I said. As Bartell started to turn in that direction I stammered, 'Y-you don't have to carry my groceries. I've lugged much heavier than this around, trust me.'

His eyebrow lifted. 'It's no bother. Besides, I thought we could talk as we walk. You did leave me a message earlier, did you not? Or have you thought it over and decided that whatever information you wanted to impart wasn't all that important after all?'

My lips thinned to a straight line. 'Oh, I think it's important enough. But I really don't think it's the type of info that can be dispensed walking around town.'

Was it my imagination, or did his lips quirk ever so slightly. 'How about riding around town, then?' he asked. He paused next to a large black sedan. 'My car. I can drive you to yours, and we can talk. Satisfied?'

It looked as if I didn't have much of a choice. I nodded, and Bartell clicked open his trunk. He loaded all the bags in, then opened the passenger door and held it open for me. I slid into the seat and had just finished adjusting my seat belt when Bartell slid in behind the wheel. He adjusted his own seat belt, and then slowly pulled away from the curb.

'OK, Ms Austin. What is it you think I need to know about this Robert person?'

'Roberto,' I amended. 'His name is Roberto.'

'Fine. What's so urgent about *Roberto*?'

I exhaled a deep breath. *Count to ten, Tiffany.* I looked over at Bartell's profile. 'For one thing, I saw them having a heck of an argument Monday night.'

Bartell shifted his gaze from the road to look at me, then back to the road again. 'You did?'

'Yes. Both my friend Hilary and I were at Bueno, Bonito y Barato Monday night. Jenny Lee was there as well, with Chef Frederick Longo. When Hilary and I were leaving, we saw Jenny Lee and Roberto having a rather heated discussion on the sidewalk in front of the restaurant.'

Bartell turned on to the street where the magazine office was located. 'How heated would you say this discussion was?'

'Pretty much so. She raised her fist at him and shouted that he'd be sorry and that he'd pay.'

'Pay for what?'

'I have no idea. Then he shouted back that it was her who'd end up paying. Jenny Lee didn't answer, just hopped into the car and it took off.' I paused. 'I saw Roberto make a cutting motion across his throat as she sped away.'

Bartell didn't speak for several seconds. We approached the employee parking lot, and he pulled in. 'Which one is your car?' he asked.

I pointed to my maroon convertible, parked on the far end. There was an empty space next to it, and Bartell slid into it. I couldn't take it any longer. 'Well?' I demanded. 'Wouldn't you consider that important?'

He turned and his steel gaze bored into mine. 'I would consider it somewhat significant, yes.'

Somewhat significant? Was he kidding? I lifted my chin. 'There's more.'

'More?' He said it as if he couldn't believe it.

'Yes,' I snapped. 'I finally found out who this Roberto is. His name is Roberto Manchetti, and he's the son of Enzo Manchetti, the chairman of the board of *Southern Style*.'

Bartell's eyes narrowed. 'My, my. Seems as if you've been doing a bit of investigating.'

I flushed at his sarcastic tone. 'I certainly didn't do it on purpose,' I lied. 'The information just happened to fall into my lap.'

'Did it now?' His lips grew taut, and he reached up to rub behind his ear. 'Nice of you to finally tell me.'

'Hey, I called you. You took your sweet time getting back to me.'

His brow arched. 'You might have told me about Ms Plumm's argument with this Roberto when you were questioned initially.'

'Well, I'm sorry about that,' I bristled. 'In retrospect you're right. I should have. But it was my first time at the rodeo. I was a bit intimidated at being hauled down to the police station and questioned as if I were suspect number one.' And investigating is the only way I can ensure I don't continue to be considered suspect numero uno, I added silently.

His gaze raked over me again. Then he said in a somewhat softer tone, 'Somehow I doubt that much intimidates you, Tiffany Austin.'

Oh, wouldn't you be surprised. 'I try,' I murmured. 'I don't always succeed.' I waited a moment and then said, 'So, are you going to question Roberto Manchetti?'

He gave me what I assumed was his version of a tolerant look. 'I can't reveal details of an ongoing investigation.'

'Why?' I bit out. 'Because I'm still considered a suspect?'

'Because it's protocol not to discuss details of an investigation with civilians,' he said evenly.

I couldn't help but notice it was the second time he'd avoided discussing my suspect status. 'OK, you can't reveal details. How about confirming them?'

He frowned. 'What do you mean?'

'Well, I heard that Jenny Lee died eating something.'

The expression on his face changed almost immediately. His brows drew together and the corners of his lips turned downward. He was angry, all right, and trying not to show it. 'Where did you hear that?'

'Oh, around,' I said lightly. I certainly wasn't about to tell him I'd heard it from Bob and Nita. 'Jenny Lee wasn't exactly a big eater, or even a fast one. She was downright birdlike, actually. It doesn't seem logical to me that she'd have choked to death, so the other alternative is she might have been poisoned?'

Bartell's hand shot up and he rubbed absently at his forehead. 'I'm sorry, Ms Austin. As I said, I can't reveal details of an ongoing investigation.'

My hand closed around the door handle. 'OK, then. I guess we're done here – for now.'

Bartell reached across me and grabbed my hand just as I was about to open the door. 'Listen, Ms Austin, I will concede that the information you gave me today is actually quite helpful.'

I relaxed my grip on the door handle. 'Thank you.'

'But . . . playing detective, especially with a killer on the loose, can be a dangerous pastime. I would advise you, quite strongly, to leave the detecting to the professionals.'

I eyed him and then said in my frostiest tone, 'Well, considering that I and some of my friends are currently under suspicion, that's a bit hard to do.'

Bartell bit down hard on his lower lip. 'Try,' he said softly. 'I'd hate to receive a call and be standing over your body next.'

I snorted. 'Like you'd care.'

'Quite the contrary. I would care.'

I gasped. Our eyes met, and for just a second – a very brief one – I could swear there was something in Bartell's eyes. A flicker of what? Interest? In me? I blinked. I had to have been mistaken. Still, if circumstances were different, that was exactly how I would have interpreted that oh-so-brief glance. Definite interest.

Flustered suddenly, I twisted the door handle and the door flew open. I clambered out, and then thrust my head back inside the car. 'Thank you so much for the ride, Detective. As for not playing Nancy Drew, well, I'll see what I can do.'

'I'm not kidding, Tiffany. Stay clear of this.'

I turned and flounced over to my car without a single backward glance. It wasn't until I reached my vehicle that I realized he'd finally referred to me by my first name. I heard a motor gun and stole a look over my shoulder, just in time to see Bartell carom out of the lot. I walked around to the driver's side, slid behind the wheel and then slammed my hand down on it, hard.

'Darn it! I left my bags in his trunk!'

Well, no way was I calling him. He probably wouldn't answer anyway. No doubt he'd find them when he opened his trunk later. Maybe if it wasn't midnight, he'd send one of his flunkies over to my house with them. In the meantime, though, what was I going to do for dinner?

And then my phone buzzed with an incoming text that drove all thoughts of dinner straight from my mind. It was from Hilary:

MEET ME AT MY HOUSE. GOT INFO. JENNY LEE DIED EATING POISONED EMPANADA.

ELEVEN

F ifteen minutes later I parked my car in front of a charming white stucco house with a large enclosed porch. Hilary rented a one-bedroom apartment on the second floor, with a private entrance that was located around the side of the house. I hopped out of my car and hurried up the gravel driveway. Hilary must have been watching for me, because I no sooner stepped up on the stoop than the door was flung open, and my friend grabbed my arm and pulled me inside.

'About time you got here,' she said. 'Come on up. I've got lots to tell you.'

'I can't wait to hear it.' I took note of her flushed cheeks and sparkling eyes. 'An empanada? Are you sure?'

'Well, according to Howard . . .' Hilary stopped speaking and frowned. She put a finger to her lips and pointed to the door to the left of the stairway. It was open a crack. We remained silent for a few seconds, and then the door slowly inched open and Mrs Polk, Hilary's landlady, thrust her head out. 'Hilary, dear is that you?'

Hilary turned slightly so the woman couldn't see and gave me a wink. 'Yes, Mrs Polk, it's me.'

'Is everything all right? You're usually not home at this time on a Saturday . . .' Her voice trailed off as she caught sight of me standing next to Hilary. She peered at me through her thick, tortoise-rimmed glasses. 'Oh, I'm sorry. I didn't know you had company.'

Hilary shot me a look that clearly said, *yeah, right*, and then gestured toward me. 'This is my friend, Tiffany Austin.'

'Tiffany Austin?' She turned to peer more closely at me. 'Not the Tiffany Austin who writes that delightful food blog?'

I smiled and held up both hands. 'Guilty.'

Mrs Polk's weathered features relaxed into a smile. 'My dear, it's so nice to meet you. I just loved your article on

Spanish cooking last month. Made me race right out and buy the ingredients for paella.' She smacked her lips. 'Just thinking of it is making me hungry.'

Hilary's fingers dug into my forearm. 'We were just on our way upstairs, Mrs Polk. Did you need something?'

Mrs Polk shook her head. 'No, dear. I'm fine. But I think I will go out and check on the mail.'

She pushed past us and, after giving us another quick smile, hobbled out the door and down the driveway. Hilary watched her go and shook her head. 'Mail schmail. She knows I work for the magazine and was probably hoping to hear some juicy gossip. I love the woman. She's always leaving me dinners I can heat up and her baked goods are out of this world. Plus, she charges a pittance for rent. But she's so *nosy*.'

I giggled. 'Maybe she thought you were having some afternoon delight.'

Hilary let out a loud Hmpf. 'Don't I wish!' Then she added with a wink, 'Knowing her, she'd probably want to join in.'

'Ew! TMI!'

Hilary laughed and gave me a little push in the direction of the stairs. 'Come on, let's get upstairs before she comes back and invites us in for tea.'

We hurried up the stairs and into Hilary's apartment. My friend decorates in what I like to call 'charming clutter'. Hand-knit throws and embroidered pillows adorned the small sofa and rocking chair. The top of the mission-style coffee table was covered with magazines, and a wicker rack wedged in between the sofa and wall was near to overflowing with various issues of *Southern Style*, as well as *Vogue*, *Harper's Bazaar* and *Glamour*. A tall covered object stood in the far corner. Hilary walked over to it and lifted the cover up. 'Hello, Seamus. How are you doing?'

An enormous green and red parrot opened one eye and looked lazily at us, then let out a sharp whistle. 'Wow! What a couple lookers!' he said. 'Come onna my place honey. Squawk.'

I laughed. 'I see Seamus McGee is in rare form.'

Hilary grimaced. 'Oh, yeah. That's the last time I let him watch a Charlie Sheen movie. David said he could pick up phrases just like that,' she snapped her fingers for emphasis, 'but I never really believed him.'

Seamus had originally belonged to David Prattle, a reporter on *Southern Style*. When he'd gotten a job with KLV news as a foreign correspondent, he'd been asked to move to France – and he couldn't take Seamus with him. Hilary often liked to grumble that David had guilted her into taking the bird, but I rather fancied she was fond of the parrot – for his shock value, if nothing else.

'Well, Seamus should be around for a good long time,' I told my friend. 'Some parrots live between fifty to a hundred years.'

'Figures he'll outlive me,' Hilary said. She shook her finger at the bird. 'You'd better be good, buddy, or who will want you after I'm gone?'

'Everyone wants me,' the parrot croaked. 'I'm sexy.'

'That's it. Definitely no more Martin Sheen for you. Take a nap, now. Tiffany and I have important business to discuss.'

'Monkey business,' the parrot croaked. Hilary groaned, threw the cover back over the birdcage and motioned for me to have a seat on the sofa. She disappeared into her tiny galley kitchen, returning a few minutes later with a bottle of wine, two glasses, and a small platter of sliced cheese on a tray. She set it down on the coffee table, poured us each a glass of wine, and then leaned back on the sofa next to me. She raised her glass.

'Here's to crime,' she said, taking a large sip. I took a sip as well, and then sat, cradling my glass in my hands.

'OK, what happened?' I asked. 'I'm dying of suspense here.'

'Yeah, who would have ever figured Jenny Lee for an empanada gal? Taco, maybe. A burrito even. But an empanada?'

I shot Hilary a stern look. 'OK, let's get serious. What exactly did Howard tell you?'

Hilary ran her hand through her hair, messing up her spikes. 'Howard didn't tell me anything. He's a real stickler for going by the book, that one! Midway through brunch I started asking some general questions, and he shut down tighter than a clam!'

I'd started to take a sip of wine but now I stopped and set the glass back on the coffee table. 'Wait, I'm confused. I thought you said Howard told you Jenny Lee died eating a poisoned empanada.'

Hilary avoided my gaze and looked down at her hands. 'We-ell, Howard didn't tell me, not exactly.'

I bit down on my lower lip. I was getting more than a little vexed at my friend. 'Then how on earth did you find that out?'

Hilary raised her gaze to meet mine. She reached out and took both my hands in hers. 'You know I would only do something like this for you, don't you?' she said softly.

I sucked in my breath. 'Oh gosh, Hilary. You didn't . . . you couldn't . . .'

Hilary let go of my hands and put hers on her hips. 'You think I slept with him? Heck no. I love you like mad, Tiff, but there are some things I wouldn't do, even for you.' She let out a breath. 'No, I just played up to his ego. I could see questioning him wasn't going to get me anywhere so, after we finished eating, I told him I was thinking of doing a piece on careers, and I wondered what it was like to work in the coroner's office.'

'Oh,' I cried. 'You mean you got him to take you to the morgue?'

Hilary wrinkled her nose. 'Not the morgue per se, just his office. I mean, I might have gotten to the actual morgue, but once I found out what I needed to know, I made an excuse and hightailed it out of there.'

'Dare I ask how you found out these details?'

'I noticed that he kept a notebook in his side drawer, and that his desk wasn't locked. I feigned a coughing fit and he hurried out to get me some water. It gave me just enough time to look through his notebook.'

I looked at her, and then my face broke out in a wide grin. 'Well, look at you, Nancy Drew!'

'I felt more like Mata Hari. Anyway, the last page in that book had his notes on Jenny Lee Plumm. Her sole stomach contents were an empanada, and he found minute traces of aconite in it.'

'Aconite?'

'I looked it up. It's a toxin derived from the monkshood plant, more commonly known as wolfsbane. It leaves only one post-mortem sign, that of asphyxia. It causes an arrhythmic heart function which leads to suffocation. It's an extremely fast-acting poison, nearly undetectable.'

'Undetectable huh? Then how did he find it?'

'Apparently Bartell told him to pay very close attention to the autopsy, so he had the stomach remains gone over with a fine-tooth comb.'

'Interesting. How do you administer that poison, I wonder?'

'I looked that up too. Aconite can be administered in water. It might leave a bitter taste, though. Or you can crush wolfsbane leaves and sprinkle the juice in food. That's probably what happened.' She paused. 'I also looked up where you could get wolfsbane. Some people grow it in their gardens, taking proper precautions, of course. It produces very attractive flowers.'

'So it's not hard to get, if you know what you're looking for.' I leaned back against the sofa cushions, and pulled one of Hilary's embroidered pillows on to my lap. The gaily sewn saying read, SAVOR EVERY DAY. I turned the pillow upside down and remarked, 'You know what this means.'

'Yep. It was cold-blooded murder, all right. But who would do such a thing, even to a viper like Jenny Lee?'

I tapped my finger against the pillow. 'And to put it in an empanada, no less. That's hardly the type of cuisine I'd have associated with Jenny Lee. Wasn't she always hanging out in those fancy French and Italian restaurants?'

Hilary picked up her glass and took a sip before she answered. 'Apparently there was another side to Ms Jenny Lee Plumm that we never knew about. A wild and crazy side, a chick who went around eating empanadas and, who knows, maybe even drinking chocolate milkshakes too.'

'And a chick who pissed somebody off enough to kill her,' I added. 'She told me that she was working on a big story, a career-changing story. It had to be kept quiet, though, till she had all her facts.'

Hilary leaned forward so quickly she almost toppled her glass over. 'Maybe it was some sort of exposé. Maybe that's who killed her! They arranged to meet her and bam! Poisoned her.'

I glanced across the room and saw Hilary's tablet lying on the desk amid a sea of papers. I walked over and picked it up. 'Maybe we can find the answer somewhere in her blog,' I said. 'She kept saying how easy it was to incorporate tidbits about food into her column. Maybe there's something in one of them that will yield a clue.'

I handed the tablet to Hilary. She put in her password and, a few seconds later, had Jenny Lee's blog up on the screen. 'Search older posts,' I directed. 'We're looking for anything that might have mention of food in it.'

Hilary looked at me. 'You think she wrote about an empanada joint? I don't even think Branson has one.'

'I've never heard of one, but who knows? Maybe she found someplace trendy that serves them and she liked them.'

Hilary cut me an eye roll. 'Sounds like a long shot, but what the heck?'

After about twenty minutes of concentrated searching, we were both forced to admit defeat. There were a few blogs that mentioned food, but they were all about high-class eateries in Branson and who was hanging out where drinking what (and possibly sleeping with whom).

'No dice.' Hilary pushed aside some magazines and set the tablet on the coffee table. She stretched her arms out in front of her. 'It was worth a shot, though.'

'Maybe there's still hope.' I picked up the tablet and clicked on the tab on Jenny Lee's website that read 'Photos'. There were twelve pages. I went through them all painstakingly, with Hilary looking over my shoulder. I was ready to admit defeat, but there was one more page to go. I clicked on it, and almost immediately my eyes were drawn to a photo down at the bottom. It depicted Jenny Lee, smiling widely, pointing to an object she held in her hand. The caption below read, 'Who knew it would taste so good!' I recognized the object in her hand immediately – an empanada.

'Wow, looks like you hit pay dirt!' exclaimed Hilary.

I frowned. 'Partly. There's no mention of where this photo was taken. It could have been anywhere.'

Hilary squinted at the photo, and then tapped a nail on the screen. 'The background looks kind of familiar,' she said. 'I've seen that knotty wood paneling somewhere before, I just can't think where.' She tapped at her temple. 'It'll come to me . . . eventually.'

I groaned inwardly. I knew it might take weeks for my friend to remember where she'd seen those walls. 'I haven't got that long,' I said. I set the tablet down. 'It might be easier to narrow the location down if we knew where her body was found.'

'Oh, gee, I almost forgot.' Hilary slapped the side of her head. 'It was in Howard's notes. They got an anonymous tip and found her body in an alley off Copeland.'

'OK,' I said. 'So she must have gotten poisoned in a restaurant near there that serves empanadas. Her killer must have slipped the poison in it somehow.'

'And it hit her when she left, and she stumbled into an alley and died?' Hilary sighed. 'Kind of sad, even for Jenny Lee.'

'It's possible. What are you doing for dinner tonight? We can canvass the restaurants that are close by Barry's in the vicinity of Copeland. Maybe we'll get lucky and find this one. I'm hoping someone might remember seeing her there and, if we get real lucky, remember who she was with.'

'Ordinarily I'd be on board, but I've got a command perform-ance at Mom's tonight.' Hilary's nose wrinkled as if she smelled something disgusting. 'Arleen will be there too. I've got a feeling this could be a set-up. Arleen's been talking about this new, single guy in her class. Anyway, you know I'd much rather go restaurant slumming with you, but I can't blow this dinner off. My mother would strangle me.'

I made a shooing motion with my hand. 'I certainly don't want to be responsible for your demise at your mother's hands. You go on to your mom's. Say hello to her and Arleen for me. I'll do all the slumming myself. Might as well, seeing as the dinner I originally planned to cook is now residing in the back of Bartell's car.'

'Say what? Did I hear right? Bartell's car? Detective Hunk Bartell?'

My lips thinned to a straight line. 'You did.'

Hilary choked back a laugh. 'You're kidding! Any details you want to share on that?'

'Not at the moment.' I shot her a tentative smile. 'Let's just say it was a rough morning.'

The smile she shot me was enigmatic. 'Well, then let's hope your *evening* fares better.'

TWELVE

Hilary printed out a copy of the photo of Jenny Lee with empanada in hand. I tucked it into my purse and drove back home, where Cooper greeted me enthusiastically at the door. I realized with a guilty pang that I hadn't taken the poor dog out for a walk all day. Lily was snoozing in Cooper's dog bed, and didn't even look up when I snapped his leash on and led him out the door. He made an immediate dash for the yard, but stopped abruptly when I called out for him to heel. He scampered back to me and I lavished praise upon him for his good behavior. We went out the gate and walked briskly two blocks north to a nearby park. The park had a dog run, and as we approached I could see other owners out and about with their dogs. Cooper did his business beside a shady elm, and I scooped up the remains into one of the plastic bags I'd stuffed into my jacket pocket. Then, to reward him for being such a good and patient doggy, I let him off his leash and let him exercise a bit with some of his doggy friends.

While Cooper romped and played with a Siberian husky, I sat on a nearby bench and went over everything I'd learned the past few hours. The most startling and significant thing, at least to me, was that she'd died eating a poisoned empanada. It must have been a truly spectacular empanada, because that was the type of food Jenny Lee usually said she'd never be caught dead eating (ironic, wasn't it, now that I thought about it). As I'd told Hilary, her killer must have not only known where to get one, but he or she had to be someone Jenny Lee must have trusted. Would she have trusted Roberto? Not if that fight was any indication, although they might have kissed and made up afterward. Longo? They'd argued over something, and both had seemed pretty angry with each other if the last encounter I saw was any indication. I knew I could write Mac, Dale and myself off the suspect list. Bob Gillette from Po'Boys too. Even though he hadn't spoken kindly of Jenny Lee, I didn't get the sense that he hated her enough to kill her.

That left only one other person that I knew about so far – the mystery woman who'd driven the convertible Monday night. Jenny Lee obviously trusted her, because she must have called her to come pick her up. And then my spine stiffened as I thought about one other possibility.

'The subject of her big story,' I murmured. 'The one she said would put her on the map. Would she have trusted that person? Or might Jenny Lee, in her zeal to get a big story, have gotten careless?'

'Penny for your thoughts,' said a deep voice behind me, and I jumped.

'Sorry.' I turned around and looked into the dark gaze of Detective Eric Dalton. He shot me a sheepish grin. 'I didn't mean to startle you, but you looked really out there.'

I pulled my jacket tighter around me. 'Yeah, well, being a suspect in a murder investigation tends to make one a bit introspective.'

He inclined his head toward the dog run, where Cooper and Laski, the husky, were engaged in a game of tug of war with a stick. 'Your dog's the spaniel, right? He looks like he can hold his own with the bigger dog.'

'Cooper and Laski are old buddies,' I said. 'They enjoy playing together.' We were silent for a few moments, watching the dogs, and then I asked, 'So what are you doing here? Keeping suspects under surveillance?'

Dalton reached up to flick a stray hair out of one eye. 'I'm on my break. I like to walk in the park. It relaxes me.' He let out a sigh. 'There's not much chance for relaxation at work these days.'

'I can imagine,' I said. I resumed looking at Cooper frolicking, but watched Dalton out of the corner of my eye. 'How's the investigation coming? Oh, wait!' I held up my hand, traffic-cop style. 'You can't discuss it with civilians, or potential suspects, am I right?'

Now he did laugh. 'I see you know the drill.'

'I've heard it before.'

Dalton eyed me. 'Bartell tells me you've been doing a bit of . . . investigating.'

'You could call it that,' I admitted. 'I haven't had much luck so far, though.' I gave him a tight smile. 'I don't much fancy being on a suspect list.'

He jammed his hands in his pockets. 'Not many people do,' he said. 'But they rarely start investigating on their own.'

'I was never one to sit back and let things happen,' I admitted. 'Particularly when my reputation is at stake.' My lips twitched slightly. 'You can ask anyone, my friend Hilary in particular. Once I get involved in something, I've been known to have the tenacity of a pit bull.'

'A pit bull, eh?' Dalton's hand came out of his pocket, rubbed at his chin. 'Sometimes that's a good thing, but in this case . . .' He gave a swift glance around, and then leaned in a bit closer to me. 'Bartell would have my head if he knew I was telling you this, but . . . as a suspect, you're not very high on the list. As a matter of fact, in the grand scheme of things, I don't think you made the cut at all.'

Relief flooded through me. 'Thank you,' I breathed, and then I narrowed my eyes. 'Just why are you telling me this?'

Dalton shrugged. 'I thought you seemed worried about all this the other night, and I was right. You're concerned enough to go poking around where you shouldn't. Getting involved in a murder investigation is serious business. It's nothing to fool around with. You should listen to Detective Bartell and quit while you're ahead.' He paused and then added with a boyish grin, 'Besides, I rather like you. I'd hate to see you get hurt.'

Well, that comment had certainly come out of left field, and I had to admit it rendered me speechless. 'Gee . . . thanks,' I finally managed to stammer. 'I have to admit, though, knowing I'm not number one on the suspect hit parade takes a lot of pressure off.'

His grin vanished. 'You're not officially in the clear yet, so please don't say anything to anybody. Like I said, if Bartell knew I spoke to you . . .' he shrugged.

I made a crossing motion over my heart. 'I'll never tell,' I promised. I was pleasantly surprised that Dalton was so forth-coming with me. It was a refreshing change from Bartell's stodginess. I wondered if it stemmed from the fact that Dalton appeared to have an interest in me as more than a suspect. 'But you do have some legitimate suspects, right?'

'Besides you, you mean? A few.'

'I don't suppose any of them have an interest in botany?'

Dalton looked at me sharply. 'Why would you ask that?'

I was about to whip out the photo of Jenny Lee and her empanada and tell him what I'd learned about aconite when a buzzing sound suddenly emanated from his jacket pocket. He reached inside, whipped out his cell, glanced at the screen and let out a sigh.

'Sorry to cut our chat short,' he said. He held up his phone. 'Duty calls. I've got to get back to the station.' He hesitated a moment and then said softly, 'Would you mind if I called you sometime, maybe go out for coffee? When this is all over, of course?'

'Not at all,' I murmured. The interruption didn't disturb me in the least. Maybe it was for the best. If I'd mentioned the aconite, he might want to know just where I'd found that out, and no way would I rat on Hilary.

He shot me a grin, touched two fingers to his forehead in a gesture of farewell, then turned and walked out of the park. I watched him go out the gate and slide behind the wheel of a dark sedan parked at the curb.

'Odd,' I murmured as a sudden thought struck me. 'He must really like this park. The police station's across town, and there's another park five minutes from there, yet he drove here. Why?'

The obvious answer was that Dalton was following me. He'd said I wasn't under serious consideration as a suspect, but had he been telling the truth? Or had he been handing me a line so I'd drop investigating? I was inclined to go with the latter, and I also had a pretty good idea that he'd been ordered to keep me under surveillance by none other than Philip Bartell.

So much for being cut off the suspect list. If I were no longer under suspicion, why would Bartell have Dalton shadow me? Obviously I was still on the list, and if that were the case, well, I certainly wasn't going to stop trying to clear my name. I bit down on my lower lip, hard. I'd have to be careful I wasn't followed when I went out later. I whistled for Cooper, who came running. He bounded up to me, tongue lolling. I patted him on the head and snapped on his leash. Cooper gave a sharp yip and, as we turned to go, I caught sight of a man standing a few feet away, lounging against an elm. He turned abruptly and walked swiftly away before I could get a closer look, but I was fairly certain I'd recognized Frederick Longo. What on earth was he doing in the park? Was he following me too? He'd have no reason to, unless Longo was more involved in Jenny Lee's murder than I originally thought.

Cooper gave another short yip and I bent down and patted his head. 'Yes, we're going, Coop. Mommy's got to get some rest. It looks like I've got a busy night ahead of me.'

I lay down on the couch, intending to close my eyes for a few minutes, but when I woke up it was five thirty. I swung my feet off the couch and shook my head to clear it. I'd needed the rest, though, to recharge my batteries, and it seemed to have worked. I felt newly invigorated as I shrugged out of my clothes and made a beeline for the shower.

An hour later, freshly showered and dressed in navy cargo pants, a white button-down shirt and a powder-blue cashmere pullover, my hair curled and my makeup flawless, I sat back down on the couch with my trusty tablet. I plugged in the address of Barry's Café and asked the search engine for names of all type of eateries and cafés within a five-block radius of Copeland. A few seconds later, no fewer than twenty-five names popped up on my screen. Now to narrow them down.

I typed in cafés and eateries that served Spanish food, and was rewarded with a ten-name list. I printed it out and then looked it over carefully. There was one, Roy's Brew Barn, which boasted a wide range of American and Spanish specialties, including empanadas. The address placed it two blocks from Barry's Café, and one block south of Copeland.

'Looks like Roy's Brew Barn is the perfect place to start,' I said to both Cooper and Lily, who were at my feet, looking up at me expectantly. I set my tablet aside, went into the kitchen, and got dinner out for the children. Then I grabbed my suede jacket and car keys.

'Wish me luck,' I said, but both of them were hunkered

over their food bowls, immersed in their dinner and totally ignoring me. I thought I heard a soft meow, though, followed by a sharp yip as I slipped out the back door.

I almost walked right past Roy's Brew Barn. For one thing, the neon sign above the entrance had most of the lights out, proclaiming it, 'Ry's Bw Brn'. For another thing, the chipped paint on the outside and the untrimmed hedges on either side of the badly scarred wooden door weren't exactly enticing. No wonder this place had never been on my radar to review, I thought, as I squared my shoulders and pushed through the door.

I stood in the doorway for a few moments, letting my eyes adjust to the extremely dim lighting. There was a jukebox in the far corner, and a woman in a denim mini-skirt was busy plugging coins into it. A few seconds later, Jimmy Buffett's 'Margaritaville' came blasting out at a nearly ear-splitting level. I could make out the sound of billiard balls being racked in a back room off to one side of the jukebox. A U-shaped bar took up most of the room, and there was a large group of people, both male and female, gathered around it, laughing and chatting away as they scarfed down beers and chips loaded with salsa. A few tables covered with plastic red and white checked tablecloths were scattered on the other side of the room, and each one was filled. But what drew my attention were the wood-paneled walls, some of which were covered with a mosaic of tin signs sporting sayings like, 'Don't kill the Messenger – Buy him a Drink' and 'I'm not dead, I'm just sleeping'. I reached into my bag and pulled out the photo of Jenny Lee. It was hard to be absolutely certain, but it sure looked like the paneling in the photo was a match for the paneling here. I took another quick look around, and I didn't see any video surveillance cameras. Apparently Roy's Brew Barn didn't feel the need to beef up their security.

There was a menu tacked up on one side of the entrance, so I took a look at it. The menu was indeed varied, offering everything from burgers and Philly steak sandwiches to tacos, burritos and yes, empanadas. I looked back at the bar and spied an empty seat in the far corner, near the entrance to what I assumed must be the kitchen. I glanced back at the dining area. From the looks of things, it would most likely be a while before a table opened up. I opted for the empty seat at the bar, and slid on to the stool just as the bartender emerged from the kitchen – or should I say barmaid? It was a curvy woman with hair the color of my old Raggedy Ann doll. Her generous bosom looked as if it were about to spill over her low-cut, too-tight white blouse. She wiped her hands on the apron tied around her waist, looked over the bar area, spotted me sitting there without a drink in front of me, and immediately hustled over. 'Hey there.' Her voice was deep and husky, as if she'd smoked one too many cigarettes in her day. She leaned across the bar and peered closely at me. 'I never have seen you in here before. First time?'

I nodded. 'Yes. I – ah – heard the Spanish food in here is to die for.' *Literally.*

She threw back her head and emitted a loud, guttural laugh. 'You got that right. José, he came straight over the border from Mexico. We're lucky to have him.' She leaned in a bit closer to me. 'He makes a killer taco.'

Killer, huh? Boy, you got that right. 'I, ah, heard the empanadas are good,' I ventured.

She waved her hand in a careless circle. 'Honey, they're the best! Why, everyone who has ever eaten one raves about 'em. And just between you and me, we've gotten some hoity-toity types in here who never thought they'd like the food, but . . .' She spread her hands. 'They keep coming back for more.'

Except for Jenny Lee, I thought. She won't be coming back. I glanced at the name-tag pinned on her shirt and said, 'Well, Dixie, what do you recommend?'

'For a first timer? Let's see.' Dixie pursed her thick lips as she thought. 'I'd definitely recommend you start out with a margarita. We've got two types. There's traditional, and raspberry-flavored.' She licked her highly glossed lips. 'I personally prefer the traditional, myself, but the boss says we have to cater to the young, hip crowd too, so raspberry's been a big seller.'

'I'm with you. I prefer the traditional, myself,' I said. 'What about eats?'

She gave a slow wink. 'All depends what you're in the mood for, sugar. If you want American, José makes some of the most flavorful burgers in the area. Pink and juicy on the inside, perfectly charcoal broiled on the outside. Don't know how he does it, and I don't much care. If you want to try our Spanish cuisine, well, practically everything on that menu's a winner. Like I said, the tacos are especially good.'

'I'm sure they are,' I murmured. I tapped the menu. 'What about the empanadas? Are they good?'

'Are they ever! They even have their own menu, see.' She reached underneath the counter and whipped out a laminated sheet which she laid in front of me. **EMPANADA CENTRAL** was scrawled in bold block letters at the top of the page. 'We got a special, three for $9.99, and most people mix 'em up. Or you can just try the sampler.' She tapped the paper. 'You study that, and I'll be right back with your drink.'

Dixie moved away to the other end of the bar. I picked up the sheet and studied it. The fillings were indeed varied, ranging from chicken or beef spiced with cumin and paprika to ones filled with different types of fish, onions, boiled eggs, olives and ham. Dixie returned with a large margarita glass which she placed in front of me with a flourish. I picked it up and took a sip. 'Damn that's good,' I said. I wasn't lying. It was one of the best margaritas I'd ever had.

Dixie beamed. 'Thanks, sugar. Decide on your eats yet?'

'I think so, but I've got a question.' I pointed to one entry on the menu. 'What's humita?'

'That's a sweetcorn with a white sauce. José puts spinach in it too. It's very popular with the vegetarian crowd. We've got dessert empanadas, too. Filled with strawberries, blueberries, peaches. They're delish.'

I set the menu down. 'You've convinced me to try the empanadas.' Even as I said that, I felt my stomach lurch a bit at eating the same food that had killed Jenny Lee. But then again, no one was trying to poison me, right? 'I think I'll try the sampler. One chicken, one beef and one fish, right?'

'Right. Tonight the fish is cod. That OK with you?'

'Perfect.'

Dixie scribbled my order down on a pad and then pushed

through the double door to the kitchen. I picked up my margarita and sipped the drink slowly. One thing for sure, they didn't skimp on alcohol. I imagined that fact played a large part in their booming business as well.

The man sitting next to me gulped down the last of his beer, threw a twenty on the counter and then slid off his stool. He gave me a poke on the shoulder. 'Could you make sure Dixie gets that?' he asked. 'I gotta leave, but sometimes the other barmaid comes in and hogs the tips.'

I nodded. 'No problem.' He smiled and left and I snatched up the twenty and scissored the bill between my fingers. When Dixie pushed through the doors back into the bar, I motioned her over and extended the twenty to her. 'The fellow who was sitting next to me wanted to make sure you got this,' I said.

'Aw, that's Randy. He's a regular and a real dear. He knows that Ginger comes in early and sometimes she takes my tips.' Dixie took the twenty and jammed it down the front of her blouse. She let out a loud laugh. 'She'll never get it there.'

I slid the photograph of Jenny Lee out of my purse and unfolded it. 'I was wondering, Dixie, if you could possibly tell me if you'd ever seen this woman in here.'

Dixie's demeanor, formerly so friendly, underwent a one-eighty-degree change. She narrowed her eyes at me. 'You a cop?' she asked.

I shook my head. 'No, actually, I write a column for *Southern Style*. A food column.'

The frown vanished and Dixie's eyes widened. 'No shit? You're a food critic? Like Julia Roberts in *My Best Friend's Wedding*?'

'We-ell, not on that grand a scale. I blog about restaurants and I give my honest reviews.' I tapped the edge of the photo. 'The woman in this photograph is the one who recommended this place to me. Actually, she recommended the empanadas, but she never said where she ate them. She raved about them, and trust me, she's tough to please. I've been going nuts, trying to pin it down so I can do a food review.' I touched my nose to assure myself it hadn't grown after the string of lies I'd just told and turned the photo so Dixie could see. 'Ever see her in here?'

Dixie bent down and squinted at the photo. After a few seconds she looked up at me. 'Oh yeah, she's been in here. Rhoda knows her.'

'Rhoda? Who's Rhoda?'

'She's . . . excuse me.' Dixie reached into her pocket, pulled out a cell phone. She looked at the screen, grimaced, then looked at me. 'Sorry – my old man. I gotta take this.'

Dixie moved away, back into the kitchen. I took a large sip of my margarita, feeling euphoric. It looked as if this might be the place where Jenny Lee had gotten her poisoned empanada. I wondered if this Rhoda might be one of the waitresses, and if she'd waited on her that night. Maybe she was the one who'd be able to fill in the missing pieces of the puzzle.

'Who ordered the empanada sampler?'

I glanced up to see a different woman, not Dixie, holding a large plate aloft. I raised my hand and wiggled my fingers. 'That would be me.'

The woman, who had platinum-blonde hair with several pink streaks running through it, set the platter in front of me. I saw by the name-tag pinned above one breast that this was the infamous Ginger. 'Enjoy,' she said.

She started to turn away but I reached out and touched her arm. 'Is Dixie coming back?' I asked.

Ginger shook her head. 'Naw, she hadda leave. Her old man got drunk again.' She shook her head. 'I don't know why she sticks by that old coot. He's out work and in jail on D&D's more often than Carter has liver pills. If I were her, I'd give him the old heave-ho.'

I wasn't much interested in Dixie's private life, or anyone else's for that matter. 'Is Rhoda working tonight?' I asked.

Ginger frowned. 'Nope.' she said.

A man at the far end raised his empty beer mug in the air and Ginger murmured, 'Excuse me.' As she hurried off toward the opposite end of the bar, I picked up one of the empanadas and took a bite. OMG! I felt like I'd died and gone to heaven. The beef inside was juicy, succulent and seasoned to perfection. I gobbled it down in two bites and picked up the chicken. That was even more delicious than the beef.

'This is a hidden treasure,' I murmured. I could see how even a fussy eater like Jenny Lee might have loved these. I polished off the cod empanada in record time, and wiped my hands on a paper napkin. I'd have to come back another time and do a proper review. I had a feeling once Roy's Brew Barn appeared in my column, they'd have even more customers, maybe more than they could handle. Hopefully it wouldn't come out in the papers that Jenny Lee had been poisoned with their food!

'Excuse me.' I waved at Ginger as she sailed past me on her way to the kitchen. 'I'll take the check, please.'

Ginger dug a pad out of her apron pocket. 'You had a margarita and a sampler? That's fourteen ninety-nine altogether. Cash or credit card?'

I pulled a twenty out of my wallet and slid it across the bar. 'Cash. Keep the change.' I leaned forward. 'I'd really like to speak with the manager. Is he around?'

Ginger frowned. 'You wanna speak to the manager? Why? Was there something wrong with your food?'

'Quite the contrary. I loved it. As I told Dixie, I write a food blog for *Southern Style*. I'd like to speak with your manager about doing a feature on Roy's.'

'Really?' Ginger's eyes widened. 'That would be real sweet. You can talk to Dixie about it. Stuff like that goes through her.' She shrugged. 'I guess you could say she's sorta the unofficial assistant manager. She's in charge when Brenda ain't around, and Brenda's off this week.'

'I see. So this Brenda is the manager?' Ginger nodded. 'And Dixie won't be back tonight?'

'Doubtful. And tomorrow's her day off, but . . . she lives in the apartments over on South Street. You know the ones I mean?'

I did indeed. They were a real dump. 'What's her last name?'

'Garrett. I'd give you her phone, but it's unlisted and she'd take a fit.'

I held up my hand. 'That's OK. I'm sure I'll be able to find her. Thanks.' I started to slide off the stool, then stopped. I reached in my purse and whipped out Jenny Lee's photo. 'By the way, Ginger, have you ever seen this woman in here?'

Ginger leaned forward and squinted at the photo. She tapped at her chin with one long, silver-tipped nail. 'Oh yeah. A gal like that's hard to forget.' She tapped at Jenny Lee's face with her nail. 'She loved her empanadas.'

'I don't suppose you noticed her in here Friday night?'

'This past Friday?' Ginger shook her head. 'That was my night off, sorry.' Then she brightened. 'I think Dixie was working, though. She might know.'

I replaced the photo in my bag and pulled out the one of Jenny Lee and Roberto. 'What about the man in this photo? Have you ever seen him in here before?'

Ginger took the photo and studied it. 'Wow, he's real good looking, even in a profile shot.' She looked at the photo for another few seconds and then handed it back to me. 'You know, I can't be positive, but . . . yeah, I think I've seen him in here.' She hesitated, then waggled her fingers. 'Can I see it again?' I handed it back to her and she took it, studied it for another minute, then handed it back. 'Oh, yeah,' she said. 'I've seen him, all right. He's just my type,' she remarked, closing one eye in a wink. 'Tall, dark . . . dreamy.'

I mentally cursed the fact the restaurant didn't have CCTV as I replaced that photo in my bag and whipped out my cell phone. I called up my Google app and typed in, 'Frederick Longo – images.' When they came up on the screen, I passed the phone to Ginger. 'How about him?'

Ginger's response was immediate. 'Gee, yeah. He was here yesterday,' she said, her head bobbing up and down. 'Had two soft tacos and an unsweetened iced tea.' She passed the phone back to me. 'I always remember the big tippers.'

'He was only in here yesterday? Not any other time?'

Ginger's lips screwed into a pout. 'Well, he might have been in here a couple of times before. I'm not one hundred percent certain. I know definitely he was here yesterday, because I waited on him.'

I slid my phone back into my pocket. 'Thanks for your help.'

Ginger hesitated, and I got the sense there was something else she wanted to say. After a moment, though, she shot me a smile and then vanished into the kitchen. I slid off the stool and headed for the door. I had to admit, I felt a bit jazzed. Tonight had turned out a lot better than I'd expected. I was pretty certain I'd found the spot where Jenny Lee had gotten her poisoned empanada. I'd also managed to place two out of my three suspects as having been there. I was hopeful another interview with Dixie might produce some more info, and that the manager, Brenda, might also be able to shed some light.

I stepped outside and paused, still congratulating myself on a job well done, when a black sedan pulled over to the curb and slid to a stop in front of Roy's. I glanced at the car briefly, still too wound up in my good fortune to pay it much mind. As I started to cross the street, though, the window on the driver's side of the sedan rolled down and, lo and behold, whose head should pop out but none other than Philip Bartell's.

'Well, well, if it isn't Branson's version of Nancy Drew. And just what, may I ask, are you doing here?'

All my feelings of euphoria vanished at the sarcastic tone in his voice. Still, I forced what I hoped was a pleasant smile to my lips and said blithely, 'Detective Bartell. It's nice to see you too. I thought you were working late tonight.'

He quirked one shaggy brow. 'Who says I'm not working right now?'

'Are you?'

'Actually, I am. I was on my way to interview a suspect when I saw you coming out of that place.' He jerked his thumb toward Roy's. 'It doesn't seem like the type of place you'd frequent.'

'How would you know what type of place I'd frequent?' I bristled. 'We're not friends, you know.'

He reached up and scratched absently at his forehead. 'No, I guess we're not,' he said slowly. 'But you seem like a classy lady to me, and Roy's is definitely not a classy joint.'

I balled my hand into a fist and banged at the side of my temple. 'Excuse me, I think my hearing must be going. Was that an actual compliment I heard coming out of your lips?'

'Actually, I was stating a fact.'

'Which fact? That I'm classy or that Roy's isn't a classy place?'

His lips twitched. 'I think I'll plead the fifth on that one.'

I cocked my head at him. 'You said you were on your way to interview a suspect? Is it someone in the Jenny Lee case?'

'You know I can't answer that,' he said. He paused and then added, 'Just so you know, the Plumm case isn't the only one I'm working on. We're shorthanded, and all my men are spread rather thin.'

'Working on murder cases?'

'Various cases.' There was silence for a few seconds and then he said, 'Get in. I'll give you a ride to your car.'

'No need. I'm in the municipal lot around the corner.' I patted my stomach. 'I should walk off this meal, anyway.'

'I take it you don't want the bags of groceries you left in my car earlier today, then?'

Hoo-boy, I'd almost forgotten about them. 'Oh, no, I want them,' I said quickly. 'I can still make the gumbo and freeze it.'

'Great. I'd like to get them out of my trunk as well. Get in and I'll drive you to your car.' As I hesitated he said, 'You're surely not going to walk carrying these heavy bags, are you? I promise . . . I don't bite.'

He reached over and pushed open the passenger door, leaving me little choice but to acquiesce. I got in, strapped on the seat belt, and then Bartell glided away from the curb. He slid me a sideways glance. 'You're not fooling me, you know,' he said.

I sat, my hands folded demurely in my lap. 'I'm not trying to.'

'So you're telling me you went to Roy's for their cuisine?'

'Not initially,' I admitted. 'But I have to admit I'm glad I did. Those empanadas are to . . . too much,' I finished lamely. I'd almost said *to die for*. 'I'm seriously considering writing them up in my blog.'

'Hah. Hans Anders would love that.'

'Who's Hans Anders?'

'The owner.'

My eyes widened. 'A guy named Hans owns Roy's Brew Barn?'

'You find that odd?'

'Not really. I guess I just assumed since it was named Roy's, the owner's name would be the same.'

'He bought it for a song after the original owner went to prison for selling drugs to teens. It was originally called Casa Nueva, but he changed the name because he wanted to dissociate his new place with the former owner's rep. As for him naming it Roy's . . . well, he was always a big Roy Rogers fan.' Bartell chuckled. 'I've actually known Hans all my life.'

'Oh? He was from Birmingham as well?'

'No, he used to own a luncheonette in Gilbert Arizona, which is where I grew up.'

'Oh, so you're originally from the West Coast. That explains a lot.'

He glanced over at me. 'Such as?'

'Oh, your manner in general. You're definitely not a good ole Southern boy. I imagine coming from a rough-and-tumble state like Arizona shaped your personality.' I shot him a slow grin. 'I bet you learned to handle a gun at a real young age, right?'

'Arizona is a carry state. They taught us young.'

'So you're handy with a gun. Is that why they offered you a boatload of money to join the Branson force? I'm surprised they didn't promote someone already on the force. Surely there were some just as qualified as you.'

He shrugged. 'I'm sure there were. I can't speak as to why they looked to the outside. As for the boatload of money, I'm afraid that's exaggerated.' He paused. 'We're getting off track here. I asked you what you were doing in Roy's.'

'Eating. What else would I be doing?'

'Snooping, perhaps. Sticking your nose where it doesn't belong.'

'I was in there sampling food. I heard their empanadas were fabulous and I wanted to see for myself so I could blog about it. Go in and ask the barmaid if you don't believe me,' I said. 'I told her what I wanted and asked for the manager's name so I could contact her. Apparently she's out this week, but there's a woman who's acting as manager in her stead. Dixie Garrett.'

Bartell nodded as if confirming what I'd just said. 'Well, good. I'm glad to hear that.'

What I should have done was drop the subject right then

and there, but of course I didn't. 'Whatever did you think I was doing in there, Detective Bartell? Asking questions about the night Jenny Lee died? She died either there or somewhere close by, didn't she?'

Bartell slammed on the brakes. Thank God no one was behind us. He pulled over to the curb, shut off the motor, then leaned his elbow on the steering wheel as he shifted in his seat to look at me. 'What makes you think that?' he asked.

'I know Jenny Lee died after eating something. I looked on her blog and saw a photo of her eating an empanada and she raved about the place, so I thought maybe that might bear checking out. I did a little homework and I found Roy's.' I reached into my bag and whipped out the photo, stuck it under his nose. 'The paneling in Roy's matches the one in the photo.'

Bartell barely glanced at the photo. 'That wood paneling is common in lots of eateries around here.'

'But Jenny Lee didn't rave about the empanadas in every eatery.'

His eyes narrowed. 'So you deduced she died eating an empanada from seeing a photo on her blog?'

'Not just that,' I grumbled. 'It was the way she raved about the place.'

His lips thinned. 'That's either quite a deduction or an excellent example of dumb luck.'

I slumped back in my seat. 'Maybe,' I grumbled.

Bartell started the car up again and pulled out into the street. 'So, Nancy Drew, what else did you learn?'

I eyed him. 'Oh, I'm supposed to share anything I learn with you but you can't reciprocate? That doesn't seem fair.'

'I know, but I'm the one with the badge.' He tapped his breast pocket. 'Trust me, Tiffany, you want to stay out of this.'

I glanced up sharply at his use of my first name. I had to admit, I kind of liked the way he lingered over saying it. 'I'm not sure I can,' I said. 'After all, I'm still considered a suspect . . . right?'

Bartell's eyebrow rose, but he didn't make any comment. We drove in stony silence the few blocks to the municipal garage. Bartell pulled inside. 'Where's your car?' he asked.

I pointed to my convertible, parked over on the far wall. 'Over there.'

Bartell drove over and parked right in back of my car. He popped open his trunk and got out. By the time I squirmed out of my seat, he was standing next to my car holding both bags of groceries. I opened my car door, popped my trunk, and Bartell set both bags inside, then slammed down the lid, hard. Then he turned to look at me, his arms crossed over his chest. 'How did you find out we had Jenny Lee's phone?' he snapped.

I met his gaze unflinchingly. 'Dale told me about her habit of recording her conversations, and that she was never without her phone. I assumed that, since she'd sent me a text just minutes before she died, you found the phone on her body.' I paused. 'And I just assumed you'd listened to it.'

'Hmpf.' He glared at me for a few seconds before barking out, 'I've told you this before, and I'm going to repeat myself,' he said. 'I can't reveal any details to you, but you have to trust me. You've got to stop nosing around. You might be making a murderer nervous. As I told you earlier, I'd hate to get a call and find myself standing over your dead body next.'

Bartell looked so serious that, in spite of the gruesome picture his remark conjured up, I felt a sudden urge to tease him. I leaned forward, laid a hand on his arm and said in a breathy tone, 'Why, Detective Bartell. You like me. You really like me.'

I was totally unprepared for what happened next. Bartell stared at me for a few seconds then, before I realized what was happening, he swept me into his arms and tilted my head back. The kiss he planted on me was deep and extremely pleasant. When he released me, I staggered back, my knees shaking, my lips tingling.

'Dammit, I really, really do,' he murmured, so softly I had to strain to catch the words. Then he hopped in his car and drove off, leaving me staring after him, shaken and more than a bit confused.

'Down, girl,' I whispered. 'It was only an impulsive kiss. It doesn't mean anything.'

I turned to open my car door and, as I did so, a movement

at the far corner of the garage caught my eye. I glanced up just in time to see a man slide behind the wheel of a BMW. A few seconds later, he gunned the motor and flew out of the garage. I'd only had a fleeting glimpse as he whizzed past, but I thought he resembled Roberto Manchetti. And if it were Roberto, what in heck had he been doing here?

THIRTEEN

'Oh my God! He kissed you! What was it like? Did you just want to die!'

I was sitting in my kitchen and Hilary was across from me. It was nine thirty, and a large pot of gumbo was simmering on my stove, and there was a half-empty bottle of Chablis on the kitchen table. I picked up my glass, drained it, and reached for the bottle. I refilled my glass and took a sip before I answered.

'It definitely took me by surprise. I wasn't expecting it, but I'll say this. The man's an excellent kisser.'

'Ooh, it just sounds so romantic.' Hilary rubbed her arms and pretended to swoon. 'Why, it's like he's Rhett Butler and you're Scarlett O'Hara. You're the headstrong gal who won't listen to reason, and he's the charming gent who sweeps you off your feet and makes you listen – or tries to, anyway.'

I ran my finger around the rim of my glass. 'It was hardly romantic. We were in the municipal lot standing next to my car, and he was lecturing me about staying out of the Jenny Lee investigation. Next thing I knew, I was in his arms.'

Hilary sniffed. 'Sounds pretty romantic to me. Unless, of course, you think he was using the kiss as a distraction. To get your mind off the Jenny Lee thing.'

Oddly enough, that observation disappointed me. 'I'm not sure,' I said at last. 'But if that was his intent, it didn't work.'

Hilary picked up her own glass of wine and raised it at me. 'Face it, honey. The guy's got the hots for you.' She paused. 'And I think you kind of like him too.'

'What! Are you nuts?' I pushed back my chair and clomped over to the stove to check on my gumbo. After giving the pot a few quick stirs, I turned back to my friend. 'I don't want to talk about Bartell anymore,' I declared. 'It's pointless at best. Our time would be much better served going over what I learned at Roy's Brew Barn.'

Hilary leaned back in the chair and kicked off her shoes. 'Well, compared to the evening I had to endure listening to my mother and Arleen prattle on about my sorry single state, talking about a murder would be like watching a Disney movie. So, go ahead, shoot. What did you find out?'

I sat back down and hit the highlights of my evening at Roy's. 'Ginger remembered seeing Jenny Lee in there a few times,' I finished. 'She also remembered seeing Roberto and Longo in there. I'm hoping Dixie and this Brenda will be able to substantiate seeing Roberto and Longo as well. And who knows, maybe one of them will even remember if Jenny Lee was in there Friday night and, if I'm real lucky, if she was with someone.'

'Maybe Jenny Lee's killer is someone who works at Roy's,' suggested Hilary. 'Is it possible she had something on the owner?'

'Hans Anders? Doubtful. Bartell knows the guy personally and seems to think he's an upstanding citizen. As for the killer being one of the other employees, I'm more inclined to think the killer might have bribed one of them to slip the poison into Jenny Lee's food. That kitchen's revolving door was pretty busy, as I recall. Maybe the killer him- or herself even slipped back there to do the deed.' I sighed. 'Why oh why didn't Hans Anders install CCTV?'

Hilary crossed her arms over her chest. 'You know you really should mention all this to Detective Bartell.'

'I was going to tell him,' I admitted. 'But then he got on his high horse about me sticking my nose in where it doesn't belong.'

'Plus, after he kissed you, that drove anything else right out of your mind. Admit it!' Hilary crowed as she stuck her finger in my face.

I pushed her hand aside. 'All right, I do admit his kiss . . . distracted me a bit.'

'A bit?'

'OK, a lot,' I grumbled. 'But there's also the question of Bartell's attitude. He acts like I'm an interfering idiot.'

'Oh, I'm sure he doesn't think you're an idiot. Interfering now, maybe.'

I stuck my tongue out at her. 'Bartell didn't come right out and say it, but he kind of hinted that I was off the hook, suspect-wise.'

'Which confirms what Dalton told you, right?'

I nodded. 'True, but I can't depend on that. I'm still not one hundred percent certain that Bartell didn't tell Dalton to keep an eye on me. I mean, I've never seen him at that park before and he just shows up? When there's a perfectly good park about a block away from the station?'

'It does seem kind of odd,' Hilary said after a moment. 'Of course, it could just have been a coincidence. Maybe he was in the area too, checking out suspects.'

'Maybe. We'll still have to be extra careful when we go out to make certain we aren't being shadowed. And speaking of being shadowed . . .' I told Hilary about seeing Longo at the dog park and Roberto at the parking garage. 'Was the fact they just happened to be there coincidence? Or are they following me too?'

'Maybe having a policeman on your tail is a good thing,' Hilary protested. 'Especially if either Longo or Roberto should be the killer and they think you're getting too close to the truth.'

'No danger of that right now. I haven't got anything concrete about either of them, just supposition.' I started to tick off on my fingers. 'Take Fred Longo. He had two arguments with her that I overheard. Did she discover something about him worth killing over? Same goes for Roberto Manchetti. Did she discover something about him that could potentially bring harm to the magazine, or to his father?' I sighed. 'I wonder if either of them has a garden—'

'Love of botany aside, I vote for Roberto,' Hilary cut in. 'After all, we heard them argue and it wasn't pretty. And he made that cutting motion across his throat. I bet he knows lots of people who could have steered him toward that poison.'

'I like him too, but sometimes the most obvious suspect is not the one. I considered Bob Gillette.'

'The sweetie who owns Po'Boys!' Hilary cried. 'You're kidding.'

'I said I considered him. He sounded so venomous talking

about Jenny Lee. And he does grow his own herbs. But I eliminated him just as fast. He would have to have been gone at least twenty minutes to a half-hour, and Nita said they were super busy that night. She'd have noticed if he were missing for that length of time.'

'She could be covering for him,' Hilary suggested.

I shook my head. 'I thought about that too, but Nita's not the type. If he had ducked out and left her all alone, she'd call him out on it and tell everyone how hard she had to work. So that leaves us with the mystery woman.'

'Mystery woman? Oh, you mean the chick in the convertible who picked Jenny Lee up that night?' Hilary said. 'Why do you have her on your list?'

'Because she is a mystery woman, in every sense,' I replied. 'We don't know who she is, or what her connection to Jenny Lee was, other than the fact she apparently came running when Jenny called her. There had to be a reason for that, and I'm thinking it wasn't a deep friendship.'

'Blackmail?'

'Possibly.' I paused. 'And then there's Dale and myself. Dale thinks the police have Jenny Lee's phone. He said that she had a habit of recording her conversations, and he's pretty certain she recorded his parting shot to her, as well as mine.'

'Maybe so, but I can't believe the police would consider either of you serious suspects based on that. Besides, didn't Dalton practically admit you were off the hook?'

I shrugged and pushed my wineglass aside. 'It's all so jumbled. But there's got to be some clue, somewhere, that will break this case wide open.'

'And you want to be the one to find it.'

'Yes,' I admitted, 'I do. If for no other reason than to wipe that smug smile off Bartell's face.'

Hilary chuckled. 'Are you sure you wouldn't rather kiss it off?' As I shot her a look, she held up both hands. 'OK, OK, Sherlock. What's our next move?'

'*Our* next move?'

'Well, sure,' Hilary said with a grin. 'I can't let you walk into danger alone, now can I? What sort of friend would I be if I did that?'

I reached over and squeezed her hand. 'The gumbo's almost done,' I said. 'How about a nice big bowl before we take off.'

'Sounds great. I didn't eat much over at my mother's. Constant aggravation and nagging isn't exactly conducive to a healthy appetite.'

I walked over to the stove, spooned out two healthy amounts of gumbo into bowls, and came back to the table. I set Hilary's bowl in front of her, and smiled as my friend sniffed the aroma and pretended to swoon.

'Smells delish.' She picked up her spoon, but before she dug in she looked at me. 'Just exactly what do you have planned, Tiff?'

'Oh, nothing drastic,' I said with a wave of my hand. I picked up my own spoon, took a taste. The gumbo tasted as delicious as it smelled. 'Just a little ride over to the Bentley Apartments over on South. Maybe if we're lucky, we can catch Dixie at home.'

The Bentley Apartments was a run-down, three-story brick building located on the very end of South Street. The street was a dead end, and the apartments were right next to a large expanse of woods that at one time had been the proposed site of a shopping center that had never materialized. The apartments had no parking lot, so the tenants had to fight for parking on the street on a first-come, first-served basis. Tonight it seemed as if every tenant in the building must be home, because both sides of the street were packed. I finally found a space on Morton Street, two blocks over, and it was a tight squeeze at that. A light wind kicked up as Hilary and I made our way to the apartment building. We climbed the few steps to the front door and the first thing we saw was the sign: RING FOR ENTRANCE.

'Wow, this is just about the last thing you'd expect in this neighborhood,' murmured Hilary. She gathered her suede jacket more tightly around her and I did the same with my wool ruana. It was almost mid-September, and the nights were starting to get cool. I looked at the names above the bells and finally located one marked 'Garrett' up at the top. I pressed the bell and waited.

No answer.

'She must not be home,' whispered Hilary. 'Maybe we should go. It's getting colder and, I don't mind telling you, it's a little scary out here. If I'm not mistaken, there was an article in the paper about a woman getting mugged a few weeks ago right in this general area.'

I pressed the bell again. No answer. I stepped back a few paces and looked upward. The number on the Garretts' bell read 3C. I looked at the apartment windows on the third floor. All had lights in them save one. That must be Dixie's. I started to move away, when I caught a flicker of movement. I raised my head just in time to see the edge of the curtain in the darkened window move ever so slightly.

I stumbled back to the stoop and gripped Hilary's arm. 'She's up there,' I said. 'She's hiding from us.'

'Why would she do that?' Hilary asked. 'And how do you know she's up there?'

'I saw the curtain in the darkened apartment move – or at least, I think I did.'

Hilary's lips tugged downward. 'Oh, that doesn't mean anything,' she said. 'It could have been the wind, or maybe she's got a cat.' She reached out and gave my arm a sharp tug. 'Let's go. If you're that determined to speak to this woman, maybe we can come back tomorrow in the daylight.'

I hesitated, but from the set to my pal's jaw, I knew she was going to stand firm on this. 'OK, fine,' I said reluctantly.

We stepped off the stoop and turned in the direction of where I'd parked the car. As we started down the street, I suddenly stopped. 'Wait. Did you hear that?'

Hilary frowned. 'Hear what?'

'I thought I heard a twig snap.'

'I didn't hear anything. Come on.'

A cool wind had sprung up. It swept through the trees, sending a chill up my spine. I walked a few steps and then paused again. I stole a glance over my shoulder, but saw nothing. And yet I had the persistent feeling I was being watched.

Hilary, more than a few paces ahead of me, paused to glance

over her shoulder. Seeing me lagging behind, she called out, 'Tiff. Come *on*.'

'I'm coming,' I called. I started forward, when not ten feet behind me I heard a loud crack, like a tree branch being split. My skin started to prickle and my pulse jumped. I whirled around and stared at the clump of trees beyond.

'Hey. What's the matter?' yelled Hilary.

I didn't answer. My vision was focused on a dark shadow at the edge of the trees. As I watched, the shadow moved. Ever so slightly, but it moved.

Hilary had walked back to me and now tugged at my arm. 'What's with you?' she demanded.

'Look. Over there,' I whispered hoarsely, and pointed in the direction of the shadow. It moved again, and now I could make out the distinct shape of a man.

'Holy cats,' Hilary cried. 'It's a mugger. Run!'

She'd spoken the last word very loudly. Upon hearing the command, the shadow suddenly charged forward.

I didn't need any further encouragement. I started to run like the dickens. Hilary and I both ran like our pants were on fire. We didn't stop until we reached Morton Street and my convertible came into view. I hit the button to unlock the doors and we tumbled into the car. I punched down the door locks and we both sat there for a few minutes, breathing heavily.

'I told you this neighborhood wasn't safe,' Hilary finally gasped. 'We could have been mugged like that old lady.'

'Maybe.' I paused, took a few deep breaths, and then twisted the key in the ignition. As the motor sprang to life, I said, 'Or maybe it wasn't just any old mugger.'

Hilary's eyes popped. 'What are you saying? That it was Jenny Lee's murderer out there? But how on earth would he have known we'd be here tonight?'

'I don't know. Maybe he followed us. There seems to be a lot of that going around lately.'

Hilary tucked a strand of hair behind one ear. 'Maybe it wasn't a mugger. Maybe it was that other detective – you know, the one you think Bartell asked to follow you.'

'I'm not certain Bartell did ask Dalton to follow me. Besides, if that were the case, I doubt he'd have let us get so frightened. I think he'd have made his presence known.'

'So you think it was the killer? But why would he follow you?' Hilary demanded as I pulled away from the curb. 'You don't know anything!'

I stared out into the darkness. 'The killer doesn't know that,' I said. 'It would appear that my inquiries are making someone uncomfortable.'

Hilary let her breath out in a whoosh. 'That's an understatement,' she grumbled.

I pulled out into the street and made a quick turn. As we passed South Street, I drove slowly by. The street, and the woods beyond, appeared quiet and deserted.

'Well, if someone was following you, he's gone now,' said Hilary. 'Did you get a look at whoever it was?'

I shook my head. 'I couldn't even tell you if it were a man or a woman. All I saw was a dark shape.'

Hilary slumped down in her seat. 'I don't suppose this little experience has put you off investigating?'

I scratched at my head. 'I suppose I should be,' I said, 'but this little incident has only made me more determined than ever. As a matter of fact, I think we should go to the office early tomorrow.'

'Tomorrow? But tomorrow's Sunday,' Hilary said. 'The office is closed.'

'I know. What better time than to snoop through Jenny Lee's office when no one is around?'

Hilary shook her head. 'The police have probably gone over her office already with a fine-tooth comb. If there was anything significant there, it's probably gone.'

'Maybe,' I said. 'But it doesn't hurt to look. After all, you never know. We could get lucky.'

'If we don't get dead first,' groused Hilary.

I dropped Hil off and then went home. It was after eleven thirty and I was pretty much exhausted; after all, I'd had a pretty full day. I peeled off my clothes, tumbled into bed and fell asleep almost immediately. It was a restless slumber, though. My dreams were peppered with visions of dark shadows; hulking, menacing shapes with glowing eyes. In one in particular, the shadow loomed large over me. Its eyes glowed like twin beacons and it slowly raised one hand. I could see it clenched a small vial, with a skull and crossbones on the label. As I watched, the shadow's face came sharply into focus: Frederick Longo. It then morphed into Roberto Manchetti, and finally into the visage of the mystery woman from Friday night. The shadow's face faded, and it leaned forward, enveloping me. I felt a warm stickiness on the side of my face and sat bolt upright, wide awake, startling Cooper.

'Oh my God it was you, Cooper.' I rubbed at the side of my face with the back of my hand. It came away sticky with doggy saliva. Cooper gave two short yips and then sat back on his haunches, head cocked. I glanced over at the clock. It was just a few minutes past six thirty. Hilary was meeting me here at ten. I pushed back the covers and swung my feet out of the bed. If I got my rear in gear, maybe I could get some work done after I took Cooper for a short walk.

Cooper, as if reading my mind, gave another short yip and jumped off the bed. I pulled on my robe and regarded the pup. 'It could have been worse,' I told him. 'I could have dreamed about that kiss instead of having suspects chase me.'

My spaniel looked puzzled, as if he didn't understand how I could equate Bartell's kiss with a murderer. Frankly, I didn't either. If I were to be totally honest with myself, I'd rather liked that kiss, maybe a little too much. After what had happened to me back in New York, though, I wasn't ready for another serious entanglement. Yet.

I showered quickly and dressed in yoga pants, a comfy, rose-colored sweatshirt with kangaroo pockets, thick pink socks with kittens embroidered on them, and sneakers. I bundled my unruly hair up in a ponytail, tucked my keys into my pocket and headed downstairs. Cooper was waiting expectantly by his food bowl, as was Lily. I said good morning to the Siamese and she rubbed against my pant leg in return. I spooned food into both their bowls and, while they chowed down, went out to the back porch to retrieve the paper. I brewed a quick cup of coffee in my Keurig as I scanned the headlines. No big murder stories on the front page and nothing further about Jenny Lee's death, save for a small article on page 10 that her viewing would be tomorrow night, with a private service on Tuesday. The article mentioned a stepsister who was flying in from Los Angeles to make arrangements, but no name was given.

I snapped on Cooper's leash and we left Lily sprawled across the linoleum floor, calmly washing herself. I walked Cooper around the block twice before he deigned to finally do his duty near a massive oak tree. All the while I was out, I kept looking over my shoulder, half expecting to see either Longo, Roberto, or maybe even Detective Dalton following me. Fortunately, the walk passed without incident, and a half-hour later Cooper was snoozing happily in his dog bed, Lily was nowhere to be found, and I was at the kitchen table with my laptop, putting the finishing touches on my pizza challenge feature.

My cell chirped and I picked it up, glanced at the screen. It read *Private Caller*. I hesitated, afraid to answer. What if it were Detective Bartell? What would I say to him? *Say, Detective, I surely enjoyed that kiss but I don't think it was a good idea. Better if we just forget about it and remain friends?* That was what my head was telling me to say but my hormones were definitely steering me in another direction. *Say, Detective Bartell, how about we go somewhere for a repeat of yesterday afternoon?*

'Goose,' I chided myself. 'If it were Bartell, the station name would pop up.' I pressed down on the answer button. 'Tiffany Austin.'

'Ah, Tiffany, I'm glad I caught you.' I recognized Frederick Longo's voice.

'Chef Longo. What can I do for you?'

'Well, for one thing, I was wondering how your latest brain-storm is coming along. Dale told me about your idea for the recipe of the month. I have to say, I think it's an excellent idea. Inspired really. It should certainly encourage home cooks to participate actively, and might even garner some subscriptions for the magazine.'

'My thoughts exactly. As a matter of fact, I was just putting the finishing touches on the article now.'

'Working so early on a Sunday? You are dedicated.' He cleared his throat. 'Actually, I was calling to see if you might be free for brunch today. We could perhaps discuss your feature, and any other ideas you might care to run past me.' He paused. 'And catch up, as well. I thought perhaps we might meet at the Adirondack Club.'

I knew that restaurant. It was about a mile and a half out of town, set far back on a lonely stretch of road. They did serve a scrumptious brunch, but there was a small part of me that wondered just why he'd chosen such an out-of-the-way place, when there were many others around locally that served an equally sumptuous meal. I struggled to remember the shadow of the evening before. I thought the figure had been about Longo's height and build, but I couldn't be certain. I cleared my throat. 'Ordinarily I'd love to, but I do have plans for later this morning.'

'Oh, dear what a shame.' Disappointment was evident in his tone. 'Well, then if you're not free for brunch, how about dinner? Let's say, seven o'clock at the Adirondack?'

I wondered why Longo seemed in such a hurry to see me. To pick my brain, find out what I'd learned about Jenny Lee's death so far? Well, two could play at that game. But in a not-so-secluded place.

'Dinner sounds good, but I'd rather meet in town, if it's all the same to you. How about Po'Boys Anonymous?' I suggested.

'Po'Boys Anonymous?' he repeated. Indecision was rife in his tone, but I suspected it had more to do with the name of the place than anything else.

'Yes. They have wonderful dinner entrées, and they've just updated their menu. I recently did a review on them.'

'So did Jenny Lee, if I'm not mistaken,' said Longo. 'She didn't much care for the place, which in itself is a ringing endorsement. I'll see you there at seven.'

Longo hung up and I tossed my phone aside. Maybe this was a golden opportunity for me to casually interrogate Longo about just what his connection had been to Jenny Lee. The real question was, could I believe what he told me? I'd done an Internet search on him last night and nothing untoward had surfaced, nor could I find any hint of a prior relationship with

Jenny Lee. Still, I couldn't eliminate him, much as I might want to. Quite honestly, I'd always liked him.

I pulled up my article on the pizza contest and went to work. I'd decided on the final format. The contestants would be challenged to bake an original pizza on the spot and present it to a panel of judges. I was hoping to entice some local pizza-makers into the role, and perhaps Chef Longo as well. There would be five separate categories: Traditional, Non-Traditional, Pan, Specialty and, because we wanted to appeal to everyone, Gluten-Free. The winners in each category then competed for a grand prize, yet to be decided. All the top finishers would have their original recipes published on my blog, as well as in the hard copy of *Southern Style*.

Before I knew it, it was nine thirty. I put the finishing touches to my 'baby' and then sent it off to Dale with a brief e-mail:

Here's my proposal for the pizza challenge. Read it and see what you think. We can discuss at length tomorrow.

I'd no sooner hit the send button than my doorbell rang. I glanced at the clock on the wall. Hilary was a good fifteen minutes early, which was definitely unusual. She was almost always late. I went to the front door and opened it.

No one was there.

I was just about to go back inside when I noticed a piece of paper hanging out of my mailbox. I went over and pulled it out. It was a photograph of Jenny Lee, with a big red X marked across her face. Below, in crude red pencil were the words:

DON'T LET WHAT HAPPENED TO HER HAPPEN TO YOU.

FOURTEEN

'Don't you think you should show that to Bartell?'
I took my eyes off the road briefly and glanced over at Hilary, seated next to me in the passenger seat. She held the paper I'd gotten earlier gingerly in her gloved hands, and handled it almost as if she were afraid it would bite her.

'I probably should,' I said, 'but after what happened yesterday, I'm a little reluctant to make contact with him,' I confessed.

'Oh, for heaven's sake,' Hilary exploded. 'You've been threatened, girl! This is a threatening note if I ever saw one. Bartell should know about this. Maybe he can get fingerprints or DNA off of it, or something to track the killer down.'

'Well, that's highly doubtful. I imagine the killer handled that note the same way you are – gingerly and with gloves. I doubt he or she would be stupid enough to leave any traceable evidence.'

'You never know,' Hilary declared. 'It's always some small detail that trips the bad guys up on *Criminal Minds*.'

'Yeah, well, I'll think about it.'

I pulled into *Southern Style*'s parking lot. Hilary let out a low whistle. 'Wow, I've never seen this parking lot so empty. We must be the only ones here.'

'Us, and maybe the cleaning crew and the guards,' I agreed. I pulled my convertible into a spot near the back entrance. Hilary looked at me questioningly, and I shrugged. 'No sense making our presence more conspicuous than necessary,' I said. I shut the car off and then wiggled my fingers at Hilary. 'Hand it over.'

Hilary handed me the note and I folded it carefully, then reached into my pocket and pulled out one of the cellophane baggies I usually reserved for Cooper's deposits. I tucked the note inside, then opened my glove compartment and slid it in.

I locked the glove compartment and we exited the car and walked around to the front entrance.

'Oh, great. Just our luck. Look who's on guard duty,' Hil whispered as we pushed through the double glass doors. 'Gil Chesterton.'

'The DA? Great.'

Gil was a seventy-something man who'd served in the Korean War and loved to relate anecdotes to anyone who would listen, and also to those who wouldn't. He'd gotten the nickname DA because of his penchant for asking a gazillion questions in rapid-fire succession, much like Herbert Hathaway, Branson's District Attorney.

'Well, we have to sign in. There's no getting around that,' I said through clenched teeth as Hilary hung back. 'Let's get it over with.'

We approached the reception desk. Gil looked up, blinked slowly, and then his craggy face split into a smile. 'Wal, if it isn't Miss Hilary and our newest employee, Miss Tiffany. Watcha all doin' here on a Sunday? Don't tell me two pretty gals like you don't have dates, or somethin'?'

I shot Gil my biggest 150-watt mega-smile. 'Now, Gil. What could be better than coming here on a Sunday morning?'

He gave me an odd look, and then barked out a dry laugh that sounded more like a cackle. 'Oh, I could think of lots of things.' He gestured beneath the desk. 'Watching the Atlanta–Dallas matchup for one. I've got my tablet all fired up and rarin' to go.'

I signed my name in the book with a flourish and handed the pen to Hilary. 'Don't let us keep you,' I cooed. 'I just want to pick up some notes I left in my new office for the article I'm writing. We won't be long.'

'New article, eh? What restaurant did you review now?'

'Oh, it's not a review. It's a contest.'

Gil's eyes lit up. 'A contest? Now that sounds interesting. What sort of contest? A bake-off?'

'Actually, it's a pizza contest. We're going to offer a prize for the home chef who makes the best original pizza.'

Gil smacked his lips together. 'Hey, that does sound interesting. I love a good pizza, myself. You know where it originated, right?'

'Italy, of course,' Hilary answered. 'Everyone knows that.'

'Ah.' Gil jabbed his finger in the air. 'The first known pizza shop opened in Port Alba in Naples, but do you know how it was invented?' Without waiting for an answer he went on, 'The Neapolitan pizza-maker Raffaele Esposito invented the Pizza Margherita to honor the Queen Consort of Italy, Margherita of Savoy.'

'Fascinating,' I murmured. I started to edge away. 'We're sort of in a hurry, so if you'll excuse us . . .'

Paying no attention he went on, 'The first pizza was garnished with tomatoes, mozzarella and basil. Know what that represented? The national colors of Italy, as on the Italian flag,' he puffed out his chest proudly. 'Maybe you could use that in your article. I've got some other anecdotes too. Like, why is it called pizza? Seems that—'

He paused as the phone on the desk suddenly jangled. Gil frowned. 'Now who could be calling?' he muttered. He picked up the phone and barked, 'Hello. *Southern Style*.' His features screwed into a surprised expression. 'Good morning, Mr Swenson.'

I mentally blessed Dale for whatever reason he'd decided to call the office. I motioned to Gil that we were going upstairs. He waved us on and continued talking to Dale. Hilary and I practically ran down the corridor to the elevator. Once we were inside the car going up, Hilary let out a sigh.

'Whew, that was a close one. I thought we'd be stuck listening to the history of pizza for at least an hour.'

'I don't know why Dale was calling, but I'm glad he did,' I said. 'Although I must admit, it might be a good idea to include some of that stuff Gil mentioned in my article. I'll have to do a bit of rewriting later.'

We'd reached the fourth floor where Jenny Lee's office was located. The doors slid open and we exited into a very dark hallway. I pointed to the ceiling. 'Some bulbs are out,' I said.

Hilary glanced upward, and then rubbed her hands together. 'Great. It just adds to our cat burglar atmosphere.'

'Where is her office, do you know?'

'I think it's all the way at the end of the hall.'

We hurried down the corridor and finally saw a dark oak

door next to a glass-enclosed conference room. The shiny brass placard on the door read, JENNY LEE PLUMM.

'We're at the right place,' I announced. I reached into my pocket, pulled out my leather gloves and slipped them on. Then I gave the doorknob a sharp twist, and groaned. 'It's locked.'

'Of course it is,' murmured Hilary. She cast an apprehensive look over her shoulder. 'Let's get out of here. This is giving me the creeps. Unlike you, I'm just not cut out for a life of crime.'

'In a minute.' I felt in my hair, found a bobby pin, and knelt in front of the lock. After a few minutes of jiggling, I heard a sharp click! I stood up, twisted the knob, and the door swung slowly inward.

'I don't even want to know how you learned to do that,' Hilary hissed at me as we stepped inside the office. The room was pitch black. 'Light switch should be here somewhere,' Hilary mumbled.

'We don't need that.' I felt in my bag and pulled out my phone. 'Flashlight app works much better.'

I switched on the bright beam and swung it around the room. There wasn't much to see. The top of Jenny Lee's massive oak desk was bare except for a blotter. The tops of the two filing cabinets were bare as well. A small bookshelf off to my left held a collection of books and magazines, all stacked neatly. There weren't even any pictures on the walls.

'Not much to see here,' Hilary said. 'I told you, she hardly used this place. Did mostly everything from home. Besides, Bartell's men would have removed anything significant.'

'Maybe.' I swung the light around as I walked over to the desk. I bent over and started opening the drawers. The top one held a blank pad of paper and two Bic pens. The second drawer had some plastic bags. The third held a small desk calendar. I reached inside the drawer and pulled it out. 'I wonder why the police didn't take this,' I murmured.

Hilary walked over to me and peered over my shoulder as I flipped through the pages. 'Maybe because there's nothing in it. See, the pages are blank,' she suggested.

I bent to replace it in the drawer and, as I did so, the light from my flashlight app shone on something white caught in the space between the drawer and the floor. I thrust my hand in the opening and carefully removed it. 'Look at this,' I said.

Hilary peered over my shoulder. 'What? It's a scrap of paper?'

'It's torn from a calendar; see the date at the top? This past Friday.'

'The day Jenny Lee died.' Hilary leaned further over and squinted at the scrap. 'Something's written there, but I can't make it out.'

I tilted the paper to one side and studied the scrawled letters. 'The letters look like c-h-i-l.'

'She was making a note to herself to chill?' Hilary observed as she leaned her head on my shoulder.

'Chill is spelled with two l's. This has one.'

Hilary shrugged. 'Maybe she was a lousy speller.'

'Or maybe this word is unfinished.' I spied a calendar on the far corner of the desk. I reached over and flipped it to Friday's date. The page was intact. 'It didn't come from this calendar,' I said. 'I wonder how it got down there.'

'Who knows? Jenny Lee probably dropped it there.'

'Or hid it,' I said thoughtfully.

'Why would she hide a scrap of paper with an unfinished word?' Hilary tugged at my arm. 'Let's get out of here. Gil will be certain to ask more questions if we're up here too long.'

'In a minute.'

I slid the paper into my pocket and shut the drawer. I flashed my light around once more, pausing when it caught a glint of something metallic underneath the file cabinet in the far corner. I hurried over, thrust my hand underneath, and came away with a small ring of two keys. 'Look at this,' I cried.

Hilary hurried over and we examined my find. The keys were attached to a leather key fob. I turned the fob over and saw a printed address: 584 Carmella Towers.

'That's a hoity-toity apartment building over on the North Side,' said Hilary. 'Come to think of it, I think that's where Jenny Lee lived.'

I turned the keys over in my palm. 'Hm, so this might be

a spare set of keys. I wonder what they were doing under the file cabinet.'

'Maybe she hid them there just in case she misplaced hers. I do that too, although it's usually in the back of the file cabinet, not under it.' She paused to stare intently at me. 'Please tell me you're not thinking what I think you are.'

'Oh, but I am.' I twirled the keys in my hand. 'Come on, Hil. Haven't you always wanted to take a gander at those luxury apartments?'

Hil sighed. 'I'm begging you, Tiff. Call Detective Bartell. Let him do the apartment breaking. He gets paid for that.'

'I'm sure his men have already been there,' I said. 'They missed finding those keys, and that slip of paper. Who knows, maybe they missed something significant in her apartment as well?'

'So you're what? Going to help them do their job?'

I grinned. 'Someone obviously has to.'

We exited Jenny Lee's office and hurried over to the elevator. 'Here's hoping Gil is busy watching the game and doesn't pepper us with a thousand questions when we try to leave,' said Hilary.

The elevator doors opened and we stepped out. I glanced over at the reception desk and nudged my friend. 'Looks like we have nothing to worry about,' I whispered. Gil was deep in conversation with a thin, pinched-face woman. She had on a light tan coat, and a white dress peeped out from underneath. She had thick-soled white sneakers on her feet.

Hilary giggled. 'I wonder if she's Gil's girlfriend.'

'I doubt it. That white dress and sneaks look like some sort of uniform. It's more likely she's part of the cleaning crew.'

We slipped past Gil and the woman, neither of whom looked once in our direction. Once we were outside, Hilary slapped her palm against her forehead. 'Geez, we forgot to sign out.'

'Well, we're not going back. If anyone says anything, we'll just say we forgot.' I jangled the keys in the air. 'Right now, we've got more important things to do.'

'Oh, yeah, embarking on my new life of crime. I almost forgot.'

We climbed into my convertible and, just as I started to

back out of the space, a sleek black Jaguar XF convertible roared past, nearly clipping my rear bumper. 'Holy cats,' cried Hilary. She craned her neck around, trying to see the car. 'He almost got you good.'

'Thank God he didn't,' I grumbled. The Jaguar slid into Dale's reserved spot near the entrance. I shook my head. 'Obviously whoever it is has no regard for reserved spaces.'

Hilary shrugged. 'Well, it is Sunday,' she said.

'But still.'

The driver door opened and a thin, well-dressed woman emerged. I slowed down, squinting for a better look. The woman wore a scarf wound tightly around her head and wore large dark sunglasses that almost totally obscured her face. The simple white coat she wore screamed designer – Armani, perhaps? And her five-inch heels resembled a pair of Louboutins I'd seen last month in one of the fashion magazines, which cost more than I made in two months as an assistant chef. She shut her car door, turned, and walked purposefully toward the entrance. I frowned and turned my gaze to the convertible. 'It kind of looks like the one we saw the other night, doesn't it,' I murmured.

Hilary squinted at it. 'Maybe.' She let out a sharp gasp and grabbed my arm. 'Oh my gosh! You think she could be the mystery woman? The one who picked Jenny Lee up?'

I frowned. 'Maybe. I'm not sure.'

I hesitated, debating. Should I park, go back inside, and see if I could find out if this woman was the same one who'd rescued Jenny Lee that night? Or would my time be better spent seeing what, if any, clues I might find at Jenny Lee's apartment?

The apartment won, and I gunned the motor.

Carmella Towers was a four-story whitewashed building that at one time had housed government offices. It had been abandoned, sold to a developer, who'd gutted the whole thing and restored it into a high-class apartment complex. I'd heard rents started somewhere around four thousand a month, and I could believe it. I'd Googled the complex on my phone, and the sample apartment that you could take a virtual tour of was simply gorgeous, like something out of a movie. The lobby boasted tall, Corinthian columns and a doorman; there was an Olympic-sized swimming pool on the rooftop for the tenants, as well as a private health club. The common area boasted a huge seventy-two-inch flat-screen TV and a gigantic fireplace.

The sample apartment was just as opulent: the bedroom was huge and boasted a round, king-sized bed; the sunken bathtub with its jets was huge enough for two (or three, if you were so inclined); the kitchen was about the size of the entire first floor of my house and boasted every appliance one could imagine using, and some that I confess never even crossed my mind as a professional chef.

'You stay here,' I directed Hilary after I'd parked in a spot marked 'Visitors'. 'Call my cell if you see anyone suspicious.'

'And that would be?'

'Chef Longo, Roberto, that mystery woman, or – God forbid – Bartell or Dalton.'

'You got it.'

Hilary seemed relieved not to accompany me on the actual housebreaking. I had to admit, the whole episode had me kind of jazzed. Maybe I would find a clue that Bartell and his men had overlooked, and solve this thing once and for all!

I swaggered up to the front entrance, just like I belonged there. I figured one of the two keys on the ring was for the front door, and I got it on the first shot. I saw the stool that was obviously the doorman's post; however, he was conspicuously absent. Probably on a break, thank goodness. I walked through the lobby, over to the bank of elevators and was whisked up to the fourth floor without encountering any neighbors.

I found Jenny Lee's apartment and my heart was pounding and my pulse racing as I inserted the key in the lock and turned the knob. I walked inside swiftly, shutting the door behind me, and stood still for a moment, listening. All I heard was the hum of the very expensive stainless-steel refrigerator in the kitchen.

After debating for a few moments, I flicked on the light

switch and looked around. The apartment was gorgeous – of that I'd had no doubt – and it certainly reflected Jenny Lee's flamboyant tastes. The living room was done in bold shades of maroon and teal. The couch was massive, upholstered in a pattern of black and teal, and there were black, maroon and teal throw pillows scattered all over it. A black Barcolounger recliner sat off to one side, covered with a fluffy garnet throw. The carpet was a rich teal, a sharp contrast to the stark white walls. Abstract paintings in teal, black and maroon covered the walls.

I moved forward and stole a peek at the kitchen. It looked exactly like the model, and the appliances showed no sign of wear. I walked over to the refrigerator and jerked the door open. It was empty save for a few bottles of wine – and very expensive wine at that – and two bottles of Heineken beer. I fancied Jenny Lee hadn't been much of a cook, probably choosing either to order or eat out. And she'd wanted to be a food critic!

I moved down the long hallway. There were three closed doors. I opened the first one and snapped the light on. This had to be the master bedroom. The bed was king-sized, covered with a beautiful dove gray coverlet, and looked to be soft and inviting. I noticed that the closet door was slightly ajar. I walked over and gently opened it. I stood there and stared at the dozens of dresses, skirts, blouses and pants that hung there. It was almost like walking into the ladies' department at Tyler's, Branson's most exclusive clothing store. I was pretty certain that most of Jenny Lee's clothing had come from Tyler's too. One dress in particular caught my eye. It was a simple shift dress, burgundy in color, with a lace bodice. I succumbed to temptation and reached for it. I walked over to the full-length mirror and held the dress in front of me. It had two pockets, cut on the side so they were hardly noticeable. One seemed to bulge out slightly. I stuck my hand inside, and pulled out a small leather notebook.

I tossed the dress on the bed and sat down on the edge. My hands trembled as I thumbed through the notebook. One page had Longo's name on it. Beneath that were the names of several different women. Next to each name were dates and times. I skimmed the list quickly. I recognized a few of the names as other apprentice chefs in New York. At the bottom of the page was a phone number with another name: Christine L. I was pretty sure Christine was the name of Longo's wife. I frowned. Could this list be what Longo and Jenny Lee had argued over?

I thumbed through a few more pages and found a notation on Roberto Manchetti. Jenny Lee had written there, *'Roberto is a disgrace, not only to his father but to the family name. Just need a little more time.'* A little more time for what? I had the feeling this could have something to do with the argument I'd witnessed, but just what, I had no idea. The next few pages were blank, and on the last page was scrawled, *'Golden Goose about to be cooked. Just need to confirm one last detail.'*

I pulled out my phone and snapped a few quick photos of the pages that interested me, then slid the notebook back into the pocket of the dress and replaced it in the closet. I went back into the hall and moved on to the next door. This had to be Jenny Lee's home office. A massive oak desk sat in the middle of the room, and I made my way swiftly toward it. There was a stack of papers on the top of the desk, arranged neatly, a Cross pen on top. I walked over and thumbed hastily through them, but they were all printouts of her blog articles. Nothing earth-shattering here. At the bottom of a stack was a folded slip of paper. 'Important' was written across it. Curious, I picked it up and unfolded it. Cricket's Department Store was scrawled across the top of the page, and below it, ES CL REC $15. What was so important about this, I wondered? After a few seconds, I folded the paper and tucked it in my jacket pocket.

I made certain I left the desk exactly as I found it, shut the light and then retraced my steps to the living room. I was just about to leave when I heard a noise in the hallway. Instinctively, I retreated a step just as the apartment door was flung open. The next instant I was staring at a woman in police uniform, the barrel of the .45 she held in her hand pointed right at my heart.

'Police. Freeze where you are and put your hands in the air where I can see them!'

FIFTEEN

The female officer crouched in a combat stance, her gun trained on me. 'Step into the center of the room, hands on your head,' she barked.

I did as she instructed. My heart was pounding so loudly I figured it could be heard all the way back to my parents' house in Gilson. What the heck had happened to Hilary, I wondered? Wasn't she supposed to warn me if the police were on their way?

I shuffled forward. 'I can explain,' I squeaked, and started to lower my hand to my pocket.

'Time for that at the station. Hands on your head,' she barked again.

I slapped my hand back on my skull just as another officer, a male, pushed past me and started down the long hallway. I glanced past the female officer's shoulder and gasped as I saw a large shadow loom in the doorway behind her. My feeling of unease dissipated quickly as the shadow stepped into the light and I found myself looking at Detective Eric Dalton.

Dalton, for his part, seemed surprised to see me. 'Miss Austin?' he asked as he lowered his gun. '*You're* the burglar?'

'I'm not a burglar, if you'd just let me explain,' I began.

Dalton motioned to the female officer. She put down her gun (rather reluctantly, I thought) and turned her attention to examining the front door. Dalton looked at me. 'We received a report of an intruder in this apartment.'

'I'm not an intruder,' I protested. 'At least, not in the strictest sense of the word.'

'What sense then? You're in this apartment without permission. That spells "intruder" to me,' said a frosty voice from behind Dalton. He stepped to one side and I bit back a cry as I recognized who stood behind him. It was the woman I'd seen going into *Southern Style*'s offices, the woman who'd nearly clipped my bumper with her Jaguar XE. The sunglasses were gone, but the scarf was still draped around her head and she had her white coat (cashmere, I thought, now that I could see it better) wound tightly around her thin body. The woman touched Dalton's arm. 'Officer, I want this woman arrested.'

'It's Detective, ma'am,' Eric Dalton said politely. 'Don't worry, we'll get this all straightened out.'

'I saw you a little while ago,' I blurted out. 'You were going into *Southern Style*'s offices. You almost clipped my bumper,' I added accusingly.

The woman raised one pencil-thin eyebrow. 'That was you? What were you doing? Following me? You knew I was occupied, so you figured this was a good time to make your move?'

I drew myself up straight, no easy feat because I still had my hands on my head. 'Not at all. You've got it all wrong.'

'I do, do I?' The woman moved closer to me, and her words dropped like chips of ice. 'Then can you kindly explain to me just what you are doing here in my sister's apartment?'

I gasped as light suddenly dawned. 'Oh my gosh! You're Jenny Lee's stepsister! You flew in from LA to make funeral arrangements.'

'Yes, I'm Isolde Carter.' She tapped the toe of her Louboutin impatiently on the thick carpet. 'I needed to get into this apartment, but there were no keys found on Jenny Lee's body and I couldn't get ahold of the manager of this complex. Finally I called Dale Swenson. Jenny used the same cleaning service as *Southern Style*, so he contacted the cleaning woman to drop the key off for me at the office.' She fixed me with a dagger stare. 'Imagine my surprise when I glanced up to discover an apartment that should have been shrouded in darkness had a light on – several, in fact. I called the police immediately. Just how did you get in here, anyway?'

'We'd like to know that too,' barked the female officer. 'There's no sign of forced entry.'

The stare got even icier. 'If you have her keys, then how did you get them? From her cold, dead hand?'

Eric Dalton looked at me. 'Do you have anything to say?'

I raised my chin. 'I refuse to answer on the grounds it may tend to incriminate me,' I said stiffly.

Eric sighed. 'OK, lower your hands.' He stepped forward

and took my arm. 'I'm going to have to insist you come down to the station with me.'

Isolde glared daggers at me. 'You're going to arrest her, aren't you, officer? I want you to throw the book at her. Why, she might be the person responsible for my sister's untimely demise.'

I spun on my heel and glared at her. 'I assure you, I did not kill your sister,' I said.

Isolde threw up her hands. 'Officer, please instruct this woman not to speak to me.'

'It's Detective,' Eric corrected her again. 'We're going to take her down to the station, ma'am, and sort all this out.' His tone was neutral, but I could tell from the set of his jaw he was pissed. 'Would you like to come downtown with us?'

Isolde made a motion as if she were shrugging off a fly. 'I don't think that's necessary. I'm already behind in what I need to do around here. I've got to get everything in order for the viewing and the funeral, and then the reading of her will. Then I've got to catch a red-eye back to LA Wednesday night.'

'Your busy schedule aside, can you take a quick look around, tell us if anything's missing?'

Isolde made a little mewling noise. 'You've got to be kidding! How would I know if anything is missing? This is the first time I've ever been in this apartment. I would have no idea!' She paused, and her eyes narrowed to slits. 'Oh, wait, I see what's going on here.' She raised her finger and pointed it accusingly at Eric. 'You're on her side. You can't arrest her for burglary if nothing's missing, right? But you *can* arrest her for breaking and entering.'

Eric's jaw set. The other policeman came back into the room, shook his head at Eric. Eric turned back to Isolde and said, almost gleefully, 'Apparently there's no sign of forced entry anywhere.'

Isolde made a tsking sound deep in her throat, then raised her hand and pointed dramatically at me. 'Of course not. Because she let herself in with the keys she took from my sister after she killed her.'

'I did not,' I growled.

'So what? Jenny came back from the grave and let you in?' Isolde sneered.

I started toward Isolde but Eric caught my arm and pulled me back. He looked at Isolde and said stiffly, 'I assure you, ma'am, we'll get to the bottom of it.'

'I certainly hope so,' she sniffed. With a final scathing look at me, she turned on her heel and flounced down the hallway. A few seconds later, we heard a door slam.

Eric looked at me. 'OK, she's gone. Now tell me, how did you get in here?'

I swallowed. 'I used Jenny Lee's key.'

Eric's eyes widened. 'How did you get . . .?' He held up his hand. 'Never mind. I don't think I want to know. What exactly were you doing here?'

We heard a door open, and the sound of heels clicking on the polished floor. A second later, Isolde came into view. She walked right over to me and held out her hand. 'Give it to me,' she demanded.

I stared at her. 'Give you what?'

'My sister's diamond and platinum watch. It wasn't found on her body, and she hardly ever took that thing off. It was the final birthday gift our father ever gave her. If you had a key to this apartment, then you probably killed her. Which means you must have her watch, so hand it over,' Isolde cried.

I took a step back. 'Lady, calm down. I don't have Jenny Lee's watch.'

'Then where is it?' she snarled. 'I just looked through her jewelry box. It's not there. If she wasn't wearing it the night she died, it would be there, unless . . .' Isolde whirled around and jabbed her bony finger at Eric Dalton. 'I want that woman searched,' she growled.

I held out both arms. 'Feel free.'

Eric shot me an apologetic look, and then patted me down. I turned my pockets inside out, and dumped the entire contents of my tote bag on the floor. Eric sifted through them, then replaced everything in the bag and handed it back to me. He looked at Isolde. 'There's no watch,' he said.

Isolde's lips thinned. 'Whatever. But I still want her arrested.'

She flounced off and Eric gestured toward the door. 'Come on, I'll drive you downtown.'

I paused. A large knot started to form in my stomach. 'Downtown?' I squeaked. 'I thought you were going to take my statement here?'

'Under the circumstances, I think it's best if Detective Bartell does that.'

I felt the knot explode. I forced a taut smile to my lips. 'Terrific. Lead the way.'

We adjourned to the police station. I rode with Dalton in the front seat. I did a quick canvass of the parking lot as we left, and neither Hilary nor my car was anywhere to be seen. Boy, did she have some explaining to do to me later!

First, though, I was going to have to deal with Bartell. And I was not happy about that.

We went in through a side door and Dalton led me to a small room that held a table and two chairs. He waved me to the seat facing the wall on the far side of the table. 'Detective Bartell will be with you shortly.'

I leaned back and made a show of putting my hands behind my head in a relaxed fashion. 'I'll be here.' I propped my feet up on the chair next to me.

Dalton's lips twisted into a faint smile. 'I'm sure you will.'

Once the door closed behind Dalton, I slumped in my seat and leaned back so my head rested against the chair's wooden back. I closed my eyes, trying to figure out just what I could say to Bartell.

Fancy seeing you here, Detective Bartell. We meet again. And so soon after that kiss.

I thrust my hands in my pockets and my fingers closed around my phone, which made me think of the notebook. Maybe once Bartell saw what I'd found, he'd be a bit more charitable. One could only hope. OK, maybe I'd found it by unorthodox means, but hey! His people hadn't found it. He should be thanking me, right? Right?

I leaned back and closed my eyes. A few minutes later I heard the slight creak of a door and then a gruff voice: 'Sorry to disturb your beauty sleep, Ms Austin.'

My eyes flew open and I struggled to sit up straight in the chair. Bartell walked around the other side of the table and faced me. I had to admit, he looked pretty darn good. He had on khaki pants and a matching jacket. He took off the jacket and laid it across the back of his chair. I admired the light green pullover he wore. It was molded to every bit of his lean, muscular body. There was a slight hint of stubble around his jawline and dark circles underneath his eyes. 'Looks as if you haven't gotten any sleep, beauty or otherwise,' I blurted.

He pinned me with his sharp gaze. 'Observant as usual, I see,' he said. He reached up and rubbed his fingers along his jawline. 'You're right. I didn't get much sleep last night. I was busy thinking about . . . things.'

What things? That kiss? I wanted to scream out, but I didn't. I kept my voice surprisingly calm as I replied, 'Jenny Lee's murder?'

'That and other matters.' He pulled out the chair and eased his frame into it, and then he folded his hands on the table in front of him. 'I understand you've decided to add breaking and entering to your list of accomplishments.'

I shifted in the chair. 'I didn't break and enter. I told Detective Dalton that.' I sat up straighter as a sudden thought occurred to me. 'What was Dalton doing there at a supposed B&E anyway? He's homicide, right?'

'We recognized the address as Jenny Lee's. He was in the area, so he took the call. Have I mentioned we're working shorthanded?' Bartell said frostily. 'Now you said you didn't break in, so how did you get in the apartment?'

'I had a key.'

'I see.' He drummed his fingers on the tabletop. 'Jenny Lee had given you a key to her apartment?'

'Not exactly.' I let out a breath. 'I sort of . . . found it.'

The finger drumming abruptly stopped. 'You found it? Where?'

I burrowed deeper into the chair and wrapped my arms around my torso. 'In her office.'

Bartell's eyebrow rose. He leaned forward. 'And just when were you in Jenny Lee's office?'

I looked down at the floor to avoid his razor-sharp gaze. 'I went to the *Southern Style* offices earlier today. I thought maybe I'd just take a quick look around, see if I could find anything your men might have missed.'

There were a few seconds of silence, and then Bartell resumed drumming his fingers on the table. 'I do believe I left instructions that her office be locked. Are you telling me that my men were lax, and it was open?'

'No, I'm trying to avoid telling you just how I got in there.'

'So you broke into and entered Jenny Lee Plumm's office.' It was a statement, not a question.

'If you want to get technical about it, I suppose that's as good a way to put it as any,' I grumbled.

Bartell shook his head. I half expected him to start yelling, but instead he spoke in a quiet tone. 'What am I going to do with you, Ms Austin? I'm trying to help you, and you continue to thwart me at every turn.'

Now I did look straight at him. 'Help me? How?'

He leaned back in his chair. 'You told me, did you not, that you resented being considered a suspect?'

My front teeth worried at my lower lip. I couldn't come right out and tell him that Detective Dalton had hinted I'd nothing to worry about on that score. I shrugged. 'Surely I'm not a serious contender?'

Bartell didn't answer, just steepled his fingers beneath his chin. 'So you found the key in her office. Might I ask where? My men went over that place with a fine-tooth comb.'

'Apparently not fine enough,' I said with a curl of my lip. 'I found them underneath a file cabinet.'

His confident expression faltered just a bit. 'Underneath a cabinet?'

'Must you repeat everything I say? Yes, they were shoved under a file cabinet,' I said irritably.

Bartell's jaw set. 'OK, so you found her keys, and instead of turning them over to us, you decided to do a little investigating on your own?'

'Yes, and it's a darn good thing I did, too. I found something else your men overlooked. A notebook.'

Bartell's cheeks started to redden. 'A notebook?'

'Yes. It had some jottings in it. There was a page on Fred

Longo and a page on Roberto Manchetti. Also one on someone
who Jenny Lee referred to as her "Golden Goose".'

'Golden Goose?'

'It was a code name she had for some big story she was
working on.'

The spots of color on Bartell's cheeks heightened. 'And just
where, may I ask, did you find this notebook?'

'It was shoved in the pocket of one of her dresses. Apparently
your men weren't as *thorough* as you thought,' I added with
a sneer.

Bartell sat quietly for a few minutes. It appeared that he
was inwardly counting to ten, or maybe twenty. At last
he said, 'I should throw the book at you for what you've done.
Breaking and entering. Tampering with evidence.'

'OK, it's not breaking and entering when you have a key,
and I didn't tamper with the evidence, not exactly. I just took
a quick look and put it right back. You might want to send
someone over there to get it before Isolde Carter gets her
hands on it,' I added. 'Those notes could provide a motive for
Jenny Lee's murder.'

'You broke and entered into her office to find the key, and
you might have disturbed fingerprints on that notebook. That
aside . . . you did find something significant that my men
overlooked.' He paused. 'I suppose I should thank you for
that.'

I hadn't been expecting that. 'You're welcome,' I said.

'Like I said, I should charge you but, in light of your mean-
ingful contribution to the case, I'm going to overlook this.'

I let out a breath. 'Great.'

He held up a finger. 'This one time. If you pull something
like this again, Tiffany, I'll be forced to take more serious
action. I mean it.' He scraped back his chair. 'You're free to
go. And remember – no more playing Nancy Drew.'

I knew I couldn't make that promise, so instead I said, 'You
know, you didn't answer me before. You can't possibly think
I could have killed Jenny Lee.'

He looked me straight in the eye. 'Who's Jeff?' he asked.

My mouth went dry and for a few moments I couldn't speak.
'Jeff?'

'Yes. Do you know anyone by that name? Have you had a significant relationship with anyone by that name?'

'I know a few people named Jeff. Why do you ask?'

'Because this was waiting for me when I got home last night.'

He reached into his jacket pocket and pulled out a plastic baggie, which he slid across the table to me. There was a piece of paper inside, and scrawled on it were two sentences:

Check out someone named Jeff. Tiffany is hiding something about her relationship with him. Could be significant.

And while I couldn't be absolutely certain, I thought I recognized the handwriting. Jenny Lee's.

SIXTEEN

'Well?' Bartell growled when I remained silent. 'Don't tell me you have nothing to say.'

I looked up at him and scowled. 'Oh, I've got plenty to say, all right. Mainly that Jenny Lee was mad that I had a job at *Southern Style* and she didn't. She was grabbing at any straw she could, trying to get something on me that would ruin my career. Her words, not mine.'

Bartell was silent for several seconds. Then he tapped at the baggie with his index finger. 'Do you recognize this handwriting?'

'Yes. It's Jenny Lee's.' I frowned. 'You said this was waiting for you at your home?'

'Someone slid it in my mail slot. Of course, once I read it, I immediately bagged it and brought it here to the lab to test for fingerprints.'

'And?'

'The only ones on the paper were mine.'

I let out a breath. 'Of course. It would be too much to hope for that the killer would make a mistake and leave his or her fingerprints that easily.' I looked straight into Bartell's eyes when I added, 'You see what this is, don't you? It's an attempt by her killer to give *me* a motive.'

Bartell leaned across the table so that his nose was almost level with mine. 'So, if I were to investigate this, would I find someone in your past named Jeff that you had a significant relationship with?'

I squirmed in the chair, debating my options. Finally I said, 'The note could refer to Jeffrey Marki.'

'Jeffrey Marki. Who is he?'

'Jeff is the son of my former employer, and a darn good chef. We . . . we worked together in New York.'

His eyebrow rose. 'You worked together? That's it?'

'We went on a few dates,' I admitted. I crossed my fingers

underneath the table as I added, 'Casual, friend-type stuff. There was nothing serious between us.'

His gaze swept over me. 'Nothing serious? You're certain?'

I gave him what I hoped was an indulgent smile. 'I think I would know if I were in a serious relationship.'

'So you're telling me, if I were to question some of your former co-workers regarding your relationship with this Jeffrey Marki, they would back up what you're saying.'

I was silent for a few seconds, considering what to say. Finally I blurted, 'There were some people who thought Jeff and I spent too much time together. Jeff was an apprentice chef, a few years younger than me, and I was his boss. Several people thought I showed a bit of favoritism toward him.'

'Did you?'

'Jeff's an excellent chef, but he was a bit on the lazy side. He needed a fire lit under him to get him to really shine. Did I show favoritism toward him? Yes, I did, but he earned it. And he stepped up after I left. Longo told me that he's done a remarkable one-eighty turnaround. I'm sure his father is well pleased.' I exhaled a breath. 'Several of the female chefs were jealous of the closeness between us. I can only imagine the stories that went on. I assure you that Jeff didn't pine away over my leaving. As a matter of fact, he just got engaged. You can check out the announcement in the New York papers.' This all might come back to bite me in the rear one day, I thought. But considering the state of our relationship, if one could call what we had a relationship, I wasn't comfortable telling Bartell the truth. Not yet.

Bartell studied me for what seemed an eternity, and then gave a brief nod. 'OK, Tiffany. If you say there was nothing serious going on, that's good enough for me.'

I choked back a sigh of relief. 'It is? Since when?'

He barked out a dry laugh and then said in a softer tone, 'I'm not the enemy here, Tiffany. But you've got someone rattled enough by your snooping to try and make it appear that you should be bumped up on the suspect list.'

'Yeah, well, if they only knew how unsuccessful I am at

playing Sherlock Holmes, maybe they'd take a different tack. Pick on someone else.'

'They're probably afraid that, if you continue to ask questions, eventually you'll ask the right one and expose them,' Bartell remarked.

'So you don't seriously consider I might have a motive for murder?'

'I believe you were angry enough at the woman to threaten her, but to actually kill her . . .' He shrugged.

I wiggled my fingers at the baggie. 'Could I see that again?'

Bartell passed it over to me, and I studied it for a long moment before passing it back. 'I can't be absolutely certain, but it looks like the same kind of paper that was in the note-book I found. I noticed a few pages had been torn out.' I started as a sudden thought occurred to me. 'Maybe Jenny Lee had this on her when she died. This might have been the "thing" she wanted to talk to me about.'

Bartell inclined his head. 'That would make sense.'

'Oh, and about that watch Isolde accused me of taking . . . I didn't.'

'I know. Dalton told me he searched you.'

'She claims that Jenny Lee never took it off. Wasn't it found on her body?'

Bartell didn't answer. He picked up the baggie, pushed back his chair and stood up. 'OK, I think we're done here. I want to caution you again, Tiffany. No more playing detective. You can see this person means business. At the risk of repeating myself . . .'

'You don't want to be standing over my dead body next. Yeah, I get that. I'll try.' I started to rise and then stopped. 'There's something you should know,' I said.

Bartell looked at me, sighed, and sat back down. 'What?'

I pointed to the baggie. 'You said you got that last night. I also found something sticking out of my mailbox this morning. A picture of Jenny Lee with a red x drawn through it, and printed underneath the words, "Don't let what happened to her happen to you".'

Bartell's face darkened. 'WHAT?'

'I was going to give it to you,' I said meekly. 'I had it in the car when I went to Jenny Lee's apartment but . . . in the ensuing melee, it slipped my mind.' I saw no need to add that my car, along with my sidekick, had done a disappearing act.

I saw a muscle jump in Bartell's jaw as he clamped his lips together. Finally he spit out, 'You received a threatening note and you waited this long to tell me about it? Why didn't you call me right away?'

I hung my head. 'I know I should have. I was . . . sort of afraid to contact you.'

He looked at me quizzically. 'Afraid?'

I rubbed my hands together. 'Because of . . . well, you know.'

He gave me a funny look and then said in a soft tone, 'I'm afraid I don't. Enlighten me, please.'

I rolled my eyes. 'Well, if I have to do that, what's the point?'

I pushed back my chair and stood up. Bartell did likewise. We just stood there, staring at each other for a few moments. Then Bartell took a step closer to me, lifted his hand, tucked a finger under my chin and raised it so that our eyes locked.

'The point,' he said softly, 'is that while you're not under serious consideration, you are nonetheless still on the suspect list. And unfortunately, since I've received this . . .' he held up the baggie and shook it, 'for us to be any more than detective and suspect at the present time would be . . . unethical.'

I swallowed. 'We can't have that, now, can we?'

'No, we can't.'

He leaned in closer, and the air suddenly seemed charged with electricity. He bent over, till his lips were only scant inches from mine. I looked deeply into his eyes, and then mine closed. I swayed slightly toward him and then . . .

The door banged open, and we jumped apart like two teen-agers caught necking underneath the bleachers at a football game.

Dalton looked a trifle embarrassed. 'Oh . . . sorry.' He waved a sheaf of papers he held in his hand. 'I have those reports you asked for. You said to bring them to you as soon as they came in.'

Bartell lifted up his free hand to rub his chin. 'So I did, so I did. Thank you, Eric, for your . . . promptness.' He motioned to me. 'If you wouldn't mind escorting Ms Austin out. We're done here. For now, anyway.'

He took the papers from Dalton and, as I walked past him he said, 'Remember what I said, Ms Austin. Oh, and I'll send someone by to pick up that article later today.'

I turned and, being careful not to let Dalton see, batted my eyelashes at him. 'I'll have it waiting and ready for you. Oh, and I'll also definitely take your advice under advisement, *Detective* Bartell. Good day.'

Then I followed Dalton into the hall and pulled the door shut.

'Sounds like you had the last word back there.' Dalton grinned at me as we shuffled down the hall back to the main entrance.

'You think so? I'm not so sure,' I said. 'It's hard to get the last word in with Bartell.'

'Tell me about it.'

We'd reached the main lobby. Dalton smiled at me. 'Do you need a ride back to your house?'

I was just about to accept when Dalton's beeper went off. He pulled it out, looked at it, made a face. 'Sorry. Boss Man needs me.' He touched my arm. 'You'll be OK?'

I nodded. 'Yes, thanks.'

He leaned a bit closer to me. 'You know, I meant what I said the other day. When this is all over, I'd like to take you out for a coffee. Or maybe even a drink.' He paused. 'Unless there's some reason why I shouldn't be asking.'

His beeper went off again before I could answer, which I thought a good thing, since I really didn't know how to answer him. He gave me a brief wave and shuffled off. I went over to one of the benches that lined the wall, dug my cell phone out of my pocket, and punched in Hilary's number. I let out a soft grr as the call went to voicemail.

'What the heck happened to you?' I growled into the phone. 'I'm just getting done at the police station. Bartell is sending one of his men over to pick up that note, so my car'd better be in my driveway when I get home.' I paused. 'And I'll see you later.' I hung up and dialed the Come Quick cab service. They proved to live up to their name, arriving a scant five minutes later, and I breathed a sigh of relief when they pulled up in front of my house. I got out, paid the fare (along with a generous tip for Pepe, my driver) and gave him a friendly wave as he sped off. The first thing I noticed as I turned toward my house was that my car was indeed sitting in my driveway. The second thing I noticed as I approached it was the large paper tucked between the wiper blades. I have to confess, I approached it with caution, hoping it wasn't yet another threatening note. It turned out to be a note of a different kind, from Hilary: *Sorry about the disappearing act. Will explain everything tomorrow. H.*

'Swell,' I grumbled. I opened the driver's door and snatched the keys out of the ignition where Hilary had left them. Then I opened the glove compartment and retrieved the baggie containing the note I'd received. I stuffed it into my tote bag and hurried up the steps and into my house, where a party of two were anxiously awaiting my arrival. I bent down to receive Cooper's sloppy doggy kisses and Lily rubbed her head insistently against my knee.

'So sorry, guys,' I said. 'I was hoping to be home a lot sooner than this, but . . . life happened. And a murder investigation. And another encounter of the strange kind with Detective Philip Bartell.'

Cooper let out a sharp yip and Lily a soft merow. My kids were sympathetic, but they had needs that had to be fulfilled. They followed me into the kitchen, where I promptly refilled their empty food and water bowls. As they hunkered down, I pulled out a chair and sat down at my kitchen table. I propped my feet up on the chair across from me, dug my phone back out, switched it to camera mode and called up the photos I'd taken of the pages in Jenny Lee's notebook.

I looked at the page that had Longo's name on it first. I pulled over a pad that was lying on the table and jotted down the names that appeared there. There were six in all, each with a different date and time next to it. I set the phone on the table and went into the living room, returning a few minutes later with my laptop. I booted it up and, once I'd called up Google, typed in the first name: Eva Weiss. I went to her website, evaweisschef.com and had a look around. She posted mostly news about the fancy hotel she was now head chef at, and I noticed there was one tab marked 'Photos'. I clicked on that, and a montage of photos appeared. One in particular caught my eye, down near the bottom of the page. It showed Eva, in full chef regalia, holding a glass of champagne aloft. Beside her was none other than Frederick Longo, and next to Longo was a very pretty redhead in a green dress with a neckline that showed a generous amount of bosom. I clicked on the photo and a larger version appeared, beneath which was a caption:

With my mentor, Chef Frederick Longo, and his wife Christine, celebrating my first night as head chef at La Scala.

I went down the list of other names. All the women had websites, and all had a photo of them with Longo on them. In each instance they referred to him as their 'mentor', although Eva's was the only one that had a photo of Longo and his wife on it.

Hm, I thought. Had Jenny Lee been trying to prove that Longo was more than just a mentor to these women? The dates must be significant. Assignations, perhaps? And how had Jenny Lee gotten hold of this information? I remembered Twyla Fay saying that Jenny Lee had a huge network of informants. How huge, I wondered?

I picked up my phone and called up the photo of the page with Roberto Manchetti's name on it.

Roberto is a disgrace, not only to his father but to the family name. Just need a little more time.

I sat back in my chair and frowned. A little more time for what? I nibbled at my lower lip as I thought. What would make someone disgrace not only their father, but their family name? It had to be some sort of scandal that involved the magazine. Drugs? Women? Roberto seemed to be the volatile type who could easily be involved with either. He had a temper, as I'd witnessed, and if he suspected that Jenny Lee was about to blow the whistle on him . . .

Finally I looked at the page that mentioned the mysterious 'Golden Goose'. Jenny's big story might be the most likely suspect, if only I had more information on it. What type of story was it? Big enough to kill over? She'd intimated it was huge, career-changing. What could it be?

My phone jangled, and I saw my parents' name pop up on the caller ID. I sighed. Better to answer it and get it over with or they'd just keep calling. I depressed the answer button and tried to make my tone cheerful. 'Hey! How are you guys?'

'Wondering when we'd hear from you,' said my mother.

'Hear from me?' I slapped at my forehead. 'Oh, right. About the party.'

'You forgot, didn't you?' My mother's tone was accusatory. 'Dan, she forgot. I told you we should have called earlier.'

'Sorry, Mom, but it's been a little busy over here,' I said. I hesitated, and then figured I'd just better get it all over with. 'Now's not a really good time for a party. I think you should put it off for another week at least, maybe two would be better.'

'Why? What's wrong?' my mother asked. 'Has something happened? Don't tell me you lost that job already?'

Gee, thanks for the vote of confidence, Mom. 'No, it's nothing like that.' I let the breath I'd been holding come out in a whoosh. 'I-I've been instructed not to leave town.'

'*What?* Dan, come here!'

My mother put me on speakerphone and a few seconds later I heard my father's concerned voice. 'Punkin, what's the matter? You can't leave town? Why?'

I bit down on my lower lip-hard. 'I . . . ah, I'm sort of involved in a murder investigation.'

'*What?*' both of them shouted. 'Involved *how?*' my mother cried. 'Whose murder?'

'Jenny Lee Plumm.'

My mother let out a gasp that almost shattered my eardrum. 'Isn't she the woman who worked with you at *Southern Style?*'

'We didn't exactly work together. As a matter of fact, we hardly had contact with each other.'

I could hear the exasperation in my mother's tone. 'Then how on earth could the police consider you a suspect?'

'It's a long story.'

Dead silence and then my father said, in a calm tone, 'Tell us what's going on, baby girl.'

I related the pertinent facts, leaving out, of course, the fact that I was not so much a suspect as I was amateur investigator. 'So, I've been ordered to stick around Branson until this is all cleared up,' I finished.

'Ridiculous,' my mother said. 'I'd like to call up this Detective Bartell and tell him a thing or two. The fact that you're even considered a suspect is ludicrous. Why, you couldn't even kill a spider when you were ten! Don't they have more serious matters to look into in that town instead of persecuting innocent people?'

'More serious than a murder, Mom?'

'Well, just as serious. I remember reading about drug dealing going on in that town. And it seems to me I recall hearing something shady that had to do with the police department too, although right now I can't remember just what it was. What's that man's number?'

'Mom!'

'Now, now, Emily, calm down.' I heard my father's soothing voice in the background, and then he came over the line. 'You know your mother, Punkin. She's like a lioness, protecting her baby cub. She's always been like that with you and your brother too.'

'Dad, you're not going to let her call Detective Bartell, are you?' I grabbed a hunk of hair in my hand and gave it a sharp tug. 'That would be so embarrassing!'

'Don't worry,' he said with a soft chuckle. 'But you call us in a few days and keep us up to speed, all right! Your mother won't rest until she gets this party out of her system.'

'I will, I promise. Love you.'

'Love you too,' they both chorused, and then the line went dead. I'd just set the phone back on the table when there came a sharp rap at the kitchen door. I went over and opened it to find Eric Dalton on my doorstep.

'Hey,' he said with a sheepish grin. 'Bartell said you had something for him. I volunteered to come get it.'

'Oh, right.'

I went over and got the baggie containing the note I'd

received. Dalton glanced at it, shook his head, then dropped it inside a large manila envelope. 'Looks like you're getting under someone's skin,' he observed.

'It would seem that way.'

'I know I've said this before, but . . . you're not a trained investigator, Tiffany. You should take Bartell's advice and stay out of it. You could get hurt.'

'Yeah, well, I promised Bartell I'd let up on playing Nancy Drew.' I had my hands behind my back, all my fingers crossed. 'I just got off the phone with my parents. They're disappointed that I can't leave town till all this is over.'

'Hopefully it won't be much longer,' Dalton said as he tucked the manila envelope under his arm. 'We're hoping to catch a break soon, maybe either tomorrow night or Tuesday. In the meantime, keep your chin up.' He looked as if he wanted to say something more, but he didn't. He just gave me a friendly wave and left.

I leaned against the door. Tomorrow night or Tuesday? What was happening then? Oh, yeah, I remembered. Jenny Lee's viewing and funeral. Well, maybe I'd just go and pay my respects as well. I'd heard that murderers often liked to visit those events. Maybe something would break at that.

I glanced at the clock. It was quarter to seven, and I remembered with a pang of guilt I was supposed to be meeting Longo at Po'Boys in fifteen minutes. I waggled my finger at Cooper and Lily, who were looking at me expectantly.

'I know, I know. Looks like I'm gonna be late.'

I let Cooper out in the backyard for a quick run while I changed my clothes. By the time I got to Po'Boys it was an hour later. The restaurant was crowded as usual and I pushed through the door, my apology to Longo prepared. No sooner had I stepped inside than Nita hurried over to me.

'Were you supposed to meet a gentleman here at seven?' she asked. When I nodded, she pressed a slip of paper into my hand. 'He asked that I give you that, along with his apologies.'

I unfolded the slip of paper and read:

Tiffany: Sorry but we'll have to reschedule dinner. Something's come up that I can't avoid. FL

I folded the note and tucked it inside my pocket. I wondered if the 'something' that had come up had to do with Bartell and the page on Longo in Jenny Lee's notebook. Well, I was certain I'd find out everything tomorrow.

In the meantime, I ordered a roast beef and shrimp po'boy to go. After all, I had to keep my strength up, didn't I?

SEVENTEEN

I went to bed early and, in spite of the day's harrowing event, slept like a stone. I dropped off as soon as my head touched the pillow, and I didn't wake up until my Bose alarm went off at six thirty. Cooper was on me as soon as I pushed back the covers, his tail wagging, his eyes shining.

'Good boy,' I cooed at him. 'You let Mommie get some much-needed shut-eye. Your sister too.'

Lily was curled up in a tight ball at the foot of the bed. She opened one eye, regarded me lazily, then rose and did her kitty stretch. They followed me downstairs, where I fed them and made myself a cup of mocha nut coffee in my Keurig. As I sipped the hot brew, I reviewed the events of the day before, particularly the note that Bartell had received. Someone wanted me out of the way pretty badly. Maybe Bartell was right, and they were afraid that eventually I'd ask someone the question that would break this wide open. It made me more determined than ever to keep on snooping, in spite of Bartell and Dalton's warnings.

I let Cooper out in the backyard for his morning run, and went back upstairs to get ready for work. As the hot water in the shower pulsed down on my tired body, I thought about Fred Longo and our missed dinner date. Had Bartell pulled him in for questioning regarding the pages in Jenny Lee's notebook, I wondered? I resolved to try and contact Longo later in the day. First things first. I had a pizza contest column to finalize.

I let Cooper back in, told him and Lily to be good kids till I got home, and then grabbed my laptop and briefcase and headed out the door. Today would mark my first official week as a permanent employee, and a little thrill of anticipation nickered up my spine as I headed my car in the direction of *Southern Style*'s offices. I arrived at the building at a quarter to nine, fifteen minutes before my official start time. I went immediately to my office on the third floor, took off my coat and booted up my laptop, and called up my piece on the pizza contest.

I flexed my arms out in front of me. 'OK, Tiff old girl,' I said. 'Time to put all thoughts of murder aside and concentrate on your bread and butter.'

Truth be told, I'd rather liked the pizza tidbits that Gil had shared the day before. I thought adding in a bit of history about pizza would be a nice touch, maybe inspiring some home cooks who might be on the fence about entering to throw caution to the wind and sign up. I spent the next hour researching 'the history of pizza' on the Internet and was able to come up with some additional facts. For example, I was pretty sure not many people knew the precursor of pizza was focaccia, which was known to the Romans as *panis focacius*. The thin kind of pizza that we know was developed in Naples, when tomato was added in the late eighteenth century. Until around 1830, pizza was sold from open-air stands and out of bakeries that specialized in pizza and only pizza. Antica Pizzeria Port'Alba in Naples is widely regarded as the city's first pizzeria.

I'd just finished my rewrite when I heard a timid knock at my door, and a few seconds later it creaked open and Hilary stuck her head in. 'Hey,' she said. 'Are you still speaking to me?'

I was tempted to say no, but she looked so ashamed that I didn't have the heart. 'I shouldn't be,' I said, wagging my finger, 'but you know us BFFs. We forgive almost any indiscretion. Even desertion.'

Hilary pushed the door open and stood in the doorway. She put a hand against her breast and let out an audible sigh. 'Whew, thank God. If the roles had been reversed, well, I'd be darn mad at you.'

I cocked an eyebrow at her. 'Oh, I didn't say I wasn't angry at you,' I assured her. 'I just said I forgive you.'

Hilary hung her head. 'I can explain.'

'Good. Get your buns in here and tell me why you deserted me in my time of need.'

Hilary stepped inside and pulled my door shut. She crossed

the room and slid into the chair opposite mine, then crossed her legs at the ankles. 'First off, you know, don't you, that I wouldn't have left you if I didn't have to.'

I fixed her with a piercing stare. BFF or not, she wasn't getting off the hook so easily. 'Go on,' I said. 'I got ambushed up there. I thought you were supposed to warn me if anyone like the police showed up, or had you already left before they did?'

'Oh no, I saw the cruiser drive up,' Hilary admitted. 'And I did try to call you, I really did, but it kept going to voicemail.'

I frowned. 'It did?' I drummed my fingers on the desktop. 'Hm. I did switch it into camera mode to take some pictures. I was in a hurry, so it's possible I might have put it in silent mode when I switched it back.'

Hilary shot me a grin. 'Aha! So I'm off the hook for that, at least.'

'Maybe,' I said grudgingly. 'But what made you take off like that?'

Hilary sighed. 'I got a text from my sister telling me that my mom had been admitted to the ER. I guess I panicked and I just took off in your car.'

'Oh, no,' I cried. I felt a pang of guilt. 'Is your mom OK?'

Hilary nodded. 'She climbed up on a stepladder to get something out of one of the cabinets and she slipped and fell. Fortunately my sister was there and she took her to the ER. Of course, Arleen made the incident out to be worse than it really was,' Hilary said, cutting me an eye roll. 'Mom ended up with a sprained ankle and a foot cast. To hear Arleen describe the incident, you would think the surgeons were about to amputate her leg.'

In spite of myself, I couldn't help but chuckle. 'At least she's going to be OK. But why didn't you call or text . . . oh, right. It all went to voicemail. You should have left a message.'

'I know. I wasn't thinking, I guess. To top it off, I got a call from Mac. The reporter who was supposed to cover the fashion show at the Royale with him got sick, and Dale told him to call me to fill in. I dropped your car back at your house and had him pick me up there.' She gave me a lopsided grin.

'Afterwards we went out for a few drinks. It was past midnight when I got home, and I figured it was too late to call you and explain.'

'Yeah, I was fast asleep by then, sleeping the sleep of the dead. And it was well deserved, let me tell you.'

I encapsulated the events of the day before for my friend, carefully omitting the part about me and Bartell getting a little more up close and personal than we should have. Hilary listened, her jaw dropping more and more until I'd finished. Then she cleared her throat and said, 'Holy cats! So Bartell got a note too! And it hinted at what went on with Jeff?'

I nodded. 'Yes, and it was definitely in Jenny Lee's handwriting, so I'm assuming that was what she wanted to talk about that night.'

'Wow!' Hilary reached up to brush an errant strand of hair out of her eyes. 'How did she find out about Jeff, I wonder?'

I shrugged. 'Longo told me that she tried to pump him, and he suggested that she contact some of my former co-workers. Apparently that's what she did.'

'I'll bet it was that Gretchen you worked with,' Hilary said, her lip curling. 'Didn't you always say she had a major crush on Jeff and was always giving you the evil eye?'

'It could have been quite a few of the women,' I admitted. 'I wouldn't rule out Fiona, either. Or even her father.'

Hilary uncrossed her legs and stretched them out in front of her. 'That could have gotten really ugly.'

'Tell me about it,' I said. 'Fortunately, I was able to offer Bartell an explanation he bought.'

Hilary cocked her head at me and gave me a knowing glance. 'So, was he?'

I looked at her. 'Was who what?'

'Bartell, silly. Was he jealous?'

I felt my cheeks start to grow hot. 'I don't know,' I said. 'Why would he be jealous?'

'His reaction to that note screams jealous.' Hilary leaned forward to peer at me. 'You look a bit flushed, too. Are you sure you shouldn't have told Bartell the truth?'

'I'm sure I should have, but I just didn't think it was the right time. After all, it's not like we're dating or anything.'

'Yet,' said Hilary. She gave me a long look. 'Sure there's nothing else about your encounter with Mr Hunk Detective Philip Bartell you want to tell me?'

'No,' I said, a bit too quickly. 'There's nothing else to tell.'

Hilary leaned back in the chair and crossed her arms over her chest. 'Uh-huh. And I'm in the running to be the next Miss America.'

My gaze swept over her outfit, the tight black leather skirt and the tighter ivory cashmere V-necked sweater. 'In that outfit, you could be.'

'Flattery will get you nowhere.' Hilary pushed herself up and out of the chair. 'Well, now that I've done my mea culpas, I have to get back to work. Want to go for a drink later after work?'

'Actually, I was thinking of going to Jenny Lee's viewing. It starts at seven tonight.'

Hilary wrinkled her nose. 'Not exactly my idea of a fun evening, but . . . I don't suppose you need a wingman?' She held up her hand and made a quick crossing motion over her heart. 'No deserting you this time, I promise.'

'OK. I'll pick you up at six thirty. We can go out for a drink afterward, if you want.'

'I want,' Hilary said as she breezed out the door. 'Something tells me we'll need one – or more.'

After Hilary left, I called Dale. Callie answered the phone. 'Dale will be in a little late today,' she said. 'He had an appointment with Dr Farnsworth at nine thirty.'

Dr Farnsworth was Dale's dentist. I knew Dale, like most people, dreaded going to the dentist. 'OK, I'll just email him my pizza article,' I told her. 'Make sure he looks at it when he gets in, OK?'

Callie chuckled. 'You know Dale after a visit to Dr Farnsworth. But I'll do my best.'

I'd no sooner hung up the phone than there was another tentative knock at my door. Before I could say, 'Come in,' the door opened and Frederick Longo stood in the doorway.

'Chef Longo,' I said, rising. 'I was going to call you today.'

He held up his hand. 'Please. I just dropped by to offer my

apologies for not keeping our appointment yesterday. I did try to call you, but it kept going to voicemail.'

I winced. 'Sorry about that. Apparently there was some sort of problem with my phone yesterday.'

He moved all the way into my office and gestured toward the chair Hilary had sat in earlier. 'May I?' At my nod, he eased his tall frame into it and stretched his legs out in front of him. 'I do apologize for ruining your evening, but I'm afraid it was unavoidable.' He pulled a face. 'I spent the better part of last evening being grilled by Detective Bartell.'

'Over Jenny Lee's notebook?' The words tumbled out of my mouth before I could stop them.

The bland look on Longo's face morphed into one of astonishment. 'Yes, but how on earth did you—'

'I'm afraid I probably should be the one apologizing to you,' I said. 'I'm the one who found her notebook.'

'You? How?'

'The details aren't important,' I said. I looked him straight in the eye. 'Was that what you and Jenny Lee were arguing over? The women who were listed there?'

He passed a hand over his eyes. 'Yes,' he said.

I leaned forward. 'I'm sorry, but I have to ask. Was Jenny Lee trying to prove you were unfaithful to your wife with any of those women?'

Longo stared at his hands, twisted in his lap, for a few seconds before raising his gaze to meet mine. 'Jenny Lee learned that I was on the short list to replace Jeremy Slater. So, of course, she felt the need to cultivate a new ally. And there was only one way, I'm afraid, that Jenny Lee went about it.'

'Blackmail?'

Longo nodded. 'Yes, that was her modus operandi. She went into full operative mode, calling up all her sources and tracking down names and dates. She compiled a list of women chefs, most of whom worked as apprentices under me, and tried to prove that I'd been . . . improper with them, to put it delicately.'

I looked him straight in the eye. 'And was she successful?'

'Heavens, no!' Longo actually looked horrified. 'There was

nothing to her claims. She tried her best to prove otherwise, but she couldn't, because there was nothing to her suspicions. She threatened to keep digging, said she was positive she'd unearth something. I invited her to try. I told her that I was no Slater.'

'She had something on him, then? Or were they having an affair?'

'Affair?' Longo let out a snicker. 'Jeremy wouldn't have touched that woman with a ten-foot pole. He did, however, have an affair with a woman in his wife's book club, and Jenny Lee discovered it. She used it to coerce him into taking her side with the board. Lord knows – if it weren't for his influence, she'd probably have been fired long ago. Anyway, when Slater's wife inherited all that money, he confessed all. She gave him an ultimatum: the magazine and Jenny Lee, or her. You know what he chose.'

I picked up a pencil, tapped it on my desk. 'So, since she no longer had a hold over Slater, she set her sights on you.'

'She did, and she was annoyed that she couldn't pull the same shenanigans with me that she did with Slater. Now, I don't mean to come off as an angel,' he added. 'I can't say that I wasn't tempted by any of those women, because I was. Several times, in fact. But it just wasn't worth it.' His lips twisted into a wry smile. 'My wife has many wonderful attributes, but I can't say that forgiveness is high on the list. If I were to have an indiscretion and Christine found out about it . . . well, needless to say, I'd lose everything.'

'She had Christine's name and number in that notebook,' I said. 'I'm assuming she threatened to call your wife.'

'Yes. She said that planting the seed of doubt in my wife's mind might be just as effective as the real thing. I told her that if she continued to interfere in my private life, I would have no choice but to retaliate.' He formed his hands into a steeple beneath his chin. 'I told all this to Detective Bartell last night, along with stressing the fact that I did not kill Jenny Lee. He asked me where I was between the timeframe of nine and ten last Friday and, unfortunately, I had no alibi.'

I looked at him sharply. 'You don't?'

'No. I'd decided to take a walk to clear my head. I went

over to the park on the south side of town and ended up sitting on the bench by the pond, just thinking. No one saw me that I know of.' He let out a sigh. 'I only hope he believed me.'

I reached out and touched Longo lightly on the knee. 'I believe you,' I said softly. 'For what it's worth.'

His eyes widened slightly. 'It means a great deal, actually.' He paused and then added, 'I owe you an apology, Tiffany.'

'For what?'

'I'm afraid that I might have caused some difficulty for you with Jenny Lee.' Longo shifted in the chair. 'She called me again that Friday night – around nine, I believe. Wanted to know if I knew anything about you having an intimate relationship with someone named Jeff. She said that she'd taken my advice and talked to some of your former co-workers. Most were reluctant to say anything about you, but one intimated that you and Jeff had more going on than met the eye.'

'Let me guess. Fiona?'

Bartell nodded. 'She wanted to know if I thought Fiona was credible. I told her that I didn't know her all that well, but I'd also never caught her in a lie either. She asked me if I thought what Fiona said might be true. I told her as far as I knew, you and Jeff were co-workers and nothing more. Then I mentioned the fact that Fiona was always jealous of your relationship, and that only seemed to encourage her in the belief that there might have been something between you.' He let out a long breath. 'I guess I helped put you in her sights, and for that I am truly sorry.'

'You have nothing to apologize for, Chef Longo,' I said lightly. 'Fiona always had a huge crush on Jeff. She was jealous of any woman he was friendly with, not only me. If Jenny Lee bothered to investigate fully, she would have found that out.' I paused and then added softly, 'It's all moot now, anyway. Fiona and Jeff are engaged.'

'So I understand.' Longo rose from the chair. 'Personally, I always thought Jeff liked you a bit more than was proper for a boss–employee relationship, but that's just my opinion. Which, I might add, I certainly did not share with Jenny Lee.'

He walked to the door, laid his hand on the knob and then turned to me again. 'I would like to reschedule our dinner, though, when you have some time. I definitely would like to discuss your ideas going forward for the blog.'

'I'd like that,' I said. 'I'd like to run the pizza contest by you as well, once Dale approves it. Maybe convince you to be one of the judges.'

Longo smiled. 'My dear girl. I won't need much convincing. Believe it or not, pizza is one of my favorite foods.'

He touched two fingers to his forehead in a brief salute and then left. I let out the breath I'd been holding. My secret was still safe, although Longo's remark did bug me a little. If he'd noticed something between us, had anyone else?

I glanced over at my laptop and saw an Insta-Message flash from Callie: *Dale in office now. Come on down!*

'No need to ask me twice,' I said. I grabbed the printout of my article and started for the door. I pulled it open, almost colliding with the tall, broad-shouldered man who stood just outside, his arm raised as if poised to knock.

I gasped as I recognized him: Roberto Manchetti!

'Mr Manchetti,' I stammered. 'Wh-what are you doing here?'

Manchetti didn't answer at once, just pinned me with a hawkish stare. His nostrils flared and I saw a vein throb in his high forehead. He pointed a finger dramatically at me.

'You,' he hissed. 'Mind your own business . . . or else!'

EIGHTEEN

For a second all I could do was stare in astonishment at the angry man before me, and then my own temper started to rise.

'Excuse me,' I flared. 'What are you talking about?'

Roberto Manchetti pointed to the brass placard on my door. 'You are Tiffany Austin, are you not?'

'Yes, but—'

He jabbed his finger under my nose. 'You! You're the one who sicced the police on me!'

Ah, apparently Bartell had been a busy boy last night. I drew myself up straight and said in a haughty tone, 'I beg your pardon?'

'Oh, don't play coy with me,' Manchetti said irritably. 'You know darn well what I'm talking about.'

I folded my arms across my chest and glared at him. 'Sorry, but I haven't a clue. Enlighten me, won't you?'

'So you need it spelled out?' he sneered. 'Fine. You're trying like heck to drag me into Jenny Lee's murder!'

I stared at him. 'What?'

'You heard me. Do you think I don't know that you've been running around town, asking questions about me?' He raised one hand, ran it through his thick head of hair. 'Bartell sent his minions to my apartment last night and dragged me down to the station. Again. I spent the better part of two hours there, rehashing last Friday night all over for them.'

'I'm sure,' I said coldly, 'that Detective Bartell wouldn't have wasted his time if new evidence hadn't come to light.'

'Oh, new evidence came to light all right – courtesy of you. You had to snoop around and find her notebook! Bartell showed me that page. Asked me point-blank what I might be involved in that would disgrace my family.'

'And what did you tell him?'

'What do you think? I told him there was nothing to it,

that Jenny Lee was just grasping at straws, but I could tell he didn't believe me.' He balled his hand into a fist and pounded it against his chest. 'It's so unfair! I'm innocent. I had nothing whatsoever to do with Jenny Lee's death. I'm being framed.' He paused to eye me. 'And I can just about guess who's behind it.'

'Certainly not me,' I shot back.

Roberto Manchetti looked me up and down, and then dropped his hands to his sides. 'Hmpf,' he grumbled. 'And why should I believe you?'

'Probably for the same reason you want me to believe you. I'm innocent.'

His brows drew together, cutting a sharp v in the middle of his forehead. 'I really am innocent,' he said, his voice a low growl. 'Jenny Lee and I had a rather . . . volatile relationship. We fought hard, and we fought a lot. But we made up hard, too. I would no more harm her than I would my own mother.'

'Funny, it didn't look that way to me,' I said boldly. 'I saw both you and Jenny Lee arguing the other night. It seemed quite intense to me. I heard each of you shout that the other would pay.'

Manchetti looked puzzled for a few seconds, and then he waved his hand in a careless circle. 'Oh, you mean outside that restaurant? That was nothing. A mere difference of opinion, in comparison to some of the battles we had.'

'I see. So it was commonplace for you to make a cutting motion across your throat at her?'

His face darkened. 'See, that's what I mean. I bet you told the police that, didn't you! No wonder Bartell treated me like public enemy number one.'

I eyed him. 'You do know that as long as your alibi for Friday night checks out, you have nothing to worry about. Unless, of course . . . you have no alibi?'

His upper lip rose, and he bared his teeth. I'd obviously hit a sore spot. 'I don't need to prove my whereabouts,' he hissed. 'I had nothing to do with her death.' He jabbed his finger at me again. 'And I'm telling you for the last time, mind your own business. Keep away from me.'

I didn't flinch. 'Are you threatening me, Mr Manchetti?'

His jaw hardened and then he responded, 'Oh, I would *never* do that, Ms Austin. I'm merely giving you some good advice, which I hope you'll take.'

He turned on his heel and started to move away. I probably should have let him go, but I just couldn't. I hurried after him. 'One thing, Mr Manchetti,' I shouted at his retreating back. 'Just how is it you know all these things?'

'What things?' he flung over his shoulder without turning around.

'That I've been asking questions about you, that I found that notebook? There's only one way you could know all that. You've been following me.'

Manchetti stopped walking and slowly turned to face me. His eyes blinked rapidly as he said stiffly, 'Sorry, sister. I've got better things to do with my time.'

'Have you now? Somehow I doubt that.' I stepped boldly forward and shoved my finger under his nose. 'I saw you the other afternoon, in the parking garage. And I'm pretty sure you followed me and my friend the other night and tried to scare us.'

I had to admit, he did look genuinely baffled. 'Followed you the other night? Where?'

'The apartments over on South Street. You must know the ones I mean.'

'Yeah, and I know that neighborhood. I wouldn't be caught dead there.'

'Really? Then just where were you around ten p.m. on Saturday night?'

'None of your business.' His tongue darted out, licked at his bottom lip. 'You flatter yourself, Ms Austin. I wouldn't waste my time following you.'

'It doesn't look that way to me, and I'll bet Bartell wouldn't view it that way either.'

'You'd tell him that, too, wouldn't you?' Manchetti's hands balled into fists at his side and he took a step toward me. 'Why, I ought to . . .'

'Something wrong here?'

We both turned to see Gil Chesterton shuffling up behind us. His eyes narrowed as he looked from me to Manchetti and back to me again. 'Everything OK?'

I forced a smile to my lips. 'Yes, Gil. Mr Manchetti was just leaving.'

'Darn straight I was.' Manchetti started to turn, then did a sharp pivot and waved his arm at me. 'Just mind your own business,' he said through clenched teeth. Then he spun around and stalked off without a backward glance.

Gil shook his head. 'That guy's a piece of work. Thinks he can browbeat people just because of his father's position here. It's not the first time I've had to interrupt him having a . . . discussion.'

'Let me guess. He had similar ones with Jenny Lee?'

Gil nodded. 'Among others, but with Jenny Lee it happened at least once a week. She could give as good as she got, though. If you ask me, the two of them were made for each other.' He made a whirring motion beside his temple. 'Two nuts.'

'Tell me, Gil, do you think Manchetti would ever have harmed Jenny Lee?'

Gil reached up and stroked at his chin. 'Manchetti's mainly all bluster and no substance, but I'll tell you . . . there were a couple of occasions when it sure did look as if he could cheerfully strangle her. And she him.' He let out a soft chuckle. 'Of course, not to speak ill of the dead, but she had that effect on a lot of people.'

I couldn't argue that point. As Gil started to leave, I reached out and touched his arm. 'Gil, did you ever hear Jenny Lee talking about some big story she was working on?'

'Big story?' Gil pressed his lips together as he thought. 'Come to think of it, I did hear her on her phone one day. We were the only two people in the elevator, and Jenny Lee was pretty excited. I tried not to listen, but she was a bit loud. I remember she said something like, 'Are you sure that's the right name?'

'I don't suppose you remember the name?' I asked hopefully.

Gil thought for a few minutes. 'Sorry.' He shrugged and tapped his finger against the side of his temple. 'I don't recall. The gray cells aren't what they used to be and, like I said, I wasn't trying to eavesdrop.'

I nodded. 'I understand.' Gil gave me a wave and moved

off, and I hurried down to Dale's office. So close and yet so
far, I thought, as I stepped into the elevator. Maybe it was
time to go grab another empanada at Roy's Brew Barn. If I
were lucky, maybe both Dixie and the mysterious Brenda
would be in residence.

I spent the next hour and a half in Dale's office. In spite of
being on Novocain overload, he was even more enthusiastic
about the pizza contest than before, and informed me that he'd
be bringing my outline before the board the next afternoon. I
managed to climb out of my euphoric state long enough to
drop by Hilary's office to invite her to come along to Roy's,
but was informed by Missy Braeden that Hil had left for lunch
with Mac MacKenzie not ten minutes before. I made a mental
note to bust Hil over her budding 'friendship' with the handsome photographer at the first available opportunity.

    Roy's was packed when I arrived shortly before one. Every
single table was occupied, and the bar didn't look much better.
Just as I debated coming back another time, a burly chested
man got up from his seat at the end of the bar, tossed a ten
on the counter and headed for the restroom area. I didn't even
hesitate. I slid on to the stool just as Ginger emerged from
the kitchen, her cell phone glued to one ear.

    'Listen,' I heard her say, 'I know just where you'll be later.
I'll meet you, and you'd better come through with what I
want, or else. And I'm not kidding, either.' She shut the
phone with a snap, frowned as she slid it back into her apron
pocket.

    'Ginger,' I called out. The woman turned and regarded me
with a blank stare. 'I was in here the other day. You waited
on me.' The stare didn't waver. I leaned closer to her and
whispered, 'You gave me Dixie's address.'

    Now her expression cleared. 'Oh, yeah, I remember you.
How ya doin' hon?'

    'Fine. I was wondering if Dixie was working this
afternoon.'

    'Actually, she's late. She should have been here a half-hour
ago. That's why I'm pulling bar duty in addition to my regular
lunchtime tables.' Three men at the other end of the bar waved

simultaneously, and she shot me an apologetic look. 'Excuse me, I gotta deliver these. Got some thirsty boys a'waitin'.'

I didn't remove my hand from her arm. 'But Dixie is coming in today?'

Ginger cast an anxious eye at the clock on the far wall. 'Should be here any minute,' she said. 'I hope.'

'How about Brenda? I still want to talk to them about doing a formal review on this place.'

'Not sure about Brenda,' Ginger replied. 'She doesn't confide in me like she does some people.'

I took my hand away and Ginger moved off toward the other end of the restaurant, hips swinging. I craned my neck to read the specials that were printed in pink chalk on the blackboard next to the bar. Even though my mouth watered at the thought of those empanadas, I probably should try some of Roy's other fare. I was considering a hearty bowl of gazpacho when I heard a familiar voice say, 'Can't make up your mind, huh? I recommend the prawns in fried garlic. Or the tortilla Española.'

I glanced up and saw Dixie's smiling face. 'Hello again,' I said.

Dixie frowned. 'Have we met?'

Gee, was I that unforgettable? 'Yes, the other night. Don't you remember? I came here because a friend of mine recommended the empanadas.'

Dixie snapped her fingers. 'Oh, that's right. You ordered the samplers.' Her lips split in a wide grin. 'I guess you liked it, huh, because here you are.'

'Yes, here I am. I have to tell you, those empanadas are out of this world.'

'Everyone loves 'em,' Dixie said. She reached up and tapped at the board with a long red nail. 'You'll like the tortilla Española too.'

'What's that?'

'A Spanish omelet. They slow-cook caramelized onion and potato in EVOO – that's extra virgin olive oil – and then they add egg and cook it into a thick omelet. You can get it plain or as a bocadillo. That's a sandwich. They usually serve it on Spanish crusty bread.' She licked her lips. 'It's to die for, trust me.'

'Sold. I'll have a beer to go with. What's on tap?'

'Bud, Coors, Heineken. Or, if you feel like edging out of your comfort zone, try a nice Corona with a lime wedge.'

'The Corona sounds good.'

'Smart girl.' Dixie reached beneath the bar, pulled up a bottle of Corona. She opened it, then added a lime wedge and placed it in front of me. 'Bon appetit,' she said with a grin. 'I'll get your order for tortilla Española in right away.'

I held up my hand. 'Before you do that, though, we never finished our conversation of the other evening.'

Dixie tucked her pen behind one ear. 'We didn't? Guess you'll have to refresh my memory, then. What were we talking about?'

I whipped out the photograph of Jenny Lee from my purse and laid it on the counter. 'I asked you if you'd ever seen this woman in here.'

Dixie squinted at the photo. 'Oh, right. Yeah, she's been in here. I've seen her and Rhoda talking.'

'This woman, Rhoda – where can I find her? Is she working today?'

Dixie shook her head. 'Actually, her name's not Rhoda. That's just a nickname because she looks so much like Valerie Harper, you know the actress who played Rhoda on *The Mary Tyler Moore Show*? Her name's actually Brenda Klemm. She's the night manager, but she hasn't been working a lot lately. Sprained her wrist and had to take some time off.' She looked at Jenny Lee's picture again, then leaned forward and said in a confidential tone, 'She and Brenda got to be pretty tight, although the last few weeks, I think they had a falling out. I remember them going at it pretty good one night.' She tapped at her lips. 'Last Friday, I think.'

My heart almost leaped into my throat and I strove to keep my voice calm. 'Last Friday? Are you sure? Because Ginger said that Brenda wasn't here, that she took the week off.'

'She wasn't working, but she dropped by in the evening. Said she needed something out of her locker. I did see them over in the back booth. They were arguing about something. Both of 'em looked like they could commit murder.'

Maybe one of them did, I thought. Aloud I said, 'Are you sure?'

'Yeah, funny thing too,' Dixie went on. 'I remember Brenda left and was gone for a while. When she came back, she went straight into the kitchen and then left again by the back door.'

'I don't suppose you recall what time that was,' I asked casually.

Dixie twirled a strand of red hair around one finger. 'Hm. It was late – eight, eight thirty maybe. Stuck me as odd – Brenda hardly ever goes in the kitchen.'

Odd indeed, unless Brenda had a reason to visit the kitchen? To doctor an empanada, perhaps?

'I'd really like to talk to her about doing a food review for *Southern Style*,' I said. 'I don't suppose you can give me her address or phone?'

Dixie's pert nose wrinkled. 'I doubt she'd answer if you called. She's pretty picky about answering calls from people she doesn't know. It might be better for you to catch her at home. She doesn't live far from here. Three blocks up on Mulholland. It's the house with all the fancy plants growing in the backyard.'

My ears perked up. 'Plants?'

'Oh, yeah.' Dixie chuckled. 'Brenda loves to garden. She grows all her own herbs, and sometimes even brings 'em in here. She's got some green thumb all right. Why, some of the things she grows I never even heard of.'

'How about wolfsbane?' The question popped out of my mouth.

Dixie looked at me. 'That's a funny name for a plant.'

'It's more commonly known as monkshood, I believe.'

Dixie rolled her eyes. 'That's funny-sounding too. Truthfully, I have no idea, but it wouldn't surprise me.'

Dixie went into the kitchen to put my lunch order in, and I took a long sip of my Corona. I might finally be getting somewhere after all.

After finishing the tortilla Española (which, by the way, was supremely delicious!), I walked the three blocks to Mulholland. The address Dixie had given me turned out to be a cozy-looking little cottage with light blue shutters and gabled windows. A gray picket fence opened on to a graveled walkway, along which grew brightly colored flowers. I stepped up to the front door and rang the bell. I could hear the chimes echo inside, playing a soft melody of 'Evergreen'. I waited a few minutes, rang the bell again. No answer.

I stepped down from the porch and circled around the side of the house. I could see the garden that Dixie had mentioned. From where I stood, it looked like a veritable jungle. I hesitated only briefly before pushing open the white gate and stepping inside the backyard for a closer look.

One glance assured me that Rhoda, or Brenda, was really into plants and flowers. There were roses, daisies, even some chrysanthemums scattered around. I wondered if Brenda might run a florist business on the side. I was about to leave when, out of the corner of my eye, I noticed a small patch of flowers set apart from the rest, under the shade of a large tree. I slowly made my way over and paused before a large group of medium to dark blue-purple flowers. Something pinged at my brain. 'It couldn't be,' I whispered. I whipped out my phone and Googled images. A few seconds later I had an exact match on my screen for the flowers before me.

Monkshood, aka wolfsbane.

I snapped a few quick photos and then beat feet out of there. I walked quickly back to the *Southern Style* offices, my heart pounding the entire time. Once I was safely in my office, I hit speed dial for Bartell.

Of course, the call went to voicemail.

'Detective Bartell,' I said, once the answering machine kicked in, 'this is Tiffany Austin. I've just come from Brenda Klemm's house. I'm fairly certain she's got deadly wolfsbane growing in her garden. I'm sending you a photo. Call me, please.'

I disconnected and then called up the photos I'd taken. I selected the best one and emailed it off to Bartell. Then I flopped into the chair behind my desk and leaned back, my eyes closed, thinking.

It couldn't be a coincidence. For one thing, I, like Sherlock Holmes, didn't believe in them. What were the chances that Jenny Lee had died from wolfsbane poisoning, and Brenda

Klemm just happened to grow the plant in her garden? And why did she grow such a dangerous plant?

My eyes flew open. 'Motive,' I muttered. 'What would her motive have been for offing Jenny Lee?' Dixie had said the relationship between Brenda and Jenny Lee had been strained of late, and it had been particularly noticeable on the Friday she'd died. Had something happened between them that had pushed Brenda over the edge, to murder? If so, what?

I was pretty certain of one thing: the only way I was ever going to get an answer to that question was from Brenda Klemm. But would she tell me?

'If she doesn't tell me, then she's going to have to tell the police,' I said, slamming my hand down on my desk.

'Whoa, whoa,' came a voice from my doorway. 'Who's going to have to talk to the police?'

I looked up and saw Hilary in my doorway. I motioned for her to come in and she did, shutting the door behind her. She walked over to my side chair and eased into it, her expression serious. 'Girl, what's wrong? You look like someone just died . . . again.'

'I think I might have gotten a break in Jenny Lee's murder.'

I related the details of my meeting with Dixie and my subsequent trip to Brenda's house. I ended by showing Hilary the photos I'd taken. 'Of course, I'm not one hundred percent positive, but it sure looks like she's growing monkshood in her garden,' I said.

Hilary studied the photo, then handed me back the phone. 'It doesn't make sense. If she's such a plant aficionado, she must know it's deadly. Why is she growing it in the first place?'

I scratched at my head. 'That's true,' I said slowly. I snapped my fingers. 'Maybe she's growing the plant for someone else!'

Hilary frowned. 'You mean Manchetti?'

'Maybe. Establishing a connection between Brenda and Manchetti would be nice.' I pushed back my chair and stood up. 'It's pointless for us to speculate. I think Bartell should look into this.'

'Oh, I definitely agree,' Hilary said. She paused. 'Assuming this Brenda grew the monkshood with malice aforethought, what would her motive be?'

'According to Dixie, they had quite an argument the night Jenny Lee died.'

'So this Brenda was so mad at Jenny Lee that she went back to her house, got some wolfsbane and sprinkled it in her empanada?'

'I agree, my theory needs some work,' I admitted. 'But you've got to admit, this is the best lead so far.'

Hilary shook her head. 'No matter what, I'm still putting my money on Manchetti. That guy's a nutcase.' She sighed. 'The one I really feel sorry for is his father. Marcia Allen always said Enzo was a real sweetheart. I spoke with her earlier, and she said that Enzo's very upset about all this.'

'I'm sure he is. He probably believes his son is innocent.'

Hilary frowned. 'Marcia didn't say that. I kind of got the impression that Enzo doesn't know what to believe.'

'I wonder if either Manchetti will attend the viewing tonight,' I said thoughtfully.

'I guess we'll find out,' said Hilary. She looked at her bright red and white skirt and red T-shirt. 'I better leave a little early to dig out something somber to wear. Although I imagine Jenny Lee would approve of this outfit.'

Hilary left, and I flopped back into my chair. I dialed Bartell's number again, and once again it went into voicemail. I sighed. I'd have to corral him at the viewing. And speaking of the viewing, I had to find out which funeral parlor Hil and I would be visiting tonight. I switched on my laptop and pulled up the notice of Jenny Lee's viewing. I read the brief announcement:

Plumm, Jenny Lee: 12 September. Viewing this Monday evening at the Calhoun Funeral Home on Park Place. Private Service and interment on Tuesday. Beloved sister of Isolde Chalmers Carter.

I started as I read the last part. Isolde *Chalmers* Carter? I grabbed my tote bag and thrust my hand into the zippered compartment. I pulled out the scrap of paper that I'd taken from Jenny Lee's desk and laid it on my desk. 'I almost forgot about you,' I whispered. I studied the cramped handwriting. I'd thought they spelled 'Chil' but maybe it was 'Chal'?

Could Jenny Lee's scrawled note refer to her half-sister?

Taking that a step further, what if said half-sister was involved in some way with Jenny Lee's 'big story'? And was that story important enough to kill over?

I shook my head as I replaced the paper in my tote bag. Now there were even more questions I didn't have answers for.

Yet.

NINETEEN

The scent of sweet flowers – lilies no doubt, accompanied by gardenias – assaulted my nostrils the second I stepped inside the Calhoun Funeral Home. I could hear organ music playing softly in the background and I paused to get my bearings. I confess, funeral parlors aren't exactly my favorite place in the world to visit, ranking right up there with hospitals and prisons. 'Organ music doesn't help either,' I grumbled, and then I felt a sharp jab in my ribs.

'Whew, it smells like the botanical gardens in here,' Hilary exclaimed. She tugged with one hand at the jacket of the tailored black suit she wore, and gestured with the other toward the viewing room. 'Looks like Jenny Lee's sister went all out.'

'The product of a guilty conscience, perhaps?' I'd spent the better part of the afternoon looking up information on Isolde Chalmers Carter on the Internet, which I'd shared with my BFF on the ride over. At the ripe old age of thirty-five, she'd already been married – and widowed – twice. Each marriage, the first to Douglas Harriman Chalmers and the second to Ralston Enley Carter, had left her wealthier than the last. She was the COO of Ralston Carter's PR firm, located in Los Angeles. Their client roster was fairly large, and included several prominent names in show business, some of which were popular talk-show hosts. I'd looked and looked, but there wasn't a shred of impropriety to be found about Isolde. She was as clean as the proverbial whistle . . . maybe a little too clean?

Hilary shot me a look. 'You can't seriously think that Isolde might have offed both her husbands?' she whispered. 'Even if that were true, I doubt it would be the career-changing story Jenny Lee was hinting at.'

'Maybe it had nothing to do with the big story,' I hissed back. 'Maybe Jenny Lee got some proof and was blackmailing her sister, and Isolde got tired of it and had had enough. Isolde didn't exactly strike me as the patient type.'

Hilary glanced around. 'Not too many people are here yet,' she observed.

'I doubt there will be a large crowd at all,' I said. 'I know Dale isn't coming.' I noticed a wooden podium with a white guest book resting on top. 'Maybe we should sign in.'

We walked over to the podium, and I picked up the pen and scrawled my name in the book. 'Looks as if we're the first ones here,' I observed.

'Just as long as we're not the only ones,' Hilary said as she took the pen. She signed her name and then angled a glance toward Parlor B and the sign that read 'Jenny Lee Plumm'. 'Shall we venture in?'

'Might as well.'

We stepped through the arched doorway into a room that felt like the freezer aisle at the local Wegman's. It was done in shades of burgundy, black and gray, and I was reminded of the color scheme of Jenny Lee's condo. Beside me I heard Hilary's sharp intake of breath. 'What's wrong?' I asked.

'Open casket,' Hilary muttered. As I snickered she looked at me sharply. 'What?'

'I was just thinking that the gal who can sit through all six *Saw* movies gets shaken up at the thought of seeing a body in a coffin.'

'Not just any body – Jenny Lee's. Oh, well, let's get it over with.'

Hilary took my elbow and resolutely steered me toward the casket. Flickering white candles stood atop gleaming tapers at either end of the ornate brass coffin. There were dozens upon dozens of flowers banked behind it, lilies and geraniums and carnations, which I knew to be Jenny Lee's favorite flower. A burgundy satin cloth covered the lower half of the bier. I steeled myself and looked down.

Jenny Lee looked much more peaceful now than at any other time I'd ever seen her, and certainly more so than at our last encounter. Her skin appeared fragile, albeit waxy-looking in spite of the skillfully applied makeup. Her hair was simply coiffed, brushed away from her face, and I noticed that her lashes were extremely long, unless Isolde had had falsies put on for some odd reason. I knelt beside Hilary and said a quick prayer for her soul, then rose. As I turned, my gaze fell on the front row of chairs a few scant feet away, and the woman who sat alone there. Isolde Chalmers Carter looked properly sedate in a simple black suit. Her head was bowed, as if in prayer, but I had the feeling she was more alert than she let on. I hesitated, and then made up my mind. I walked boldly over and extended my hand to her.

'My condolences, Isolde.'

She looked at me blankly as she shook my hand. 'Do I know you?'

I smiled thinly. 'We met last night. At Jenny Lee's apartment.'

Her eyes flickered with sudden recognition, but I had to hand it to her. She was shrewd enough not to make a scene. 'Sorry,' she said tightly, 'I don't recall. But thank you for coming.'

'My pleasure.'

I moved off to the far corner where Hilary was waiting. She gave me a nudge. 'Dragon Lady not remember you?'

'Oh, she remembers. She just chooses not to acknowledge it here.'

'That's probably smart.' She nodded toward Isolde. 'That suit she's wearing – Dior. It costs over two thousand dollars. Jenny Lee did a piece on them a few months ago.' She looked down at her own tailored suit, which I knew she'd gotten on sale at Dillard's for fifty bucks. Her lips parted and she emitted a strangled sigh. 'Must be nice.'

'Must be.' I glanced toward the doorway and my blood froze as I recognized the man standing there. I reached out and gripped Hilary's shoulder. 'Roberto Manchetti at twelve o'clock,' I whispered.

Hilary glanced up, sucked in a breath. 'Wow – he actually showed up.'

I had to admit Roberto Manchetti looked exceedingly handsome. He wore a navy blue suit with a white shirt and a navy and white pinstriped tie. The barmaid Ginger had said that Jenny Lee's type was tall, dark and dreamy, and Roberto certainly filled that bill. He walked over to the podium, signed the book, and then made his way over to the coffin. He knelt there for several minutes, and then rose. He walked straight over to Isolde, took her hand and kissed it. Then he sat down right next to her.

'Talk about making yourself at home,' Hilary whispered.

I looked at the two of them. Their heads were bent close together. Manchetti whispered something to Isolde and then patted her shoulder. She laid her hand on top of his and looked at him with an almost worshipful gaze. I frowned. They seemed pretty intimate for people who hardly knew each other.

'Will you look at that?' Hilary's voice cut into my thoughts. 'Maybe she's setting him up to be husband number three.'

'Doubtful. If her MO is marrying for money, then she'd have her sights set on his father.'

Hilary bounced her eyebrows. 'Maybe Roberto has other attributes she's more interested in.'

'Ew.'

I turned my attention back to Manchetti and Isolde. Whatever Manchetti was saying to Isolde, it was not going over well. Isolde shook her head emphatically, and then turned away, her eyes blazing. Manchetti touched her on the shoulder, but she did not turn around.

'Whoa, get a load of that outfit,' Hilary suddenly hissed. I glanced up and immediately saw what my friend was referring to. The woman who stood uncertainly in the doorway to the parlor wore a flame-orange, low-cut dress that contrasted sharply with the pink streaks in her hair. It was Ginger, the barmaid from Roy's. What was she doing here? It hadn't seemed to me as if she'd be inclined to pay her respects to Jenny Lee. And then I remembered the snippet of conversation I'd overheard earlier. She'd mentioned meeting someone, but here?

A beak-nosed man wearing a Roman collar and carrying a Bible approached them – the minister, no doubt. He sat down next to Isolde and started to speak to her in low tones. Midway through the conversation, Manchetti rose and walked off toward the rear of the viewing room. He reached the podium and turned around. His gaze fastened on Isolde and the look he shot her was one of thinly veiled contempt. Then he vanished through the doorway.

'Looks as if there's trouble in paradise,' I remarked.

'Maybe she turned down his indecent proposal,' Hilary suggested with a laugh.

I started to turn away, and then, out of the corner of my eye, I saw Ginger follow Manchetti through the doorway. Was he the person she was meeting? I was tempted to follow but, before I could move, Hilary laid a hand on my arm and said, in a wicked tone, 'Oh, and speaking of indecent proposals, here comes a friend of yours.'

I looked up and saw Philip Bartell coming straight toward me. He looked every bit as dapper as Manchetti in a gray suit, white shirt and solid gray tie. Close on his heels was Eric Dalton, equally as dapper in a black suit. Bartell came right up to me and bowed. 'Ms Austin.'

I inclined my head. 'Detective Bartell.'

He pinned me with his sharp gaze. 'Sorry I couldn't return your earlier call, but it's been very hectic down at the station. If you have a few moments, now, however . . .' Without waiting for me to answer, Bartell reached out, cupped my elbow with his hand and gently steered me over to the far corner of the viewing room. Once he had me against the far wall he growled, 'I thought you told me you weren't going to play detective anymore.'

'I believe I said I'd try. And I did,' I added hastily as Bartell shot me a dark look. 'But when things just fall into my lap, what can I do?'

'I see. And investigating the contents of this Brenda Klemm's garden just fell into your lap, so to speak?'

'I went there to talk to her but she wasn't home. According to Dixie Garrett, she was pretty friendly with Jenny Lee, and they'd had quite an argument the day Jenny Lee died. Dixie said that this Brenda was supposed to be off that night, but she came back and spent some time in the kitchen. Don't you think it's possible that she might have slipped the aconite into Jenny Lee's food?'

'I try not to make assumptions unless I have corroborating evidence,' Bartell replied.

'But you are going to check her out,' I persisted. 'After all, who grows poisonous plants in their yard for the fun of it?'

'Possibly people who sell them to taxidermists.'

My jaw dropped. 'What?'

'Aconite is sometimes used in taxidermy. I made some inquiries after I got your e-mail. It seems Ms Klemm has several side enterprises, one of which is supplying a taxidermist over in Closter with aconite.'

'Well, OK. That could explain why she grows it, but that doesn't mean she couldn't have used it to poison Jenny Lee.'

Bartell held up his finger. 'There is the question of motive. You say they were arguing, but what about? And how do you know the argument escalated to the point of murder?'

'I don't, or at least I don't yet. I haven't had the opportunity to question Brenda Klemm.' I looked at him sharply. 'Is that why you're here? You're hoping to run into her here, aren't you?'

'Possibly. She wasn't at home when I went calling, either.' Bartell put both his hands on my shoulders. 'Honestly, Tiffany, do I have to arrest you to make you see reason? You're treading in dangerous waters here. Go home, please, and let me handle this investigation.'

I cocked my head at him. 'You would really arrest me?' I asked.

His lips twitched. 'In a heartbeat.'

'On what charge?'

'Charges. Trespassing. Interfering with a police investigation. Breaking and entering.'

I let out a breath. 'Once again, it's not breaking and entering when you have a key.'

'You didn't have a key to Jenny Lee's office.'

My face fell. 'Oh. Right.'

He took my arm and gave me a little push into the hallway. 'You've paid your respects to your former co-worker and her sister, so go on home now. Nothing more to be done here.'

I spun around to face him. 'Speaking of the grief-ridden sister. Have you checked her out?'

Bartell's left eyebrow rose to Spockian proportions. 'Checked out Isolde?'

I nodded. 'Did you know that both of her husbands died rather abruptly?'

'Her first husband died in a boating accident and her second husband had a heart attack.'

'Her second husband had no history of heart disease, though.'

'He wouldn't be the first person who met his end that way.' Bartell pursed his lips. 'So what are you getting at, Tiffany? You think Jenny Lee's sister killed her? She wasn't even in Branson on the day she died.'

'How do you know? Did you check flights? Or better yet, show her photo around. She might have flown in under an assumed name.'

Bartell shook his head at me, like I was some deranged lunatic escaped from the asylum. 'I'm probably going to regret asking this, but what put this idea into your head?'

I hesitated, then reached inside my cross-body bag and pulled out the scrap of paper I'd found in Jenny Lee's desk. 'I found this wedged in one of Jenny Lee's desk drawers. It's dated the day she died.'

Bartell stared at me for a long moment, and then looked at the paper. 'C-H-I-L,' he spelled.

'Or maybe it's C-H-A-L,' I ventured. 'The writing's not too clear. Maybe she was writing down her sister's name.'

'For what purpose?'

I shifted my weight from one foot to the other. 'I thought maybe it might have something to do with the big story she was working on.'

Bartell nodded slowly. 'I see. So you think she found out something about her sister, something so horrible that her sister either flew in to murder her, or hired someone to do it?'

'Hey, it's happened.'

'On an episode of *Columbo* or *Murder, She Wrote*, maybe,' Bartell growled. 'And by the way, I love the fact you think I'm so inept at my job that I wouldn't have checked out Isolde, or asked her where she happened to be on the night Jenny Lee was murdered.'

'You did?' I yelped. 'Where was she?'

'Not that it's any of your business, but she was at a charity event. There were several hundred witnesses.'

'OK. But that doesn't mean she couldn't have hired someone. Manchetti!' I cried.

'What about Manchetti?'

'They were talking before, and they seemed pretty chummy for people who'd never met before.'

'You're assuming they hadn't met before,' Bartell said. 'If Jenny Lee was in a relationship with Manchetti, she might at some point have introduced him to her sister.'

I shook my head. 'I don't think Jenny Lee and Isolde were all that close.'

'Once again, an assumption. Now, is there anything else you're keeping from me? Any more suspects you've chased down, any more evidence you've withheld?'

'No. And I didn't purposely withhold evidence. I just . . . forgot.'

'Be that as it may. Your detecting days are over.' Bartell spun me back around and gave me another push. 'Now get your friend and go home.'

Before I could say another word, Bartell turned on his heel and marched back into the viewing room. I was tempted to follow, and then checked myself. I could hear my father's voice cautioning me: *Pick your battles, Tiffany.*

'Maybe my detecting days are over for tonight,' I muttered. I poked my head back in the viewing room, but Hilary was nowhere to be seen. 'Swell,' I muttered. I fished in my bag for my cell phone. I'd have to give her a quick call, tell her to meet me out front. I was just about to hit her number on my speed dial when a movement off to my left caught my attention. I spun around and let out a sharp gasp.

Standing in the funeral parlor's foyer was a woman. She wore a tailored black suit, a gray and black scarf wound tightly around her head, and large black sunglasses obscuring the upper portion of her face. She turned so that I could see her profile, and recognition flashed through me.

This was the mystery woman – the one who'd picked Jenny Lee up that night!

She disappeared through the door. I didn't even hesitate, I followed. I caught sight of her in the parking lot, heading straight for a dark car that looked like a Jaguar XF – the same car that Isolde drove. I quickened my steps, breaking into a half-run. I reached the car at the same moment she opened the car door on the driver's side and was about to slip in.

The woman turned at the sound of my voice. She paused, one hand fisted on a slender hip. 'Pardon me?' she asked.

I didn't answer. I reached out, and in one quick motion snatched the scarf from her head. She put her hands up, and I grabbed the glasses. And stared at a face that I'd never seen before.

'Holy Moly,' I cried. 'Who the heck are *you*?'

'Brenda Klemm.' She reached out and, in one swift motion, snatched back the scarf and glasses. 'And who, may I ask, are you?'

Startled, for a second all I could do was stare at her. Brenda Klemm was about the same height and build as Isolde, so it was easy to see how I'd made that mistake. By *assuming*, as I'm sure Philip Bartell would cheerfully point out to me. In the harsh glare from the light overhead, I could see that the suit she wore, while similar to Isolde's, was definitely not designer. In fact, up close and personal, it looked to be a bit baggy around the hips.

'Brenda Klemm,' I said. 'I-I've been looking for you.'

Brenda's eyes narrowed into two green slits. 'Oh, no, please don't tell me that you're with the police. I already answered that detective's questions, and he seemed fine with it, so please, leave me alone.'

She started to slide inside the car but I grabbed her arm. 'My name is Tiffany Austin,' I said. 'Dixie down at Roy's told me you'd be the one I should speak to about doing an article?'

She paused to stare at me. 'You want to do an article on Roy's?'

I nodded. 'Yes. Roy's place was recommended to me, and I went there, twice in fact, and each time the food was better than the last. I'd love to do a blog on the restaurant for *Southern Style*.'

Her jaw hardened a bit. 'You work for *Southern Style*?'

'Yes. I write a food blog – Bon Appetempting? Maybe you've heard of it.'

'I have.' She hesitated, and then Brenda Klemm let out a long breath. 'Sorry I snapped,' she said. 'It's just . . . it's been

a long day. I came here to pay my respects, but I didn't want
to run into the police yet again. I was going to head home to
bed.'

'Oh, no,' I cried. As Brenda looked at me sharply, I added
quickly, 'Why not let me buy you a drink first, at Roy's? We
can discuss the blog. It won't take long, I promise.'

Her front teeth worried her lower lip for a moment, then
her expression cleared and she shrugged. 'OK, sure. I'll meet
you there in ten minutes?'

'Great.'

Brenda hopped in her car and sped off. I walked over to
mine and, as I opened the car door, heard my cell phone
chirp. I fished it out of my bag and saw Hilary's name on
the caller ID.

'Where are you?' she demanded when I answered.

'Where were you?' I countered. 'I was looking for you.'

'I had to visit the little girls' room. For such a fancy funeral
parlor, they should really put in more than two stalls. Where
are you? Are you ready to go to Trends?'

'Ah, listen. Do me a favor. I need you to stay at Calhoun's
a little bit longer and keep an eye on Bartell for me.'

'Keep an eye on Bartell? Why? Where are you?' Hilary
asked again, suspicion rife in her tone.

'I've got a lead on the mystery woman, and I don't need
another lecture from Bartell tonight,' I said. 'Please, Hil. If
you do this for me, why . . . I'll buy you breakfast and lunch
for a week.'

Hilary let out a long, drawn-out sigh. 'Make it two weeks,
and you've got a deal.'

TWENTY

Fifteen minutes later, I was sitting with Brenda Klemm in a back booth at Roy's. An older woman, Gerda, who could have passed for my late Aunt Melanie's twin, took our orders: I had my usual Heineken, and Brenda ordered chili fries and a Jack and Coke. Once Gerda shuffled off, I turned to Brenda with a smile. 'I have to admit, I was a bit leery the first time I came here but the food's made me a convert.'

Brenda allowed herself a small smile. 'That's pretty much what happens to everyone,' she admitted. 'We really made our name with the empanadas. No one has ever sent them back that I know of. The other food's good too.'

'I know, I've sampled some of it. I'd really like to come in some night and do a "tasting". That means I sample several different dishes and then write up a review.'

'Sounds good. Of course I'll have to speak with the owner, but I'm sure he'll love the idea. Just let me know when you'd want to come in and we can work out the billing details.'

'Great.' Gerda brought our drinks and set them in front of us. Brenda looked up at her with a smile. 'I'm surprised to see you here tonight, Gerda,' she said. 'I thought it was your night off.'

'It was,' the older woman said with a sniff. 'But Ginger called. She said she had an appointment she couldn't break, and asked me to cover the first part of her shift.' She glanced impatiently at the watch on her wrist. 'She should have been here a half-hour ago. Oh, well. More tips for me.' She muttered something under her breath and shuffled off. Once she was out of earshot, I looked at Brenda. 'I thought I saw Ginger tonight, at Jenny Lee's wake.'

Brenda's brows drew together. 'Really? That's odd. They weren't friends as far as I know. Are you sure it was her?'

'Pretty hard to miss those pink streaks in her hair. Yeah, I'm sure. She wasn't exactly dressed for a wake, though.'

Brenda shrugged. 'Maybe she was on her way somewhere and stopped in out of curiosity. Ginger's pretty nosy, and she loves to gossip.'

'Maybe.' I took a sip of my Heineken and then asked, 'You were friendly with Jenny Lee?'

Brenda took a long sip of her Jack and Coke before she answered. 'We were, at one time. Pretty close, as a matter of fact, or at least I thought so. The last few months . . .' Her voice trailed off and she bit down hard on her lower lip. 'It's my fault. I have only myself to blame for us drifting apart.'

'Why do you say that?'

Brenda glanced around and then said in a low tone, 'I did something that I shouldn't have, and Jenny Lee found out about it. Instead of being supportive, you know, like a real friend would, she, well, she—'

'Blackmailed you?' I finished.

Brenda sighed. 'I only have myself to blame, like I said. I put myself in a vulnerable situation. I'm recently divorced and I have two small children. Money's been tight. My ex isn't exactly on time with the child-support checks.'

'So you grow herbs and sell them for extra money?' I asked. At her surprised look I added, 'Dixie mentioned you were good with plants, and I went by your house to try and talk to you.'

'Oh. Well, yes, that's correct. I do grow herbs, and I sell them to some of the restaurants around here. I even sell some here.'

'You also sell plants to places other than restaurants, right?'

She nodded. 'Yes. There's a taxidermist over in Closter who uses the leaves of a certain plant in his work. He pays me to grow it for him. Pretty handsomely too, I might add.'

'I see. So, what did Jenny Lee find out about you, if you don't mind my asking?'

Brenda drew a circle on the checked tablecloth with the edge of her nail. 'I guess there's no harm telling you, since the matter's been resolved. I told you things had been tight for me, money-wise. Well, Jenny Lee overheard me talking one night on my cell. Found out that I'd been, ah, "borrowing" money from the till here.'

194 T.C. LoTempio

'Embezzling?'

'That's the word she used,' Brenda almost spat the sentence out. 'Anyway, I told her as soon as I got Junior's first check I was gonna replace the money, but that wasn't good enough for her. She'd recorded everything on her phone, damn her, and she was gonna play it for the manager unless I "played ball with her".' Brenda drew air quotes around the phrase. 'I tell you, I was never so mad at anyone in my entire life.'

'Oh, I can imagine. Jenny Lee had that way about her.'

'Yeah, she did. Anyway, she wanted me to do just odd things for her. I think what she wanted was a personal gofer. Every time she needed something picked up, or she got stuck and needed a ride, she called me and *boom!* I had to show up or else.'

'That does sound like Jenny Lee,' I said. 'I'm sorry you had to go through that.'

'Yeah, me too. In retrospect, I should have just confessed all. Hans Anders is a good guy. I bet I could have worked something out with him, but . . . Jenny Lee put the fear of God into me. Said that she'd go to the police, and I'd get arrested.'

Impulsively I reached out to cover her hand with my own. 'That was her MO, I'm afraid. You're lucky being a gofer is all she wanted from you.'

Brenda paused, her glass halfway to her lips. 'Oh, she wanted more. She wanted me to be a spy for her.'

'A spy!'

'Yep. She wanted me to watch some of the people who came in here. She said that she needed to get intel on them for stories she was thinking of doing. Told me it was a small price to pay for my silence. She even wanted to give me some fancy schmancy device to listen in and record conversations, but I told her no way. I wasn't going that far.' Brenda's lips screwed into a half-smile. 'She sure wasn't too happy last Friday when I met her here and told her that I'd done my last little job for her. I'd finally gotten Junior's check, and I replaced the money I'd borrowed. So she had no more hold over me. Man, was she pissed. Told me I was deserting her in her hour of need, just when she was "this close" to a break in her story.' Brenda held up her thumb and index finger pressed together.

I pulled out my phone and called up a photo of Roberto Manchetti. 'Tell me – was this one of the people she wanted watched?'

Brenda glanced at the phone and nodded. 'Oh yeah. Him. She wanted to know the dates and times he came in here, and if he ever met anyone.'

'Did he?'

Brenda nodded. 'Yep. Some surly looking guys that looked like either bouncers or' – her voice dropped to a whisper – 'mob bill collectors, if you get what I mean.'

I did indeed. 'He met them here?'

'Always on a Wednesday night, late, at the booth in the far corner in the back. It's right by the side entrance. All the better for a quick getaway. Ginger usually waited on them. I told Jenny Lee to ask her, but no, she wanted me to take photos with my phone and email them to her.'

Things were starting to fall into place, now. 'Do you still have the photos?'

'Oh, sure. I guess I could send 'em to you. Wouldn't do any harm now.'

I wrote down my email address for her. 'Was there anyone else besides that man she wanted you to keep an eye on?'

'Only one other person.'

'Not this woman?' I called up a photo of Isolde and showed it to Brenda.

Brenda looked at the photo and shook her head emphatically. 'Oh, no. It was a guy. She wanted . . .' She paused as her own cell jangled. She pulled it out and made a face. 'Oh gee, it's my kid. I gotta take this.'

Brenda got up and moved away. I was pondering the best way to break this new development to Bartell when a shadow fell across the table.

'Well, well, Tiffany Austin,' Bartell said. 'What are you up to now?'

I swallowed. 'Detective Bartell. I was just thinking about you.'

'How convenient.'

Bartell slid into the seat that Brenda had just left. My cell buzzed with an incoming text. I glanced at the screen.

Bartell got away from me. Can't find him anywhere. What do you want me to do? H.

I texted back: *Meet me in an hour at Trends.* Then I looked at Bartell.

'Don't get mad,' I told him. 'But I just might have solved the case.'

Bartell stared at me, his eyes as hard as flint. 'What do you mean, you just might have solved the case?'

'Exactly what I said,' I replied. 'I'm thinking Manchetti did Jenny Lee in because he was involved in something with the mob.'

Bartell's lips thinned. 'That's a pretty serious accusation. Do you have any proof this time, or is this another of your armchair deductions?'

'A little of both, actually. Ah, here's my proof now,' I said as Brenda made her way back to the table. She paused and stood uncertainly in the aisle when she saw Bartell.

Bartell rose from the seat and nodded at Brenda. 'Ms Klemm. I must say, I didn't expect to see you again so soon.'

'Neither did I, Detective.' Brenda glanced from me to Bartell then back to me. 'Say, what is this?'

'This would be a civilian sticking her nose a bit too deeply into a police investigation,' Bartell ground out. 'I apologize, Ms Klemm, if it's caused you any undue embarrassment.'

Brenda waved her hand. 'Oh, not at all.' She looked at me. 'Why didn't you tell me you were working with the police?'

'Because she's not,' Bartell cut in before I could answer. 'Ms Austin is definitely not working with us.'

'He's right,' I said to Brenda. 'I'm not working with them, but I am trying to help them. It all started out because I was considered a suspect in Jenny Lee's murder.'

Brenda's eyes widened. 'You too!'

I nodded. 'We had an argument the day she died, and I said that I could kill her. Apparently she recorded my statement.'

'That's how she got me to help her. She always had the recorder on her damn cell phone switched on,' Brenda replied.

Bartell looked at Brenda. 'You say Jenny Lee got you to help her? Help her with what?'

'She used some information she had on Brenda to get her to spy on some people for her.' I was the one who answered, even though the question was directed at Brenda. 'And guess who one of those people was. Roberto Manchetti.'

Bartell turned to Brenda again, and his serious expression didn't waver one iota. 'Is that true?'

'Jenny Lee never told me their names. Just pointed them out, and told me to watch them.' She pulled out her phone and tapped at the screen. 'Here. See for yourself.'

She passed the phone to Bartell. I peered over his shoulder. There were half a dozen photos of Roberto Manchetti, deep in conversation with some men who definitely looked like tough customers. In a few of the photos, Roberto was either passing a manila envelope to one of the men, or receiving one.

'Well, I'll be,' Bartell swore softly under his breath, but I heard him.

'Who are those guys?' I asked. 'They look like mob enforcers.'

'Two of them are,' Bartell admitted. He tapped at one's face. 'This guy is actually one of the junior members of the Giovinchini family. They're suspected of being involved in some pretty heavy stuff.'

'Drugs?'

'Among other things.' He eyed Brenda. 'Why didn't you tell us any of this when you were down at the station earlier?'

Brenda shrugged, and then turned her head slightly so Bartell couldn't see her wink at me. 'You didn't ask,' she said demurely.

Bartell's lips tugged downward, and he rolled his eyes. I thought he was fighting off the impulse to yell 'Women!' at the top of his lungs. He looked straight at Brenda and said, 'Well, now I'm asking. Do you have time to come down to headquarters now and amend your earlier statement?'

Brenda grinned. 'Only if Ms Austin can come along. I feel better with her here.'

Bartell turned to me. 'Do you have time to come along to

the station?' he asked with a tight smile that looked more like a sneer.

Was it wrong of me to enjoy this so much? I gave Brenda's arm a squeeze and batted my eyelashes at Bartell. 'Since you asked so nicely . . . of course.'

I laid a twenty on the table for Gerda and then we all headed for the door. We'd barely stepped outside when a blood-curling shriek rent the air. Brenda grabbed at my arm. 'Good God! What is that? A wild animal?'

'I don't know,' I replied. The shriek sounded again and I jabbed my finger in the air. 'It's coming from the back alley.'

Bartell reached inside his jacket, pulled out a revolver. 'You two stay back,' he said, moving forward.

'The hell we will,' I muttered. With Brenda still clinging to my arm, we followed a few paces behind Bartell. As I rounded the corner, the first thing I saw was the large, green dumpster. Beside it, a dim outline slumped against the building's brick wall. A few feet away, on the back steps, stood Gerda. Her hands were jammed into her mouth, her shoulders were shaking, and a large bag of garbage overflowed at her feet and down the short flight of steps. She glanced up, saw Brenda, and she practically leapt over the spilled garbage to rush to her side. I moved aside a second before she enveloped Brenda in a bear hug, sobbing and babbling incoherently all the while.

I dragged my gaze away from Gerda and focused on Bartell. He'd put away his gun and was down on one knee beside the still form. As I approached he whipped out his cell phone and rose, giving me an unobstructed view, and what I saw made me gasp.

The slumped-over form belonged to Ginger. And, from the looks of her, she was most certainly dead.

TWENTY-ONE

'I can't believe you actually found a body.'

It was a little before midnight, and Hilary and I were at a table in Trends. Hilary had ordered a pitcher of margaritas and a platter of one of my favorite appetizers, potato skins. I reached for a potato skin and nibbled absently at it. 'Technically I didn't find it. Gerda the waitress did, when she went to throw out the garbage. Poor Ginger was propped up beside the dumpster.' I shuddered. 'I'll never forget those vacant, staring eyes, or those bruises on her neck.'

'Strangled, huh? The poor thing.' Hilary gave a small shudder as well. 'How did Bartell home in on Manchetti so fast?'

'Her phone was on the ground, behind the dumpster. There were a few texts to him, and the last one said to meet her in that back alley. Brenda said that Ginger always waited on Manchetti when he met with his mob friends in Roy's. From a conversation I overheard earlier, I figure maybe she tried blackmailing him and he wasn't exactly receptive to the idea.'

'So then the case is solved! You did it, Tiff!' Hilary got up out of her chair, walked over to me, pulled me up and gave me a gigantic bear hug.

'Let's not celebrate just yet,' I said. I extricated myself from Hilary's grasp and we both sat back down. Hilary poured each of us a drink from the frothy pitcher. 'When I left Bartell, he was going to pull Manchetti in for questioning.'

Hilary paused, mid-sip. 'Surely he's got enough evidence to charge him? There's the text, there's the fact you saw Ginger following him at the wake, and let's not forget those photographs!'

'Texts have been faked, and no one actually saw Manchetti with Ginger.' I picked at the salt on the rim of my glass with my nail. 'As for the photographs, all they really prove is that Roberto met with those men. He could say anything was in those envelopes and, for all we know, maybe that's true.'

Hilary took a long sip of her margarita, and then slammed the glass down on the table. 'Oh, come on. You don't believe that, do you?'

'Well, no I don't, and neither does Bartell, but he's right. To go to the DA he needs more concrete evidence. A report from your friend Howard Sample showing Manchetti's DNA on Ginger's person would really do it, but I'm betting he was smart enough to wear gloves.'

'Maybe Manchetti will crack once Bartell shows him those photos?'

I considered that for a moment. 'I think he'll probably sweat a bit,' I said finally. 'But I bet the first thing he'll do will be to lawyer up.'

'Yeah, and Daddy will make sure he has the best lawyers money can buy,' Hilary said with a sigh. 'If he did kill both those women, I'd hate to see him go free.'

'I'm sure Bartell won't let that happen.'

We were both silent for a few moments, enjoying our margaritas. I picked up another potato skin and had just taken a bite when Hilary leaned over and said, 'So, I guess this means the other suspects are off the hook?'

'For the moment, although I'm still not sure I completely trust Isolde. And she and Manchetti were pretty tight at the wake.' I popped the rest of the potato skin into my mouth, chewed, swallowed and then added, 'To quote Bartell, "No one is eliminated until we have a complete confession".'

'But once he gets it, and he will, then you are no longer relegated to suspect status. Which would mean you and Bartell would be free,' Hilary said with a wide smile.

I arched a brow at her. 'Free? Free to do what?'

Hilary cut me an eye roll. 'Oh my God, do I have to draw you a diagram? Free to date, of course.'

I could feel heat rise to my cheeks and I coughed lightly to cover my confusion. 'You're doing what Bartell always accuses me of. Making an assumption. What makes you think he wants to date me?'

Hilary gave me the look she usually reserved for her four-year-old niece, and then shook her head. 'What makes you think he doesn't want to date you? He's already kissed you.'

'That was . . . I don't know. Weird. Sort of in the heat of the moment.'

'And you liked it, didn't you?'

I bit down on my lower lip, hard. 'Well . . . yeah.'

'You wouldn't turn down a date with him if he asked you, would you?'

I tapped at the stem of my margarita glass with my nail. 'I-I don't know. I hadn't thought about it.'

Hilary leaned back in her chair. 'Well, you better start. Cause once this is all wrapped up and you are officially no longer a suspect, I'm betting a whole month's salary he'll be knocking at your door.'

'That's what I'm afraid of,' I blurted. As Hilary stared at me, I lowered my gaze. 'I-I'm not sure I'm ready to get involved again.'

'Tiff, get over it. One bad apple does not a whole bushel make,' Hilary said. 'Just because things didn't work out with Jeff doesn't mean it will be that way with someone else.'

'I guess that's true,' I said grudgingly.

'Besides, Jeff wasn't the problem,' Hilary continued. 'It was everyone else who ruined your relationship. Bartell doesn't have any women working with him lusting after him, does he? Or does he?'

'Well, he was named one of Branson's Ten Most Eligible Bachelors,' I remarked. 'But he certainly doesn't give off the air of being a ladies' man.'

'He didn't seem the type to me who would kiss someone in a parking garage, either,' chuckled Hilary. 'I have the feeling that he really has to like someone before he'd do that.'

I glanced up and let out a soft chuckle. 'Speaking of really liking someone . . . here comes your new sweetie now.'

'Wha-a-a-t?' cried Hilary. Then her cheeks turned red as a beet as Mac Mackenzie approached our table.

'Hey girls,' he said. Mac looked dashingly handsome as always, tonight particularly so in a beige turtleneck and a cashmere jacket. He held a frothy mug of beer in one hand and he gestured toward the empty chair next to Hilary with the other. 'Mind if I join you?'

'Not at all.' I flashed Mac a wide smile. 'You're more than welcome here, isn't he, Hilary?'

'Oh. Yeah. Sure. Sit,' Hilary mumbled.

Silence settled over the table. Hilary seemed to be at a loss for words, a rare occurrence for my bestie. I cleared my throat and smiled at Mac. 'So, you've got a free night? No pressing story that requires your photographic skills?'

'No, thank goodness.' He took a sip of his beer and stretched his long legs out in front of him. 'A good thing, too. I feel like I've been working non-stop.' He glanced over at Hilary and smiled. 'Thanks for filling in the other night. I'd much rather work with you than Donna Murphy. She's always giving me that evil eye of hers.'

I couldn't resist a chuckle. Donna Murphy was close to sixty, but she was what my father would have referred to as 'well preserved'. It was also a known fact that Donna was somewhat of a cougar, preferring men thirty years younger than herself to those her age.

'Oh, no problem,' Hilary said, studiously avoiding my gaze. 'I'll work with you anytime, you know that.'

'Did you go to Jenny Lee's viewing?' I asked him.

Mac nodded. 'I stopped in for a minute, just to pay my respects. After all, I did date her for a bit.' He shook his head. 'She was a pretty driven woman. Always trying to catch that brass ring that would set her apart from the rest. All she ever talked about on our dates was work.'

'Work, really?' Hilary leaned forward and cupped her chin in her hand. 'I would have thought she'd talk about herself.'

'She did that too,' Mac said with a laugh. 'But the last few times she was consumed with work. She was pressing me to ask my aunt for some names down at City Hall and the police station.'

My ears perked up a bit. 'She was? What sort of names?' I asked.

'Well, she knew my aunt served on the town council for a bit, so she wanted me to ask her for some names of people she considered trustworthy. Just between us . . .' Mac leaned in a bit closer and lowered his voice as he added, 'I think she was on the lookout for someone to be an informant for her.'

'At City Hall and the police station? Really?' I said.

Mac nodded. 'Jenny Lee had an idea in her head that something fishy might be going on there.'

'Fishy? Like how?'

Mac shrugged. 'Dunno. To be honest, I never paid much attention to her when she rambled on. The last time we went out, I told her that I wasn't getting my aunt involved. She got pretty mad at me and walked out.' His lips twigged downward. 'I feel bad that our last words were harsh ones.'

Hilary patted Mac's arm. 'Don't feel bad, Mac. You're not alone. I'm sure plenty of other people had last words with her that weren't pleasant.'

Mac and Hilary started to chat, and I leaned back in my chair, thinking. City Hall and the police station were not places that would normally interest Jenny Lee. Why was she looking for an informant? Could that have something to do with her 'big story'?

A feeling of unease washed over me. Maybe Manchetti was right in protesting his innocence. Maybe he didn't do it. And if that were true . . .

Jenny Lee's killer, and possibly Ginger's too, was still out there.

TWENTY-TWO

Cooper woke me the next morning by sticking his face about an inch away from mine so that when I opened my eyes, the first thing I saw were his limpid brown ones. Lily, not to be outdone, got into the act too. She stretched out full length on the pillow above my head and meowed at me, so I got a good blast of her kitty breath too.

'Oy, Lily. What have you been eating?' I cried. 'I think you need some kitty breath mints.'

Lily let out a sharp merow, indicating she wasn't fond of that idea. I rolled over on my back, stretched, and glanced over at the clock. It was a few minutes past seven. I'd been so beat when I finally got home last night I'd just tumbled into bed and forgotten to set the alarm.

Cooper jumped off the bed and padded over to the bedroom door, pausing only long enough to glance over his shoulder. 'Woof,' he said. Then he kept on going. Lily jumped off my pillow and followed, tail held high. Animal speak for 'get up, you lazy human' if ever I heard it. I grabbed my bathrobe and made a beeline for the shower.

When I arrived in the kitchen some twenty minutes later, both Cooper and Lily were squatted by their food bowls. I spooned out their breakfast and, as they hunkered down, popped a slice of rye bread in the toaster and a pod of Newman's Special Blend in the Keurig. I leaned against the counter and let my thoughts drift to the viewing last night and the subsequent events. If Roberto Manchetti was indeed involved in some way with the mob, and Jenny Lee had found out about it, it would certainly be a prime motive for murder. Roberto had always been at the top of my own personal suspect list, and yet . . .

'Something's off,' I said out loud. Both Cooper and Lily glanced up from their food bowls. Cooper cocked his head at me.

'It just seems too easy, somehow,' I said to the dog. 'Manchetti's motive, his anger at Jenny Lee, the fact that he doesn't have an alibi for the time of death, the texts to him from Ginger – it's all just, oh, I don't know . . . too pat?'

'Rrrowr,' said Cooper.

I sighed. 'Yes, I know. That's just the way it works sometimes. And yet, I can't help but wonder about Jenny Lee's big story. Could it have had something to do with the police, or someone down at City Hall? Why else would she have been after Mac's aunt for some names of people she considered trustworthy? Was there something underhanded going on down there?'

Now Lily glanced up. 'Merow.'

'I know. Maybe Manchetti protesting his innocence isn't an act. Maybe Bartell should be looking in another direction. After all, I never actually heard Ginger say Manchetti's name when she was on the phone. She could have been talking to someone else.'

My coffee was ready. I picked up the mug, carried it over to the refrigerator, where I added some milk. Then I took it over to the table, sat down, and added two packets of sugar. I stirred the mixture thoughtfully. Something was niggling at the back of my brain, something I'd overlooked, but for the life of me I couldn't think what it was.

'But it's something important,' I murmured. 'I know it is.'

I glanced at the clock and started as I saw the time. I hastily gulped down my coffee and hurried back to my bedroom to finish dressing for the day. I had a lot of meetings scheduled. Maybe if I immersed myself in work, whatever was bothering me would rise to the surface.

The first person I saw as I entered the office building was Twyla Fay Thorpe. She was standing by the elevator, hard to miss in an orange and pink printed caftan-style dress with large orange hoop earrings dangling from her ears. I considered making a sharp left and taking the stairs, but I hesitated a moment too long. Twyla Fay hurried over to me, a concerned look on her face.

'My dear, have you heard! It's simply scandalous,' she cried.

I tried for an innocent expression and hoped that I succeeded. 'Heard what?' I asked.

Twyla Fay's heavily made-up eyes fairly popped. 'Why, about Roberto Manchetti, of course! I heard . . .' She glanced around, then grabbed my elbow and propelled me into a nearby alcove. 'I heard that he was dragged back down to the police station last night, for more questioning.'

'No!' I hoped I sounded properly astonished.

'Yes! And what's more, I heard there's some sort of evidence that definitely links him to Jenny Lee's death, and that barmaid's too.'

I formed my lips into a perfect o shape. 'Really?'

'Oh yes. Apparently Roberto was involved with some not so very nice people. And Jenny Lee found out about it.' She shook her head, and the orange hoops dangled to and fro. 'It's not looking good for him. I hear poor Enzo is a wreck.'

I started to say that I did feel sorry for Enzo, but Twyla Fay cut me off before I could get the words out. 'Oh, there's Simone from Business Development. She might have heard some more. Catch you later, sweetie.'

Twyla Fay hurried off to pigeonhole Simone, and I made good my escape. Once I reached my office, I checked my phone messages. There was one from Hilary: *Wow, did you stir up a hornet's nest! Call me.* One from Dale: *We are having our nine thirty meeting as scheduled, in spite of recent developments. Please be on time.* And the final one was from none other than Detective Philip Bartell: *Ms Austin. Kindly call me at your earliest convenience.*

I pulled out my chair, plopped down in the leather seat and dialed Bartell's number. For a change he answered on the second ring. 'Bartell.'

'Detective. It's Tiffany Austin. You rang?'

'Yes. I thought, since it was you who discovered the lead, that it would be only fair to tell you what transpired last night.'

I leaned back and kicked off my heels. 'I'm all ears, Detective.'

'I took those photos to the DA, who was extremely interested in them, and in the texts on Ms Mancuso's phone as well.'

'Ms Mancuso?'

'Ginger. Mancuso was her last name. Then, armed with a warrant, Detective Dalton and I paid a little visit to Mr Manchetti at his residence.'

'Oh, I bet he loved that.'

'Indeed. He threatened to sue both Detective Dalton and myself and bring us both up on charges of police harassment. His tune didn't change very much after we showed him the warrant.'

'So I gather he wasn't exactly the picture of co-operation?'

'That's putting it mildly. He knew nothing about texts from Ms Mancuso and he flatly denied meeting her in the alley. Detective Dalton and I went through Manchetti's apartment from top to bottom. It was clean as a whistle.'

My face fell. 'Nothing incriminating?'

Bartell sounded amused. 'You sound disappointed, Ms Austin.'

'I guess I am. Of course, I didn't expect that Manchetti would have evidence of his being involved with a drug lord out in plain sight, but—'

'You're right about that,' Bartell interrupted. 'It wasn't out in plain sight. But when we went through his home office, Detective Dalton discovered a false bottom in one of the drawers.'

I snapped to attention. 'You're kidding! And did you find something concealed there?'

'Oh, yes.' Bartell sounded almost gleeful. 'A set of ledgers that appear to be bookkeeping records of *Southern Style*. Little Roberto was keeping a second set of books.'

'Really?' That surprised me somewhat. I hadn't thought Roberto was that smart.

'Long story short, we found evidence that not only indicates Roberto's been laundering some money for Chilton King, a drug lord; he's also been forging his father's name to some very substantial checks. Apparently he hasn't been making enough to support himself in the style to which he's become accustomed.'

I sat up straight. 'Did you say Chilton King?' That name would certainly fit in with what had been written on the paper I'd found in Jenny Lee's desk.

'Yes. But here's the best part. You remember the diamond watch Jenny Lee's sister mentioned was missing?'

'The one she accused me of taking from her sister's cold dead body, you mean? That one?'

'Yes. Jenny Lee was wearing a watch at the time of her death, but there was no watch found on the body.'

'How do you know that?'

'There was an indentation on her wrist indicating a watch was there. Anyway, Detective Dalton found it shoved in the back of the drawer behind the ledger.'

I let out a low whistle. 'Could he explain how the watch got there?'

'No. He just kept insisting he was being framed. We took him down to the station last night. He's charged with embezzlement and fraud, and the DA wants him charged with Jenny Lee's murder. First degree.'

'Not Ginger's murder?'

'Not yet, but I'm hopeful the coroner will turn up something.' Bartell paused. 'So, Ms Austin, it looks as if the Jenny Lee case is closed at least.'

I pushed an errant curl out of one eye. 'So that means that I'm . . .'

'Officially no longer on the suspect list,' Bartell finished.

There was an awkward pause. I held my breath, wondering what would come next. Now that there was no longer a conflict of interest between us, what would Bartell do? Would he ask me out? Or should I make the first move? He didn't seem to be the shy type, but maybe when push came to shove . . .

Just as I was about to bite the proverbial bullet and ask Bartell to join me for coffee, he cleared his throat and said, 'The reason I called . . . I want to thank you.'

I started. 'You're thanking me?'

'Yes. Without your dogged interference, we might not have solved this case so quickly. And we are working shorthanded, so any case that we can get resolved is a relief.'

My front teeth came out, worried at my lower lip. This was definitely not what I'd expected. 'Well . . . you're welcome,' I said at last. There was another awkward pause and then I continued, 'If that's all, Detective Bartell, I have a meeting to get ready for.'

'Understood. I have a memorial service to attend.' He hesitated briefly and then said, 'Oh, and Tiffany?'

'Yes?'

'Take care of yourself,' Bartell said softly. Then the line went dead.

I sat and stared at the phone for a full minute, then slammed it back down. 'So much for mutual attraction,' I grumbled. I glanced at my watch. Nine fifteen. I had just enough time to gather my notes and make it to Dale's office on time. The memorial service Bartell mentioned was no doubt Jenny Lee's. I figured that Roberto Manchetti would not be attending. Aside from Isolde, Bartell and maybe Dalton, there probably wouldn't be very much of a showing.

I picked up my notebook and started for the door. I jerked it open and almost collided with the man standing on the other side. I stopped, startled, and stared at him. He was a tall, distinguished-looking older gentleman. The suit he had on looked to be Brooks Brothers, and fitted him impeccably. His storm-gray eyes reminded me of Bartell's, and his stare was just as piercing. He raised his hand, and my eyes popped at the large gold watch on his wrist. It looked like a genuine Cartier. 'Tiffany Austin?' he barked out, in a voice rich with Italian accent.

I felt my stomach start to roil. I had an idea I knew the identity of my visitor. 'Yes. You are Enzo Manchetti?'

He nodded. 'May I have a few minutes of your time?'

I hesitated and then looked at my own watch. 'I do have a meeting with Mr Swenson at nine thirty,' I began.

Enzo Manchetti waved his hand. 'This won't take long. Just tell Mr Swenson I detained you.'

What choice did I have? Who could refuse a subtle command from the chairman of the board? I nodded and moved aside to let him enter. Manchetti walked over to my side chair and lowered himself into it. After a few seconds, I walked over to my desk, set my notebook down and pulled out my own chair. I sat and folded my hands meekly on the desk in front of me. 'What can I do for you, Mr Manchetti?'

Manchetti looked me straight in the eye. 'You know my son was arrested last night.'

I swallowed. 'Yes, I-I heard.'

'I've been told you had something to do with that.'

I felt my cheeks flame. 'Oh, I wouldn't say that, exactly.'

'No?' He leaned forward, propped one elbow on the edge of my desk. 'You haven't been nosing around, asking questions, trying to find out who murdered Jenny Lee Plumm?'

'That's true, I did take a rather active interest in the investigation, but it was to clear my own name.'

'Yes, I'm aware you were one of the first people to be questioned.' Enzo Manchetti let out a heartfelt sigh and leaned back in the chair. 'Forgive me, Ms Austin. I do not mean to browbeat you. I am upset over what has happened with my son.'

'That's understandable.'

'I have to take some of the blame,' Manchetti went on. 'After his mother's death, I'm afraid I spoiled the boy. Indulged him a bit too much. Anything he wanted, I got him. I didn't teach him a good work ethic, and I didn't teach him the value of a dollar. I was too busy trying to make up for the fact that his mother had died and left us.'

I felt a wave of pity for the man. 'You shouldn't blame yourself, Mr Manchetti,' I said. 'After all, Roberto had a mind of his own. He knows right from wrong.'

Manchetti drummed his fingers against the edge of my desk. 'Ms Austin. I have no grand illusions about my son.'

I stared at him. 'What?'

'I have no illusions about Roberto,' he repeated. 'I know my son isn't – how can I say this? He isn't the sharpest pencil in the box, the brightest bulb in the lamp.'

'Oh, I wouldn't say that.'

'I would. I tried to make up for my neglect and indulgence. I'm afraid it was a case of too little too late. I cut off his allowance, made him work here. I tried to teach him how to earn an honest living. And what does the dumb bunny do? He makes a second set of books, writes checks out on the company account to pay for his Mercedes and condo, and ends up laundering money for a drug lord.' Manchetti pushed himself up and out of my chair. 'I want you to know, Ms Austin, that I am grateful to you.'

I thought I'd heard wrong. 'I'm sorry?'

'If it hadn't been for your persistence in the Jenny Lee matter, none of this would have come out until it was too late. Roberto would have surely brought about the ruin of *Southern Style*. I want you to know that I have no intention of getting him out of this, or cutting any sort of deal with the DA. Roberto deserves to have the book thrown at him for his fraud and embezzlement.' He paused. 'Murder, however, is another story. My son is stupid and spoiled, and he has always looked for the easy way out of situations. That is exactly why I cannot believe he would murder one woman, let alone two. I am afraid the police have made a mistake thinking he is.'

I gestured helplessly. 'I'm so sorry. I wish there were something I could do for you, Mr Manchetti.'

Manchetti rose. He pulled on his jacket lapels, turned and started for my door. He put his hand on the knob, and then turned to face me. I could see tears shining in his eyes as he said, 'Perhaps there is something you can do for me, Ms Austin. You seem to be very adept at ferreting out information. Put your talent for snooping to good use. Find the person who *really* killed Jenny Lee and that other woman, and clear my son's name of murder.'

TWENTY-THREE

'Oh, that poor man. He's in denial.'

It was a few minutes past eleven. I'd only been ten minutes late to the staff meeting, and Dale had been very understanding. Of course it had helped that Marcia Allen had called down and told him that Enzo Manchetti was meeting with me. Afterwards, of course, Hilary wanted to know all the details, so she followed me back to my office where I related not only my meeting with Manchetti, but Bartell's phone call as well.

I tossed her a wry smile. 'Are you talking about Enzo Manchetti or Bartell?' I asked.

'Either. Both,' Hilary answered. 'On second thought, I mean Manchetti. Bartell's just being a jerk.'

'On that point we agree.'

Hilary jumped up from her chair and started to pace around my office. 'I mean seriously. Is Bartell so threatened by you that he's afraid to ask you out on a date?'

'What makes you think Bartell is threatened by me?'

Hilary stopped pacing and fisted her hand on her hip. 'Well, duh! You solved the case for him, didn't you? If you hadn't gone out and done all the legwork, he and Detective Dalton wouldn't have made that arrest, which will, no doubt, result in a nice feather in their cap.'

I passed a hand over my eyes. 'I hope it does, but to tell you the truth, I'm not so sure.'

'What do you mean?'

'I mean, maybe Enzo has a point. Roberto *is* lazy and stupid. You have to be somewhat bright to plot one murder, let alone two.'

Hilary's jaw dropped. 'You can't be serious! Now you think Roberto's innocent? Might I remind you of the scene you witnessed outside the restaurant only a short week ago? The slicing motion Roberto made across his throat?'

'I know that I said before Roberto was at the top of my list, but now that I've had time to think about it, I'm not so sure anymore.'

'Well, the police are,' Hilary shot back. 'Jenny Lee knowing about Roberto's little money laundering scheme gives him a nice motive. Then there's the missing watch. They found it in his desk.'

'That's what I mean. Roberto's stupid, true, but stupid enough to leave a key piece of incriminating evidence lying around?'

'It wasn't lying around; it was hidden with the second set of books in the drawer! And as for Ginger, well . . . she probably made the mistake of trying to blackmail him. I'm guessing Roberto doesn't play nice when he feels cornered.' Hilary gave her hand an impatient wave. 'Look, I know you feel sorry for Enzo. Heck, the entire staff of *Southern Style* feels sorry for him. Enzo's a likeable guy. It's not his fault that his son didn't turn out to be a chip off the old block.'

'Enzo doesn't think that way,' I pointed out. 'He blames himself for Roberto getting involved with the mob. But he doesn't think his son is a murderer, and even though I hate to admit it, I don't either.'

Hilary let loose with an enormous sigh, then plopped back in my side chair. 'OK, fine. Let's just say for argument's sake that Roberto's innocent. Who did it?' Hilary started to tick off on her fingers. 'It's not the sister, she's got an alibi. It's not Brenda Klemm. It's not you, it's not Dale, and it's not Frederick Longo. So, who's left?'

'It could only be one person. The subject of Jenny Lee's big story.'

Hilary raised a brow. 'What about Ginger?'

'Maybe hers too. Remember, she never mentioned who she was meeting by name. Maybe it was someone else at the wake.'

'And God only knows who that is,' Hilary cried, throwing both hands up in the air. 'You haven't got a single clue as to who that might be.'

'No,' I said miserably, 'You're right, I don't. And yet, I think that there is something, somewhere, some valuable clue that I'm overlooking.'

'Well, until you figure out what that might be, the DA is going to go ahead and charge Roberto with Jenny Lee's murder. It was all over the news just now.'

'Twyla Fay knew about it early,' I said. 'She accosted me first thing when I walked in the building.'

Hilary grinned. 'Yep, that's our Twyla Fay. You know, sometimes I think she has better informants than Jenny Lee did. She always has her pulse on what's happening in town.'

My head jerked up. 'Yes, she does, doesn't she?' I murmured. I looked at my BFF. 'You remember what Mac was saying last night, about Jenny Lee and his aunt?'

'Yeah, that Jenny Lee wanted names of people his aunt knew down at City Hall. What's that got to do with anything?'

'Maybe nothing, maybe something,' I muttered. 'My mother mentioned some trouble awhile back having to do with the police department here. Does that ring any bells with you?'

Hilary's brows drew together. 'No. Should it?'

'I'm probably grabbing at straws, but . . .' I pushed back my chair, stood up, and now I started to pace around my office. Suddenly I paused and jabbed my finger in the air. 'The police have been working shorthanded for a while now, Bartell said. Why, I wonder?'

Hilary shrugged. 'Vacations, maybe some of 'em are sick. You know you could call Bartell and ask him,' she suggested with a perfectly straight face.

'I could,' I said. 'Or I could do the next best thing.'

'Which is?'

'Ask his sidekick, Detective Dalton.'

After I managed to convince Hilary that I did not need a chaperone and it was all strictly business, I called the police station. Eric Dalton returned my phone call far faster than Philip Bartell ever had. No, he wasn't attending Jenny Lee's memorial. Sure, he could meet me for lunch at Po'Boys. Would twelve thirty be all right? I assured him it would.

I spent the next half-hour finishing up my final copy for the pizza bake-off. At five to twelve I sent it down to the copy editor, and then I sat for a few more minutes, scrawling ideas for a few more cooking contests. If this one took off, we could have a Christmas bake-off and maybe something Valentine Day related. I remembered Jeff making heart-shaped gnocchi for me for our first Valentine's Day, and the thought made my eyes water. I brushed the memory aside and grabbed my suede jacket and purse. Time to meet Detective Dalton.

He was already seated at a corner table when I walked in a few minutes past twelve thirty, and he waved me over enthusiastically. 'I thought for a second I might be getting stood up,' he said once I was seated.

I took off my jacket and draped it across the back of my chair. 'Now why would you think that? I was only a few minutes late.'

He waved his hand as if to brush my comment aside. 'Oh, it's happened before.'

'Really? I find that hard to believe, to such a good-looking guy as yourself.'

He chuckled. 'It's not the looks that turn them off, it's the moment they learn I'm a homicide detective. Dealing with dead bodies isn't a turn-on for most women.' He paused and looked at me speculatively. 'That fact doesn't seem to bother you, though.'

'Oh, I wouldn't say that. I'm not all that fond of dead bodies, trust me.'

Nita came over and placed menus in front of us. We spent a few minutes studying them, and when Nita returned gave our orders: I decided on the sausage and shrimp po'boy, while Eric opted for the special, the French fry po'boy, which consisted of French fries, gravy and condiments within the French loaf bread. As Nita collected the menus, she leaned toward me. 'I heard they got Jenny Lee's killer,' she said.

'It appears that way,' I said carefully.

Dalton smiled at Nita. 'We got him,' he said confidently. 'Dead to rights. Good thing too. We're all glad that case is wrapped up.'

'Any news about Ginger's autopsy?'

'Not yet, but we're confident Manchetti's guilty of that as well.'

Once Nita had departed, I picked up my glass of water and took a sip. I set the glass down and remarked, 'Detective

Bartell said now the Jenny Lee case is closed you guys can
move on to other things.'

Eric nodded. 'That's true. We can.'

'He mentioned you've been working shorthanded?'

'Yep, for a few months now.'

'People on vacation? Or out sick?'

'Not really.'

He lapsed into silence and we sat for a few moments, me
sipping water and Eric rubbing his forefinger along the rim
of his glass. Finally he looked at me and said, 'Bartell would
have my head if he knew I was sharing this with you. I can't
go into detail, but suffice it to say there was an investigation,
and a few of the men were suspended pending further notice.'

I held up my hand. 'Say no more. I don't want to get you
in any trouble, I was just curious.'

He let out a long breath. 'Yep, you're a curious type of gal,
aren't you?'

'I suppose I am.' I tapped my finger idly against the side
of my glass. 'I confess, I was also a bit puzzled as to why the
city council would go all the way to Birmingham to hire a
new chief of detectives, but now I think I understand. It's
because of this investigation, right?'

Eric's front teeth jutted out, worried his lower lip a bit. 'You
didn't hear that from me,' he said.

'I imagine there was a bit of resentment when he was hired?'

'You could say that.' Eric picked up his glass, took a sip,
set it down. 'Lots of guys resented him, including me. But
Bartell's a smart cookie, and he's really not bad to work for.
And he's extremely ethical, which is the main reason they
wanted him, I think.'

I smiled thinly. 'Yes, I got that impression.'

Nita arrived with our lunches, and the topic of conversation
shifted first to the food, then the weather, then the Atlanta
Falcon's chances of getting into the Super Bowl this year. The
hour passed quickly, and when the check arrived Eric reached
for it. 'Allow me.'

I smiled. I really didn't want to hurt his feelings. 'Thanks.
That's nice of you.'

'I enjoyed it. As a matter of fact, tonight's my night off.

How would you feel about taking in that new Hugh Jackman movie at the Strand?' As I hesitated he said, 'Or is there a reason you aren't interested? You already have a date?'

I thought about Bartell's earlier brush-off and shook my head. 'No. No other date. Sure, I'm always up for Hugh Jackman.'

'Great. It starts at eight, so I'll pick you up at seven.' He waggled his finger at me. 'Just don't get involved in any more murders between now and then.'

I smiled thinly. 'I'll try my best.'

Eric slid his credit card into the leather check holder. 'I kind of got the sense you weren't too satisfied with the outcome of the Jenny Lee case.'

Nita bustled over, picked up the leather case and, as she hurried off, I said, 'I wouldn't say that, exactly. I always suspected Roberto Manchetti was up to no good. It's just, well, his father came to see me today,' I admitted.

Dalton nodded. 'To plead his son's case?'

'Sort of. He admitted that he thought his son was stupid enough to get himself involved in a money laundering scheme with the mob, but not bright enough to commit murder once, let alone twice.'

'Of course he'd say that. It's his son.'

'True. I have to admit, though, I thought the same thing. Roberto just didn't seem the murderous type.'

Dalton's lips twitched slightly. 'And you'd know the murderous type, how, exactly?'

'I wouldn't,' I admitted. Then, before I could stop myself, I blurted out, 'Golden Goose.'

Eric stared at me. 'I'm sorry?'

'Golden Goose. It's a code name, I guess, for some big exposé story that Jenny Lee was working on. And I can't help but wonder . . .'

'Ah, you think this Golden Goose might have been the one who killed her and Ginger?' Eric frowned. 'Did you ever stop to think that possibly Roberto Manchetti was this Golden Goose? Exposing his fraud and duplicity would have been a big story.'

'True, but I got the sense, somehow, that it was something bigger than that.'

Eric stroked at his chin thoughtfully. 'Like what?'

I shrugged. 'I have no idea,' I said. We turned to go, and once again I felt a niggling feeling gnaw away at me, telling me I was missing something important, something that was right under my nose.

Of all people, who should be standing in the office lobby when I got back from lunch but Twyla Fay. This time, instead of trying to avoid her, I made a beeline for her. 'Twyla Fay,' I called. Twyla Fay turned and waved. I took in the sedate (for Twyla Fay) black caftan dotted with purple hydrangeas and asked, 'Did you happen to attend Jenny Lee's memorial?'

Twyla Fay let out a long sigh. 'Yes, I did. I know the woman was the lowest life-form going, but I just felt bad. I figured no one would show up and I was right. It was only me, her sister and the girl who cleaned her apartment twice a week. Oh, yes, and that handsome detective.' She cast me a sly look. 'You know the one I mean.'

'Yes, Detective Bartell. That's it? No one else?'

'Well, no way was Enzo Manchetti going to go. I'm sure Roberto might have gone if he'd been able.' She shook her head. 'I still can't believe he really killed her.'

You're not the only one, I thought. Aloud I said, 'I'm surprised you didn't figure it out. After all, you always seem to know everything before it happens.'

Twyla Fay preened. 'That's true, I guess,' she agreed. 'I try to keep my pulse on current events.'

'And you do a splendid job. Why, take for example that business with the police force a few months ago. I bet you know all the details about that investigation.'

'You mean the Internal Affairs one?' Twyla Fay waved her hand dismissively. 'I still can't believe they aren't any closer to finding the guilty party. The mayor is having fits, too. I mean, they know one or more of the cops were taking kickbacks, but so far they haven't a shred of concrete evidence on anyone.'

'Kickbacks?' As Twyla Fay shot me a sharp look I added, 'I'm sorry, I'm a little vague on the details. Maybe you could refresh my memory?'

'Sure. Some of the detectives on the force were accused of

taking kickbacks from local drug lords. They were looking the other way and drugs were getting into the high school big time. They had a few suspects, but they couldn't make anything stick.'

'And that's why they brought in Bartell.'

'Yep. There were a few guys qualified, but once under the finger of suspicion . . .' she shrugged. 'Bartell came highly recommended.'

'And he's very ethical.'

'Yep, and the mayor figured that's what they need right now.'

'So this IA investigation is still going on?'

'As far as I know. I heard a few weeks ago that there might be a break in the case, but then that rumor died.'

'Who did you hear that from, if you don't mind my asking?'

Twyla Fay's heavily made-up lips parted in a grin. 'You can ask. It was Jenny Lee. Of all people, right? I would never have figured she'd be interested in local politics.' She shook her head, and then suddenly her hand dived into her pocket. She whipped out her cell, looked at the screen. 'Sorry, hon. Gotta go.'

Twyla Fay hurried off, and I mulled over what I'd just learned. Police corruption certainly was what one would call a big story – had that been Jenny Lee's? It seemed likely. I got in the elevator and rode up to the third floor. Once I was in my office, I whipped out my own cell and dialed Brenda Klemm. She answered on the second ring.

'Hi Brenda. I hate to bother you, but there's something I forgot to ask you.'

'Sure. What is it?'

'Last night you mentioned that Jenny Lee wanted you to spy on some other people in addition to Manchetti?'

'One other,' Brenda amended. 'He was a guy she met there a couple of times, and he came in separately as well. As a matter of fact, he met with some of the same people that Mr Manchetti did.'

My heart was pounding so loudly I could barely hear myself speak. 'I don't suppose you know his name or what he looked like?'

She barked out a laugh. 'He might have been handsome or he might have been ugly. Every time he came in, he wore a hat pulled down low over his face and sunglasses, so I never got a good look at his face. Hard to tell the build under the heavy coat he wore, but he seemed athletic.'

'So he didn't want to be recognized,' I said thoughtfully.

'Guess not. Oh, wait!' She sounded excited as she added, 'I almost forgot. He did come in one time, sat way in the back, and he did take off those glasses briefly. Only for a minute, but I managed to snap a photo of him with my phone.'

'I don't suppose you still have that picture?'

'I'm not sure. I deleted a lot of stuff. Maybe. I'll take a look and, if I do, I'll send it to you.'

'Great. Thanks. Oh, one more thing. Do you know if Ginger ever waited on him?'

'I believe she did. As a matter of fact, I know she did. She commented on the fact that he looked like Claude Rains, the Invisible Man, in his getup, but he was a good tipper so why should she care?'

I hung up and sat back in my chair. I picked up a pencil and gently gnawed at the end of it. There was something else, I knew it. If I could only put my finger on it . . .

I thrust my hand into the pocket of my suede jacket and I felt the tiny tear in the lining. Darn, I'd meant to take this to the dry cleaner to have it fixed but I'd forgotten. As I went to pull my hand out of the pocket, I touched something hard stuck in the lining. My fingers closed over it and I pulled out a slip of paper. It was marked 'Important'. I frowned, and then I remembered where I'd found this: in Jenny Lee's apartment. I unfolded it and looked at it again. There was the Cricket's Department Store heading, and ES CL REC $15 scribbled beneath. I whipped out my phone and dialed the store number. When the operator answered I asked to speak to the manager of the electronics department. A few minutes later a bored voice said, 'Briggs. Electronics. How can I help you?'

'I was wondering if you have any sort of equipment in your store that would go by the initials ES CL REC. It's priced at fifteen dollars.'

'ES CL REC, you say? Just a moment.' Muzak came on

and I found myself humming along to 'Rhapsody in Blue' for a full five minutes before the clerk came back on the line. 'We have one item that fits your description,' he said. 'The ES Call Record model. It's a call intercept device.'

'Call intercept?'

'Yes. It allows one to spy on phone calls that take place on any Android, iPhone or Blackberry, incoming or outgoing.' He paused. 'It's not fifteen dollars, though. It's fifteen thousand.'

'Dollars?' I practically shrieked. 'That's a lot of money.'

'Well, you're getting a lot of bang for your buck, especially with this particular model. It can be used as a cell phone, but in actuality it's so much more. It's got software on it that allows you to record conversations as well as listen in.'

'Sounds very tech-y.'

'Oh, it is. The software is pretty sophisticated. You put in the number of the phone you want to listen in on and the software notifies you when calls come in. You look like you're talking on a regular cell phone, so no one is the wiser.'

'Very James Bond-ish. I don't suppose you have any of these in stock?'

He barked out a laugh. 'You're joking, right? These babies aren't readily available. You have to have connections to get your hands on one, if you get my drift.'

'You mean they're illegal.'

'You said it, not me.' He lowered his voice. 'If you're really interested, though, I do know a guy who might be able to help you.'

'Not necessary,' I said. I was about to hang up when a thought occurred to me. 'Has anyone else inquired about this type of spyware in the past few months?'

He was silent for a few seconds, then said, 'Now that you mention it, there was a woman who called a while back. She was very insistent that she absolutely had to have one of these babies. I put her in touch with my contact.'

'Thanks very much. I might circle back to you later.' I hung up before he could say anything more. I had the feeling that – in this particular instance – the less I knew the better. However, in Jenny Lee's case, and considering her proclivity for recording her conversations, owning equipment like this made perfect sense. Dale had mentioned Jenny Lee liked to record her conversations, and Bartell hadn't denied that he'd listened to the conversations she'd recorded with Dale and me on her cell. Using a sophisticated piece of equipment to spy on private conversations must have been just like a walk in the park for Jenny Lee.

I went to my computer and Googled 'ES Call Record device'. A few minutes later I had it up on my screen. This model looked like a cell phone, but was in actuality so much more. Just as the clerk had said, one could listen to any call made to or from the phone targeted, live and as it happens. All one had to do was input the phone number to be spied upon into the database. It was as easy as sending a secret SMS, or flipping a switch in the online dashboard. The targeted phone would have no idea anyone was listening in. The whole concept was rather scary, and yet very Jenny Lee.

I leaned back, tapping idly at my chin. I wondered just how many conversations Jenny Lee had listened to using this device, or had she bought it specifically for the purpose of targeting whoever she thought was behind the kickbacks on the police force? Most likely the latter, I thought. If this device was going to get her the evidence she needed to break this big story – and now I was ready to agree that it was, indeed, big – she would have taken special care with it. Unlike Roberto, she wouldn't have left it just anywhere a person could find it. She'd have made damn sure it was hidden, and hidden well, but where?

My first thought was a safety deposit box, but then I nixed that idea. Getting into a safety deposit box took time, and Jenny Lee had been an impatient sort of person. I couldn't see her putting anything into a safe deposit box.

The next logical place would be somewhere on her person, or in that oversized Gucci tote she always carted around with her. But the more I thought about it, the more I eighty-sixed that idea as well. What if she happened to misplace the bag or someone took it? Both possibilities were highly unlikely, true, but would Jenny Lee have taken that chance with such valuable evidence? I thought not. That left only two other possibilities: her home, or her office.

I swung myself up and out of my chair. Since Jenny Lee's office was only one floor away, there was no time like the present to do another quick search. The best time, probably, since her murder was now officially marked 'solved' on the books. Her office had, no doubt, been formally released and would probably be cleaned out within the week. Spurred on by that thought, I grabbed my own purse and headed straight for the stairwell. I took the stairs two at a time and burst through the door leading on to the fourth floor just in time to see Jenny Lee's office door swing shut. Someone else had gone in there. Who? Throwing caution to the wind, I barreled down the hallway, pushed open the door – and stopped dead still as I recognized the person standing behind the desk.

TWENTY-FOUR

'Tiffany?' Marcia Allen glanced up and shifted the file folders she was holding in her hands. She shoved them into the box that was square in the center of the desk and then fisted one hand on a slender hip. 'What are you doing here?'

I thought fast. 'I was just about to ask you the same thing,' I said quickly. 'I saw the door close and thought maybe someone might be prowling around in here.'

Marcia's lips twisted in a wry grin. 'No prowler, just me. Isolde Carter rang up Mr Manchetti and told him that she wouldn't be taking anything out of Jenny Lee's office, so he sent me down here to get everything boxed up and out of here.'

'Lucky you,' I murmured. I glanced around the sparsely furnished room. 'So, what's going to happen to all her stuff?'

Marcia shrugged. 'It'll go into storage and, if no one wants anything, and I doubt anyone will, there's not much of anything here, we'll donate it to Goodwill.' She gestured toward the files. 'These are all stories she was working on. Society pieces. They'll get shredded. To be honest, cleaning out this place shouldn't take me more than an hour. Jenny Lee didn't keep much here.'

I glanced at the leather chair and the brown sweater casually draped across its back. 'That sweater's nice. Looks like cashmere.'

Marcia bent down and looked at the label. 'What do you know? You've got a good eye, Tiffany, it is.' She hesitated and then said, 'Would you want it?'

I shook my head. 'No thanks.'

Marcia lifted it off the back of the chair and held it up to her. 'It's my size. I might just take it. I've got a brown tweed skirt this would look great with.'

The thought of wearing this particular dead woman's clothes

made me shudder, but it obviously didn't bother Marcia. 'Hey, go for it,' I told her.

Her lips curved in a smile. 'I think I will. This is two-ply, at least four hundred bucks. I couldn't afford anything like that. And the folks who'd get this from Goodwill wouldn't have a clue how expensive it is.'

Marcia put the sweater off to one side and finished loading the files into the box. I stepped all the way inside the room and closed the door behind me. 'It's good of you to do this,' I said. 'I know how terribly busy you must be.'

'You got that right,' Marcia's head bobbed up and down. 'I've got a gazillion things to finish up before I can get out of here tonight. Really, the last thing I need is to be boxing up Jenny Lee's personal effects, but . . .' She spread her hands. 'Mr Manchetti's orders. I think he wants anything that reminds him of just how big a jerk his son has been out of here.'

'I could understand that.' I moved closer to her. 'You know,' I ventured, 'I finished my recipe pitch so I've got some free time. I'd be glad to help you with this so you can get done faster.'

Marcia's eyes lit up. 'Really? You wouldn't mind?'

'Not at all.'

'Wow, well, sure. I really need to get out of here by five.' She lowered her voice and said in a conspiratorial whisper, 'I've got a date with Frank Lewis from Marketing at five thirty. I've been flirting with him for months, and he finally asked me out! I really don't want to cancel.'

I held up my hand. 'I so understand that. What can I do to help speed this along?'

Marcia made a sweeping gesture with her hand, 'If you want to tackle the closet and the file cabinet, I'll just finish up with the desk.'

I noticed there was a computer monitor shoved off to the side of the desk. 'What happened to her computer?'

'If the police don't still have it, they probably returned it to her sister. Jenny Lee didn't have a company computer. She didn't want one. She used her own personal laptop.'

No doubt the police had gone over it with a fine-tooth comb, but I was pretty certain Jenny Lee wouldn't have kept anything about her big story on a computer she also used for day-to-day work. I was betting she either had a second laptop, or maybe she kept her 'special' files on a thumb drive. I walked over to the closet, opened the door. A navy blue raincoat hung there, and a blue and white printed umbrella lay on the floor. Otherwise, the closet was bare. I took the items out of the closet and laid them on a nearby chair. I went over to the file cabinet, opened every drawer. I really didn't expect to find anything important, and I wasn't disappointed. The top two held some manila folders containing printouts of old stories. The bottom two drawers were empty. No other set of house keys. I figured I could only get lucky like that once.

Marcia had taken the blotter off the desktop and set it on the floor. 'That's one beautiful desk,' I observed. 'It's certainly a heck of a lot nicer than the one in my office.'

'That's because Jenny Lee bought this,' Marcia said. 'I remember the day it was delivered. She claimed she thought better on designer furniture.'

I let out a soft chuckle. 'Sounds like Jenny Lee. I'm surprised her sister isn't taking this desk. She could sell it for a good sum.'

'We asked her, but she said she didn't need two.'

I raised an eyebrow and shot Marcia an inquisitive look. 'Two?'

'Yep. Jenny Lee ordered a desk for her home office at the same time she ordered this one. If you think this desk is nice, you should see the other one. She showed me a picture one day. Got it custom-made from the same place Roberto Manchetti got his.'

'Really!' That was interesting. Hadn't Bartell said Dalton had found a false bottom in one of the drawers of Manchetti's desk? Could Jenny Lee's have one as well? 'I don't suppose you remember the name of the place?' As Marcia gave me a look, I added, 'I was thinking of getting a new desk for my home office.'

'This place is expensive. I mean really expensive. You'd be better off going to Office World, unless you have a problem writing on anything but designer furniture too,' Marcia said.

'Maybe so, but I'd still like to check it out.'

'Whatever. It was Cabrini Specialty Cabinet and Desk, I think.'

I reached for a pad and pen still on the desktop, scribbled down the name and tucked the paper into my jacket pocket. 'Thanks. So I take it Isolde is taking the other desk? The one at Jenny Lee's apartment?'

Marcia shrugged. 'I guess so. She did call yesterday and ask for the name of a reputable moving company, so I'm assuming she is taking her sister's furniture, or at least some of it. Oh, that reminds me!' Marcia dug her fingers into the pocket of the oversized charcoal cardigan she wore and pulled out a ring of keys. 'The cleaning service turned these in this morning. Apparently they had two sets to Jenny Lee's apartment. Darn, I promised Isolde I'd drop these off at the apartment today. Between doing this and my other work, I forgot.' Marcia bit her lip in vexation.

'I could run them over there, if you'd like,' I said, trying not to sound too eager. I needed to see that desk before Isolde had it packed up and shipped off to California. Hopefully I wasn't too late.

Marcia's eyes lit up. 'Would you? That would be a huge help to me – if you're sure you wouldn't mind.'

I held out my hand, and Marcia dropped the key ring into it. 'Believe me, I don't mind at all,' I said.

Before I made a return visit to Carmella Towers, I stopped in my office and pulled up Cabrini Specialty Cabinet and Desk's website. All furniture custom-made and to order. I looked through the online catalog, and on the second page I found a desk that had two drawers with false bottoms – Roberto's desk, no doubt. On the next-to-last page I came across another model that boasted a secret drawer. I had to admit, from the photo it was impossible to tell. The desk came in either oak or cherrywood, and I was betting this might be the model that currently resided in Jenny Lee's home office – if it wasn't already on a truck to Los Angeles. I made a call to Cabrini's and was connected with a very chatty salesman named Ivan, who was able to confirm that yes, Jenny Lee did indeed order the same model as Manchetti, in oak, for her personal office.

'Would you like to order a similar model?' he asked. 'If so, you're in luck, because we just happen to have some in the warehouse.'

'When you say similar . . . would that model have secret drawers as well?'

'Well, yes, but . . . I should have mentioned that every model is different.'

'Different? Different how? Do you mean some don't have secret drawers?'

'Oh, no, they all have them,' he hastily assured me. 'It's just that the designer sometimes switches the location of the drawers around. It's not always as it appears in the sample.'

Swell. 'So does that mean the secret drawers in Ms Plumm's desk might be in a different location than the ones in Mr Manchetti's?'

'That's correct.'

'I don't suppose you'd have any paperwork on how the desk might be constructed?'

'I'm sorry no. The designer doesn't update us when he makes a change. Now, if you're interested, we just completed an order for a place that went out of business, so we're stuck with the inventory. That being the case, we've reduced the price drastically. You can get one of those desks for only five thousand dollars – plus tax and shipping, of course.'

Only five grand? I almost choked. 'Thanks. I'll think it over.'

'Don't think too long,' Ivan cautioned me. 'Deals like this don't grow on trees.'

'I'm sure they don't.'

I rang off after assuring Ivan I wouldn't dawdle too long, and then stole a glance at my watch. If I hurried, I could just make it back in time to get ready for my date with Eric Dalton with some time to spare. I felt a sharp pang of guilt at how lackluster I felt about my date. It wasn't Eric's fault that I was more attracted to his insufferable supervisor. After all, Eric was pretty good looking himself. If it hadn't been for Bartell's kiss, maybe I'd feel differently.

Maybe.

I pulled up in front of Carmella Towers and breathed a

sigh of relief when I didn't see a moving van parked in the lot. My heart did a brief flip-flop, though, when I saw the familiar black Jaguar XF convertible parked near the entrance. The last thing I needed was to run into Isolde! Luck was with me, though, because a few minutes later the woman herself came out lugging a large cardboard box. She put the box in the backseat, and then whipped out her cell phone. After a few seconds she flung the phone into the car, slid behind the wheel, and tore out of the lot like her pants were on fire.

'Something's gotten her riled up,' I observed. 'Bad for her, good for me.'

I locked my car and then tripped up the steps to the entrance just like I belonged there. Keys in hand, I made my way to Jenny Lee's apartment and, after giving a cautious look around, opened the door and stepped inside, pulling the door shut behind me. I was going to have to be quick. There was no telling when Isolde might return. Remembering how the lights had alerted her to my presence in the apartment the last time, I switched on the flashlight app on my phone and shone the beam around. There were boxes everywhere, and I noted that all the artwork was missing from the walls. I carefully picked my way around the sea of cardboard until I came to the office door. I opened it and stepped inside. There were boxes stacked against the wall in here too, but the object of my search was still there, albeit looking a little bare. I shut the door behind me and made my way over to the desk. I took a moment to admire the workmanship. It really was a beautiful piece of furniture, although I would never have paid five thousand dollars for it. And that was the sale price! Jenny Lee certainly had liked to spend money. I shone my light around the desk. Since the odds were that Jenny Lee's secret drawers were in a different place, I'd have to carefully examine the entire piece of furniture.

There was some decorative molding around the desk's sides. I leaned over and pressed my hand against the molding on the left side. Nothing. I did the same to the one on the right. Again nothing.

'OK, not you.' I ran my hand along the sides of the desk,

then underneath. I gasped as my fingers touched what felt like a little bump in the wood. I got down on my knees and shone the light underneath the desk. Sure enough, there was a tiny knob. I tugged at it, but the drawer seemed to be stuck fast. I set my jaw, gripped the knob and gave it a quick jerk sideways, then gasped as a little door shot up, revealing a recess below. I reached inside the hole and let out a little cry of triumph as my fingers touched something hard. I pulled my hand out and looked at the object clenched there. It looked like an ordinary cell phone, but in actuality it was so much more.

I turned the recording device over in my hand, mentally berating myself that I hadn't looked up instructions on how to actually listen to it. But surely the police would know what to do. I had to get this down to Bartell right away, and then I paused as a thought occurred to me. What if Bartell had something to do with the police corruption?

As quickly as that entered my head, I dismissed it. Bartell hadn't seemed the type of person who'd take a bribe, but yet . . . one never knew. I bit my lip and then brightened. I'd take it to Dale. He'd know how to proceed.

I slipped the recording device into my jacket pocket, and then my cell in the other pocket pinged. I drew it out and looked at the message on screen:

Found the photo. It's attached. Brenda

The hairs on the back of my neck started to prickle. I had the feeling that I should be hot-footing it out of Jenny Lee's apartment and back to the office, but curiosity won out. I opened the attachment and a few seconds later I was looking at the photo of the person Jenny Lee had referred to as her 'Golden Goose', the person who was most likely involved with the police corruption scandal. It was a profile shot taken at a distance and not all that clear, but clear enough that recognition kicked in. I couldn't mistake that chiseled profile, that strong jaw.

The Golden Goose was none other than Eric Dalton, my date for tonight.

It took a few seconds for my brain to process all this, and then, like a blur, I shoved my phone in my pocket and headed for the door. I flung it open, and then stopped dead in my tracks.

Eric Dalton stood on the other side of the door. I caught a flash of blue steel and looked down. The gun he held was leveled directly at my heart.

TWENTY-FIVE

Eric made a little clucking sound in his throat. The gun he held didn't waver once as he said, 'Tiffany, Tiffany. You just couldn't mind your own business.'

My throat felt dry, constricted. Even as the last piece of the puzzle clicked into place, I could hardly get the words out. 'Eric. It's you. You knew Jenny Lee. You knew Ginger. You're—'

'The Golden Goose,' he finished. His lips twisted in an expression of distaste. 'Silly nickname but then again, it was Jenny Lee. She loved those *Grimm's Fairy Tales*. Myself, I'd have used King Midas. Everything he touched turned to gold, right?' He held out his hand. 'I'll take that recording device you found.'

My knees were so wobbly, I thought for sure I'd fall down. 'How . . . how do you know I found anything?'

'Oh, puh-lease! Don't lie. You came here looking for it and, knowing you, I'm certain you succeeded.'

I couldn't suppress a gasp. 'How did you know that?'

He reached into his pocket and pulled out a cell phone. 'Easy. I have one of these too. As a matter of fact, Jenny Lee found out about this device from me, back before she started blackmailing me. I programmed your cell number into it, and I've been tracking your calls for a while now. I had a feeling that, sooner or later, you'd prove very useful.'

'Oh my God, you've been spying on me?' My hands clenched into fists at my sides. 'Is that why you asked me out?'

He looked surprised. 'Heck no. I asked you out because, well, because I do like you. No one's more disappointed than me at this outcome, believe me. I tried to warn you to stop your snooping several times, in fact.'

'You . . . you followed Hilary and me that night! And you put that photo of Jenny Lee in my mailbox!' I cried. 'You killed Ginger, too!'

'Guilty, guilty and guilty,' Eric admitted. 'I thought it might discourage you, but it had the opposite effect. You just didn't stop snooping. As for Ginger, well . . . she asked for it. After you started asking questions, she put two and two together and decided to try and blackmail me. She had to be dealt with.' He clucked his tongue. 'Poor Tiffany. You've got amateur detective syndrome. You can't help yourself, can you?'

My eyes darted around, looking for some possible avenue of escape, but the only way out of the apartment other than the door would be one of the windows, and it was a good forty-foot drop on to concrete below. Not a good choice if I wanted a shot at getting out of this alive. My best chance was to keep him talking, and maybe Isolde would come back. 'Why on earth would you do this, Eric?'

His laugh was mirthless. 'Why do you think, Tiffany? For money, lots of it. I mean, we're not talking small sums here. Drug trafficking is big buck business.'

'Big enough for you to jeopardize your career?'

His lips twisted into a sneer. 'My career? Hah! They never appreciated me. I've been on the force since I was twenty-one, and I had to work my ass off to make detective. I've been passed over for promotions four times.' He made a fist, pounded it against his chest. 'Four times!'

'Is that why you decided to start taking kickbacks?' I asked. 'Because you felt underappreciated?'

'At first,' he admitted. 'When Chilton King's men first approached me, my first instinct was to turn 'em in, but I gave them the benefit of a listen. Once I learned just how much money was to be had, well, my decision was easy. I make ten times what I'd have made if I'd gotten Bartell's job – not that they would have ever considered me. King appreciated my smarts, he needed a guy like me on the inside, and he was willing to pay big for it.' His lips twisted into a bitter smile. 'It was easy for me to point the finger of suspicion on those other detectives, almost as easy as it was for me to get into the position of Bartell's right-hand man.' He puffed out his chest. 'No one ever suspected me, least of all Bartell, hotshot that he's supposed to be. I think, before I take off, I'll put everyone out of their misery and pick a patsy to take the fall. Maybe Cal Henderson. He's always hated me.'

There was a wild, almost maniacal light in Eric's eyes. I could see that there was no reasoning with him, at least none on a sane level. *Feed to his ego*, I thought. *Keep him talking.* 'It seems as if they have definitely underestimated you,' I said.

'That's obvious.' He gestured with his free hand. 'No more stalling now, Tiffany. Isolde won't be back for a long time, if at all. She got a call that her hotel room caught on fire. Hand over Jenny Lee's phone.'

I should have known he'd have managed to get Isolde out of the way. My hand closed over the phone in my pocket and I said in my sweetest tone, 'Of course I will. I know when I'm beaten, but first, won't you tell me how you did it? I'm *so* curious as to how you managed to get that poison in her empanada. It's such an ingenious way to murder someone.'

Eric grinned. 'I thought so,' he said. 'Jenny Lee was always looking over her shoulder, afraid someone might try to get her. She never dreamed it would be me.' He shook his head. 'I guess it won't do any harm to tell you, since you won't be repeating this to Bartell or anyone else.' He waved the gun, indicating for me to take a seat. I backed into the living room and slid on to the loveseat. Eric seated himself in the chair across from me.

'I won't bore you with all the details,' he said. 'Suffice it to say that Jenny Lee was no saint herself. The witch was blackmailing me. She kept my involvement with King quiet so long as I paid her a very healthy sum each month. Once her sugar daddy retired, though, she called me and said that now she was out of a steady job, she had no choice but to expose me and the police corruption. She had the idea that this story would inject some life into her now-dead career. She had no idea that, at that moment, she'd signed her own death warrant.'

'So that was when you decided to kill her?'

Eric shrugged. 'I won't deny the thought had crossed my mind before. Now, though, it was going to be either her or me. She was desperate to break the story. She figured it was her ticket to landing a job with a major news magazine.' He let out a long breath. 'She said that, because I'd been so co-operative with her, she'd hold off breaking the story for forty-eight hours. Give me time to make a getaway. She said she owed me that much. Can you imagine? So then I knew what I had to do.

'I'd hung around Roy's long enough to know about Brenda and her monkshood plants. I knew she grew 'em for that taxidermist, and I also knew what part of her garden she kept 'em in. I snuck in and got some of the leaves, then ground them up real fine, taking care to wear gloves all the time. I met Jenny Lee at Roy's that night and I told her I'd decided to go to South America. She said fine, she'd wait a day before she broke the story. We'd had a few drinks, and she got up to go to the ladies' room. I'd arranged with the cook to bring her empanadas out. After he dropped them off, I slipped the ground aconite into the empanada. I knew she'd gobble 'em down once she came back, and she didn't disappoint me. God, she loved those damn things! Anyway, she finished eating and then she started to complain about not feeling well, but she said that she had another stop to make.

'I followed her outside. She didn't take more than ten steps when she collapsed. I dragged her body into a nearby alley and then used a burner phone I'd picked up to send the anonymous tip.'

I swallowed. 'I was the other stop she had to make, right? She was going to grill me about Jeff.'

He nodded. 'Jenny had her phone in her hand when she collapsed. She'd just sent you that text. I found the note about you in her purse and, I confess, I held on to it. I thought it might come in handy.'

'You sent it to Bartell to direct suspicion at me,' I accused.

'I used it as a diversion. I knew you weren't high on the suspect list, but I also knew that Bartell had some feelings for you. I figured this would be a good distraction.'

I tried not to home in on what he'd said about Bartell having feelings for me. 'It worked. Bartell was upset. You took Jenny Lee's watch too.'

'Yep. At first I was planning to hock it; it was worth a fortune. I found a far better use for it, though, when I went to Manchetti's apartment.'

'You planted it.'

'Sure did. Figured that would close the case and, wham!, the heat would be off and I'd be in the clear. But no, you weren't satisfied. You had to keep snooping.' He rubbed absently at his forehead. 'Too bad you had to get yourself so involved. I meant it when I said I really liked you. If you hadn't had to play junior detective, we might have had a good time together.'

'You and me? I don't think so,' I sniffed.

He shrugged. 'Your loss,' he said through clenched teeth. 'OK, so now you know. Hand over Jenny Lee's phone.'

My hand dipped into the pocket that contained my own cell phone. I whipped it out, held it up. 'You want it,' I said. 'Go get it.' And with that, I pulled my arm back and threw my phone into the far corner of the living room.

'Tut-tut, bad move,' Eric growled. He rose from his chair and was standing over me in a second. As he reached for my arm, I brought my knee up and hit him hard in the groin.

'Yow-owww,' he cried. He doubled over, and the gun fell from his hand and skidded underneath the sofa. I jumped up, but before I could make a run for it, his hand shot out and he grasped my ankle, causing me to lose my balance. As I went down, my arm flailed out and pushed a floor lamp sideways. I heard the glass shade smash as it hit the hardwood floor, and the sound caused Eric to loosen his grip on my ankle. I twisted free but it was a short-lived victory, as Eric straightened up and started to charge after me. I saw some boxes stacked off to my left and I swept both my hands at them, knocking them in front of Eric. As he stumbled I turned, but my foot skidded on the edge of the carpet and I fell, banging my arm on an end table.

Eric lunged for me, his fingers digging into the edge of my shirt, and he pulled me toward him. 'You foolish, foolish girl,' he muttered. His other hand came up and tried to close around my throat.

I twisted away from him and slammed into two more boxes. My elbow pushed down the flap of the top one, and I saw the edge of a large brass bowl peep out. I grabbed it and swung my arm up and out as hard as I could, making very satisfying contact with the top of Eric's head. His eyes rolled back and his arms dropped to his sides as he fell to the floor.

And just then, the door to Jenny Lee's apartment burst open and Philip Bartell and another officer stood in the doorway, guns drawn. Bartell's eyes widened as he took in my disheveled appearance and Eric lying prostrate on the floor.

I stumbled toward Bartell. 'Manchetti didn't kill Jenny Lee or Ginger. Eric Dalton did.' I reached into my pocket, pulled out Jenny Lee's recording device, and pressed it into Bartell's hand. 'Jenny Lee has evidence of his taking kickbacks from that drug lord Chilton King on this. Plus Eric made a full confession to me. I'm pretty sure I got it all on my cell recording app, as long as my phone's OK.' I gave Bartell a tight smile. 'I don't know if I could have fought him off much longer. He wanted to kill me. Don't take this the wrong way, but I've never been so happy to see anyone in my life.'

Bartell slid Jenny's phone into his pocket, keeping his eyes locked on mine. Then he reached out and took me in his arms. 'Didn't I tell you that snooping wasn't good for you?' he growled.

And then he kissed me.

TWENTY-SIX

'Oh my God and he had you at gunpoint! I would have died!'

It was the following afternoon. After the events of the day before, Dale had told me to take the rest of the week off. I was more than happy to comply with his wishes. Hilary dropped by around noon and listened wide-eyed as I recounted the events of the evening before with an occasional yip from Cooper, sprawled across my lap, and a merow from Lily who had made herself comfortable at my feet.

'I won't lie, I was pretty frightened,' I admitted. 'If Bartell hadn't shown up when he did, I doubt I would have succeeded in fighting Eric off.'

Hilary tugged at her jacket. 'So Eric Dalton was the corrupt detective all this time?' She shook her head. 'What a waste! And he was so good-looking, too.'

'True that. Oh, and by the way, remember the night we went to Dixie's apartment building? It was Eric who followed us. He thought it might scare me off.'

Hilary grinned. 'Boy, did he get fooled.'

Cooper let out a loud yip at that, and we both laughed. The doorbell rang, and I pulled a face. 'Who could that be? Truthfully, I'm not up to visitors right now, present company excepted, of course.'

Hilary jumped up. 'Don't worry, I'll get rid of 'em,' she assured me. No sooner had she disappeared than my cell rang. I saw my parents' name pop up on the caller ID and I immediately answered.

'Hey, I was going to call you,' I began.

'We just heard it on the news.' My mother's voice was anxious. 'The report said that you were instrumental in bringing about this Dalton man's arrest.'

'Instrumental? Really?' I felt a swell of pride. 'I wouldn't say that, exactly.'

'Apparently this Detective Bartell thinks a great deal of you.' My father's voice came over the line. 'Your mother and I didn't realize we had an amateur detective in the family.'

'Well, I'm pretty sure this was a one-time thing,' I said. 'My real vocation is cooking, as you know. As a matter of fact, next week I'm going full steam ahead with my plans for the pizza bake-off, and I can't wait. It's going to be a really big event, and of course, you and mom are invited.'

'We wouldn't miss it,' my father said with a chuckle. 'Oh, and speaking of big events, your mother wants to know if you're up to having that celebration party this weekend.'

My first inclination was to say no, but I knew my mother. If I didn't agree to this weekend, she'd just keep pestering me until I finally capitulated. I might as well get it over with now. 'Sure, why not,' I said. 'Who knows, I might even enjoy myself.'

'You might at that,' my mother said coolly. I grimaced. I should have known she'd be listening in. 'Make sure you bring your friend Hilary,' she went on blithely. 'Oh, and you might want to ask that Detective Bartell, since he said such nice things about you.'

I made a face. 'I wouldn't count on Bartell, but I'm pretty sure Hilary will come.'

'Well, you won't know if the detective will or won't unless you ask him,' my mother remarked. 'Unless you'd like me to extend an invitation.'

'No, no. I'll take care of it.'

We exchanged a few more pleasantries and then I rang off. I'd just set my phone on the cocktail table when Hilary appeared in the foyer. 'I didn't think you'd want me to turn this visitor away,' she said.

I grimaced. 'Who is it – Dale?'

'Better,' she said with a wide smile, and stepped aside to let Bartell enter. He held a bouquet of flowers – carnations and pansies – in one hand. 'I have to get back to work, so I'll leave you in the detective's capable hands.' Hilary gave me a quick wave and made a swooning gesture before hurrying out the door. Bartell set the bouquet down on the coffee table and stood over me with what I could only describe as a lopsided grin.

'So, Nancy Drew junior, how are we feeling?'

I stretched my arms wide in front of me. 'Exhausted. I don't know how you do it, catching criminals for a living twenty-four seven.'

Bartell's lips quirked. 'It's easy when you have competent help.'

I raised an eyebrow. 'I understand you said some pretty nice things about me to the press.'

'I believe in giving credit where credit is due.'

'And it didn't even pain you to say it,' I marveled. 'I'm touched.'

'Don't get me wrong. I would much have preferred it if you'd stayed out of the matter entirely, and stayed safe. But, I have to admit, we might never have found the evidence we need to convict Eric if it weren't for your, ah, dogged persistence.'

'Thanks. I think. So, Eric made a formal confession?'

'He had no choice, really. Between your cell phone recording and Jenny Lee's, we've got him dead to rights, not only on the drug trafficking but two murders. He's insisting Ginger's wasn't premeditated, though. He said that Ginger had seen him fiddling with Jenny Lee's empanada. She confronted Eric about it and then tried to blackmail him, which made him see red so soon after Jenny Lee tried it. They argued, it got rough and, before he realized it, she was dead. He figured Manchetti was the logical suspect, so he faked those texts to incriminate him.' Bartell let out a sigh. 'Who knew Eric was so devious? He'll be in a cage for a long time to come, and it's a darn shame. He was a good detective. If only his ego hadn't gotten in the way, who knows how far in the department he might have gone?'

'I never suspected him until I saw the photograph Brenda Klemm sent me, although thinking back on it, I should have sooner.'

Bartell's brows drew together. 'Why do you say that?'

'Because when I was in Po'Boys after Jenny Lee's murder, Nita told me that you and Dalton had been in, discussing her death. Nita said she overheard Dalton make a comment on Jenny Lee dying eating something she loved. I didn't think much of it at the time because we were all fixated on the possibility she'd choked to death, but when I was staring down the barrel of his gun, I realized that remark of his was what had been bothering me. How could Eric possibly have known Jenny Lee loved empanadas unless he knew her?'

Bartell nodded. 'Good point. I didn't pick up on that, and I should have. I guess now is as good a time as any to tell you that we've had Eric on our radar for some time – for the drugs, not Jenny Lee's murder.'

'Really? And here he thought he'd pulled the wool over everyone's eyes.'

'To be perfectly honest, it's one of the reasons I was hired, and why I made Eric my assistant. I was trying to get some hard evidence on him, but in that regard he was pretty clever. He knew how to cover his tracks, all right.'

My lips twisted into a grin. 'Too bad you didn't just ask Jenny Lee.'

Bartell stretched his long legs out in front of him. 'According to Eric, one of Jenny Lee's many contacts put her in touch with Ross Fein. Fein worked for one of King's suppliers, and he wanted out in the worst way. He met with Jenny Lee, told her that there was a key member of the Branson police force that was taking kickbacks, allowing the drugs to filter into the schools. He'd planned to name Eric, but met with a fatal traffic accident before he could do so.'

I shuddered. I didn't want any details on that. Instead I asked, 'So how did she home in on Eric?'

'She pestered people on the force and in City Hall, trying to get a lead. She knew it was someone in the homicide division, because Fein had told her that much.'

I nodded. That explained why she'd wanted Mac MacKenzie to put her in touch with his aunt.

'So,' Bartell continued, 'clever woman that she was, Jenny Lee got one of her contacts to get the phone numbers of all the detectives and she programmed them into that listening device. She hit pay dirt, caught Eric on his phone, talking to King about a drop. She started out blackmailing him but, once she was fired, all bets were off.'

'One thing still puzzles me,' I said. 'Why didn't Eric take

her phone? Wasn't he afraid there would be calls from him or to him on it?'

'According to Eric, she never used that particular phone when she contacted him. Plus, he knew about her habit of recording conversations, and figured there might be something on her phone that might point a finger at someone.'

'And it did – me and Dale,' I said, wrinkling my nose. 'I hate to say Jenny Lee got what she deserved, but no one, not even her, deserves to die like that. I hope Eric rots in prison for a long, long, time.'

'Oh, I believe he will, and so does the DA. Thirty to life, in fact.'

Cooper trotted over to Bartell, sniffed at his trousers, then jumped up and put a paw on his leg.

'Cooper, get down,' I admonished the spaniel.

Bartell leaned over and gave Cooper a scratch behind his ear. 'No worries. I love dogs. Cooper looks like a fine animal. I'll bet he's devoted to you.'

'They both are.' I indicated Lily, who'd moved to the back of the sofa, with a wave of my hand. 'They're my kids.'

'They're lucky to have you for a mother,' Bartell said. He cleared his throat. 'I suppose now is also as good a time as any to discuss the elephant in the room.'

I looked at him. 'The elephant?'

He leaned over, planted a soft kiss on my lips, then drew back. 'I meant what I said. I do like you, Tiffany Austin. And I'd like to get to know you better, when you're not running around sticking your nose in police business or being held at gunpoint by criminals, that is.'

I could feel the heat rising to my cheeks. 'That makes two of us,' I managed to croak out. 'I'd like to get to know you too, Detective Bartell. When you're not on my case for snooping around in a police investigation, that is.'

He reached for my hand, gave it a squeeze. 'Then perhaps you'll consent to go to dinner with me sometime? We can test the waters, see where things might lead.'

'If we don't kill each other first, you mean? That was a joke,' I added hastily as he shot me a look. 'To be honest, dinner with you sounds . . . good.'

Bartell's shoulders relaxed. 'Excellent. You can pick the place, since you're the undisputed food expert.'

'I'll have to check my social calendar, and I'm going to be pretty busy the next couple of weeks with the pizza contest,' I said primly, and then my face split in a major grin. 'Oh, hang all that. What are you doing Saturday? You see, there's this party at my parents' house . . .'

Recipes From Tiffany's Blog – Bon Appetempting

Tiffany's Southern Gumbo

You will need:

¼ cup all-purpose flour
1 cup canola oil
3 celery stalks, chopped
2 green peppers, chopped
1 medium white onion, chopped
¾ cup chicken broth
2 minced garlic cloves
Salt and pepper to taste
1 teaspoon cayenne pepper
2 lbs uncooked shrimp, peeled and deveined
1 lb andouille sausage, pre-cooked
1 tomato, chopped
1½ teaspoons gumbo filé powder
Cooked rice

In a dutch oven over medium heat, cook and stir flour and oil until caramel-colored, stirring occasionally for about 10 minutes (do not burn). Add the celery, onion and peppers and stir until tender, about 6 minutes. Stir in the broth, garlic, salt, pepper and cayenne, bring to a boil. Reduce heat. Slice the andouille sausage and add to skillet. Cover and let simmer for 25 minutes.

Then stir in the shrimp and tomato. Let boil, then reduce heat, cover and simmer until the shrimp turn pink. Stir in the filé powder. Serve with rice.

Brew Barn Easy Empanadas

You will need:

  1 package pre-made pie crust
  1 lb of lean ground beef (if you prefer chicken or shrimp,
    you can substitute)
  ¼ cup diced onions
  ½ medium diced bell pepper
  1 teaspoon cumin
  1 teaspoon minced garlic
  ¼ teaspoon salt
  ¼ teaspoon chili powder
  1 cup Mexican blended cheese
  1 egg

Preheat your oven to 350°F. Prepare a cookie sheet with parchment paper or non-stick foil. Set aside.

In a large skillet, cook the ground beef, onions and pepper until beef is fully cooked. Drain any excess fat. Add the cumin, garlic, salt, pepper and chili powder to the mixture and cook for approximately 2–3 minutes, then remove from burner.

Roll out pie crusts. Trace circles on to pie crust. Lay the circles down on cookie sheet. Add 2–3 tablespoons of beef mixture to each circle. Top with ½ tablespoon of cheese. Fold pie crust circle in half, keeping filling inside, and press edges down. Beat egg in small bowl and brush on top of empanadas.

Bake in oven at 350°F until golden brown, about 12 minutes. Remove and serve with salad or guacamole.

Trends Famous Cajun Burger

You will need:

Seasoning:

  2 tablespoons ground cumin
  2 tablespoons ground oregano
  1 tablespoon garlic powder

1 tablespoon paprika
1 tablespoon salt
1 teaspoon cayenne

Burger:

1 lb ground beef
1 cup finely chopped onion
1 teaspoon salt
1 teaspoon Cajun seasoning
½ teaspoon hot pepper sauce
1 minced garlic clove

Hamburger buns

Optional:

Sauteed onions or raw onion cut into slices

Combine all seasoning ingredients in bowl; mix well.

Combine all burger ingredients into bowl, mix well and shape into patties. Cook in skillet or on grill for 4–5 minutes or until burgers are done to your liking.

Serve on buns. You can top with either sautéed or raw onion if desired.

Tiffany's Southern Style Mac and Cheese

You will need:

1 lb macaroni
1 stick of butter, melted
4 cups of extra sharp Cheddar cheese
2 cups of Colby cheese
1 cup of Pepper Jack cheese
3 eggs
2 cups milk
1 teaspoon salt
1 teaspoon pepper

Preheat oven to 350°F. Cook macaroni in large pan of salted water until al dente. Drain, rinse and set aside.

Combine pasta and butter, salt and pepper in pasta pot. Stir in 2 cups of the Cheddar cheese.

Grease baking dish and add half of macaroni mixture. Sprinkle some of the Colby and Pepperjack over mixture, then cover with another layer of macaroni. Sprinkle with remaining cheese mixture. Beat eggs and milk in another bowl and spread evenly over pasta.

Cover baking dish with foil and bake in oven for 20–30 minutes. Remove from oven and sprinkle remaining Cheddar cheese on top. Put under broiler and bake until golden brown.